PRAISE FOR CARO...

'It is no secret that I love anything this lady writes. I find that her style carries me along beautifully. From the very first moment I felt Rebecca's tension I did not breathe properly until I read the very last word. As ever I was entranced by the sharp characterisations that convinced me I knew these people personally. This book was thrilling, tense, exciting, dark and twisted in the best possible way. It is only now, the following day, that I am able to breathe normally again.'

—Angela Marsons

'*Silent Victim* is fast-paced, twisty, and it chilled me to the bone . . . I loved every minute of it!'

—Robert Bryndza

'The very definition of a page-turner. Unreliable narrators mean you never quite know where you stand until it all builds to a richly satisfying climax. A fantastic psychological thriller.'

—John Marrs

'A dark yet compelling domestic drama that had me hooked straight off. The tension built up and up, the fear and sense of dread layered throughout, and the ending had me breathless. I devoured every page.'

—Mel Sherratt

TRUTH
AND
LIES

ALSO BY
CAROLINE MITCHELL

TRUTH
AND
LIES

CAROLINE MITCHELL

THOMAS & MERCER

Text copyright © 2018 by Caroline Mitchell

Published by Thomas & Mercer, Seattle

www.apub.com

Amazon, the Amazon logo, and Thomas & Mercer are trademarks of Amazon.com, Inc., or its affiliates.

ISBN-13: 9781503903142
ISBN-10: 1503903141

Cover design by Tom Sanderson

Printed in the United States of America

For Jessica,
Because short people rock. x

'One lie spoils a thousand truths.'

—African proverb

29 October 1987
Beasts of Brentwood killer receives life sentence

Lillian Grimes, one half of the deadly duo nicknamed the 'Beasts of Brentwood', has been sentenced to life imprisonment at Chelmsford Crown Court for the murder of nine young women. Justice Michael Devine told the prolific serial killer, who denied all involvement, that she was a danger to the public and should never be released. Bodies of six young women, aged from thirteen to twenty-three, were found on the grounds of 13 Newbold Street in Brentwood, home to Lillian and husband Jack Grimes from 1972. They included the remains of their daughter, Sally-Ann Grimes, which were discovered behind a boarded-up fireplace.

The 34-year-old mother of four repeatedly voiced her innocence as she was convicted, despite overwhelming evidence against her. Evidence that, according to her solicitor, was manipulated by police to obtain a successful charge. She will be appealing the verdict.

Lillian's husband Jack, 39, was found dead in his cell two months before trial, when he was reportedly preparing to disclose the whereabouts of three of the victims. According to officials, his death was caused by an undiagnosed heart condition.

Jack and Lillian Grimes were arrested following a social care visit to their home in connection with the disappearance of fifteen-year-old Sally-Ann Grimes. The couple's remaining three children have been taken into care.

A jury of five men and six women were subjected to sickening evidence in court, including details of how the couple had lured eight of the nine victims to their house before subjecting them to horrific sexual violence. They were then brutally murdered and buried in the garden, inside the wall cavities and beneath the floorboards of their home. Lillian Grimes maintained that Sally-Ann's death was an accident, yet forensic evidence revealed she received a severe blow to the head. Jurors rejected Grimes's claims of innocence when questioned about the deaths, and after eleven hours of deliberation found her guilty.

The investigating officer, Detective Chief Inspector Robert Winter of Essex Police, has stated that further investigations are underway with regards to the whereabouts of the three victims whose bodies have yet to be found.

CHAPTER ONE

1986

It was the scratching noise that brought Poppy down to the place where she wasn't allowed to go. She wrinkled her nose as her bare feet touched the steps, wishing she could blot out the stinky smell. She did not want to think about the spider that had produced the giant cobwebs hanging from the basement rafters. Glancing around the room, she took in the flaked paint and cardboard boxes piled high against the walls. 'Hammy,' she whispered, her heart fluttering like a butterfly in her chest. She had poured away her special bedtime drink, because she didn't want the nightmares that it brought. Lying in bed unable to sleep, she had not been able to stop thinking about her pet, lost and alone in the dark. 'Hammy,' she whispered a second time, the basement floor cold beneath her soles.

Peering in the dim light, she tiptoed past the old single mattress on the floor. She didn't know why her father kept a bed in the room where he worked, but the presence of red stains made her scared. Glancing back up the basement steps, she wondered if her hamster could have made it all the way down here on his own. Scratch . . . scratch . . .

scratch . . . The noise crept from a large wooden chest in the corner of the room, but it seemed very loud for a hamster. Poppy stiffened. If it wasn't Hammy making that noise, then what was it?

'What are you doing down here?' Sally-Ann rasped from the top of the steps, making Poppy jump. Her older sister was more like a mother to her, seeing to her needs when Mummy and Daddy were away. But today, Sally-Ann's eyes seemed as big as saucers, and the colour had left her face.

Poppy bit the corner of her lip. She had broken the rules. She was in big trouble now. 'Hammy got out,' she whispered, pointing to the corner of the room. 'He's over there.' But the scratching had stopped and been replaced with a low moan. Poppy wound the sleeves of her My Little Pony nightdress over her hands, her fingers withdrawing as she bunched her fists inside. She was desperate to put her thumb in her mouth, but that would bring another telling-off, and she was in enough trouble as it was.

Sally-Ann's feet barely touched the steps as she joined her. 'That's not Hammy,' she whispered, glancing up to the shaft of light at the top of the steps, then back to Poppy's face. 'And you shouldn't be here.' Her voice turned into a squeak as a door slammed upstairs. 'It's Dad. Gawd, if he catches us, we're done for.' Grabbing Poppy by the arm, she dragged her back to flee the way they had come. But it was too late. Heavy footsteps grew louder as they echoed down the hall.

Poppy's fingernails bit into the palms of her hands as her fists tightened in response. If Daddy caught them down here, he would beat them with his belt.

'Quick, hide,' Sally-Ann whispered, her fingers pinching Poppy's skin as she pulled her away.

'You're hurting me,' Poppy squeaked, tears rising. What she wanted to say was that she was scared: more scared than she had been in all her life. The look of fear in her sister's eyes told her there was more than a beating at risk. She knew that Sally-Ann had seen things, secret things she could not share. The footsteps were getting closer now. Her father was just seconds away. 'Hide in here,' Sally-Ann gasped, plunging her hands beneath Poppy's armpits as she lifted her into the air. 'Don't cry. Don't make a sound, no matter what happens. Do you hear? No matter what, or you'll be done for, too!'

Poppy found herself being plunged into a washing basket half-filled with dirty sheets. The stains were the same colour as the ones on the mattress: burgundy red. Her heart hammered as she squashed herself into the narrow space. In a thought too horrific for her four-year-old brain, she realised that the dried crusted substance was blood. She choked back a whimper as Sally-Ann covered her with a sheet and placed the lid back on. Blinking back her tears, she broke through the material tangled around her. A gap in the wicker allowed her a narrow glimpse of her father as he swaggered down the stairs. Tall and broad, he seemed like a giant of a man as he took a swig from the bottle in his hand. His features twisted as he glanced around the room, and Poppy prayed that her sister had found a hiding place in time. She couldn't allow herself to think about the blood on the sheets and why her father was dragging the chest from the corner of the room. A smile curled on his face, but it was a bad smile. Her chin trembled as she sucked in a silent breath, wishing she were back in bed.

When her father heaved the naked and bloodied body from the chest, Poppy clamped one hand, and then two, across her mouth to stem her scream. But Sally-Ann was not as instinctive when it came to taking her own advice, and Poppy winced as she heard her sister's sudden intake of breath. Her father's reaction was swift. He strode behind the boxes and pulled Sally-Ann out by her plaits, picking up the bottle he had left on the ground. Bellowing with rage, he tugged hard on her hair, while raising the bottle in the air.

Closing her eyes tightly, Poppy stuck her fingers in her ears to blot out the noise. This wasn't happening. It couldn't be. Warm urine trickled between her thighs, accompanying the clawing sensation of fear.

Poppy knew it was all too real. Involuntarily, her eyes blinked open, and she caught sight of her mother descending the stairs.

'What have you done?' Lillian gasped with obvious horror, taking in the scene.

Swallowing back her tears, Poppy followed her mother's gaze to see Sally-Ann, crumpled and lifeless on the basement floor.

CHAPTER TWO

September 2018

The pitter-patter of rain drummed like fingernails on black umbrellas, failing to drown out the mourners' sobs. Envying their tears, Amy bowed her head as a mark of respect. Her dad's Met colleagues, who were also hers, had done him proud. Leaning forward, she picked up a handful of damp earth and threw it on the coffin. A scattering of roses followed it, and Amy took comfort from the wall of rain-speckled police uniforms as they gathered to pay their last respects.

She failed to stop herself from stiffening as her brother, Craig, placed his arm around her shoulder. Giving her a quick squeeze, he immediately withdrew, and she responded with an apologetic half-smile. What kind of a freak was she? Unable to cry at her father's funeral, and now incapable of accepting an affectionate hug. Pulling off her gloves, she stuffed them in her coat pocket, touching the hard edges of the 007 key ring her father had given her six months before. She cleared her throat, feeling it constrict as she pushed her grief down. Who would watch Bond movies with her now?

Just twenty-four hours after the funeral, Amy found herself parked on a leather armchair in Dougie Griffiths's bungalow. It was the exact spot where her father had sat when visiting his ex-partner once a week for the last eight years.

Amy's grey eyes danced across the photos gracing the fireplace, Dougie's whole life story on display: a blurry photo of his parents, having emigrated from Jamaica in the hope of a better life, the East London flat Dougie grew up in, and a picture of his first day at school. The next photo brought a smile as Amy saw a fresh-faced Dougie's first day in police uniform, his afro crammed under his helmet, his chest swollen with pride. Having met Amy's father in Essex Police, they had transferred at the same time to the Met. But their working relationship was cut short when Dougie received an injury that rendered him permanently wheelchair-bound. Amy's eyes fell on the last picture, of Dougie and her father, glasses raised in the pub, celebrating their latest collar. It was beyond her how a heart that had beat so fiercely for justice could stop without warning, depriving them of the opportunity to say goodbye. Amy sighed. A spirit as strong as his could not just fizzle out. There had to be a part of him somewhere, willing her to carry on.

'I'd tell you to go home, but I suppose I'd be wasting my breath.' Dougie's East London accent broke her free from her thoughts.

'Ta,' Amy said, taking a sip of the hot, sweet beverage, and giving him a knowing smile. 'You know how Dad loved his traditions. I'm not going to break this one now.'

Dougie manoeuvred his wheelchair beside her, spilling not a drop of tea on the tray balanced on his lap. These minor victories had been a long time coming, and her father had been instrumental in each one. Dougie's voice was soft now, a depth of sympathy in his honeyed brown eyes.

'Sweetheart, your father's just died. You're entitled to some time to grieve. Don't feel you're obliged to carry things on.'

'I'm afraid you're stuck with me,' Amy said, her eyes twinkling as she kept her tears at bay. 'And don't think it's out of obligation. Nobody makes a cuppa like you.'

Dougie chuckled. 'In that case, my door is open anytime.' He paused to sip his tea. 'How are you settling in with your new team? Taken command of any big cases yet?'

Amy relaxed into the chair, the subject of work a welcome one. 'I'm getting on well with my DS. Do you know him? Patrick Byrne? He used to be my tutor. Worked in firearms for a few years before transferring to serious crime. Dark hair, forty-five-ish . . . ' It was not unusual for officers to occupy different roles during their career in the police.

'Paddy Byrne? Yeah, I know the chap. You'll do just fine with him as your anchor man.'

Amy nodded. Patrick 'Paddy' Byrne was her most trusted colleague, although when out and about they made an unusual coupling. At ten years older and a whole foot taller, he dwarfed her five-foot-two-inch frame; but what Amy lacked in height she made up for in spirit, and in the face of criminality, they were a formidable pair. 'The rest of the team seem happy to have me at the helm, although that's more to do with Dad's reputation than anything else.'

'You'll prove yourself in time.' Dougie gave her a knowing look. 'How's Craig? I didn't get to talk to him at the funeral.'

Like her, Amy's brother had joined the police on his eighteenth birthday. But given that Craig was five years her senior, he'd had a good head start. Their competitiveness was a source of friction between them, and he had only recently been promoted to Detective Inspector of CID. 'He left early,' she said, not wishing to go into detail. She loved him and would not gossip behind his back.

Seeming to sense her discomfort, Dougie changed the subject. 'I'm going to miss your dad. It won't be the same without him.'

Amy drained the last of her tea. She could imagine Dougie and her dad replaying old war stories as they swung the lamp. A shadow crossed her face at the prospect of never seeing him again. She turned to Dougie, her eyes locking onto his. 'I'm going to make him proud. I won't let him down.'

'He was always proud. Look at all of the things you've overcome.' He shook his head. 'You didn't have the easiest start in life, that's for sure.'

Setting her empty cup onto the coffee table, Amy stared at him with a mixture of curiosity and surprise. 'What do you mean?'

Dougie shifted in his chair as he averted his gaze. 'Look at me being all maudlin. Let me get us a proper drink, and we'll raise a toast to your dad.'

Amy knew better than to offer to help him retrieve the bottle of Jamaican rum from the cupboard in the kitchen. As he rifled for glasses and ice, she felt a cold shiver dart down her spine. Her hands disappeared into the sleeves of the woollen sweater that she had changed into an hour before. Bunching her fists, she was unable to put her finger on the sudden streak of fear running through her. Unaccustomed to anxiety, she caught her breath as it took her by surprise. Releasing her hand, she accepted the tumbler of rum and ice as it was offered to her, forcing a smile to her lips.

'To your dad.' Dougie raised his eyes to the ceiling as he held up his glass. 'And to your future.'

Amy clinked her tumbler against Dougie's as she repeated his words. But the chill had invoked a strange feeling inside her. One that said the past wasn't done with her yet.

CHAPTER THREE

The bars of the prison cell window were cool against Lillian's cheeks. It had been fifty-eight minutes since she saw the sun. She lived for her moments in the exercise yard, when she could fill her lungs with fresh clean air. She could still smell the aftermath of the rain, although these days she didn't dare close her eyes as she inhaled a breath. The last time she did that, she received a punch to the stomach and several kicks to the spine when she went down. She touched the bald patch on the back of her head, feeling the prickles of new hair growth. It was one of many injuries she had suffered this week. The wardens kept an eye on her, but staff cutbacks made it hard. It was the funeral of that copper that sparked it off. That, and the silly cow who sold her story to the press. Gladys Thompson had barely known her, yet the papers had lapped up news of her terminal illness, and her dying wish to give her little girl a proper burial. Lillian snorted. If she was such a great mother, then why had her twelve-year-old daughter been wandering the streets alone? Decades had passed since the murders, yet even now, the public could not let it go.

The prison beatings, the newspaper reports and the constant stream of hate mail were doing her head in. Why did Jack have to die, leaving her to face the music alone? It was the stress of his arrest that did it, and just when he was about to spill the beans. Had he suffered an attack of conscience, or was he giving up the burial sites in exchange for a better deal? Keeping quiet was Lillian's act of defiance. Why should she help the police after all they did to her? At least that's what she had thought – until now. She would give Gladys what she wanted, but only because it suited her. She turned to the spindly legged table, smoothing her hand over the letter she had written an hour before. She had left it there to rest, allowing the words to speak to her as they replayed in her mind. Rereading it one last time, she knew she had done the right thing.

Dear Amy,

I know this will come as a shock. I doubt your family have been truthful about your background, or even told you that you were adopted at all. I do not want to end my days in this prison cell without seeing you one more time. I am your birth mother. The person who gave you life.

You were just a few years old when you were ripped from my arms. Look at you now. I know that as you read this letter, you will want to discard what I have told you. Perhaps you will feel disgusted, or has denial come to the forefront of your mind? It is easier to face the future believing you come from untainted blood. But you were never one to take the easy way out, were you? My Poppy. My child.

Deep in your heart, you cannot deny me, regardless of how uncomfortable the truth makes you feel. My blood runs through your veins. Mine and your father's. Whatever lies your adoptive parents have told you, we both loved you very much.

I know you will refuse to visit, so I am bringing you to me the only way I know how. There are three more bodies buried. Three more families you can help put at rest. I will help you find them. But do not keep me waiting. Respond within a week, or I will take my secrets to the grave.

Yours always,

Lillian

CHAPTER FOUR

A shaft of early morning sunlight beamed across the row of treadmills that were spaced with perfect precision in the newly equipped gym. Britney Spears provided motivation with 'Work Bitch' drumming a beat through the overhead speakers. Amy grabbed a heated towel from the rolled-up pile next to the water cooler. Five Star Gym was a vast improvement on using the equipment in her parent's cellar, where spiders lurked in every corner.

'I didn't expect to see you today.' It was the voice of Amy's DCI, Hazel Pike. It had a husky quality from a cigarette habit she had knocked on the head when workplace smoking was banned.

'Why not? It's Thursday. We always train on Thursdays,' Amy said, avoiding the real reason for Pike's concern. Being invited to use the gym out of hours was something she had taken advantage of over the last couple of months. The gym belonged to Pike's son and only those in Pike's favour were granted out-of-hours access free of charge. Amy had enjoyed the camaraderie, as well as the insight into her DCI's job.

'You know what I mean,' Pike said, her eyes as hazel as her Christian name. Her wavy brown hair was long on top, short back and sides, her figure curvy but toned. For as long as Amy had known her, she called everyone by their surnames and expected the same in return. For Amy, it was no problem, but Pike was not the prettiest of last names.

'Dad would want me to soldier on.' It was true. She drew strength from work routines and schedules, and as long as she was meeting her commitments, the ground felt firm beneath her feet.

'Well, if you're sure.' Pike rolled her eyes as the track changed to an upbeat tune from will.i.am. 'I don't know why we have to listen to this rubbish. What's wrong with George Michael? He always makes me work up a sweat.'

Amy smiled, checking her watch. 'Fancy a quick session on the treadmill before some pad work?'

Many of their chats took place as they ran side by side, Pike speaking effortlessly while Amy tried to keep up with her long stride. Without wasting time, she set the treadmill to her usual speed. Today she felt like running in silence, but ten minutes in, Pike began to chat. It felt too soon after her dad's death to make small talk, and in the absence of a work conversation, she did not know what to say.

'How's your mum?' Pike asked, after filling Amy in on her home life.

Poor Mum, Amy thought. 'She's holding it together.' She averted her gaze in an effort to conceal the lie. Last night as she padded across the landing, she had heard her sobbing in her room. 'How's work?' she said, changing the subject out of respect for her mother.

'Do you really want to know?' Hazel's feet pounded the treadmill, but she was barely breaking a sweat. There were few DCIs left as the rank was slowly being removed from the force. Pike had been fortunate to keep her role, serving as crime manager of her department. As such she was more involved in the administrative aspect than leading multiple investigations.

Amy panted, jabbing the speed button as she cranked it up another notch. 'Are things that bad?'

'Gladwell's covering in your absence. You know what he's like. He doesn't like to say no.'

Young in service, DI Andrew Gladwell had a willingness to help that could work to the detriment of her team. Amy's squad was six months old, formed to deal with specialist cases likely to hit the media in a big way. The unit had become a necessity after a recent spate of bad publicity in the press. Amy groaned at the thought of her department falling into disarray. 'We're not there as an overflow,' she said, imagining her team armpit-high in files that should be dealt with by CID.

'They're handling it,' Hazel replied, between steady breaths. But the expression on her face said otherwise. Amy knew her tell. It came in the form of a small knot that formed in the crease of her brow when she was stressed.

'I'm coming back. Today.' Amy's arms pumped by her sides as she injected her frustration into her tiring limbs. She swiped at the sweat stinging her eyes before checking Hazel's progress. It provided enough motivation to carry on.

'It's too soon,' Hazel said. 'But pop in for a cuppa tomorrow if you like. The command team is asking for daily updates on our progress.' She paused to catch a breath. 'There's a lot of pressure to prove our worth.'

Amy checked the display as it beeped to inform her she had met her run target today. The treadmill slowed automatically, and the two women walked in unison as they cooled down. The need to find out more itched like a rash. As the treadmill came to a halt she picked up her towel and dabbed her forehead. 'So . . . erm . . . about work.'

'I wouldn't have told you if I thought you were going to worry,' Hazel said, crossing the room and pulling on a pair of red boxing gloves.

'I'm not worried,' Amy lied, wishing she had Hazel's resources. Until her private gym sessions, she had made do with practising on the old punch bag hanging from the ceiling of her parents' empty wine cellar. Her father's makeshift gym was old but functional, and it was

Amy who had persuaded her DCI to give boxing a try. As she raised the pads, she planted her feet wide, steadying herself to absorb the punches coming her way. Her biceps tensing, Amy took the blows, a small sense of satisfaction gained. As fit as she was, her DCI still could not punch as hard or as fast as her.

'Your ex was a journalist, wasn't he?' Hazel said, pausing to remove her gloves as they swapped roles. 'I remember your dad saying. It must have given you a good insight into how they work.'

'You could say that.' Amy tried to hide her discomfort as Hazel relayed what her father had said. For a split second, she made a mental note to speak to him about over-sharing, before remembering he had passed away. Taking a deep breath, she led with her left leg and delivered a series of jabs and right crosses that made Pike step back for a reprieve.

'Remind me never to piss you off,' she said, before raising the pads for the second time, a trickle of sweat running down her face.

Amy smiled before pulling back her fist and delivering a right hook. Keeping her head down, she followed it up with several more. Left, right, left, right, she threw punches, her pent-up emotions finally finding release. Twisting her hip and back foot, her body moved harmoniously just as her father had taught her. She enjoyed the feeling of power as her glove made contact with the pad. A dance track invoked a spike of energy and Amy became aware of the smell of her own sweat.

'I'll pop in around eight,' she said, wiping the perspiration from her brow as their session came to an end. 'See how the team are getting along.'

'It's too soon,' Pike replied, mirroring her actions. 'Go home, have a cry. Open a bottle of wine. We'll manage without you for a while.'

'But *I* won't,' Amy said, her words unintentionally firm. She paused, offering up a watery smile. 'I've never lost anyone before.' Although deep down it felt like a lie. There were memories, dark and festering in the recesses of her mind. Lately it was becoming harder to keep them at bay. She paused for breath, her chest feeling tight. 'I don't know how to handle it. Grief . . . it's all consuming. The only thing that will keep me sane right now is work.'

'All right, Winter, have it your way,' Pike said. 'It's easy to see where you inherited your stubborn streak from!'

'I'll take that as a compliment.' Amy feigned a smile. She knew Hazel missed her father. Everyone did. Going to work was the only way to stop her grief from swallowing her whole.

CHAPTER FIVE

Amy smiled as her mother slid a food-laden plate onto the table before her. Sausages, bacon, mushrooms and beans released a sweet aroma that smelt like home.

'Are you sure you want to go back in already?' Flora said, pouring two cups of tea from the pot on the table. 'It's only been a few days.'

'You have to be your strongest when you're feeling your weakest,' Amy said, quoting her father. 'Besides, they need me. Dad wouldn't have it any other way.' Reluctantly, she curled her fingers around her knife and fork. After her workout, the last thing she wanted was a big breakfast. A snuffling sound from under the table told her that Dotty, her beloved pug, was already lining up to help her out.

Flora's eyes glistened at the mention of Robert's name, and she swallowed back the words on her tongue. She couldn't yet talk about him without crying.

Amy had yet to shed a tear. Her inability to cry had provided amusement to her peers during her school years and was still a source of embarrassment for her.

'You don't need to cook for me either. *I* should be looking after *you*.' Amy prodded her fork into a sausage and snuck it under the table while her mother's back was turned. A quick gulping sound signalled that Dotty had made short work of it. 'Will you be OK for a few hours without me?'

'You don't need to worry about me, Winifred's coming around later.' Flora closed the kitchen window as droplets of rain spat against the glass. Amy sighed as she took in her mother's form. Like her, she was short in stature, but where Amy had muscle, Flora was fading away. Anxiety was a constant factor in her mother's life and Robert's death had taken its toll. She wished she could hug her, tell her everything would be OK, but subletting her flat to move in with her mum was the best she could offer for now. God knows her brother would not have been able to sacrifice his rampant sex life to stay and comfort her.

At least Flora knew many of her fellow residents of Royal Crescent, the curved terrace where they lived in Holland Park. It was mind boggling to imagine her parent's property was worth in excess of two million pounds. Many homes on the terrace had been converted into flats, but some houses still remained, the residents sharing the communal gardens on sunny days. For Amy, it was no great hardship moving back in. Each room was bright and tastefully decorated, her own private nook situated on the fourth floor. She glanced beyond her mother to the sash window. It was still raining. Today she would cycle to work. After eating some beans, she slipped a sliver of bacon under the table before rising to leave.

'Are you going love? You've barely touched your food.'

'Sorry.' Amy shrugged. 'I'm not up to a big breakfast after a workout.'

'It's a good thing Dotty is then!' Flora said, her eyes lighting on the pug as she danced around her heels for more.

Amy's short walk from the bicycle shed to her office was interrupted four times before she pressed her tag against the security pad on the door. Having gracefully accepted her colleagues' condolences, she carried on her journey with a serene expression that belied the emotional turbulence she was battling within. Taking a deep breath, she straightened her posture, tilting her chin upwards before striding inside. She was wearing her usual uniform of starched white shirt, charcoal suit and leather ankle boots, which added a couple of inches to her height. Her hair was straightened and rested on her shoulders, her make-up lightly applied. All she wanted was to inject some normality into her day. The first face she saw was that of DS Paddy Byrne, the one person in the police who had seen her with her guard down. Having spent the first few years of her career being taken under his wing, she was thrilled to be reunited with him as part of her team. But while Amy was organised, Paddy was anything but. A dab of bloodstained tissue still clung to his neck from a shaving nick. His shirt was ironed, most likely not by him, but his rumpled navy suit jacket looked as if his dog had made a bed of it overnight.

'Are you psychic?' she said, gratefully accepting a mug of coffee from his grip. Her James Bond mug had been a gift from her father, another bit of 007 memorabilia.

'I heard you talking in the hall.'

Amy smiled in appreciation. 'Here's to another day of outward smiles and internal screaming.'

Her sarcasm made Paddy's face crease in concern. 'You OK?'

'Yes, fine.' Amy dipped her head towards her mug as she sipped. 'But if one more person asks me if I've come back too soon, I'm going to implode.'

'How's the exercise regime going?' she said, changing the subject. Paddy had been threatening to get fit since leaving the firearms department five years ago. It made little difference to his expanding waistline, but her teasing lightened the mood.

'I've got into a routine,' he chuckled. 'Ten minutes every morning of sitting up in bed thinking about how tired I am.'

Amy smiled in bemusement. 'Briefing at eight?'

Paddy nodded. 'Nothing unusual on at the moment, but there's still time. We're just trying to sort through the shit storm of jobs Gladwell volunteered us for.'

'Don't worry about those. If they don't fit the criteria I'll be delegating them to CID.' Amy watched as the team's half a dozen officers began to filter in. Their office in Notting Hill Police Station was compact but functional, housing several desks, a small communal kitchen and her tiny office, which could have been assembled from a flat pack. Given the nature of their role, they had access to workspace in any station across the Metropolitan Police's jurisdiction, and existing teams had no choice but to make room as they assisted with high-profile cases. Cutbacks dictated that it was rare for colleagues to get precious with their workload, being more a case of all hands on deck. 'I need some alone time with my coffee,' Amy said, before going to her office.

Closing the door, she rested her forehead against the cool wooden surface and exhaled lengthily. She could do this. What choice did she have? But her father's death had hit her like a sledgehammer, manifesting as a physical pain in her chest. Her eyes trailed over the array of yellow Post-it notes gracing the planner on the wall. Reaching out, she peeled away one that was curling at the corners. It was dated for today. *Lunch in town – Dad.* Scrunching it up, she threw it in the bin. The last time she was here, she was blissfully unaware that he had passed away. It was only when she was preparing to cycle home that she picked up her mother's panicked voicemail, telling her to get to the hospital as quickly as she could. But by then it had been too late. Amy sighed; thoughts of the past descending like silken webs. Out of nowhere they would come, and each time she had to make a conscious effort to brush them away. Leaning against her desk, her gaze fell on the words printed across the mouse mat that had been a gift when she first moved in:

My New Year's resolution is to:
1. Stop making lists.
B. Be more consistent.
7. Learn to count.

The joke was old, but it brought a sad smile to her lips. The pile of mail next to it caught her attention. One letter displayed a postmark that gave it priority over everything else. Who would be writing to her from prison?

As she picked it up, there was something about the spidery scrawl that made her heart jump. Running her thumb beneath the rim of the envelope, she tore a jagged line and pulled the notepaper out. Her eyes darted from left to right as she scanned the words, her frown deepening as she read. Her lips parted to accommodate a sudden intake of breath. It wasn't true. It couldn't be. And yet . . . a sense of the past rising up to greet her brought with it a feeling of dread.

'Poppy.'

As the whisper left her lips, the envelope fell to the floor.

CHAPTER SIX

Rapping his knuckles against the door, Paddy poked his head into Amy's office, the scent of a just-smoked cigarette on his breath. 'Gladwell's coming over for briefing. Will I tell him you're covering it today? Ma'am?' His voice seemed distant, as if coming from the mouth of a tunnel. Normally, Amy would tell him off for using such a formal title. Instead, she failed to acknowledge him as she stared unblinkingly into space.

As he stepped forward, Amy snapped out of her trance and spun around. 'Sorry,' she said, battling a sudden sense of foreboding. 'I can't. I . . . I've got to be somewhere.' Bending to pick up the letter, she shoved it into her jacket pocket along with the envelope it had come in. Heads raised from computer terminals as she burst from her office, but Amy kept her eyes fixed on the door. It was too much. This was all too much. She needed to get home. To confront her mother about what she'd found.

◆ ◆ ◆

'Mum?' Amy's voice echoed in the hall, her heels clicking on the tiles as she closed the front door. Their bright and spacious home still carried the fragrance of the many flowers they had been sent following her father's death. Pushing open the living room door, she was surprised to find her mother alone.

'Why aren't you dressed? I thought Winifred was coming over,' Amy said, a slight tremble on her breath. Stunned by what she had read, she could barely remember the short journey home.

As she stared at the blank television screen, Flora's grief was evident in her red-rimmed eyes. Sitting on the floral-patterned sofa, her fingers tightened around a tissue that had seen better days. 'I lied,' she sniffed, trying to gain her composure. 'I have to get used to being on my own.'

Sitting there, still wearing her slippers and pink frilly dressing gown, her mother looked so small and fragile that Amy's heart melted. She wanted to throw away the letter that was burning a hole in her pocket, forget everything except their shared grief, but she knew it was not that easy. She could not erase the words blazing at the forefront of her mind. 'Mum?' she said tentatively, taking a seat next to her.

Blinking back her tears, Flora focused on her daughter's face. 'You're as white as a sheet. Are you all right?'

'No, I'm not,' Amy said firmly, forcing herself to push on. She took a breath, a pause to gather her strength. 'I was sent this letter . . .' Pulling it from her pocket, she thrust it into her mother's hands. 'Tell me it's not true.'

Picking up her glasses from the arm of the sofa, Flora cleaned them with the corner of her dressing gown before resting them on the bridge of her nose. Confusion etched her features, her lips moving silently as she read. Slack-jawed, she shook her head and lowered the paper to her lap. 'No,' she said quietly, as if beaten by life. 'Not now.'

Amy's hopes plummeted. She wanted her mother to tell her it was some kind of sick joke. 'Why is Lillian Grimes writing to me from prison?' Her body tensed as the reassurance she had hoped for failed to materialise.

'We didn't want you to find out like this.' Casting the letter aside, Flora reached for Amy's hands.

Amy stiffened. 'Find out what?' Her heart thundered against her rib cage. She had been aware she was adopted from an early age, but she had compartmentalised the memories of her past life a long time ago. Jack and Lillian Grimes were nothing short of monsters. She clenched her fists, her nails biting into the palms of her hands as she waited for Flora to speak.

'You were taken into care at four years of age, old enough to have a handle on things,' Flora said. 'But you didn't want to talk about your birth family. Your dad said it was a blessing. A reason to start again.'

'No,' Amy said, her voice brittle. 'It can't be. Those monsters. They're not related to me.'

'By blood only.' Flora tightened her grip on Amy's clenched hands. 'We were advised that your memory would return, but that time never came. Apart from some pictures you drew and an odd mention of your name . . .'

'Poppy,' Amy said, the word staining her lips. A sudden flap of the front door letterbox made her jump as the postman delivered their mail. Dotty leapt from her slumber in the kitchen, her bark sounding like a smoker's cough as her nails clacked rapidly against the hall tiles.

'Dotty!' Amy called, grateful for her presence. Satisfied she had chased the postman away, her pug flounced into the living room and clambered onto Amy's lap. It was as good an excuse as any for Amy to release her fingers from her mother's tight grip.

'We tried to tell you when you were ten,' Flora continued. 'But every time we brought it up you refused to listen, preferring to weave your own story of your past.'

Amy remembered the wistful fantasies she had dreamed up when she hit her teens. The child of a famous Hollywood actress, she was abandoned by her mother in favour of life on screen. Or perhaps she had come from royalty, a scandalous love child, put up for adoption to save the family's reputation. As she got older Amy focused on her future, dismissing her magical thinking. But she was always vaguely aware of something dark and monstrous buried deep inside. Something that made her blood turn cold. Amy tuned out of Flora's narrative, watching her lips move as she apologised for failing her. She sensed old scars about to be ripped open. But how could she blame her mother, when the truth was too ugly to face?

'Please try and understand,' Flora continued. 'Robert was adopted too, remember? I trusted him when he said it was best to let things lie.'

'His upbringing was a bit different to mine,' Amy replied. Like her, he never felt the need to find his biological mum and dad. But Amy was pretty sure his genes were not tainted by serial killer parents.

'Exactly,' Flora replied. 'How could we force you through the trauma of reliving it all over again?'

'You must have wondered if I would turn out like them.' Stroking Dotty's head, Amy finally met her mother's gaze. 'Did you hide the knives? Keep your bedroom door locked at night?'

Shaking her head, Flora tutted in disgust. 'Oh, Amy, if only you could have seen yourself back then. You were nothing but a scrap of a girl, as white as a ghost from lack of sun. You'd been brought up in a bubble, afforded so little contact with the normal world.' Her features softened at the memory. 'It took your father months to persuade you to stop swearing. You had your little ways, but you always put a smile on his face.'

'It's why he wanted me to join the police,' Amy said, her thoughts running wild. 'To keep me on the right path. Because deep down he knew I could turn.' She paused, shaking her head as another venomous thought reared its head. 'No wonder I'm so good at dealing with serial killers. Their blood runs through my veins. Rapists and murderers. They're part of me.'

Flora's features creased in an agonised frown. 'Sweetheart, please don't torture yourself. 'Your father and I love you very much. He'd hate to hear you talk like this.'

'But Dad investigated their case,' Amy said, recalling the newspaper headlines. 'Is that how he came to adopt me?'

A sudden shower tapped against the outside windowpane like tiny insistent fingers. Without the autumn sunshine to brighten the room, the temperature had plummeted. Tightening her dressing gown, Flora sighed. 'It's why we moved from Essex to London. We were willing to give up everything to give you a new start. Then your grandmother died, and we inherited this house. It seemed like fate.'

Amy knew that her parents had inherited their five-bedroom terraced home. It was definitely big enough to house both her birth siblings. What had happened to them? She strained to remember one of the many newspaper reports of the crimes. 'My brother and sister. Why didn't you adopt them too?'

'They were damaged, and I . . .' Flora's gaze fell to the floor. 'I wasn't equipped to deal with all three. Your dad worked long hours. It was just Craig and me. I was desperate for a little girl.' Tears wet her eyes as she recalled the memory. 'I wasn't able to have any more children. I'd longed for a daughter to complete our family.'

Amy knew Flora and Robert must have jumped through hoops to adopt her, but the truth of her background felt raw and exposed. 'So, Dad picked me out like a puppy in a pet shop and left the others to rot,' Amy said bitterly. 'Does Craig know?'

'No.' Flora dabbed her eyes with a well-practiced hand.

'And Dougie?' Amy said, remembering his comment about her having a rough start.

Flora nodded. 'He was with us throughout it all. He even worked on the case with your father, transferring to the Met not long after your dad left. We were all overjoyed when the adoption was finalised.'

'What am I supposed to do now?' Amy said. Bored from the lack of attention, Dotty jumped from her lap. Amy's eyes fell on the letter. 'She's given me an ultimatum. She'll tell me where the last three victims are buried if I visit her in prison. Those families deserve to be in peace.'

'But so do you,' Flora said, her features hardening. 'That woman's an evil, wicked monster.' She seemed to remember her audience and bit her lip. 'If you knew the things she did . . . It was enough to keep your father awake at night.'

Amy raised her hand, halting Flora's words. 'I'm not ready for that. Not yet.'

'Why does she have to torment you so soon after Robert's death?' Flora emitted an anguished cry. 'I can't handle this on my own.'

'If she hadn't written the letter then I wouldn't know the truth.'

Flora nodded, her face drained of colour. 'You need to arrange counselling, darling. You can't be expected to carry on as normal after a bombshell like this.'

'I owe it to the families to put them first. Now, more than ever,' Amy said. Stuffing the crumpled letter in her pocket, she rose. 'I'm going for a walk. I won't be long.' Calling for Dotty, she took her lead from its hook in the hall and clipped it on her collar. As far as Amy was concerned, the best therapist came with fur and four legs. Her shoulders weighted with the burden of the truth, she turned towards the door.

CHAPTER SEVEN

Amy welcomed the biting chill, dodging puddles as she tried to untangle her thoughts. It felt like her brain had turned into a ball of knotted wool. With Dotty trotting ahead of her, she turned onto Holland Park Avenue. The rumble of black cabs and double-decker buses reminded her she was in one of her favourite places in the world: the beating heart of the city. She could never imagine living anywhere else, but working in such a vibrant metropolis brought its own challenges. The onslaught of violent crimes was relentless, and in the last few years she had attributed her nightmares to her job. Mixing with murderers and psychopaths was bound to have a knock-on effect. Yet when she thought about it, the dreams she experienced were through the eyes of a child: stepping into a spider-infested basement, searching, always searching, unable to find her way out. The thick and cloying smell was one she had experienced many times in her line of work. It was the smell of death.

As Dotty trotted beside her, Amy's stomach lurched without warning. Frantically, she reached for the doggy poo bag in her pocket, opening the flimsy plastic just in time to throw up the breakfast her mother had made. Ignoring curious glances from passers-by, Amy tied the top of the bag and deposited it into the nearest bin. Staring at her with cartoon-like wide eyes, Dotty emitted a whine.

'It's OK.' Amy wiped her mouth with the back of her hand. 'We're going to be OK.' But her words were hollow. She had been running on empty since Robert's death. Where on earth was she going to find the strength to face Lillian Grimes? If only her father were here to talk it through. She could not help but feel a sense of betrayal. Surely he could have broken the news when she was young? Helped her deal with the past and move on? Or were they ashamed of who she really was? Kicking a stone, Amy failed to notice Dotty trailing behind her until the lead became taut.

'What's wrong?' Amy said, feeling a pang of guilt for walking so fast. 'Had enough?' Dotty's tongue lolled to one side. She was a lady who liked to take her time. 'Want to go home?'

Dotty replied with a whole-body wiggle, tugging on the lead to return the way they had come. Amy glanced up at the sky. Another shower was due. Her thoughts as heavy as the darkening clouds above, she trudged towards home, the tips of her shoes absorbing the recently shed rain.

As she turned into Royal Crescent, the onset of heavy footsteps broke into her thoughts. 'Dotty!' Amy gasped, as the lead was yanked back. Usually unimpressed by strangers, her pet's sudden flurry of excitement suggested she knew the person behind them.

Blinking against a speckle of rain, Amy turned, recognition dawning on her face. 'Oh! What are you doing here?' Her displeasure was evident in her voice.

Adam Rossi was no stranger to being rebuffed, given his profession as a journalist, though rejection was not a problem he usually encountered from the opposite sex. Shortening his stride, he fell into step beside her. He had not changed much in the six months since Amy last saw him. The same confident swagger, the same twinkle in his eyes. His Italian heritage granted him both the looks and charm needed to talk himself out of any situation. But not this time. Amy continued walking automatically, wishing she had stayed inside.

'You stopped answering my calls,' he said, 'and I'm guessing you blocked my emails, too.'

'I blocked you for a reason.' Amy's eyes locked firmly on the path ahead. There was no point in going over old ground. 'What are you doing here? I thought you transferred.'

'It didn't work out for me. I missed London . . . I missed you.' He smiled in response to Amy's thunderous glare. 'C'mon, why are you looking at me like that?'

'I'm not responsible for what my face does when you speak,' Amy replied. She focused on the cracks in the concrete, on the weeds turning their heads to the feeble morning sun. She would not allow herself to get sucked in. Not again.

'I'm sorry to hear about your dad. I know he didn't like me, but he was a good man. Your mum must be devastated.'

'She is,' Amy said primly, her steps quickening as she caught sight of home. She did not deny what he said because it was the truth. Her mum had been thrilled with their engagement, and her brother had given it his seal of approval, too. Even Dotty melted in Adam's presence. But her father . . . He was reserved from day one. Now she could see why. It wasn't the fact that Adam played around, it was his profession as a journalist that had made Robert so guarded. The possibility he would discover the truth.

'I'm back working for *The London Echo*. They gave me a promotion. I'm the head of current affairs,' Adam said.

'I'm glad things are working out for you.' Amy's fingers rested on the spiked metal railings outside her home. 'I've got to get inside so . . .'

'I was wondering,' Adam interrupted, bending to scratch Dotty's head as she danced around his feet. 'Your father's funeral has brought the Grimes case into the spotlight again. I thought it would be good to interview family members and talk about his work in apprehending' – he raised his fingers in mock quotation marks – 'the Beasts of Brentwood.'

Amy stood, aghast. Adam was insensitive at the best of times, but this was a new low. It served as a sobering reminder of why their relationship had come to an end. Another thought flashed like a shot across her bow. What if he knew the truth about who she really was? Her fists curled over the lead as she tugged Dotty away. 'You vulture,' she spat, her face stony. 'Dad's barely cold in the grave, and you're already picking over his corpse!'

'Hey, I come in peace.' Adam smiled, raising his palms. 'I had a lot of respect for Robert. I just wanted to pay tribute. We've lined up other interviews with family members of the victims . . .'

Amy rolled her eyes, stung by his disrespect. 'Tribute?' Anger flared inside her. She lifted her finger, poking his chest with each sentence she spoke. 'A tribute would be going to the funeral and paying your respects. A tribute would be staying on afterwards and comforting Mum when she was upset. Officers standing in uniform in the pouring rain – that was a tribute. You haven't got a clue.' Fumbling with her front door keys, she exhaled sharply as she tried but failed to find the right one.

'Amy, if you'll just listen,' Adam said, mild annoyance greasing his words.

'No, *you* just listen. I didn't invite you to intrude on my day. You came here and followed me. So I don't have to listen to a word you say.' Amy froze as Adam grabbed her shoulder.

'Don't touch me,' she said, and instantly his grip was released. Without looking back, Amy climbed the few steps to her door.

'Porca miseria!' The Italian swearword rose behind her. 'Call me when you've calmed down,' Adam shouted, before walking away.

Closing the door behind her, Amy heard her mother's voice filter through from the kitchen. 'Is that you, love?' she said, sounding brighter than before.

'Yes, be with you in a minute,' Amy replied. Unclipping Dotty's lead, she hung it on the hook in the hall. 'Traitor.' She glared at Dotty, who gave her an unapologetic wag of her curly tail. Amy smiled. She could never stay mad at her for long.

Dipping her fingers into her pocket, she pulled out the letter and gazed at it one more time. If Adam found out about this, she could be headline news. What would her colleagues think of her then? Her world would come toppling down, one domino after another. It would be so easy to throw the paper into the open fire, to walk away from it all. But the words taunted her. The chance to grant her father his last wish. *There are three more bodies buried. Three more families you can help put at rest.*

Opening the envelope, she was about to slide the letter back inside when she caught sight of a Post-it note. In her haste to open the letter, she had missed it the first time around. Unpeeling it, her eyes widened as she found the same spidery scrawl.

I've booked you in for a visit this Thursday at 2.30 p.m.

Thursday? That was tomorrow. She must have made the booking after she wrote, giving Amy little time to back out. Physical visiting orders were becoming obsolete, as many bookings were now made online.

'Cuppa?' Flora's voice carried from the kitchen.

'Yes, please,' Amy called, sliding the letter back in her pocket. Glancing in the hall mirror, she smoothed back her soft brown hair, which had grown frizzy from the rain. She knew Flora would try to dissuade her, warn her against seeing Lillian again. She couldn't tell her what she was about to do. Despite all the upset, she felt strangely resolute; the incentive of finding the burial sites of the three missing girls was reason enough to forge ahead. Seeing her mother dissolve in her grief made Amy the strong one, the person who would hold it all together. She had to do what was right, instead of what was easy. To put her own feelings aside, fulfil her father's last wish and bring those girls home. Kicking off her shoes, Amy padded towards the kitchen, silently repeating the mantra that would give her strength. She could do this. She *would* do this. But her legs felt weak at the prospect of coming face-to-face with the woman who could tear her life apart.

CHAPTER EIGHT

Paddy accepted the call from home, allowing it to filter through the speakers of his new Jag. Having worked twelve hours straight, he was glad to escape the office. His day had consisted of sorting out the workload that had been thrust upon them by other teams. As a sergeant, he had no choice but to accept what was delegated. The enigmatic Amy Winter could not come back quick enough as far as he was concerned.

Working as her sergeant made for a strange role reversal, given that he tutored her as a teen. But he had watched her climb the ranks over the years with pride. He knew her little ways: her obsession with list making and the rumbling thunder she tried to contain when she was pushed too far. He pushed the car into gear, the familiar sound of his wife's voice washing over him as she spoke about her day. Undoing the top button of his shirt, he slid his tie from beneath his collar before throwing it on the passenger seat. Craning his neck left to right, he pulled out of the junction, joining the rest of the work-weary London commuters on their way home.

'The Tesco shop came,' Geraldine replied. 'I wasn't expecting the roses, you shouldn't have.'

'If it put a smile on your face, then it's worth it.' Paddy replied, negotiating traffic as he made his way home.

'Dare I ask, how's work?'

'Relentless.' The words were followed by a long, tired sigh. 'Amy came back for an hour, then rushed off. She seemed upset.'

'It's only natural,' Geraldine replied. 'They were close, weren't they?'

'Mmm,' Paddy murmured in agreement. Automatically, the car wipers came to life as a smattering of rain hit the windshield. The bad weather was showing little sign of abating, and right now all he wanted was to go home and sink a beer. 'She won't admit to it, but she's taken it hard. We all have.'

'Will you make it home tonight?' Geraldine said.

'Unlikely,' Paddy replied. 'I'm on my way to a job now. A shooting in the park. The kid responsible is only twelve.' Paddy did not need to tell his wife to keep details of the case confidential after over twenty years of marriage.

'Oh dear, how awful. Well, don't worry about me, I've got plenty of food. You stay with Pete tonight and get home when you can.'

'Will do,' Paddy said. 'It'll probably be tomorrow. I'll see you then.' The remainder of their conversation was about a television programme that Geraldine had watched. With little contact with the outside world, she could only discuss fictional interactions involving soap characters on daytime TV. After saying his goodbyes Paddy ended the call. He had been telling the truth about the case, but having dealt with it earlier it was already wrapped up with a full confession and charge by the time he'd finished work.

Parking his car in the drive, he activated the central-locking system before shoving his key in the door of the two-bedroom semi he called home. 'It's only me,' he called, depositing his jacket on the coat hanger in the hall. He sniffed the arm. It stunk of smoke. A habit his other half was desperate for him to kick. He would sneak it into the linen basket later on, then pull it out before he went to work in the morning.

A crumpled jacket was a small price to pay to keep a smile on her face. The smell of home cooking welcomed him, and he kicked off his stiff leather shoes before padding into the kitchen.

He found her stirring a pot of chicken in what looked like a white wine sauce, her bobbed blonde hair casting a shadow over her face. Nuzzling her neck, he peered into the cooking pot, wrapping his arms around her generous waist. 'That smells nice,' he said, feeling a fuzzy sense of happiness that only came from being with her.

'It's a Jamie Oliver recipe,' Elaine said, turning her face to kiss him briefly before switching off the stove. 'Long day?' she asked, opening the oven door and sliding out the plates she had warmed just minutes before.

'A strange one,' Paddy said, repeating a conversation which he had already pushed to the back of his mind. 'The DI came into work today, but she didn't stay very long.'

'Bless her, her dad's just died, hasn't he? I hope you've been nice to her today.' Elaine turned her back to plate up.

'It was her decision to come back,' Paddy said. 'And I'm always nice. But not too nice; she hates that.'

'I suppose now is a bad time to ask to meet her. That is, unless you'd like to invite her round to dinner?' Elaine said, raising her eyebrows hopefully.

'She's moved in with her mum for a while. I don't think she'll be socialising much. I'll ask when things get on an even keel.'

'It would be nice to meet some of your colleagues. Anyone would think you're ashamed of me.' Elaine smiled, but her words were teasing, because she knew he was a private man.

'You know how it is,' Paddy said. 'I don't like mixing work with home. It's hard enough, some of the things we deal with . . .'

'And you like to keep it separate. I understand.' After reaching into the fridge, she handed him a bottle of beer.

'Take it as a compliment,' Paddy said, reaching for the bottle opener and pinging the cap into the bin. 'Coming home to you keeps me sane.'

'Even if I don't get to see you on weekends.' Elaine sighed. 'I don't see why they have to work you so hard. All those courses you do. You must be the most well-educated DS on the team.'

'It will be worth it when I'm promoted,' Paddy said, smiling in approval at the feast being laid before him. Elaine did not do things by halves.

'As long as they reward your dedication,' she said, finally joining him at the table. Her cheeks flushed from cooking, she poured herself a glass of wine. After dinner, Paddy would run her a bath, so she could soak while he cleaned up downstairs. Elaine's home was small but cosy, and they had nothing but happy memories there.

'Let's not talk about work,' he said, taking another sip of his beer. 'It's just good to be home.' And it was. This was all he ever wanted. He could never tell Geraldine that Pete, the work colleague she thought he was staying with, didn't exist. His wife would never understand.

CHAPTER NINE

The solid prison door was bolted behind her, shutting out all natural light and cutting her off from the outside world. Amy Winter felt like she was going to throw up for the second time in as many days. She was not just meeting Lillian Grimes, striding down the airless corridor, she was returning to the bowels of a nightmare that had plagued her for years. Fear tugged at her senses, bringing an unfamiliar feeling of insecurity. Was she doing the right thing? Last night she had not slept easy, and it had taken several glasses of gin before she could persuade herself to go to bed. Sleep came, bringing the same recurring nightmare: tip-toeing down the basement steps, then Sally-Ann, wide-eyed and terrified as she helped her to hide. The faces that were once blurry came into view with chilling clarity: the faces of the Beasts of Brentwood, Jack and Lillian Grimes.

Lillian was not the first psychopath she had encountered, but she was the first one claiming ownership over her. *Just get through today*, Amy reminded herself, flexing her fingers, which had cramped from being bunched so tightly. *I owe it to the victims to see what she has to say.*

Reports of Jack and Lillian's crimes made for grim reading. Lillian had been just one of the case studies mentioned in a recently published book, *Why Women Kill*. The author, Professor Quigley, was a leading expert in psychopathy, and until now, Amy had gobbled up his work. Although Lillian had declined to be interviewed, it came as no surprise that she had scored highly on the psychopathy tests.

It was with these thoughts in mind that Amy entered the visitor's room. She cast her eyes over the rows of low tables and soft spongy seats. A vending machine took up space in the corner, a yellowing tiled ceiling illuminated by fluorescent lights overhead. Timed air fresheners attached to the wall provided a fake woodland smell. A privately owned prison, HMP Bronzefield was the largest category A jail in Europe. Given that it was a women's-only institution, Amy had not had cause to visit it too often. The type of crimes she dealt with usually involved men. It was a small blessing that it was based in Ashford, unlike the other women's prisons, which were several hours' drive away. Not that she was planning on a return visit.

After taking a seat, Amy fixed her gaze on the door where the prisoners entered. She had dressed in a black skirt suit and sat primly, her knees together and shoulders straight. Her eyes fell on the inmates as they filtered in, involuntarily narrowing as she saw her. Lillian appeared a softer, more rounded version of the image displayed in the press. Amy touched her hair, her heart faltering at the resemblance: Lillian's hair was shorter than hers, but also parted at the side. Like her, she had high cheekbones, but where Amy had smile lines, Lillian's mouth seemed set in a permanent frown. A prison-issue blue bib covered her grey sweatshirt, and a slim-fitting pair of jeans hugged her hips. Amy stared, her mouth dry. The monster she had built up in her head looked as ordinary as anybody else.

Amy watched, stony-faced, as Lillian scanned the room. Finally, Lillian's eyes lit upon her, and she swerved between fellow inmates to Amy's table, a gentle smile on her lips.

Amy would not allow herself to be swayed. She knew what this woman was capable of.

'Poppy! It's so good to see you again,' Lillian said, her eyes filling with tears. She paused, wringing her hands. 'I suppose a hug is out of the question?'

'Take a seat,' Amy said stiffly. The woman in her dreams was always out of focus, but now that she was here, in her presence, she knew it had been Lillian all along. Something felt out of kilter though, and Amy kept up her guard, monitoring every movement she made.

Lillian did as instructed, swiping away her tears before sitting on the edge of the blue padded chair. While psychopaths could not feel empathy, they made an art of mimicking it to suit their own needs. 'Look at you,' she said, still smiling. 'My little girl is all grown up.'

It was only then that Amy noticed the yellowing bruise on her temple. She knew from experience that on a sliding scale of offences, prisoners with previous for murdering women and children would be viewed as the lowest of the low. It was hard to have sympathy for the violence she must have encountered since making the prison her home.

'My name is DI Amy Winter.' Reaching into her jacket pocket, Amy slid a small black recorder onto the table, something that had been cleared by security before her arrival. She could have asked for a legal visit, spoken privately, and got the police involved, but this would have taken longer to organise, and Amy needed to know if reporting their meeting was worthwhile. 'This is a recording device. One of the conditions of my visit.' Amy reeled off the location, time and date. 'I understand you have information regarding the whereabouts of victims Barbara Price, Vivian Holden and Wendy Thompson.' She kept her eyes on Lillian, trying hard to concentrate as the chatter of inmates filled the room. She did not interview many people as a detective inspector, but it was a skill she hadn't lost thanks to refresher sessions and guidance on the latest techniques. Crossing her legs, she rested her clasped hands on her knee. It was difficult to keep Lillian's gaze without thinking about their shared bloodline. *Sally-Ann*, she thought, her sister's face coming into view. Jack had killed her right before her eyes. The next day they had carried on as if nothing had happened at all. A deep stirring awakened inside her as long-buried memories hatched free.

'Ooh, don't you sound posh,' Lillian said. Her smile faded as Amy stared at her, stony-faced. 'Please, Poppy. I've missed you. How are you? I want to hear all about your life.'

Amy's knuckles turned white as she clasped her fingers harder. Glaring at Lillian with an ill-concealed fury, she spoke through tightened lips. 'If you call me Poppy one more time, I swear I'm going to walk.'

A nervous titter escaped as Lillian delivered a victorious smile. 'Oh, there she is, my little firecracker.' She licked her lips, straightening her bib before crossing her legs. 'Have it your way. I'll call you Amy, now I know you're listening to me.'

'I'm listening all right,' Amy said, annoyed with herself for losing her temper within seconds of Lillian sitting down. She knew from experience that a psychopath like Lillian would hone in on vulnerability. She may not feel empathy, but she was particularly adept at seeking out other people's pain. 'You promised me answers,' Amy said. 'Where have you buried the bodies?'

'Patience. You'll get your answers.' Lillian smiled, her dark eyes alight with amusement. 'And don't scowl. The wrinkles will ruin your pretty face.' She raked Amy's form as she looked her up and down. 'I see you're not wearing a wedding ring. Here,' she chortled, 'you're not one of those gays, are you?'

Amy took a deep breath in through her nostrils, briefly closing her eyes as she maintained control. 'If you won't give me what I need, then I'll just go.'

Leaning back in her chair, Lillian fell silent, her eyes narrowing as she tilted her head. She folded her arms high on her chest, a shadow crossing her face as she deliberated her next move. 'You're used to bossing people around, aren't you? Getting your own way. But would you really walk out on the victims' families after coming so close to the truth?' A smile twisted her face. 'Just admit it, you don't really want to go. I am your mother, after all.'

Amy could see what she was doing. Playing on her sense of duty to make her stay. 'You're a cold-hearted, psychopathic killer. Don't think for a second I'm interested in seeing you.'

'Really?' Lillian stiffened. 'Is that any way to talk to your own flesh and blood?'

'I'm not insulting you, I'm describing you.' Amy shrugged. 'Why *have* you dragged me here? Why now? You could have told the police about the victims' whereabouts at any time.'

'I could paper my cell walls with the letters I got from the Thompsons asking where Wendy is buried. You know, her mother actually wrote to say she forgave me for killing her. Fucking cheek. She can fuck right off.'

Amy watched as Lillian's walls came down and her voice fell back into the Essex accent embedded in her roots. This was the person in her fragmented nightmares. A flash of memory returned. Lillian, encouraging her to swear as a child, her drunken laughter sounding like a high-pitched scream. Now she knew why their initial exchanges had not felt quite right, why the nicely worded letter seemed odd. Had Lillian been making an effort to change, or was she just trying to pull the wool over her eyes?

'So why now?' Amy said, swallowing her revulsion.

'You always were the direct sort,' Lillian mused. 'Never did a thing you were told and, oh that mouth of yours . . . You used to give me hell. Remember when your hamster escaped? You were always sneaking around looking for him, delving into places you shouldn't. Do you remember, Amy? Little Hammy, how your sister gave up her life to save yours?' Lillian's voice darkened. A chill crawled up Amy's spine while the room seemed to close in around them.

'Sally-Ann would never have gone into the basement if she wasn't looking for you. She knew better than to disobey her father. Why didn't you stop him? Your daddy loved you. He would never have killed her if he knew you were there.'

Daddy. The word made Amy's stomach churn. Another flash of memory rippled. Lillian was describing a scene from Amy's nightmares. Only it wasn't a nightmare.

'I often wonder how things would have turned out if your sister hadn't chased you down into the basement. She would still be alive, for starters . . .' A smile haunted Lillian's lips, though her eyes were cold. 'I'd arranged for us to stay at a refuge, you know. I was planning to break free from your brute of a father so we could start again. We're not that unalike, Poppy . . .'

'Enough,' Amy said firmly, realising Lillian was mirroring her pose. It was an action developed to lure her in. 'This is the last time I'm going to ask you. Tell me where they are or I leave.'

'Tell you what, I'll give you the first address and we'll see how we get on after that.' Lillian rested her hands on her lap, just as Amy had done. 'But there are rules.'

'Rules?' Amy raised an eyebrow.

'Why so surprised? I've had lots of time to work this out. Firstly, I need to show you in person. And it's got to be you. I won't tell anybody else. Secondly, I want *you* to tell the victim's family when the body is found.'

Amy's thoughts raced forward, creating a mental to-do list. 'I'll need to organise a driver, and if you're on release from prison, uniformed officers will have to accompany us, too.'

'You can bring a brass band for all I care. And don't worry, mum's the word, I won't let anyone in on our little secret unless you want me to.' She finished her sentence with a wink. 'Get it? Mum's the word?'

The thought of sharing anything with Lillian Grimes made Amy cringe. But she was right about one thing – their relationship was a secret she was not ready to share with anyone else. She exhaled, her armpits damp with perspiration beneath her suit jacket. Covering the recorder with her hand, she switched it off before sliding it back into her pocket. She would dissect the conversation later in private, making notes before deleting it.

'Fine. I'll arrange it. Someone will be in touch.'

'Make sure it's you,' Lillian said as Amy stood to leave.

Amy did not look back as she left the room, holding her head high. She had done it, survived her first meeting with the murderer who claimed to be her flesh and blood. Survived an early memory that would bring most people to their knees. She felt lighter from the minor victory, but Lillian had orchestrated things so that she could not work on her own. She was going to have to confide in DCI Pike in order to progress the visit. How would she react to this? Amy would have her answer soon enough. It was time to return to work.

CHAPTER TEN

'Hey babe, was your body made in McDonald's . . . ? 'Cause I'm loving it!'

Hemmy Parker bit back her smile, embarrassed by the braces lining her teeth. The mild amusement gained from the joke was overshadowed by her discomfort at being called out on the street. The schoolboys weren't much older than her, but a flush crept up her cheeks just the same.

'Losers!' Paige Taylor retorted, hooking her arm through her friend's.

'Ignore them,' Hemmy muttered, yanking up the shoulder strap of her schoolbag. There were four badges on display. From declaring her allegiance to feminism to her love for Sherlock Holmes, they expressed an individuality frowned upon by her exclusive north-west London school. At fifteen, Hemmy was still getting used to male attention and had mixed feelings about it all. Striding up the footpath, her blonde ponytail bobbed as she walked with more confidence than she felt.

'I saw Mike eyeing you up again today,' Paige said, a tinge of envy in her voice. Long-limbed and lean, Paige did not yet appreciate the lithe grace in her step.

'He was not.' A fiery pink bloomed in Hemmy's cheeks at the mention of the sixth former's name. 'Anyway, he's waaay older than me.'

'But you like him, don't you?' Paige giggled. 'What's your mum going to say when she finds out?'

'There's nothing *to* find out,' Hemmy said, brushing a wisp of hair from her face. 'And don't you go spreading rumours.'

'Oh, come on, I know you're dying to get a ride on his bike. Amongst other things.'

'Eww!' Hemmy laughed in disgust as she pushed her friend away. She bit her bottom lip, giving her a furtive glance. 'He is nice though, isn't he?'

'Totally,' Paige replied. 'Well, this is me. See you tomorrow!' She waved her friend off as she turned to cross the road.

Hemmy climbed the steps to the terraced house she shared with her mum. Like her, Paige hadn't even kissed a boy yet, never mind anything else. She was still smiling when she walked inside. She loved their pretty tree-lined street, which came without the constant churn of traffic of their previous house. It was nearer for Mum's work, too. Hemmy had got used to their routine, and found herself enjoying the hour alone before her mum returned home from work. If she was lucky, they would have takeaway pizza tonight, a reward for her recent exam results. Dumping her schoolbag on the floor, she closed the door behind her and waited for her cat to greet her in the hall. A Persian cross, Purdy was named after her unnaturally loud purr. Hemmy kicked off her shoes, wriggling her toes where the leather had pinched. Shrugging off her blazer, she threw it over the bannister, her frown deepening in the absence of her cat. 'Purdy,' she called, padding towards the kitchen in her stockinged feet. 'Puuuurdy, where are you, girl?' Her eyes fell on the cat flap built into their kitchen door. Purdy hated being outside and was never gone for very long. The sharp ring of the house phone infiltrated her thoughts, making her jump on the spot. She hated answering, but worry about Purdy brought her tiptoeing to the hall. Tentatively, she picked up the handset, wishing her mum was home.

'You have a text message,' a robotic voice announced. Hemmy frowned as she listened. She didn't know you could text a landline. The words that followed rooted her to the spot. 'Can you come collect your cat? I found her on the road. I think she's been hit by a car. Mrs Cotterill.'

'Oh no!' Hemmy's hand flew to her mouth as the message came to an end. Mrs Cotterill lived two doors down. She was in her early seventies and sometimes got confused. Mum had popped in to see her recently. Had she sent the text by mistake? Surely it was easier to leave a normal message? Hemmy picked up the receiver to request the number to ring back, but the thought of Purdy made her pause. Her pet was hurt. She needed her. Why was she still faffing about with the phone? Absent-mindedly, Hemmy deleted the text and slammed down the handset.

Drawing back the security chain, Hemmy pulled her front door open, her eyes blurred with tears. 'Poor Purdy,' she cried, a sob building in the back of her throat. She would bring her home and call the vet. He was a nice man. He would come straight away. He would know what to do.

Her pulse pounding, Hemmy braced herself as she trotted up her neighbour's steps. The terrace was just like hers, with a solid black door and a brass knocker that creaked when lifted. Hemmy had broken one of her mother's rules, leaving her own door unlocked. But she reasoned that she would be back in seconds: bring Purdy inside, wrap her up warm, call her mother and ring the vet. She swiped away her tears. Purdy would be all right. She had to be. But why wasn't Mrs Cotterill answering? As she lifted the knocker a second time, the door creaked open an inch, and Hemmy realised that her neighbour had left it off the latch.

'Mrs Cotterill?' she called, poking her head inside. 'It's Hem—' she paused, 'Hermione Parker. You rang. I'm here to pick up my cat.' An angry meow echoed from the end of the hall, making Hemmy's heart flutter in her chest. It was true, something *had* happened. But she was very vocal. Did this mean she was going to be OK?

'Hello?' Hemmy said, stepping inside. The dampness of the streets had soaked into the soles of her socks. She realised that she had come out without her shoes. Peering into the gloom, she became aware of her heavy breathing as she crept down the length of the hall. Why was it so dark? She tried to flick on the light, but the bulb had been removed and all the doors in the hall were closed. Gingerly, she followed the sound of meows, pushing open the door to the right.

'Purdy,' Hemmy gasped, peeping inside the darkened room. Why were the curtains closed? And why was her cat in a cage on the floor? Flattening her ears, Purdy rasped a warning hiss, and with terrifying clarity, Hemmy realised her cat was perfectly well. Only now were alarm bells ringing, telling her everything about this situation was wrong. 'Mrs Cotterill?' Hemmy called, her voice shaky. Only then did she remember why her mother had called upon her neighbour: because she was going away. So who had left the message on her phone? The presence of a rasping breath told Hemmy she was not alone. She tensed, knowing what she had to do. Grab her cat and run. She stepped forward, a rush of adrenaline flooding her veins as she caught sight of a shadow from behind.

'Who's there—' Hemmy's sentence was cut short as a pair of arms grappled her from behind. Unleashing a powerful scream, she inhaled a mouthful of gas from the rubber mask being pressed against her face. Her eyes flashing in the darkness, Hemmy kicked the shins of the stranger behind her. A muffled grunt followed, and they temporarily loosened their grip. But it was too late to get away. Her senses became woozy and her eyelids grew heavy. With a thump, her head made contact with the cold tiled floor.

CHAPTER ELEVEN

Sliding the newspaper from under her arm, Amy placed it flat on her office desk and scanned the page.

Final Plea of Grief-Stricken Mother
By Adam Rossi

Reduced to tears, terminally ill Gladys Thompson told us of her final wish before she dies – to find the location of her murdered twelve-year-old daughter so they can be buried in the same grave. But the only person who knows the truth is Lillian Grimes, surviving member of the serial killer couple nicknamed the Beasts of Brentwood. After a fifteen-year reign of terror, the couple were arrested in 1987. The bodies of six young women aged between twelve and twenty-three were found buried on the grounds of their home. Having confessed to a further three murders, Jack Grimes died of natural causes prior to disclosing their burial sites.

Despite numerous pleas from the families, Lillian Grimes has refused to reveal the locations of the victims, Barbara Price, Vivian Holden and Wendy Thompson. The case was brought back into the spotlight last week when Superintendent Robert Winter suddenly passed away. After tirelessly working on the case for many years, he was unable to fulfil his promise of finding the location of the three graves. His daughter, Detective Inspector Amy Winter, has refused to comment on the case.

'Of all the scheming . . .' Amy said, feeling her hackles rise. Turning the page, she was met with a recent photo of Gladys Thompson lying in a hospital bed. She looked pale and haunted, with deep furrows of grief etching her face and a small tube protruding from her nose. Holding her hand was her son, John Thompson, and beneath the photo, his quote: *All I want is justice for my sister and mother. It's time to bring Wendy home.* In contrast, a ghoulish image of Jack and Lillian Grimes featured below. The custody picture was one Amy recognised, and she could see why the press loved to use it. The badly developed photo drove deep shadows into Lillian's eye sockets, making her dead-eyed stare bore into your very soul. Lillian had since gained a few extra wrinkles, and her severe haircut had been replaced by a shoulder-length bob. Her despicable acts were no longer exemplified by her appearance, but the public did not want to see a picture of a woman who looked just like everybody else. Regardless of her changed physical appearance, Amy knew precisely what Lillian Grimes was.

Rereading Adam's report, another flare of anger surged within. Where was the tribute he had promised? Why make her father sound like a failure when he had helped bring them to justice in the first place? And why mention her by name? Saying she had refused to comment implied she was not interested in the case. Chewing her lip, Amy tried to keep her temper in check. Adam was goading her. She would not give him the satisfaction of raging at him over the phone. The best form of revenge would be finding the burial sites and giving the story to a journalist who knew the meaning of respect. She spared a thought for her biological siblings. Would they be reading this too? She strained to remember them, accessing a back catalogue of memories mingled with crime and press reports. Damien and Amanda? No, Mandy. That was it. Both were older than her, and she lacked the sense of closeness she got when she thought about Sally-Ann. Since speaking to Lillian in prison, the lid had been lifted from her collection of repressed memories, and she felt the grief and loss of her sister all over again. Had she not led her down there into the basement . . . would she be still alive today?

'Oh, hello.' Craig seemed surprised to see her as he interrupted her thoughts. 'I thought you weren't due back until tomorrow.' Amy raised her head from the paper, noticing her brother's auburn hair had been cropped short. Smartly dressed in a black suit and tie, he looked more than capable of his new promotion as the head of CID.

'I'm not,' she said, folding up the newspaper and depositing it in the bin. 'But I came in early to sort out our workload. Those jobs you've been doling out – they're not in our remit.' She did not take any pleasure from being stern, but this was her team, and she had fought hard to establish it. While covering for her, DI Gladwell had accepted jobs from CID in an effort to ease their workload. This in itself would not be a problem, were Amy's team not being so closely monitored by her commanding officers. A lot of money had been pumped into the high priority unit, and it had to be run as intended, or not at all.

Craig's face darkened as Amy told him as much. 'We're all feeling the pressure,' he said. 'Gladwell was just helping us out.'

'But we're not here as an overflow,' Amy replied. 'The command team expect big things of us. If we don't deliver, they'll shut us down.'

Craig thrust his hands into his trouser pockets as he delivered a condescending smile. 'We're all one big family, Amy. There's no room for lone rangers here.'

Speaking of family, Amy wanted to ask why he hadn't called their mother since the funeral, much less popped around, but they had made a vow to keep their personal lives separate, and she turned her attention back to work. 'Tell me,' she said, her face taut. 'Why do you think this team was set up?'

Craig shrugged. 'The same reason they waste the budget on every other so-called specialist team. Because of a knee-jerk reaction to bad publicity.'

Amy raised an eyebrow. 'You don't approve?' She already knew the answer, but needed to hear him say it aloud.

'It's nothing personal, Sis, but I don't think it's fair that our budget is ploughed into specialist teams just to make us look good in the press.'

'It's about much more than that,' Amy said, knowing he was still feeling bitter after being turned down for the role himself. 'Our results speak for themselves. Remember Stephen Port? He used an app to lure his victims in. He didn't even have to leave his house. Social media has changed the face of our investigations. We owe it to the victims to be up to speed.'

'Killers are all the same at heart,' Craig said, shaking his head.

Amy's spirit burned with conviction for her team. 'But how they're working has changed.'

Craig checked his watch. 'I don't have time to argue the toss. Briefing's in five, and we've got lots of jobs on the go.'

'You've got more now,' Amy said. 'I came in early and sent a good half of them back.'

Craig stiffened. 'You did what?'

Amy frowned. She would not be spoken down to by anyone – not even her older brother. 'You heard me. This is my team, and I'll run it the way it was intended. If you've a problem with that, then speak to DCI Pike.'

'I won't waste my time.' Craig's lips thinned. Unlike Amy, he did not befriend work colleagues and his relationship with Pike was purely professional. He raised the paperwork in his right hand. 'You won't be interested in this high-profile kidnapping then, if you're sending everything back.'

'What kidnapping? Where are you going?' Amy said, rising from her seat.

'Back to my team. Looks like we've got some extra work on.'

CHAPTER TWELVE

Amy paused to compose herself, inhaling the aroma of freshly percolating coffee drifting through the crack in DCI Hazel Pike's office door. Her stomach grumbled in complaint, but since reading Lillian's letter, she could not face eating or drinking very much. *Getting sick on the street*, she thought, as yesterday's walk with Dotty replayed in her mind. *What the hell was that about?* She had faced some horrendous things, but nothing had ever affected her to the point of throwing up. But then this was not just about her career; it was about her identity: who she really was. Amy gently rapped her knuckles against the door before pushing it open. Light and airy, with newly laid carpet tiles, her DCI's office was twice the size of hers. She envied her view of the streets below and the generous bookcase that housed policing manuals and law journals. Only Amy knew she had a secret stash of romance novels with the spines facing inwards on the bottom shelf. Not that she had time to read them. These days, downtime was a thing of the past.

'Come in, come in,' Pike said, signalling at Amy to close the door behind her. Ensconced behind her desk, she wore light make-up, her short hair neatly styled. A cup of steaming black coffee sat at her right hand and a scattering of well-thumbed paperwork at her left. They had yet to go fully paperless, and Pike preferred things the old-fashioned way. 'Can I get you a coffee?' She removed her reading glasses, rubbing the imprint they left on the bridge of her nose.

'No thanks, I'm fine,' Amy replied, although in truth she was still feeling the after-effects of her minor tiff with Craig. Sliding her hand on the back of the black swivel chair, she summoned her courage for the conversation ahead. She hated being at odds with him. She could see where he was coming from, but he had caught her at a bad time. What would he think if he knew the truth about who she really was? Would he even consider himself her brother anymore?

'Take a seat.' Raising her mug, Pike took a tentative sip. 'That's better,' she said, before giving Amy a sympathetic smile. 'Do you need more leave? I was looking through your personnel file, and you've hardly taken any this year.'

'No ma'am, it's quite the opposite,' Amy said, knowing her boss's old-fashioned ways extended to the use of formal titles at work. Use of her first name was usually followed by a frown. 'I wanted to talk to you about a cold case that's been in the press. Also, I've been talking to Craig. He said a kidnapping has come in.'

'And it's being dealt with. Your team has enough to contend with, as you said . . .'

'Not any more,' Amy piped up. 'I've reallocated some of the work back to where it came from.'

'I know. Your brother's already been on the blower. He's insisting CID can take the kidnapping case.' Pike tilted her head as she regarded her with concern. 'Are you sure you're ready for DI Gladwell to relinquish cover? He's due in for one more day.'

'I'll soon be up to speed,' Amy replied, wondering why it was fine for her brother to come back early but not her. 'About this kidnapping, I hear it's Tessa Parker's daughter.' The first thing she had done after Craig left was look up the case herself. He was taking it out of spite. She could have let him keep it, eased back into work slowly, but as soon as she clicked on the image of fifteen-year-old Hermione Parker, she knew she had to handle the case. Now all she had to do was to persuade her DCI to allow her to take control.

'It's in the hands of CID,' Pike said, wearing her referee face.

'Please, ma'am. A high-profile case like this is ideal for our team. Plus . . . I've got another piece of news. Something that will interest you.' Amy was unashamedly using her liaison with Lillian to win her the kidnapping case. After a week of her team dealing with jobs nobody else wanted, they desperately needed strong results. Her heart began to thunder at the prospect of sharing details of her visit with Lillian Grimes. She could already feel herself becoming entangled in the case, something her DCI almost certainly would not approve of, should she learn the truth. 'I should have told you sooner, but I didn't think anything would come of it. And now that it has . . .' Amy looked at her hopefully, willing her to ask for more.

'I'm intrigued,' Pike said, downing a mouthful of coffee and licking her lips. 'But you'll have to be quick, I've got a strategy meeting in ten.'

Folding her hands across her lap, Amy paused to assemble her words. She was usually very articulate but her once orderly thoughts were jumbled and in disarray.

'Lillian Grimes has hit the press again. With Dad's passing and Mrs Thompson still begging for answers, it seems like the case is on everyone's radar.'

'Ah. I understand,' Pike said warmly. 'It's only natural for you to want to do something for your dad. I know how much not being able to find the graves of those girls tormented him. But you should be at home with your family, not opening up old cases . . .'

'I've visited Grimes in prison,' Amy blurted, as she caught Pike glancing at her watch. 'She's ready to tell us where the last three bodies are buried.'

Pike's mouth dropped open. It took two full breaths for her to realise and snap it shut. Her composure regained, she narrowed her eyes and delivered a questioning glare. 'You're telling me you've seen Grimes in prison? When? How? I don't remember seeing a visitation request.'

'This morning, during a private visit,' Amy said. 'She wrote to me and arranged it for the next day.' She fiddled with her hands as she forced the words. 'The thing is . . .' Amy paused, the truth stuck in her throat. Six words. That's all she needed to say. Lillian Grimes is my biological mother. But it felt like a lie. Flora and Robert were her mum and dad. It seemed unnatural to say otherwise.

'She heard that Dad died. I think she had an attack of conscience,' she said instead.

But her DCI was yet to be convinced. 'I remember the court case. She was completely unrepentant. She blamed everything on Jack and said the murders had nothing to do with her.'

Amy nodded. Lies did not come easily. 'Perhaps Dad's death triggered something. She's still not admitting to the murders, only that Jack told her where they were buried when he was alive.'

'Right.' Pike's eyes were alight as she accepted Amy's explanation. 'Whatever the reason, this is excellent news. So how do we do this? Have you arranged for a legal visit?'

Amy shook her head. 'She wants to show us in person. I suppose it's a trip out of prison for her. She's promised to give us the address of the first victim as soon as we can organise it.'

'You never cease to amaze me,' Pike said, a look of triumph blazing in her eyes. 'Despite everything, you've found a way to fulfil your father's last wish. He'd be so proud of you right now.'

'I don't want any credit.' Amy shied away from the sentiment. 'Although one of Lillian's conditions is that I'm present throughout.'

'Fine by me. But take credit when it's given. This could be a great opportunity for you. She wouldn't have agreed to it if she didn't connect with you in some way.'

Amy inwardly bristled at the truth that was too awful to bear. 'Can we credit the team instead? It would put us in a good light. If they need to name someone, I'd like it to be you. Without your support, the team never would have got off the ground.'

'Let's see if we can pull it off first,' Pike said, leaning back in her chair. 'She could be toying with us. Isn't Wendy Thompson's mother terminally ill? We don't have a lot of time.'

'She is,' Amy said solemnly. 'I'll get cracking on it straight away.'

Pike nodded, her gaze distant as she thought ahead. 'Get in touch with Essex Police, have the file sent over so you can familiarise yourself with the case. It's best to go into this with your eyes open. It would make for some great publicity for the force.'

'And give peace to the families involved,' Amy added. She had made the right decision to keep quiet about her background for now. Her DCI would never have let her see the file if she knew who she really was. It wasn't downright dishonesty. She had omitted to tell her the truth. All the same, it did not rest easy with her.

'She's giving me the location of the first body to begin with, then she'll tell us where the others are in follow-up visits,' Amy said, manufacturing another reason as to why Lillian Grimes would help the likes of her. 'I don't think she's having an easy time of it in prison. I noticed some bruising on her face. She could be hoping for better conditions inside.'

Slowly, Pike nodded. 'Don't make her any promises. Knowing her, she'll want something tenfold. But then I don't need to tell you that.' Pike gave her a knowing look. 'You always had a knack for dealing with the underbelly of society.'

Takes one to know one. Amy stiffened in her chair as the thought reared its head.

Pike checked her watch for the second time, and Amy took it as a signal to leave.

'Just one more thing.' Amy rose from her seat. 'The kidnapping case. Can we have it? It would be a brilliant follow-up to what we're doing with Lillian Grimes.' She looked at Pike pleadingly. Having baited the hook, she hoped she would not be able to say no.

'Very well,' Pike said, breathing out as if she didn't have the energy to argue. 'Make the call. You can lead. If they give you any grief, refer them to me.'

CHAPTER THIRTEEN

1986

Poppy shook with such a force that the wicker basket trembled around her. Her eyes tightly closed, she scrunched her body into its smallest possible form. Her heart was beating so hard beneath her ribcage she felt sure it would break free. Sally-Ann had been still, so very still on the floor of the basement that a part of her had wanted to jump out of her wicker cave. But she was no match for her father, who had silenced her sister for good. She remembered Sally-Ann's warning, *Don't make a sound. No crying or you'll be done for, too*, but she could not stay here forever. Her knickers were soaked through from sitting on the urine-stained sheets, the tang of crusted blood curling up her nose. Forcing her eyes open, Poppy peered through the gap in the basket. In the windowless basement, it was impossible to know how much time had passed, but all that was left of her sister was a stream of blood where she had lain.

Gathering a fistful of linen, Poppy stuffed it into her mouth, pushing back the sob rising in her throat. The dry, bitter taste proved a vital distraction. She swallowed back her tears, a physical pain swelling in her chest at the loss of the one person she truly loved. She knew she would never see her sister again. It was her fault. She had brought her down here. And now she was gone.

Poppy did not know how long she sat in the basket too scared to move. It was long enough for the shaking to subside. For her heart to resume a regular beat. She smacked her lips as she removed the corner of soiled linen from her mouth. Peering through the basket, she could see that the trunk her father had dragged from the corner was now back in its place. It was deathly quiet, and the scratching sounds that lured her in here had long since ceased. A fresh sense of horror bloomed. She was lost in the dark, like in the woodland stories Sally-Ann used to read to her in bed. Only Daddy was the giant in *Jack and The Beanstalk* and the wolf in *Little Red Riding Hood*. He was the Bogey Man, the Child Catcher, every bad man from every story she had ever heard. As the cellar door opened, Poppy sealed her mouth shut, sucking her lips over her teeth until her gums bled. A long, dark shadow loomed from above. The room smelt of sweat and the bitter stench that sometimes carried on her daddy's breath. He was coming for her, she felt sure of it. He had killed Sally-Ann and now it was her turn. He would break her in half, just like he did with the lady in the trunk. Nobody would see her again.

One step then two descended the wooden stairs. Panic grew inside her, making her flesh creep and her heartbeat thunder in her ears. She froze. If she closed her eyes and blocked out the sound then Daddy could not get her. She squeezed them shut, whispering a silent prayer. *I'll be a good girl. Please, please make him go away.* But her prayers had little effect as more footsteps came. They were growing closer. They were coming for her. Down the steps, over the mattress, then onwards, towards the basket in which she lay. The cloying smell of urine threatened to make her gag as Poppy shrank further into the sheets she had soiled. Pushing her face into her knees, her concentration was interrupted by a soft tickling sensation at the back of her neck. Brushing it with her hand, she realised that one of the long-legged basement spiders was crawling in her hair. A sharp squeak escaped her lips, finally betraying her. The footsteps stilled.

A switch was clicked on, and as the basket lid was lifted, a shaft of light beamed in. Poppy clenched her small grubby hands into fists. She would fight if she had to. She would scream, swear and shout. She would not give in.

'There you are,' a voice said, warm and reassuring, flooding her with relief.

Squinting up at her mother, Poppy's eyes were filled with remnants of the terror she had witnessed.

Lillian brushed the spider from the rim of the basket as it tried to make its escape. 'Shush now, don't make a sound,' she said. 'Daddy's asleep. If you wake him, he'll be cross.'

Poppy nodded in understanding, uncoiling her hands and face from the sheets in which she had been wrapped. Her legs had numbed, and as her mother lifted her from the basket, they fizzed angrily at being left in such a state for so long. She needed to be quiet. She needed not to cry. Mummy would keep her safe. She wrapped herself around her mother like a spider monkey, her fingers pinching the back of Lillian's neck as she clawed for something to grab onto.

'Ouch, not so tight,' Lillian said. 'You're pinching me.'

But Poppy was unable to let go. As her mother climbed the stairs she knew she would never go into the basement again.

Her sister's bed was empty, and a ball of grief lodged in her chest, pressing on her lungs and making it hard to breathe. Outside, a storm was in full flow, the wind screeching mournfully through the cracked single windowpane. Unfurling Poppy's fingers from around her neck, her mother worked quickly, stripping off her urine sodden nightclothes and pulling one of Sally-Ann's old pink t-shirts over her head. As Lillian laid her down, Poppy pointed towards her sister's vacant single bed. Unable to speak, she could only gesture as her mother rolled her blankets up to her chest.

'Just go to sleep,' Lillian uttered, unable to meet her eyes. Without saying another word, she turned and walked out the door.

CHAPTER FOURTEEN

It had taken Paddy several seconds to find his bearings when he awoke. Sometimes, he had to glance around the room to remind himself which bed he was in. The wrong word, an ill-timed text – the smallest action could send his house of cards toppling down. Starting his night in Elaine's bed, he had ended it in the home he shared with Geraldine. Not that he was some kind of stud. Intimacy with Geraldine had ended when they started sleeping in separate rooms. At five o'clock in the morning, the last thing he had wanted was to rush to her side; but facing the guilt of lying to Elaine about being called into work was far better than the alternative. He would never have forgiven himself if Geraldine hurt herself. Her earlier good mood had yo-yoed to threats of self-harm.

'You don't have to rush off just yet, do you?' Geraldine said now, tugging his jacket as he released it from its hook in the hall. His afternoon shift was a blessing, and he was grateful for the few hours' sleep he had been afforded before work.

Standing in her candlewick dressing gown, Geraldine did not seem to notice the mismatched slippers into which she had plugged her feet.

Perhaps later she would also come to realise that she had forgotten to brush her hair and clean her teeth.

'It's work,' Paddy said. 'You don't want me to be late now, do you? Not when I'm going for promotion.' It was a lie. Paddy had given up any hopes of career advancement years ago.

Geraldine rolled her eyes, releasing her grip on his coat. 'And Miss Winter hates latecomers, doesn't she?' Her lip arched in a sneer. 'You don't want to let her down. After all, I'm only your wife. What does that matter?'

Paddy touched her forearm. He hated seeing her like this because he knew her anger was coming from pain. 'Please, love, don't be like this. We've had a nice morning together. Let's just leave it at that.'

'I made you breakfast,' Geraldine replied, folding her arms. 'And yet here you are, sneaking off without saying goodbye.'

It was a bit late for breakfast, but pointing out that it was noon would not improve his wife's mood. 'In a minute, I'm just putting on my jacket. It's a bit nippy in here.' Another lie. He had been hoping to slip away while she was still being reasonable.

But after twenty years of marriage, Geraldine was not that easily fooled. 'Come off it. You can't get away from me quick enough. After all the trouble I've gone to, and you just turn and walk out the door.' Her voice was shrill now, her fists clenched.

'I'm not going without breakfast.' Paddy sidled past her into the kitchen. 'What have you made?'

'Porridge,' Geraldine spat as if it were a dirty word. Her temper had boiled over, much like the porridge sticking to the top of the gas stove. With a recently fitted kitchen, their terrace house in Ealing was much bigger than his home with Elaine. Not that Geraldine knew about that. It had been years since she had ventured outside the front door. The worst thing about her agoraphobia was that she saved up all of her frustrations for him. 'Is that stuck-up bitch bringing you out for breakfast? I bet you love leering at her, don't you? You dirty old man. You're not getting any from me, so you're sniffing around her like an old dog. Another thing I'm no good at. I know you're going elsewhere.'

'Please, love. I don't know what's happened to put you in such a bad mood.' Paddy sighed, trailing his fingers through his thinning hair. 'Why don't you join me for a bite to eat before I go?' His wife's moods were as changeable as the weather. For now, all he could do was bow his head and bear the storm. Pulling out a stool, he took a seat at the compact breakfast bar.

Closing her eyes, Geraldine's nostrils flared as she drew in a deep breath. Paddy guessed she was counting to five in her mind. Turning to the stove, she reached for the saucepan while Paddy waited to be served.

'Of course, you're right,' she said, her sickly sweet smile carrying on her words. 'I'm sorry. Here. Have your breakfast.'

Without warning, she tipped the contents of the saucepan over the back of his head. 'Ahh!' Paddy roared in disbelief, as what felt like molten lava slid down his skin.

Impassively, Geraldine watched as he leapt from the stool, sending it skittering across the tiled floor. His steps unsteady, he staggered to the tap, swiping away the porridge burning his skin. 'Help me,' he shouted, his face flushed with pain.

Geraldine stood motionless, limply holding the saucepan in her hand.

Pulling off his jacket, Paddy rinsed a tea towel under the cold-water tap, wincing as he eased it over his neck. Stodgy lumps of half-cooked oatmeal trailed down his shirt and onto the floor. He should have been watching her, but at least the burns were limited to the back of his neck this time. A loud clang ensued as the saucepan fell from Geraldine's grip. Her legs buckling beneath her, she slumped back onto a stool.

But there was no time to protest. Whatever anger had possessed her was now satisfied.

A cold shower eased the pain, but being late for work would bring recriminations he could ill afford.

'Sorry,' Geraldine said flatly, as Paddy descended the stairs for the second time that day. 'Is it bad?' she asked, unable to meet his eyes.

'I'll live,' Paddy said tersely. Lifting a scarf from the coat hook in the hall, he gently wrapped it around his neck. His skin would blister, stick to his shirt collar and make him wince as he tightened his tie, but it could have been worse. He had the scars to prove it. Geraldine's temper may have been satisfied for now, but leaving was the safest thing he could do. He used to have days, even weeks between such episodes, but lately, they were more frequent and impossible to predict.

'It's her anniversary,' Geraldine said. 'That's why I was upset. I thought we could talk about it over breakfast.'

Paddy stalled. He should go before she flared up again. But she was wrong this time, and he had to put her straight. 'No, it's not,' he said, his fingers twisting the latch on the door. Warily, he glanced over his shoulder to see her fists bunched into her dressing gown pockets, her lips a thin white line. What was she holding? A knife? A screwdriver? Something worse?

'I'm her mother.' Geraldine's words simmered with fresh anger. 'Don't tell me I'm wrong. It's ten years to the day since you bought our daughter that bicycle. Do you remember? How it took her so long to learn? Yet you insisted. You forced the point. If you hadn't kept on . . .'

'I'm late,' Paddy said, a sliver of cold air creeping in as he opened the door. 'I'll call you later. Why don't you clean up the mess you made?' He pulled the door wide, watching her visibly shrink at the sight of movement outside. He would feel guilty later for the satisfaction it gave him, but for now it afforded him a safe departure.

'Bastard!' she screamed, taking two steps backwards. 'Off you go, to your tart. Well, don't expect me to be waiting for you. Not after what you've done!'

CHAPTER FIFTEEN

Running her fingers through her hair, Amy toyed with the idea of a change of style. Perhaps some highlights? Layers? It was disconcerting, the similarity between her and Lillian Grimes. She thought about their shared height, the fullness of her lips. Her fingers crept to her mouth. What if their similarities weren't just skin-deep? A knock on her office door made her start. Standing sheepishly in the open doorway was DS Paddy Byrne. 'Come in.' She snapped her compact mirror shut. 'Take the weight off your feet.' She could just about fit a desk and two chairs in her poky office, which had once been used for storing files, but her diminutive space was the least of her worries today. She hoped Paddy would provide a good excuse for disrupting morning briefing by arriving halfway through. If it were anyone else she would have called them out for it. Lately, it felt that everything she worked so hard to achieve was starting to slide. She had said nothing as he slipped in, knowing he would explain later on.

'Sorry for being late,' Paddy said, offering a weak smile as he sat down. 'It won't happen again.'

'You know how bad timekeeping gets under my skin,' Amy replied. 'What sort of example are you setting, when you can't be bothered to show up yourself?'

Shoulders drooped, Paddy lowered his gaze, offering nothing but silence in return.

Amy's forehead creased. There was more to this than tardiness. 'What is it? Is there anything I need to know about? Problems at home?'

'It's nothing,' Paddy said. 'A gasket blew in the car.'

'Another one?' Amy replied, seeing through his lame excuse. It was his fourth time late for briefing this month. 'And why the scarf? Don't tell me you're cold.'

'Bit of a sore throat,' he said, fiddling with the edges of the black woollen material as he tightened it around his throat.

'You *are* looking a bit peaky,' Amy said, noticing the light sheen of sweat coating his brow. Sighing, she checked the time. A sense of dread had clouded her morning as she thought about what lay ahead. 'I take it you're up to speed on both cases? Because if you're not, then tell me now.' Briefing had been over an hour ago, long enough for him to catch up on what he had missed. The wheels of the investigation had been set in motion. Missing for almost twenty-four hours, Hermione Parker was cause for grave concern.

Paddy nodded, looking relieved to change the subject. Amy never laboured a telling-off. Like her, it was short and to the point. But people who let her down only got so many chances. She would hate to see Paddy go, but she was fed up covering for him. Pike would transfer him to another department if he failed to pull his weight.

Paddy crossed his legs, bumping his knee against her desk. 'I'm impressed that you managed to see Lillian Grimes. What was she like?'

'Outwardly, like any other sixty-five-year-old woman.' Amy tapped the side of her forehead. 'It's what's in here that sets her apart.' Her announcement that she had visited Grimes had brought a ripple of gossipy chatter to the briefing room. It was a sad state of affairs when a serial killer was as much of a celebrity as an A-list actress. 'I hope to get it tied up soon, so we can concentrate on the kidnapping case.'

'Oh, about that,' Paddy said, his face brightening. 'Mol's been talking to Hermione's best friend, Paige. She mentioned Hermione had a crush on a sixth former named Michael. She's looking into it now.'

'Surely those enquiries should have been done by CID,' Amy said, her face grim. 'Why is it only coming to our attention now?' Her brother's team had made a good start on the investigation before Amy's officers took the lead.

'Paige was too embarrassed to repeat their last conversation,' Paddy said. 'It was schoolgirl stuff, teasing each other about boys.'

Amy shook her head in disbelief. How could she be so coy when her friend's life was at risk? 'Are we still going with the theory that Hermione knew her attacker?' Early case notes suggested it was possible.

'Her mum said it's the only way she would have opened the front door.'

An image of Tessa Parker, Hermione's mum, floated in Amy's vision. The last time she saw her, she was featured on a rerun of *Dragon's Den* on the TV. 'She must be insane with worry,' Amy mumbled. Tessa may have come from humble beginnings, but she had grown into a businesswoman who was used to being in control. 'Arrange a visit to her when I get back from the prison. We should be done by late afternoon.'

'Will do.' Paddy winced slightly as he loosened his tie.

'And get something for your throat. There's some paracetamol in the first-aid cabinet.'

As he skulked out of the office, Amy leaned back into her chair. Paddy was usually conscientious, but lately he was letting things slide.

Her thoughts were interrupted by the cheerful ringtone of her mobile phone. Frowning, she made a mental note to change it to something more in keeping with her mood. The call that followed did not serve to improve it. Back from her enquiries with the sixth former, Molly was ready to drive her to the prison where they would pick up

Lillian Grimes. 'I'll be down in a minute,' Amy said, her mouth dry. Picking up a bottle of water from her desk, she tipped the lukewarm liquid down her throat.

As she slipped on her jacket, it felt like it was made of lead. There was no question of not going through with this, but what if Lillian let her identity slip? Was that what this trip was about? She threw the empty bottle in the bin, catching sight of the newspaper she had previously dumped. Adam's betrayal still burned, but she would not allow resentment to wear her down. She would deal with this, just like everything else in life that came snapping with its teeth bared. Her eyes rested on the framed photo of her father, which took pride of place on her desk. It was hard to look at it without feeling a wave of grief. 'I won't let you down,' she promised, the words barely audible on her lips.

◆ ◆ ◆

Molly Baxter had once held the position of DCI Pike's trusted driver and could be relied upon not to speak to the press. She had been a constable in uniform then, but Pike had a knack for sniffing out talent and encouraged her to study for the detective's exam. From what Amy had seen, it had been a good call.

'Relax.' Amy smiled as she sat in the passenger seat of the unmarked car. 'Hold that steering wheel any tighter and you'll rip it off.' Their movements had been planned to precision, their trip approved by the command team.

Molly gave a breathless laugh as she relaxed her grip. 'Sorry,' she said. 'This case is so famous, I can't believe I'm about to ferry Lillian Grimes about.' In a pinstripe shirt and black trousers she was smartly dressed for the role, though her pallor and wide eyes revealed her nervousness.

'Just treat her like any other prisoner, because that's all she is,' Amy said, as much to convince herself as Molly. 'Keep conversation to a bare minimum. No small talk. From what I've gathered, she's going to drip-feed us directions. I don't think she'd try to escape, but keep your guard up just the same.'

'I suppose we're lucky she's telling us anything at all.' Molly's seat belt punctuated her sentence with a click as she fastened it into place.

'She's not told us anything yet,' Amy reminded her. 'Just to recap, I'll sit in the back with Lillian after we pick her up. A marked car will accompany us to and from the destination in Essex. A local unit's going to attend when we get there as backup.' It had all been discussed at the briefing, but Amy mentally ticked the boxes one more time anyway.

'Can I just say . . .' Molly said, turning over the engine of the car. 'I'm thrilled to be a part of the team. You and the DCI have been a real inspiration.'

'That's good to know, thanks,' Amy said, acknowledging the admiration while it lasted. If Lillian blurted out the truth, their return journey would be very different.

Easing the car from its parking space, Molly drove towards the automatic gates which rolled back to allow her out.

'That's a nice Jag,' Amy said, in an effort to change the subject. She noticed the freshly polished red car was sporting a new registration plate.

'Oh, that's Paddy's. Lush, isn't it? We've nicknamed him Inspector Morse.'

'Indeed,' Amy murmured. Unlike Morse, Paddy was not a fictional character from a popular television show. He was responsible for supervising her team. There was no way a new car would be breaking down every weekend. She made a mental note to speak to him about it later. Looking left and right, Molly pulled out of the junction and into a gap in the traffic. She offered Amy an appreciative smile, and it felt like she had been waiting to speak to her alone for some time.

'I followed you throughout the John Miller case,' Molly said. 'How do you do it? Get inside their heads?' She was referring to a case that had won Amy a commendation. A family of four had been murdered, the only surviving member an eighteen-year-old boy. All the evidence pointed to his father, who had allegedly shot his family then turned the gun on himself, but there was something about John Miller that did not ring true. It was called 'The Case that Shocked the Nation.' One of the many headlines that Amy's ex, Adam, used throughout her career. Picking apart the evidence like badly sewn stitches, Amy gained a confession from the young man who was now spending the best part of his life in jail.

To Amy, the whole thing was tragic. 'The mistake most cops make is seeing things from the wrong perspective. Psychopaths' brains are wired differently to ours,' Amy said. 'The threat of punishment doesn't worry them. If you want their cooperation, you've got to make them believe there's something in it for them.'

'Which is what you did with Miller?'

'Yes,' Amy said. 'Although it wasn't easy because he was so convincing at first. People couldn't believe he was capable of such brutality. I mean, killing his own family . . . it was easier to think his dad had lost his mind.'

'It's the same with Lillian Grimes,' Molly said. 'You wonder what goes on inside these people's heads.'

'Don't let her see that you're interested,' Amy replied. 'She'll get off on your curiosity. At the end of the day, she's not a pop star. She encouraged her husband to rape those women then dump their bodies like they meant nothing at all.'

'Gives me the shivers thinking about it,' Molly said, pulling a face. 'I mean, I've dealt with some tough things in my time, but killing your own daughter on top of everything else . . .'

A vision of Sally-Ann floated into Amy's mind. She was grateful for the sudden change of traffic lights as Molly sharply applied the brakes.

'We'll talk about Lillian in the debrief. Focus on your driving for now.' It came out sharper than Amy intended, her pent-up emotions seeking release.

CHAPTER SIXTEEN

Lying in a half dream, Hemmy inhaled slowly, the smell of rotting fish creeping up her nostrils. Darkness enveloped her, a soft lapping licked the walls as left, right, left, right, her body swayed. She smacked her tongue against the roof of her mouth, rubbing her sleep-encrusted eyes. Where was she? Blinking, her head pounded as she tried to sit up. She fumbled against the cold metal edges of what felt like a single bed. *Purdy*, she thought, touching the bruise on her forehead. Vaguely, she recalled there had been something wrong with her cat. 'Hello?' she croaked. Her throat scratchy, she blinked in the darkness, trying to accustom herself to the lack of light. Why was the world moving? Each time she tried to stand, gravity nudged her back onto the bed.

Breathing rapidly, she tried to take in her surroundings, seeking out the tiniest glimmer of light. She had finished school, gone home . . . then the phone rang. She narrowed her eyes as the pain in her head forced her to pause. It was just enough time to catch her breath and allow the memory to surface: taking a step towards Purdy; a shadow hovering over her; heavy breath as gloved hands forced a rubber mask on her face. A further flash of memory made her limbs tremble. She had tried to struggle, kicking and screaming, but each breath dragged her down into a darkness from which she could not break free. Her hand flew to her throat at the vague recollection of her necklace snapping. It was gone. It was one her father had bought her. The most precious piece of jewellery she owned. What had they done with her? There was one thing she was sure of: she wasn't at Mrs Cotterill's anymore. Just how long had she been unconscious?

Her eyes wet with tears, she checked herself for injuries, exhaling in relief as she discovered she was OK. He hadn't touched her down there. She would know, wouldn't she? Was it even a 'he' that took her? She didn't know. Her chin wobbled, and she whimpered in the darkness as she tried to formulate a plan. She had to get out, but the room kept moving. Was this what a hangover felt like? She peered through the dimness. Was that a window over her head? A small chink of light escaped from the edge of a square block of wood hammered over what appeared to be a rusted circular frame. Getting to her knees, she clambered across the bed, pressing her face against the cold, unforgiving wood. The soft lapping again. Water. She could hear water. Her lack of balance was due to the waves beneath her feet. She gasped at the revelation. It was a porthole. She was in a boat. Was she alone at sea with her captor? Panic gripped her. She could be miles away from anywhere, and it wasn't as if she could swim very well. The dam of tears she had been holding in finally broke free, yet she kept her sobs contained, stemming her breathing to listen for sounds. Should she scream for help or keep her head down? Blinking away her tears, her vision adjusted to the darkness, and she made out the outline of four nails hammered into the wood. If she could pull them out, at least get her bearings . . . She shivered involuntarily, damp biting through her school uniform to her skin. The mattress springs emitted a rusty squeal as she climbed off the bed. With groping hands, she felt her way around the edges of the space. It did not feel like she was going anywhere. There was no forward movement, only a swaying side to side.

She envisioned her phone in her blazer pocket hung from the ban-nister. What had she been thinking? It was Purdy that made her lose all her common sense. She would do anything for her cat . . . Another thought filtered in. He had been watching her. He had taken Purdy to lure her two doors down. This was not a random kidnapping. Would they be delivering a ransom note? The thought increased the urgency of what she had to do: get away from this place, find a weapon, break free. Shuffling forward, she came to a halt as her fingers found the outline of a door. 'Come on. Please.' The words escaping her lips were followed by an anguished moan as she rattled the handle for all she was worth. Pushing and pulling, she expelled all her energy, her hopes fading as it refused to budge. Finally, she allowed panic to take over, ramming her fists against the heavy solid door. 'Let me out! Help! Help me, someone! Please!' But her protests went ignored. All she could hear was the sound of her heavy breath and the lapping of the water beneath. She touched her wrist to find her watch was gone. Her abductor had left her with nothing but the clothes on her back. What if they didn't come back? What if they had left her here to die? 'Hello?' she called. 'Are you there? Is anyone there? Please, somebody, talk to me.' Groping her way back to her bed, she pushed her ear against the porthole once more. Was that? Could it be? A police siren in the distance? Were they coming to set her free?

CHAPTER SEVENTEEN

Amy had been on two mystery tours in her lifetime and each one involved Lillian Grimes. Another memory broke free as she recalled her first excursion with social services. They had been in a people carrier then, though up until now, their mode of transport had manifested as a World War Two tank in her dreams. The image suited the battlefield of her early upbringing, but it made her wonder about the validity of her resurfacing thoughts. What she had previously dismissed as nightmares, she was now claiming as facts – but how accurate were her recollections? Being back in contact with Lillian had teased them out at an overwhelming rate. She brushed the memory of that first trip away. Today, she could not get away from Lillian if she tried, being tethered to her via a set of handcuffs in the back of the unmarked Ford Mondeo.

Lillian's presence was all-consuming, her silence disconcerting. Amy had half expected another trip down memory lane; but with her colleague driving in front, her biological mother had been true to her word. Having directed DC Molly Baxter to Essex, she had given nothing else away. Amy would not give Lillian the satisfaction of pleading for the full address. The silence was good. The less she said, the better, and Amy hoped that her cooperation was not part of some sick game.

Lillian had smiled as she greeted her, her eyes sparkling with an amusement she had since kept contained. She was wearing a sweatshirt and jeans, and her hair seemed different today, the scraggly endings trimmed in neat layers that framed her face. All traces of grey were gone, and it had returned to its youthful mahogany brown. Amy wondered if she'd had it styled in the prison hairdressers for the occasion. There was even a hint of blusher gracing the curved cheekbones that had been so attractive in her youth. Had she expected the press? Wanted a newer, up-to-date photo of herself? Consuming the outside view, Lillian stared through the car window, trying to connect with a world she had lost decades ago.

Is this what prison does to you? Disconnects you from humanity? After what she did, it's the least she deserves. Amy inhaled deeply, and immediately wished she hadn't. Prisoners weren't allowed perfume, but today Amy instantly recognised the sweet tang of a deodorant that invoked the past. Impulse. A new memory infiltrated her mind: Jack joking that their male visitors were attracted by Lillian's heady scent. Amy had not understood then, but a sick feeling grew in the pit of her stomach now. All at once, she knew the deodorant had been a special purchase, something to mess with her mind.

Once inside the car, Amy had undone their cuffs. Like an umbilical cord, it had tethered them. It was enough to make her scream.

'Turn left,' Lillian said, imparting directions to Molly. As they drove into Essex, Amy caught sight of Lillian in her peripheral vision. Silently, the woman took in Amy's features, watching for a change of expression, or perhaps the slightest sign of distress. Amy sat motionlessly, her breath shallow. She would not give her the pleasure; her thoughts were her own.

The minutes passed in silence, the sign for Brentwood coming into view. Amy didn't recognise it, but then Flora and Robert had not been to Essex since they left. Most of their family were based in London so there had been no reason to return. She recalled a school trip to

Clacton-on-Sea once, and how on edge her parents had been when she came home. She couldn't have known that they were terrified she would bump into someone from her past. What would her father say if he could see her now?

'There, take Woodman Road,' Lillian said, her voice calm and controlled.

Amy tried to stem her annoyance at the woman's upper hand. She could have told them where the body was buried, or at least provided the address before they left, but instead she had exercised control, giving directions minutes in advance. Where was she bringing them? Woodman Road was not an address Amy recognised from the case files. She had hated poring over them. She could not shake off the feeling that there was another secret waiting to be revealed. Amy cleared her throat, fighting the rising sense of dread.

'Turn in here, in the cemetery.' Lillian glanced at Amy with a satisfied smile.

'The graveyard?' Amy replied, her forehead creased in confusion. 'Is this some kind of joke?'

Lillian regarded her daughter with a look of mild amusement. 'You want to know where she's buried, don't you? It's not far from here, if my memory serves me right.'

Amy stared in disbelief, jolted in her seat as Molly sharply applied the brakes.

'Sorry ma'am,' she said sheepishly. 'It's just had new brake pads.'

'Ma'aaam.' Lillian drew out the word, her eyes narrowing as she delivered a sardonic smile.

Amy took another breath, another inhalation of Lillian's sickly sweet smell. She knew what she was thinking. How this scrap of a girl from the Grimes household had fooled the world.

It was a tiny victory as Lillian's fingers curled over the door handle and Amy barked at her to stay put. With the child-proof locks activated, she was not going anywhere yet.

'Mind if I have a quick ciggy, boss?' Molly said, stretching her limbs as they both got out of the car. The journey had been long, with traffic slowing their pace.

'Go ahead,' Amy replied. 'We can't take her out until the local units turn up, anyway.' Amy rested her hand on the roof of the car as she watched the occupant inside. The marked vehicle accompanying them drew up nearby; the uniformed officers from Essex Police were yet to attend. On her own, Lillian was manageable, but there was nothing to say she had not prearranged for a welcoming party at the location she had kept so close to her chest. It was not beyond the realms of possibility that a woman of such notoriety had contacts on the outside.

Changing the channel on her police airwave radio, Amy communicated with the Essex Police control room. Officers updated control that they were almost there, and within minutes, their police car had pulled up by her side.

'I wasn't expecting an armed response.' Amy said, as a man in a grey suit climbed out of the back. He had a confident stance befitting his authority, and his lightly stubbled face was sombre as he approached. Flanked by two armed officers, he held out his hand.

'DI Winter.' Amy's grey eyes regarded him coolly as she extended her hand in return.

'DI Donovan,' he replied, in a deep but well-spoken voice. He looked to be in his mid-thirties and was about half a foot taller than her. 'It's not a problem, is it?' he signalled to the officers flanking him. Dressed in black, they silently scouted the area.

She smiled politely in response. 'No, no problem at all.' She leaned forward, speaking conspiratorially, grateful she didn't have to crane her neck too far. 'I just hope this isn't a waste of time. The cemetery was the last place I expected to be brought today.'

Briefly, Donovan glanced through the window of Amy's car. 'You never can pre-empt a serial killer – although given your reputation, I've heard you've come close.'

His voice was warm, almost comforting, and Amy forced a smile. Once, she would have taken it as a compliment, but today it served to remind her of the tainted blood running through her veins. Patiently, Lillian waited in the car.

'Let's get started,' Amy said, squinting against the sun.

Lillian blinked as she exited the car, remaining mute as Amy took her forearm and clasped the handcuff over her wrist. The presence of another unit was welcome, and Amy felt strength in their numbers, reminding herself whose side she was on.

'Which way?' she said, drawing Lillian's attention from the armed officers. The woman had paled slightly. The warm early autumn afternoon seemed at odds with the grim reality of what they were about to do.

'Over there,' Lillian said, forcing Amy to raise her left hand as Lillian pointed with her right. It was a pretty graveyard, with a gravel path overlooked by trees on either side. The gentle rustle of leaves made it a peaceful place, but despite the outlook, it seemed grey and cold. Following Lillian's lead, Amy hoped she was not being taken for a ride.

'Why are we here?' Amy said, after spending ten minutes walking around the many headstones jutting out from the soil. 'Because if you're wasting my time, I'd rather know now.'

Lillian's features creased as she took in the names engraved on each one. 'She's here somewhere.'

A fresh spark of anger ignited as Amy heard her speak so casually.

'What specifically are you looking for?' Amy said, stilling her movements as she tugged on the cuffs.

Lillian straightened, groaning as she laid a hand on the small of her back. 'Barbara Price, of course. The first of the three bodies you're after. She's buried beneath one of these graves.'

Officers exchanged glances as her words floated in the air.

'Your fath—' Lillian quickly corrected herself. 'Jack used to earn cash in hand digging graves. Once, when he was drunk, he told me where he put her. Under the grave of a Patricia Golding . . .' She frowned. 'No, Spalding, that was it. I came here once, just to check for myself, and that's when I saw the grave.'

It was not what Jack Grimes had said when he was first interviewed by police. According to him, Lillian had orchestrated the lot. 'We've been all around the cemetery,' Amy said. 'Are you sure—'

'There it is,' Lillian interrupted. 'Under that tree, I remember now.' She smiled as if she had won a fairground prize. Tugging on the handcuffs, she dragged Amy towards the grave. 'Jack said he dug down an extra foot. Then he buried the body before it was covered by the coffin the next day.' She parted her lips, panting lightly as she found the grave. 'That's the one.'

'Are Wendy Thompson and Viv Holden buried here, too?' Amy said.

Lillian shook her head, swiping the hair from her eyes with her free hand. 'No. But Barbara is. I told you I'd show you to where she was. The rest is up to you.'

'But the others . . .' Amy said. 'Wendy's mother . . . She doesn't have much time.' The second the words left her mouth she regretted them. She had vowed not to plead with this heartless soul.

Lillian tilted her head to one side, enjoying the power she held. 'I'll tell you about the next one soon enough, but Wendy Thompson's mother can wait until last.'

Amy met DI Donovan's glance and saw the glimmer of hope in his eyes. The weight of responsibility was on her shoulders, and she had yet to inform the families involved. It was not just the victim's family that would be affected. They would have to get permission to exhume the grave so they could dig a foot beneath. There was no other way around it; she could only hope that the family of the deceased would understand.

Lillian glanced at her surroundings, shielding her eyes from the sun. 'It's so pretty out here, the kind of thing you take for granted unless you spend your life behind bars. My eyesight's bad, you know, from years of living in a dim cell.' Closing her eyes, she inhaled a deep breath. 'Can you smell it? The trees and the flowers. Feel the sunshine on your skin?'

'Have you anything else to tell us before we go back?' Amy said, ignoring her joy of the great outdoors. Barbara Price would never feel the sun on her skin again.

'Just remember this.' Lillian leaned in closer, a macabre smile lighting up her face. 'I've kept my word. You owe me.'

CHAPTER EIGHTEEN

Having returned Lillian to prison, Amy sat at the head of the briefing table, back in the bosom of her team. Her liaison with DI Donovan had been fruitful, and she was grateful for his assistance in arranging the excavation: for now, she had done what she set out to do. Lillian had used her knowledge as leverage to see her in person, but her biological mother was not the maternal type. Her eye was on a much bigger prize. The question was, what?

Lillian never remembered her children's birthdays or made them a cake. On the rare occasion they were afforded a home-cooked meal, they were offered the minimum amount. Most days, they were reared on a diet of sugary breakfast cereals, which they ate morning, noon and night. Details like these had a ring of truth to them when Amy had read through the case files. She thought back to Lillian's comments in the graveyard, about keeping her side of the bargain. She had an uneasy feeling. Being in Lillian's presence made Amy want to scrub her skin clean, but the luxury of a pit stop was something she could not afford.

As officers assembled for afternoon briefing, Amy was keen to fill her mind with something other than Lillian Grimes. She watched Paddy lead, providing updates on the kidnapping case. Despite having discarded his suit jacket, his scarf was still draped around his neck. She hoped he was not coming down with something. The team could not afford to be without him for very long.

Whirring into life, the overhead projector brought the latest CCTV images to the screen. Paddy turned to point at the picture, speaking loudly so everyone could hear. 'This is the petrol station where the suspect is believed to have filled up.' He paused to ensure he had their attention. 'The van was stolen, but luckily for us, almost out of fuel. This suggests that the kidnapper is an amateur, which goes in our favour.' With the handheld clicker, he brought the next image into view. Amy peered at the snapshot of a blurred figure putting diesel into the side of the van. A black cap masked their features, padded jacket and baggy jeans making it difficult to decipher their form. After pumping diesel, they sped off.

'I can't believe they nicked a van with no fuel,' Molly piped up. Like Amy, she had wasted no time in getting up to speed with the case. 'What about the payment card used? Any trace on that?'

'It was pickpocketed that morning,' Paddy said. 'Watch.' He clicked to activate the CCTV, and the image of the figure fumbling before the pump payment machine came into view.

'Looks like they used contactless,' Amy said, watching as they fanned one card then another before the machine. 'They probably have a plethora of stolen cards.'

'Which makes them little more than a common thief,' Paddy said. 'And a tenner's worth of diesel proves they've not gone far.'

Amy nodded. 'Unless they swapped modes of transport later on. I'm doubtful though. Judging by their MO, they look like someone who's got in over their head. Abducting a schoolgirl in broad daylight doesn't strike me as a professional job.'

Amy paused to flick through her notes. 'I see we've had a witness come forward. How's that panning out?'

Pausing to fix his scarf, Paddy met her gaze. 'One of the neighbours said she heard screaming through her window, and saw a window cleaner's van driving past when she looked outside. She scribbled down the name on the side and reported it today.'

'Why wait until now?' Amy frowned as she flicked through a copy of the report. The early hours of any investigation were the most important of all.

'It was her *bedroom* window.' Paddy threw her a wry smile, a ripple of laughter spreading around the room. 'She was meant to be at work. Popped back home for some afternoon delight with her gardener.'

It sounded like something out of DCI Pike's romance novels. Amy nodded in response, her expression blank. She failed to see the humour when a young girl's life could be at stake.

Paddy clicked on the next slide, and a map of London appeared. 'We've picked up the van travelling through the streets listed here, but then it seems to disappear.'

'Where are we with family members?' Amy asked, looking pointedly at DC Steve Moss, who had been nominated to work with the intelligence team to see what they could dig up. In his early forties, he was six months into his post as a DI when he was found having sex with a probationer on shift. DCI Pike had wasted no time in demoting him. A lot of negotiating had brought him to this team, and Amy hoped his wisdom as a senior officer would make up for his poor judgement when it came to relationships. A frequent marathon runner, his sandy blonde hair and athletic build frequently caught his female co-workers' eyes, but not this team. They were too focused on their caseloads to be playing around.

'Her mum's a widow,' Steve said, referring to Hermione. 'Her dad was a soldier.'

'He died a couple of years back, didn't he?' Amy said, remembering the broadcast on television.

'In Afghanistan.' Steve nodded in response. 'So there's no absent father to worry about. She gets on with her family. It's just the two of them living in the house.'

'But it's not just the two of them, is it?' Amy said, turning her attention to the inventory of items seized from her home. 'Not while she had access to the internet.' It worried Amy that many parents thought their children were safe in the space they called home. Her fingers tightened around her paperwork as she came to the image of Hermione's face. A blonde girl with blue eyes, she had a broad smile, with braces lacing her teeth. Yet there was something disconcerting about her. It was with sadness that she realised she was thinking of Sally-Ann, who had been the same age as Hermione when she died.

'Have you talked to her teachers yet?' Amy said, remaining stoic despite the turmoil she felt inside.

Steve nodded, his face grave. 'We've spoken to everyone she came into contact with forty-eight hours before her disappearance. Her mother may be on the telly, but she's not what you call rolling in it. If it were a ransom, we would have heard something by now. We've nothing concrete to go on at this stage.'

'Well, it's our job to find something,' Amy replied. 'A press release might trigger someone's memory. I don't see what other choice we have.' In an enquiry as serious as this, Amy had more than her own team's resources to hand. Such resources were split into management, intelligence, investigative and support teams. It was not rare for over two hundred officers to be involved in major enquiries, but many were brought in to carry out specific tasks. Once completed, they were released to their normal duties and back to their existing workload. It was up to Amy to ensure everything was handled smoothly while overtime budgets were kept in check.

The tannoy alerted her to a call on her office phone. Having wrapped up the briefing, she prayed for a breakthrough, because each day Hermione was missing reduced the chances of finding her alive. Was this what it was like for the families of Lillian's victims? Despite the passing of time, she had no doubt that their pain was every bit as sharp as before. She picked up her phone and called the front counter.

'I've got your mother on the line,' Leyla said, her words interspersed with chewing noises as she worked through the wad of gum on her back molars. 'I asked if you could call her back, but she said it was urgent and it couldn't wait.'

'Put her through,' Amy said, a frisson of worry rising from within. The last call she had received from her mother was to say that her father had been taken ill. Flora never rang her at work. Something was wrong.

'Mum?' Amy said. 'Is everything OK?'

'Everything's fine.' But it was not Flora, it was the low creeping voice of Lillian Grimes.

Amy felt her blood turn cold as Lillian's words crawled down the phone line.

'It's so nice to hear you call me mum again.'

'I thought you were Flora,' Amy said, her jaw tightening in response. 'What are you playing at, calling me at work?'

'Giving you information on Viv Holden. If you don't want to know where she is, I'll save my money and hang up now.'

Amy sighed, closing her office door before plopping heavily into her seat. 'Of course I want it,' she said. Just seconds into the call and she had been knocked out of kilter.

'Have they found what's left of Barbara yet? You'll be a real hero now, won't you? Kind of twisted really, given who you are.'

If she were talking to anyone else, Amy would reply that her DCI would be the hero in this affair, not her. Praise held no value to Amy, and Lillian was merely using the situation to twist the knife.

'You called to give me the address?' Amy said, choosing to ignore her remark. The latest email from DI Donovan was that the family of the deceased in the grave had given permission for them to conduct a dig. Not that she would inform Lillian Grimes. She would find out about it through the media soon enough.

'Not so fast,' Lillian said, a smile carrying on her voice. 'There are certain conditions to be met. The sooner you meet them, the sooner you will find your second collection of bones.'

'Her name is Viv.' Amy scowled. Why was she even talking to this woman? She hated that Lillian was reeling her in. *Be professional*, she reminded herself. *Don't give her a reaction.* But her base instincts were taking over, and she could not help but respond.

'Oh, I remember her name,' Lillian said. 'I remember lots of things. Are you remembering, Amy? Remembering what really happened to bring me here?'

Amy's knuckles tightened as they clenched the phone, every muscle in her body tense. 'I don't have time to talk, and I daresay your time is limited. So tell me what you want, or we'll have to leave it there.'

For a few seconds, Lillian's heavy breathing ruffled the line. Did she have a connection with this woman? The thought was too ugly to bear.

'I'm not asking for much,' Lillian replied. 'I enjoyed our reunion so much that I thought that you could do it again . . .'

Amy cut in as Lillian paused for breath. 'You want another visit in exchange for telling me where Viv and Wendy are buried?'

'You really must stop interrupting,' Lillian admonished. 'I thought I reared you better than that. My next condition is for a different type of reunion . . .'

Amy felt a knot grow between her shoulder blades as Lillian dangled her like a marionette. Just how long was she allowed to talk on the prison phone? She was about to tell her to get on with it when she responded with an ultimatum that stole the breath from her lungs.

'I'd like you to visit your sister, Mandy. Don't worry, she knows all about it. She can't wait to see you again.' Lillian's words were delivered with ill-concealed glee.

Amy's mouth dropped open. Apart from Sally-Ann, she had tried to shut off all thoughts of her birth siblings when Lillian resurfaced. This was a bad idea. She could feel it in her bones.

'You want me to visit Mandy?' she said, rubbing the base of her neck. Sally-Ann was the only member of her birth family who had truly loved her. A whisper of memory suggested she had grown up detached from her remaining siblings. Vaguely, she recalled an image of Mandy, telling her to 'quit whining' as she cried over Sally-Ann's loss. Then Damien, with his dark eyes and permanent scowl, tearing up her drawings because somebody said they were nice. Perhaps Flora was right. Her mind had been protecting her because she knew this day would come.

'You've got nieces and nephews, you know,' Lillian said. 'There's so much to catch up with. Your meeting is arranged for tomorrow at one o'clock.'

'I'm working,' Amy said stiffly.

'You're the big cheese, ma'am Winter.' The mocking words curled off Lillian's tongue. 'I'm sure you can take an hour off to visit your long-lost sister if it means you'll get burial site number two. Do we have a deal?'

Amy sighed. How did she do this? Make her feel as helpless as a four-year-old child? Would contacting Mandy be such a bad thing if it gave another family peace?

'I'll do it,' Amy said. 'But just the once.'

CHAPTER NINETEEN

Turning her collar upwards, Amy tilted her head to avoid the rain. She barely noticed the inclement weather due to the thoughts spinning round her head. She stared ahead, the lights of The Dog and Duck pub twinkling invitingly amid the gloom. Shoulders hunched, Amy fought against her internal voice screaming at her to turn on her heel and leave. She bore physical scars from fights she'd had with offenders over the years. As a DS, she had once narrowly missed being shot by an assailant during a raid. As a Detective Inspector, she had overseen cases involving psychopathic offenders whose deeds would keep any sane person awake at night. She had faced all of that over the years and never backed down; but now, waiting to come face-to-face with her sister, her legs felt like jelly. With Lillian, at least she had known what to expect. Mandy was a closed book.

Amy's heart faltered as she pushed through the pub's double doors, the ker-thunk, ker-thunk as they swung shut behind her delivering a sense of finality. There were lots of traditional pubs like these dotted around Whitechapel in East London, run-down boozers that were the heart of the community.

Having come from Notting Hill, the social divide was never more apparent than here. The bitter stench of beer rose up to greet her as she inhaled a sudden breath. There was no turning back now. *It will be over soon*, she told herself. *The worst has already happened.* But it did not stop her heart beating double time as she glanced around. To her right, a balding barman pulled on a beer pump, his fleshy features fixed in a concentrated scowl. A middle-aged man sat waiting for his pint, his rain-drenched border terrier tethered beneath his bar stool. A soft drink would be welcome, but it seemed premature to order before knowing how long her visit would last. She walked in, the soles of her shoes sticking slightly to the tiled floor. Would Mandy be angry? Hurt? Scared? Had Lillian backed her into a corner? Issued her an ultimatum of some kind too? Walking past the row of private booths, Amy headed towards the carpeted area that housed an open fire at the far end of the room. A woody, earthy smell emanated from the flames, but the cosy scene was broken by a baby's piercing cry. Amy's movements stilled at the sight of the lady leaning over the pram. Immediately she knew the petite, pale-skinned woman was her older sister. She looked to be in her mid-forties, with long, brown hair streaked with brassy blonde highlights, and a face that was make-up free. 'Shush shush shhh,' she said, plucking a dummy from the pocket of her tracksuit and pushing it into the baby's mouth. Glancing up at Amy, she delivered the tiniest of nods of recognition. Amy found herself doing the same.

'Mandy?' Amy checked as she rooted in her bag for her purse.

Mandy nodded, her eyes taking in every facet of Amy: her hair, her face, her clothes.

Having come straight from work, Amy was still wearing her trouser suit, her long woollen trench coat open at the front. Running a hand through her hair, she shook away the dampness, realising she must have looked a state. 'I forgot my umbrella,' she said, by means of explanation. Silence. She gave up fixing her hair and inhaled a deep breath. 'Can I get you a drink?' Anything to break the ice.

'Bacardi and Coke,' Mandy replied flatly. Gently rocking the pram handle, she eyed her sister warily as she straddled a stool. The skin under her eyes was dark from lack of sleep, no doubt due to the baby fussing in the pram.

'Whoops, steady, little man,' Amy said, swerving a toddler as he ran into her legs. His cheeks flushed pink, he swooped the plastic plane encased in his chubby fingers as he ran unsteadily towards the pram.

'Keep the noise down or you'll feel the back of my hand!' Mandy growled at the child, who looked no more than three years old.

Hunched over the bar, Amy grimaced inwardly. This was not going well.

After bringing their drinks over, with orange juice for the child, she joined Mandy at the small round table next to the open fire. The baby asleep, Mandy gently ceased rocking the pram and masked a yawn with the back of her hand. 'Sorry,' she said. 'I'm knackered. I've not had a wink of sleep all week.'

'How old are they?' Amy said, watching the little boy syphon his orange juice through his straw.

'Jake's just gone three. Ronnie is six weeks old.'

Amy nodded, trying to view them as dispassionately as she could. Considering them as her flesh and blood was too big an ask right now. She opened her mouth to ask if Ronnie was a boy or a girl, then changed her mind. Something dreadful had brought her and Mandy together. She was not here for small talk.

'I don't know what to say to you,' Mandy said. 'This is all so weird.'

'I know,' Amy replied. 'I'm still taking it in.'

A dry laugh escaped Mandy's lips. 'I can't believe I'm related to a bloody copper. All the times I thought about you, I never imagined you would end up like this. Pocket rocket Poppy . . . a detective inspector.' She shook her head in disbelief before taking a swig of her drink.

The name invoked an involuntary shiver down Amy's spine. The fire crackled and spat beside her as if absorbing her unease.

Resting her glass, Mandy allowed her gaze to travel over Amy's form. 'Look at you now, all prim-and-proper with your swanky clothes and designer handbag. What would Harry think if he saw me here with you?'

'And Harry is?' Amy said, hoping for no more nasty surprises.

'My old man. He thinks I'm in playgroup with Jake,' Mandy replied, bitterness lacing her tone. 'Instead, I'm sitting with a copper drinking Bacardi and Coke on a weekday.' Tipping back her head she downed the last of her drink. Crunching the ice cubes between her molars, she raised a finger at the barman to signal for more.

He raised an eyebrow towards Amy, and she signalled she'd had enough. She had barely taken a sip of her Coke. 'Is Jake allowed a bag of crisps?' she said, paling as his name left her lips. Jake. As in Jack? Their biological father's name.

Mandy raised her fingers to signal for two bags. 'And another orange juice, too.' She threw Amy a sly smile. 'You don't mind, do you? I reckon you owe him after all you've missed.'

'No problem.' As the barman approached, Amy tipped her contactless card against the hand-held payment machine and smiled in the absence of thanks.

'Do you remember me?' Mandy said, tilting her head to one side as the barman returned with their tray of drinks. 'Because I remember what you did. It was you who grassed us to the social.'

Amy dropped her gaze. Did her sister hold the same resentment as Lillian Grimes? 'I've been getting flashbacks,' she said quietly.

Mandy gazed into the distance, cradling her glass in her hands. She was skinny, too skinny – the by-product of a tough life. Her words were faint, as if she were thinking aloud. 'If you hadn't told the social when you did, I might not be alive today.' Tears gathered in the corners of her eyes, and she blinked them away. 'I was next. I could feel it. But I was too scared to open my mouth.' She gazed at her son with love in her eyes, despite her previous harsh words. 'I know I can be a gobby cow, but I'd never hurt my kids.' She sighed, suddenly looking very tired. 'I wish I'd been as brave as you back then. Maybe if I'd spoken up sooner, Sally-Ann would be still alive.'

'It's not your fault,' Amy said, the familiar ball of grief lodging in her chest, stemming her breath and making her stomach clench. So she had reported her parents to social care at just four years of age? As astounding as it was, it had a ring of truth. It was a relief Mandy was not blaming her for Sally-Ann's death, but the responsibility lay at her door just the same.

'Is that why you joined the filth? To try to put things right? I doubt you've met anyone quite like our mum and dad though, have you?'

Amy paused, choosing her words with care. 'I don't consider Jack and Lillian to be my parents.' She could not lie or reminisce. It made her sick to her stomach. It was not Mandy's fault but building a relationship and talking about old times was the last thing she wanted to do. 'Do you . . .' She forced the words. 'Do you still visit her?'

'Once a month, regular as clockwork. I have to. Been in care all me life. She's the only mum I got.' Mandy sniffed, giving Amy the once over. 'Some of us are stuck with our family, whether we like it or not.' She paused to ruffle Jake's hair as he munched his crisps. 'Mum told me about your nice posh house and your well-paid job. You ain't got no kids to take your money off you, neither.' She jabbed a thumb over her shoulder towards the pram. 'Ronnie's my grandson. My daughter got knocked up when she was fourteen. I've got two more kids at home. Six mouths to feed and a husband on the dole.'

'I'm sorry to hear that . . .' Amy began, but Mandy was in full flow.

'We're living in this shitty council tower block that should have been condemned years ago. There are mice in the kitchen, and I can't let the kids out after six.'

'Can't you apply for a move?' Having liaised with housing in the past, Amy had some knowledge of how things worked.

'We're trying. But it's a long waiting list. I thought when Chantelle had the baby we would be pushed up in the queue. They offered us a place in Jaywick. I told them there are too many bad memories in Essex. I can't go back there again.'

Mandy's features hardened as she spoke of the past. 'You've had it so easy. Makes me sick, to tell the truth.'

'Things have been hard for all of us,' Amy simply said. 'You shouldn't judge by appearances.'

'That's easy for you to say. God . . .' She laughed dryly. 'What the hell is Damien going to make of you?'

Hairs rose on the back of Amy's neck at the mention of her brother's name. It was too much too soon. She was barely clinging on to normality as it was. 'Lillian mentioned Damien, but she's not asked for us to meet.' Lifting her glass, Amy sipped her Coke. The ice cubes had melted, and it tasted flat on her tongue.

'She will,' Mandy said, raising a finger in warning. 'But don't turn your back on him. And don't go carrying no designer bag like you have today. Copper or no copper, he'll have you turned over before you walk out the door.'

Amy stiffened, a spark of defiance in her eyes. 'Whatever you think of me, I can assure you I'm perfectly capable of looking after myself.'

Mandy chuckled, looking scarily like her mother for the briefest of moments. 'There's the sister I grew up with. Nobody tells Poppy what to do.'

'My name is Amy,' she replied, pushing her glass of Coke away. Bored of adult conversation, Jake sidled down from his stool and toddled off, holding his plastic plane in the air. The top of his nappy jutted out from his tracksuit bottoms, and Amy felt a pang of sympathy for him. He should have been potty trained by now.

Mandy watched with disinterest. 'Shame really, you would have made a good godmother to mine. At least they would have got some presents over the years. You've got away light, haven't you?'

'Is that why you agreed to meet?' Amy said.

Mandy shrugged. 'You're my sister. Isn't that what families do?'

'We were never a family,' Amy said sadly. 'Just the offspring of two murdering psychopaths.'

'If only *I* were the one to catch Mr Winter's eye that day,' Mandy sighed, taking Amy's comments on the chin. Checking her watch, she rose from her stool before downing the last of her drink. 'You know, I had so many questions to ask. But there's no point, is there? You've done your duty. I'll tell mother dearest that we've met.'

Snapping open her purse, Amy plucked out three twenty-pound notes. 'Here. Buy something for the kids. Sorry, it's all I've got.' She knew she was leaving herself wide open to requests for more. There was nothing to stop Mandy blackmailing her and threatening to go to press. Though by doing so, she would bring the world's spotlight upon herself.

'This is why I didn't tell Harry I was here. He'd have me tapping you up for more.' Mandy snatched the cash and shoved it deep into her tracksuit pocket just the same.

'Goodbye, Mandy,' Amy said, before turning and walking out the door. She had one more visit to make tonight. A promise she had vowed to keep.

CHAPTER TWENTY

1986

'Quit your whining, will ya? I can't get no sleep with you sniffing all night.' Mandy's harsh whispers cut through the air.

Poppy did not like Mandy as much as Sally-Ann. Although closer in age, she lacked the warmth and compassion that her other sister once displayed.

'I wa . . . wan . . . want Sally-Ann,' Poppy said, her words jogged by a series of stutters. She had been a good girl. She had not cried a tear since being parted from her sister. But the hurt she had felt since her parting welled up inside her like a physical pain. The stutter she developed after her sister 'went away' had left her open to merciless teasing from her siblings, Mandy and Damien.

'Just go to sle . . . sle . . . sleep, little baby,' Mandy teased, her teeth flashing in the darkness as a hard smile rose to her lips. It was her mother's smile, narrow-eyed and cold, with a look that burned and made you draw your eyes away. Mummy had insisted that Mandy share her room now Sally-Ann had gone. Mandy had been glad to escape the space she shared with her brother and had moved her things in the next day. Nobody spoke about Sally-Ann, and Mummy had warned Poppy not to say a word to 'the social' when they visited that morning. Poppy did not know who 'the social' was, but she could tell from the way her mother's face became all tight and pinched that they were not very nice people at all.

◆ ◆ ◆

A strange smell wafted from the kitchen, tickling her senses as Poppy crept downstairs. Everything in the house seemed different. Proper plates had been spread on a plastic tablecloth, and the surface wiped clean. A knife and fork were laid either side of a blue patterned plate that had been taken from the high shelf on the dresser they weren't allowed to touch. Music tinkled from the radio on the counter. The cigarette butt mountains had disappeared, and all the empty bottles of wine and spirits had been cleared away. For a moment, Poppy wondered if she had woken up in a different house. It had happened before when they visited Mummy's relatives in London, and she had fallen asleep in the car. The next morning, she had awoken with no idea where she was. She still remembered how white and clean everything seemed, and the bowl of fruit that was on the table just for people to eat. So much food! The milk bottles were kept in the fridge and did not carry the stinky smell of the ones from home. As for the garden, it had proper flowers, trees and even a swing to play on. It was nothing like the mound of dirt and bricks that occupied theirs. But then, how could anything grow from the soil when Daddy never left it alone? More than once she had peeped through her bedroom window to see Jack digging under the light of the moon. Poppy headed towards their own open back door, wondering if there were flowers out there now, too. Thin fingers pinched her shoulder, making her wince. 'Where do you think you're going? I told Mandy to dress you half an hour ago. Get your backside upstairs, young lady, before the social get here.'

'But, Mummy . . .' Poppy said, her eyes wide as her father walked through the door. His presence stole her words, and she darted to her room. Dressed in his shirt and tie, he did not look like her normal daddy. The last time she saw him like this was when he put *his* mummy in a hole in the ground. A fun-er-al it was called in the paper, although there had been nothing fun about it at the time.

'Where's Sally-Ann?' Poppy said as Mandy tugged her hair into a plait.

'Fuck's sake, Pops, ain't I told you a thousand times? You're not to talk about her again. She's gone. She ain't coming back. If you want to stick around, you'll have to learn to shut your trap.'

'Mummy says the so . . . so . . .social's coming,' Poppy replied, for want of something to say. Thinking about Sally-Ann gave her a pain in the tummy and made her feel all sick inside.

'That's right.' Mandy pulled an elastic band onto the base of her plait. 'They're gonna be asking about Sally-Ann.'

'Wha . . . what will I say?' Poppy said, grateful her sister was too busy to tease her about her stutter.

'Nufink. She upped and ran away.' Grabbing her by the shoulders, Mandy span her around. 'And don't look so bloody scared!'

But Poppy did not know how to look any different. This was the face she wore all the time. First Hammy, now Sally-Ann; was she next? 'What about those other pe . . . people?' Poppy whispered, grateful to have her sister's attention, if only for today. 'The ones that come at night? Are they the so . . . so . . . social too?'

A sharp burst of laughter passed Mandy's lips. 'Don't be stupid! Of course they ain't. Best you not talk about them, either. Here, make yourself useful and squirt this around the house.' Mandy thrust a can into Poppy's hand. It was purple, with a picture of flowers on the front. Poppy squinted, trying to read the words printed on the side.

'It's air freshener, you twit. Just don't spray it in your eye.'

Ten minutes later, the can was roughly snatched from her hand as her mother went to answer the door. Poppy stood stiffly against the wall, staring down at her shoes. She risked a peep upwards as the couple at the door walked inside. The woman had frizzy black hair and wore a brooch on a plum cardigan that did not reach all the way around her waist. The man, who looked younger than her, had a neatly trimmed moustache and was long and thin. He walked with a slight stoop as if he was used to bending down to enter rooms. Poppy stood transfixed in the doorway as they gathered around the kitchen table, and Mummy placed the pie she had bought on the centre of the cloth. Poppy's mouth watered at the prospect of a bite. She had yet to eat breakfast, having been banished upstairs while Mummy, Daddy and Damien cleaned up the house.

As much as she wanted to enter the kitchen, the sharp glare from her father put Poppy in her place. Sally-Ann's name came up, and Daddy smiled as he explained that she had just run away.

Mummy looked as startled as Poppy when the woman in the purple cardigan asked to speak to Poppy alone. After being led to the sitting room, Poppy perched herself on the edge of the sofa as the woman, who introduced herself as Marjorie, spoke. Poppy liked the soft pink lipstick she wore. It was so unlike the jagged stripe of red that Mummy wore at weekends.

'You're not in any trouble,' Marjorie said. 'I just wanted five minutes with you alone.' She gestured to her colleague, who delivered a soft smile. 'This is Thomas; he works with me. We're here to find out about Sally-Ann, who's not been coming to school. Do you know where she is?'

The question invoked a bolt of fear and Poppy shook her head from left to right, her bottom lip sucked under her top. Her hands bunched under her sleeves, she folded her arms, imagining Daddy on the other side of the door.

'When was the last time you saw her?' Marjorie said. 'Can you remember?'

Poppy remembered all right, but such things were too horrific for words. She realised she was trembling and closed her eyes as she blocked the probing questions fired in her direction. Again, her worried gaze fell on the door.

A knowing glance passed between Marjorie and Thomas. 'I tell you what,' she said, 'why don't we pop outside, have a quick chat in our car?'

Poppy's eyes grew wide at the prospect, her face chalky white. Mummy and Daddy told her not to speak to the social. But Mummy and Daddy had done a terrible thing. Sally-Ann had not run away. She was dead.

Somebody needed to be told.

CHAPTER TWENTY-ONE

The numbers on the car dashboard clock glowed a reassuring 9.50 p.m. Being ahead of schedule offered Amy a small crumb of comfort. Mrs Price was expecting her, and it would not do to turn up late. Swiping at the car window, she peered through the fogged pane. After this, she would go off duty and make the hour-long journey home. Since her meeting with Mandy, the pieces of that puzzle had slotted into place. Only now did she remember the visit from social care that her sister had been talking about. She wished she could go back in time and cuddle her four-year-old self, smooth her hair and tell her it was going to be OK. Poppy was beginning to feel like a separate entity to her now, but someone she carried with her just the same.

Stepping out of her car, she was grateful for the chill kiss of the night air on her skin. Far in the distance, an ambulance siren screamed. Amy had heard enough emergency vehicles to be able to tell them apart. She stared at the three-bedroom brick semi, which looked identical to every other house on this street, though it was doubtful that Mrs Price's neighbours had experienced the loss encompassed within the walls of number 35 Albert Walk. Seventy-one-year-old Kitty Price still lived in the London house she occupied when her daughter was scooped off the streets by Jack and Lillian Grimes. Like many parents of missing children, she became chained to her home in the hope that someday her loved one would return. Now Amy was here to tell her that her daughter was never coming back.

The squeak of the black metal gate caused a twitch of curtains as Amy walked down the slug-trailed path. The sleepless snails were in abundance and she watched her step so as not to hear the horrible crack of a broken shell underfoot. *Lillian would probably enjoy that*, she thought. Her condition that Amy break the news to the victim's family was a cruel and sadistic demand. A job better placed in the hands of a family liaison officer. She could have called Lillian's bluff, but she felt connected to the victims in some way. Had she been in the house when it happened? Covered her ears to block out her screams? Barbara Price was a child in Amy's eyes, just sixteen years old. A bright and bubbly girl with freckles and auburn hair, she had run away from home after a tiff with her mother over a party she was not allowed to attend. Found wandering the streets, she was coaxed into the car and back to Jack and Lillian's house. Amy had read about their hunt for young runaways and how they lured them in with the promise of a babysitting job and a roof over their heads.

The exhumation had been swift according to DI Donovan, with the family of the deceased demonstrating sympathy for the woman who was purported to be buried beneath their own. Perhaps it was as much of a case of wanting their loved one to rest in peace as to assist the family of Barbara Price. Whatever the reason, they had requested that the process be quick, and DI Donovan had not wasted any time. The remains had been discovered a foot below the coffin, just as Lillian had said. The remnants of Barbara's jewellery and a handbag had been buried with her, making her easier to identify. A press release would be made as soon as the next of kin had been made aware, and further testing of the remains was underway.

Amy sighed at the thought of additional publicity. Lillian Grimes would have her notoriety yet again. She knew she had to stop thinking like this because it was eating her up inside. She took another breath, ready to focus on the news she was about to break. The blue flash of a television light filtered through the curtains, quickly extinguished as Amy approached the door. It was opened almost as soon as she raised her finger to the doorbell.

'Mrs Price?' Amy said, her fingers curling around her warrant card as she raised it in the air. 'I called. I'm DI Amy Winter.'

'Come in.' Slightly stooped and wide-hipped, Kitty Price was about five foot seven, with ash blonde hair permed in a soft style. Her face bore the creases of mourning, her slippered feet shuffling with the movement of someone suffering with stiffness in their joints. Amy felt a surge of sympathy, wishing she could quieten the voices in her head whispering that *she* was a part of the family that had caused so much pain.

Wiping her feet on the mat, she stepped inside. 'Would you like me to take off my shoes?' she asked, observing the plush carpet beneath her feet.

'No need,' Kitty said, her voice frail as she leaned on her walking stick. 'Come into the living room. All the family are here.'

Amy knew the Price family was large but had not expected all seven of her grown-up children to be present. With their strawberry-blonde hair and freckled skin, there was no denying their lineage. Those who could not fit on the three-piece suite sat perched on its arms, their eyes trained on Amy from the moment she entered the room. Amy acknowledged them with a nod, her gaze falling on a painting of Barbara that was scarily lifelike. It hung above the fireplace, the lamps either side casting her likeness in a soft orange glow. Barbara's eyes held a question. Amy felt them boring into her soul. *How could you? How could you stand by and let them do those things to me?*

'Have they found her?' Mrs Price said, breaking into Amy's thoughts.

A middle-aged woman rose to place a hand on her frail shoulders, a much older version of the girl painted on the wall. 'Give the lady a chance, Mum; here, come and sit down.' She turned her attention to Amy, her expression strained. 'I'm Marian, Barbara's sister. I was only six when she disappeared. Mum's been waiting a very long time. Please tell me you've found her.'

Amy responded with a grateful smile, instilling professionalism into every word. They needed to know this case was in capable hands. She stood before Barbara's picture, a fitting spot to deliver the news. 'As you know, we received information from Lillian Grimes with regards to Barbara's burial place. We acted upon that information. We've recovered what we believe to be Barbara's remains.'

A sense of sadness settled in the room as Barbara's siblings absorbed the news. 'Thank you,' Mrs Price whispered. Gazing up at Amy, her eyes filled with tears. 'When can we bring her home?'

Amy had her answer ready. 'We're working on getting her returned to you as soon as we can.'

Mrs Price nodded, her hands trembling as she accepted a tissue from her daughter. 'Will I be able to see her?'

'I don't think that's a good idea, Mum,' a bearded man said. His voice was gentle as he gazed into his mother's eyes. 'It's been years. There won't be much left . . .'

'Please,' she said, returning her gaze to Amy. 'I don't care if it's just bones. I need to touch her one more time. I don't care how bad it is. Please let me have that.'

Amy drew breath as she tried to comprehend how this woman must be feeling. So desperate to see her daughter that she would sacrifice the inevitable nightmares to come. 'Take some time to think about it,' Amy said. 'We'll do our best to accommodate your wishes, but bear in mind that sometimes it's best to preserve your last memory of your loved ones.'

Mrs Price's fingers unfurled around the tissue in her hand. 'I will.' Her voice was a whisper as two fat droplets fell on her plaid skirt. 'I'll never understand how those monsters could hurt my little girl. Did you know they brought one of their own children to lure them in? She would never have got into that car if it wasn't for her.'

A child? Amy had not read that far into the case notes. Her stomach clenched. What child was she referring to? Had they used her to commit their crimes? She clasped her hands tightly together, pressing her nails into her palms. All eyes were on her and she could not lose her composure now. 'It's best not to dwell. I know it's of little consolation, but at least you'll be able to have a proper funeral, say your goodbyes.'

'Thank you,' Mrs Price said, her sadness heavy as it filled the room. 'That means more than you know. Thank you for not giving up on my daughter.'

'Are you sure you don't want to speak to a family liaison officer? I can arrange for them to attend.' Amy knew they had dismissed their earlier offer, and to be fair, Mrs Price was not short of support.

'I'm fine,' Mrs Price said, rising to see her out. 'It's over. It's finally over.'

Amy nodded. 'A press release will be issued, but I'd appreciate it if you didn't speak to the papers. There are other victims involved. It's a delicate situation which still causes a lot of pain.'

'Of course,' Mrs Price said, dabbing her tears, her tissue twisted in her hand. It was only then that Amy realised some of her children were crying too. She swallowed hard, her emotions closing in.

Barbara's sister Marian spoke. 'There are two more aren't there? Viv Holden and Wendy Thompson. Do you think that monster will tell you their burial sites too?'

Amy sighed. 'Well, we've come this far so we're hoping she will.'

'I remember your father,' Mrs Price said. 'Such a decent man. He promised me he'd find her, and he's kept that promise through you.' She clasped Amy's hands, her fingers cool to the touch. 'Thank you,' she said, swallowing back her tears. 'He'd be very proud of what you've done.'

'You're w-welcome,' Amy said, blushing slightly as the stutter tripped off her tongue. She took a sudden breath as panic drove its way inside her. She had not stuttered since she was a little girl. Straightening her posture, she glanced at the door.

Amy nodded, unable to trust herself to speak any further. It was with great relief that she let herself out, shaking the hands of grateful family members who stood to relay their thanks. She turned to the bracing air, her legs weak beneath the weight of her emotions. Her instinct had been right. Coming here was a bad idea.

◆ ◆ ◆

Sitting in her car, Amy took a deep breath as she tried to shove the past back into the box from which it came. Although a box wasn't the right image – at the forefront of her mind was a bloodstained chest, jagged nails scratching for release from within. Was it the chest that harboured Barbara Price? Had she witnessed her abduction? Ignored her pleas for help? 'Enough!' Amy cried, bringing her hands either side of her temples. 'Leave me b-b-be!' Leaning forward, she tipped her forehead against the steering wheel, closing her eyes as she forced another calming breath. She had to get a grip before this case broke her. Straightening in her seat, she turned on the ignition, dust blasting from the interior fan as she tried to clear her view. Robotically, she checked the time, bringing herself back to ground by replaying tomorrow's schedule in her head. It was time to go home. Soon this would all be over, and she could get back to being who she was . . . couldn't she?

CHAPTER TWENTY-TWO

Intuition made Amy pause when she pressed her hand on the living room door. On her journey home, she had focused on Mandy, her visit to the Price's home too painful to think about. Not that their meeting had been much better. Mandy was simply fuelled by the need for some extra cash. Then again, Amy may have felt the same way, had she been in her shoes. But Amy's career had been littered with people like Mandy who refused to take responsibility for their actions. It was one of the classic psychopathic traits. Had Mandy really cared about Sally-Ann, or was she just trying to get her on side? Amy's recent flash of memory had recalled a harsh and cruel sibling – but perhaps Mandy had only been taking her mother's lead. She pushed away thoughts of her sister. The sound of Flora in heated conversation made her pause at the living room door. Slowly, she pressed down on the handle, the urgent tone of her mother's voice a cause for concern.

'It's only a matter of time until she finds out . . . she's been through enough.'

Amy frowned. Was she talking about her? Who else could it be?

'I have every reason to panic,' Flora insisted to her mystery caller as she paced the floor. 'But what do I do? Just leave it there? What if she finds it?' Silence followed as her caller responded.

'That's easy for you to say. You're not the one with . . .'

A sudden excited bark brought a break in conversation as Dotty caught sight of Amy through the crack in the door. Amy sighed. She had little energy for snooping anyway. She was running on empty. Facing Lillian, seeing Mandy again, not to mention the family of the victims whose screams haunted her dreams . . . Perhaps Flora was right. There were some things you were better off not knowing. She embraced the warmth of their living room, shrugging off her jacket and folding it over the back of the sofa. Scooping Dotty in her arms, she accepted her slobbery kisses before planting the wiggling dog back on the floor. Tonight, her pug would sleep on her bed, providing comfort when she woke.

Hastily, Flora ended the conversation before hanging up the phone. A set of curlers nestled on her head, and her dressing gown was open at the front revealing her full-length nightdress beneath. Her nightie, bed linen, candles and home accessories were all bought from The White Company. Amy often joked she should have shares in the place.

'It's a bit late for a phone call,' Amy said, despite her earlier vow not to snoop. 'Everything OK?'

Flora paled under the heat of Amy's gaze. 'It's just Winifred flapping. She . . .' She paused, shoving her feet into the slippers she had discarded next to the sofa. 'She's holding a surprise party for her daughter and has asked me to help out. She got one of those three tier cakes. She wants me to store it here.'

'Is that the woman who had cancer?' Amy said, remembering news of her remission.

'One and the same,' Flora replied, placing the phone back in its cradle. 'She sometimes pops around with her mum for a cuppa. I don't want her finding it in my fridge, and these things take up so much room.'

'I wouldn't say no to a slice of cake right now,' Amy said. 'I've barely had time to eat. Can I make you a coffee?'

'No thanks, love. I'm going back to bed. There's some homemade apple pie in the fridge. Night, night.' Leaning forward, she gently kissed Amy on the cheek. Gingerly, Amy patted her back. She had known from an early age that Flora had wanted a child she could squeeze and hug. Amy had been unable to fulfil her needs in many ways, yet her mother had stuck by her just the same. Kicking off her shoes, she half-filled the kettle and put it on to boil. The kitchen was just off the living room, and she found herself wandering back in and staring at the phone. Flora had said she was going *back* to bed. Surely Winifred would not have called at this late hour? Amy frowned. It had to be more than that. Picking up the phone receiver, she dialled 1471 to trace the call. Holding her breath, she awaited a response. The last number dialled was a private number. Private number? Then it couldn't be Winifred. Amy had advised her to go ex-directory after a series of phishing calls, but the woman had been determined to keep her number public at the time. Flora had lied, and not for the first time. Abandoning her tea, Amy reached into the cupboard and poured herself two fingers of gin. After topping up her glass with soda from the fridge, she sat at the table, wondering if this day would ever end.

CHAPTER TWENTY-THREE

Hemmy awoke with a start, blinking furiously. How long had she been asleep? She wrinkled her nose as the stench of rotting fish guts hit the back of her nose. Her confinement seemed different now it was light. She gazed at the porthole, now free of the wood that once covered it. *When did that happen?* Slowly, she crept to the end of the bed. The presence of food made her heart beat wildly, like a tightly wound clockwork toy. Someone had been here while she was asleep. Her eyes widened. The door. On wobbly legs she rushed towards it, stumbling over her stockinged feet. The handle was stiff and relentless beneath her fingers, and she screamed as it refused to give. Shaking her hand, particles of rust broke free. 'Let me out!' Her cries rebounded in the stinking space. Above her, a radio played a stream of eighties pop tunes, drowning out her voice.

A glance around confirmed her earlier suspicions. She was on the bottom deck of some kind of boat. Pressing her face to the porthole, she tried to glean a view of the outside world. The ceiling was low, but she barely noticed the cobwebs brushing against her head. Spiders were the least of her worries right now. The mud-smeared glass provided her with a view of the water outside and little else. Her breathing accelerated as she took in her surroundings, the bare timbers chilling the soles of her feet. The bed she had slept in was the only furniture occupying the narrow space.

She eyed the food. A Tesco tuna sandwich and a bottle of water sat next to a bag of cheese and onion crisps. Ripping open the wrapper she wolfed the sandwich down. She hated tuna. It brought her out in a rash, but she was in no position to be fussy. She recalled her mother's words, taking strength from their meaning. 'You have to be a strong woman to get ahead in a man's world.' Now was one of those times.

Unscrewing the lid from the bottle, she threw back her head and gulped, sighing in relief as the water eased her scratchy throat. A smell crept up from the floorboards to greet her. Urine. She felt so ashamed, but she'd had no choice. At least she was able to move around in her rust-coated prison, and she would do what she had to in order to get by. People looked on her mother as some wealthy celebrity, but Hemmy knew the sacrifices she had made to get to where she was. Renting a house in London, sending Hemmy to private school. Such things came with a price tag they could barely afford. If her captor was sending a ransom note, then her mum could never accommodate their demands.

Returning to the porthole, she gripped the bottle in her hand. If she could break the porthole glass . . . it would make a useful weapon, and maybe someone would hear her cries for help. But would she have the guts to stab her attacker if it came to it? She launched the plastic bottle against the circular window, a shooting pain travelling up her wrist as it bounced back, the glass intact. A shuffling noise behind the door stilled her movements. Someone was coming. She was about to meet her attacker face-to-face. Rushing back to the bed, she covered herself with a blanket, coughing as the damp spores invaded her lungs.

The sharp sound of a bolt being shoved across made Hemmy grip her knees to her chest. For the first time, she noticed the small steel-like shutter, allowing her captor to peer in. But what she saw made her blood run cold. They were wearing a black latex mask. A dry rasping breath rattled through the ventilation device. It was a gas mask. Why? Was this some kind of poison gas attack? Her mouth falling open, Hemmy's eyes met those behind the hatch. The sight of the bug-like eyepieces looked like something out of a horror film. Swallowing the scream rising in her throat, Hemmy stepped forward on unsteady feet to plead for her life. 'Please,' she said, not realising she was crying until she tasted the salt in her tears. 'Please let me go. I won't say anything, I swear.'

Like two shiny coals, the eyes behind the mask were black and glittering, filled with dark intent. Biting down on her bottom lip, Hemmy tried desperately to contain her fear. She needed to show them she was strong. Formidable. That was what her father had once called her. Formidable. A force to be reckoned with. Only she wasn't feeling quite so brave today.

'Let me go.' But her words came out as a whine as they echoed around the stinking space. 'Please? There's been some mistake.'

Shadowed by the rim of the mask, the cold, hard eyes of her kidnapper crept over her form. That breath . . . Hemmy thought. The torturous rattle dragging steadily through the respirator, driving a shiver down her spine. At last, it paused as he opened his mouth to speak.

'I'll keep you safe . . . As long as you're a good girl.' Another inhalation as the gas mask drew in air. Eerily, Hemmy's captor watched through the bony structures of the eyepieces, the two glass lenses tinted ever so slightly black.

Consumed by fear, Hemmy retreated to the back of the boat. The bump of a sudden lap of water made her grip the timber walls, and a splinter jabbed under her thumb. 'Please, let me go.' She winced at the sudden sting of pain. 'I won't tell anybody. I promise.'

'Not if you misbehave.' Her kidnapper's words were muffled and distorted, adding to her fear. 'You're for the chop if you do.'

What did they mean? Were they going to kill her? And why were they staring at her like that? She clasped her arms over her chest. Despite her school uniform, she felt exposed. Should she be grateful they were wearing a mask? She read once that if a witness could identify their captors, there was less chance of them being set free. Was this even a kidnapping? It was preferable to the other thoughts that were frightening her half to death.

'Purdy,' she said, just as the thought struck her. 'Where's my cat?'

'Asleep. If you're good, then you'll see her.' A pause for breath. 'If you're not . . .'

'If I'm not?' Hemmy said, trying to regain her balance.

'I never did like cats.' The sentence was punctuated by the sound of the hatch slamming shut.

CHAPTER TWENTY-FOUR

His brow furrowed, Paddy sighed, the weight of his burdens heavy on his shoulders. Yesterday he had returned to Elaine armed with an excuse for the burns on his neck. His job in the police had its uses. He had made up a story about a junkie coming at him with a homemade blowtorch, and she now thought he was some kind of action man. Geraldine had apologised of course, and like a gentleman, he told her they would draw a line under the whole thing. He was not blameless. He had broken their family. It was his fault she was driven to such extremes. The love between them may have died but how could he abandon her now? Scanning his tag, he opened the station door. Today he would take inspiration from his DI. Strong and professional, Amy Winter never allowed her personal life to interfere with work. She may have been suffering since the death of her father, but he knew better than to ask her to open up.

'How's it going?' he said to DC Steve Moss, hanging up his jacket and brushing the inevitable flakes of dandruff that had gathered on its shoulders. Steve always made him feel scruffy. Steve's suit was neatly pressed, unlike Paddy's, whose tie already bore evidence of the fried egg sandwich he had made for breakfast.

Highly punctual, Steve was always the first through the doors. A fan of clean living, he ate well and didn't smoke or drink, but womanising was his downfall. He spun his swivel chair towards Paddy, a look of mild irritation crossing his face.

'Slow, it's going slow,' he said. 'No new leads and a shitload of work. Where's Her Highness this morning? Off on another jaunt?'

'That's hardly fair,' Paddy said, knowing he was referring to their DI. 'She had a good result with Lillian Grimes. The command team will be singing our praises when it hits the press.'

'Come on, you and I go back a long way,' Steve said. 'Can't you see what's going on?'

'Enlighten me.' Whatever Steve had to say, he was obviously desperate to get it off his chest.

'I get demoted for nothing, yet she strolls into a prime job on the back of her father's rep. As for me . . .' He poked himself in the chest. 'I come from a family of grafters. I wasn't born with a silver spoon in my mouth.'

'Who pissed on your cornflakes this morning?' Paddy said, a smile softening his features as he shook his head. He knew Steve of old. He was a good copper but a pessimist by nature.

Leaning back in his chair, Steve's jaw cracked as he yawned. 'I feel like I'm going backwards. We're being told to focus on the kidnapping, yet our DI's chasing a case that's over thirty years old. All because Her Highness wants the glory.'

Paddy rubbed his chin. He had not slept properly in days, and the last thing he wanted was a sparring match with his old shift partner. 'This is a high-profile unit and Winter handles it well,' he said wearily. 'You can't get more notorious than Lillian Grimes. Which is why we can't mess this up.'

'I suppose you're right,' Steve said. 'I just don't see why women are getting these posts. What happened to blokes overseeing things?'

Paddy groaned. 'Things have changed since we joined the job. It's not all about brawn. It's about perception and insight. Winter's built up a connection with Grimes. The woman's actually telling her stuff. From what I've heard, that's a flaming miracle. Right now, she's trying to find Wendy Thompson's body so her mum can die in peace. Surely that's worthwhile?'

Steve snorted. 'And all while a fifteen-year-old girl's been kidnapped and having God knows what done to her.' He prodded the table before him. 'Winter should be here, overseeing the case. Hermione's the same age as my daughter. I'd be going out of my mind if that was me.'

Patience lost, the smile dropped from Paddy's face. It was too early in the morning, and his neck still hurt like hell. 'Well, put your bloody energy into the case, instead of whining to me. Why don't you tell Winter how you feel instead of sniping behind her back?'

'Because she'll run off crying to DCI Pike. You know those two are thick as thieves.'

'It goes to show that you don't know Winter at all. She doesn't cry. Not a tear. Not even at her dad's funeral, and I know that hit her hard. You're only pissed off because Pike demoted you. And that was your own stupid fault.'

'And here was me thinking it would be good for us to work together again.' Leaning over his desk, Steve picked up his empty coffee mug to make himself a brew.

'Who are you kidding?' Paddy replied. 'You didn't join this team for the pleasure of my company. Why are you really here?'

Steve shrugged. 'I thought it would help me get back into the Chief's good books, but there's not much likelihood of that, with Winter's nose stuck up her backside.'

'Maybe if you improved your attitude instead of racking up complaints you'd get somewhere,' Paddy replied. In the hall, a tannoy sounded, but the request was for someone else. He wanted to get to work instead of handbags at dawn.

'You've changed,' Steve said. 'I remember the day you said there was no place for women in the police.'

'I was wrong.' Paddy hated being reminded of the ugly, misjudged comment he'd made in his youth. 'I've watched Winter in action. She's good. Either you get with the programme or move on.'

'I was going to ask you out for a drink tonight, but I don't think I'll bother now.' A sneer rose on Steve's face. 'Is your missus still giving you grief? That's a nasty burn on the back of your neck.'

Paddy sighed. In his haste to get in early, he had forgotten to bring his scarf. 'It's nothing. And don't go spreading rumours about Geraldine. She's been through enough . . .'

'Don't worry, mate,' Steve interrupted sharply. 'I'm good at keeping things to myself.'

Paddy knew what he was doing, flexing his muscles to stay in control. Steve was one of the few people he had confided in when things got tough, but that was years ago, and he had moved on since then. He should have been pleased when his old friend joined his team. He and Steve went back a long way. The problem was that Steve had grown bitter. He knew all Paddy's secrets, too. He had a choice: bow down to Steve or tell his DI the truth. For now, he needed to focus on the task at hand.

'Have you anything positive to take into the briefing?' he said, changing the subject. 'I take it you had nothing back from DIU?' The divisional intelligence unit was a valuable resource but they were backed up with more work than they could handle, and their reports took time to obtain.

'Nothing that ties in with this,' Steve replied. 'Social media has gone crazy, there are thousands of tweets and shares. She was trending at one point. Hashtag "Find Hermione". Somewhere in the middle of all that could be a clue, but when are we gonna get time to trawl through it? Sometimes it feels like I'm pissing against the wind.'

'You've more important things on your plate than Facebook and Twitter,' Paddy said. 'We've got a new DC starting today. Gary Wilkes. He's completed part one of his sergeant's exams and is keen to get some more experience under his belt.'

'Good,' Steve said. 'We could do with some extra bodies around here. I'm going to a MAPPA meeting today to fill them in.'

There were three categories of offenders discussed at the multi-agency public protection meeting: registered sexual offenders, violent offenders and dangerous offenders known to police. Paddy liked that Steve used his initiative, but since his demotion, he had trouble getting to grips with the fact he was a DC. Rather than accepting the tasks that were set for him, he created his own. But while Steve had a hold over him, it was safer for Paddy to leave him be. 'It's just a shame there's no ransom note.' Steve locked his computer before walking away from his desk. 'Hermione could be sex trafficked for all we know.'

'The guy who did this is an amateur,' Paddy said, keeping an eye on the time. 'And who's to say there's no ransom note? Tessa wouldn't be the first parent to keep it a secret. Or maybe she's in on it herself. I've seen her finances. She's not exactly flush. Her face has been everywhere since it hit the news. Can't be doing her career any harm.'

'Which is why she's listed as a person of interest,' Steve replied, looking into his empty cup. 'This coffee isn't going to make itself. Fancy one?'

'My throat's dryer than a camel's ball sack,' Paddy responded. 'So I won't say no.' His shoulders hunched, he took a seat at his desk. Unlike DI Winter, he did not have the luxury of a separate office, and he sat at the head of the room instead. He preferred to be part of the team. He had plenty to do before they filtered in, and sending an email to Winter would timestamp his early appearance at the very least. He had to show willing. His neck was on the line, in more ways than one.

CHAPTER TWENTY-FIVE

The endorphins gained from her morning gym session with Pike dissipated as Amy pressed the phone to her ear. She tightened her fingers around the receiver, willing herself to speak. Her impromptu caller filled her with dread, the sound of her voice drilling into her brain. Amy had loathed giving Lillian Grimes her direct line, but she could not stand to have another transferred call announcing her mother was on the phone. She reminded herself that contact was temporary: as soon as the final two bodies were recovered, then all communication with Lillian Grimes would cease. But deep inside the uncomfortable truth lingered. How could she get back to normal when she no longer knew what normal was? Breaking the news about Barbara Price had made her feel like such a fraud. She had no right to be in the family's home. And as the daughter of prolific serial killers, did she even have a right to her job? As Lillian's breath ruffled the phone line, Amy felt her day go from bad to worse.

'It's me. Mother,' Lillian said, relishing the word. 'Aren't you going to speak?'

'I hope you're calling with the burial site,' Amy replied tightly. 'Because I met Mandy as agreed.' The clock on the wall ticked solemnly in the silence that fell between them. It seemed to stretch on forever. She knew Lillian would string this out for all it was worth.

'She told me,' Lillian said, after taking a measured breath. 'I was delighted to hear how well you got on. The children will be pleased to have you in their lives. They've been a bit short of birthday presents, but it's never too late to make up for your neglect.'

'I don't have much time,' Amy lied, feeling the walls of her office close in. Rising from her desk, she opened the blinds, allowing the morning sun through; anything to lift the oppression in the room. All she wanted were the remaining burial addresses. She needed to free herself from this hateful woman before the past swallowed her whole.

A beat passed between them before Lillian spoke again. 'I'd best let you go, given you're so busy. Perhaps I'll give you the address another day. I've held onto it all these years after all.' Theatrically, she sighed. 'Still, you never know what's around the corner. It would be a shame if it died with me. None of us knows how long we've got.'

'Don't go,' Amy replied, hating herself for having to beg. 'Do you want to show us? Will I arrange it with the prison?'

'You've always been the impatient one, ever since you were a little girl.' Lillian laughed mirthlessly. 'And no, to be honest, I felt a little carsick after the last time. It doesn't appeal to me anymore, being driven around like a cow to slaughter.'

The blood left Amy's face as she caught the self-pity in Lillian's voice. 'You didn't mind the drive when you were hunting for those young girls. Trust you, did they? I suppose the presence of a child helped to reel them in.'

A pause. Lillian spoke. 'I sense some animosity in your tone. Has someone upset you?'

Upset me . . . that's an understatement, Amy thought, her temper rising as she fought to gain control. 'How could you? How could you snatch those girls off the street knowing what you were about to do?

Who did you bring? Was it me? Did you . . .' Amy pursed her lips, cutting her words short as she felt a stutter gather on her tongue.

'Really, Amy, I've tried to explain, but you won't listen,' Lillian interrupted. 'Jack insisted I bring you. It was a threat. If I didn't do as I was told, one of us would get hurt.'

'That's not what Jack said, and the evidence . . .' Amy said, having gained her composure.

'Was planted. And you'll find that out soon enough,' Lillian interrupted once more. 'Tell me something, do you hate me, or the *idea* of me? For years I've been painted as a monster. That's why nobody will listen to the truth. I'd expect it from others, but not you.'

'If you think a phone call from you will change my mind then you're more deluded than I thought . . .'

A sudden eruption of swearing in the background caught Amy's attention. Lillian's voice grew tense as their conversation was cut short. 'Fuck off,' Lillian said, to whoever was moaning in the background. 'I've got five more minutes!' She sighed, reverting back to the accent she used with Amy. The much improved one. 'Try to remember what happened to Sally-Ann. I could never hurt her. It wasn't me.'

Amy did not inform Lillian that she already remembered that much. Her recollection of what had happened in the basement had been one of the first to return. Her mother finding Sally-Ann crumpled and bleeding on the ground. Her screams as her panicked voice asked Jack what he had done. Then later, plucking Amy from the wash basket and telling her to be quiet. *Don't wake your father, whatever you do.*

Amy sat in her office, watching dust motes dance in the shaft of morning light.

'Sod off,' Lillian grumbled to whoever was waiting to use the phone. 'Amy, listen to me because I'm doing this for you. You'll find Viv in the same cemetery as before. She's a few graves down from the last one.'

'But you said . . .' The words hung on Amy's lips.

'If I told you at the time you wouldn't have visited Mandy, now would you? Can't you see? I just want my family back.'

'Which grave?' Amy said, ignoring her sentiment.

'You'll find her under Joe Fletcher. I remember it because Fletch was the name of the character in that comedy, *Porridge*. Ironic, isn't it, given how I've ended up on the inside.'

A memory filtered into Amy's brain: the tune of a prison comedy show playing on a loop. It *was* ironic – and a memory Amy could do without. Just when she thought she had a handle on her, Lillian threw another curveball into the mix. Was she playing her? Sprinkling her memory with echoes of the past to drag her back there for good? Wouldn't Lillian love to hear her stutter, to swear as she did as a child.

'Is the body buried beneath the coffin the same as before?' Amy said, her voice feeling very far away.

'Yes,' Lillian hastily replied. 'Jack only had a short stint as a grave-digger. Be grateful that you didn't end up in there. I did everything I could to protect my family, and yet *I'm* the one on the inside.'

'I didn't put you inside,' Amy snapped. 'I was four years old.'

'Are you sure about that? Has that part of your memory not come back yet? Think about that day when the social came to visit. Think about what you said.'

'I wasn't the one who murdered those girls,' Amy replied righteously.

'Neither was I. But we were both there when it happened, and *I'm* the one locked up. It's time to stop running away . . .'

'I've got to go,' Amy said, pressing her pen into a pad as she scribbled the name of the grave. 'Where's Wendy? In the same graveyard?'

'No, and I'm telling you the truth this time.'

'Then where?' Amy said insistently. 'Tell me.'

But Lillian's voice was cold. 'We'll speak again soon. Just remember what I said.'

CHAPTER TWENTY-SIX

After updating Pike on the second burial site, Amy needed a change of scene. Her DCI had taken the role of Senior Investigating Officer and being in the background suited Amy just fine. Given what she knew about Lillian, being the SIO would be a conflict of interest at the very least. Amy's involvement in the case had been keeping her awake at night as it was. Her job was her life. She should have come clean from the beginning, but it was too late now.

She turned her attention to the person before her, feeling a sense of surrealism. Tessa Parker was Flora's favourite celebrity, and *Dragon's Den* was always on in the background at home. Not that she looked much like her screen persona today. Dressed in a baggy knitted jumper and faded jeans, Tessa was a shadow of herself. Her face was gaunt, her limp blonde hair scraped back from her face. Her fear and concern for her daughter were evident, and Amy reassessed her theory that she may have been involved. 'We have teams of officers working around the clock,' Amy said, in response to her request for an update. 'Floyd will update you as soon as we're in a position to share more.' Floyd, nicknamed 'Floyd the FLO', was the family liaison officer, a young West Indian man who was relatively new to the role.

Tessa nodded unblinkingly, her eyes puffy from lack of sleep. 'I feel so helpless. Floyd said you've been flooded with calls since the press release, most of them from trolls. And as for what's posted online . . . some of it is vile.'

It was true, and team members were working on getting the worst of the comments removed. DCI Pike had held a press conference in the hope of some fresh leads, but all it did was swamp the teams with false hope and burden them with work. A *Crimewatch* re-enactment was due to air in the hope of jogging memories. Most of all, Amy needed to satisfy her suspicions that this was a premeditated attack.

'It's senseless,' Amy said. 'Much like the people who post it; but we're monitoring it as it comes in.' She didn't know what trolls were until she joined the high-priority team. There was something about the excitement of a big case that brought them crawling out of the wood-work, feeding off the excitement for kicks. Each day Hermione was missing decreased the chances of her being found alive. Having com-pleted door-to-door enquiries, officers had come back with a lead that Amy was keen to explore. 'I've got something to show you,' she said, pulling back the flap of her briefcase and slipping out a clear exhibit bag. Marked with the time, date and place of where it was seized, it carried the exhibit number and identity of the officer involved. Amy's details were also there, given she had booked it out of the property system. 'We seized this from an address two doors down. Could it be Hermione's?' Amy held it up to the light: behind the transparent plastic, a broken chain with a silver 'H' could clearly be seen. At the top of the letter was a tiny diamond. It was an unusual piece, something Amy had never seen before.

Tessa's eyes grew wide at the sight of the jewellery. 'It's hers. Her father had it made when she was ten. She wouldn't take it off. Not for anyone.'

Amy nodded. Having seen the necklace in previous photos, it came as no surprise. 'Officers were holding house-to-house enquiries when your neighbour two doors down brought it to their attention.' Amy slipped the jewellery back into her bag. A statement would be taken to cover the identification, but for now, she had to forge ahead.

'Which one?' Tessa said, her face ashen.

'Mrs Cotterill. We gather that she's been away. She said she found the necklace on the floor when she came home. There'd been no sign of forced entry so we wondered if Hermione spent time in her place.'

Tessa's features creased in confusion. 'What? No. She's never been there. I went around a couple of times, once when her dog was put down, and another to collect her spare key when she was going away.'

'Oh, poor thing,' Amy said. 'What kind of a dog did she have?' It had nothing to do with the investigation, but she found herself asking just the same.

'One of those awful yappy little Yorkshire terriers. It had been sick for ages and she couldn't face it on her own . . . Sorry,' she said, her frown gathering, 'I'd rather focus on Hemmy. What was her necklace doing there?'

'That's what we're trying to find out,' Amy replied. 'Unfortunately, Mrs Cotterill gets a little confused. Officers reported that she had a burglar alarm, but she can't remember turning it on before she left. The alarm company haven't been able to help either. Do you know of anyone else who has a key or knows the code?'

'I'm afraid not.' Tessa shrugged. 'She has early dementia. I'm surprised she remembered to hand the necklace in.'

Amy made a mental note to enquire with local locksmiths to see if Mrs Cotterill had had any extra keys cut. She returned her attention to Tessa, who was picking at a fray in the knee of her jeans. 'Do you mind if I ask you a few more questions? I'd like an insight into your daughter's personality.'

For Amy, the emotional impact on the victim was highly relevant, and Hermione's inner strength had barely been touched upon in the statement provided to police. People reacted in different ways as victims of crime. The fight or flight syndrome was real. She had known victims to freeze in situations when they could have run away, others to fight when it would have been safer for them to comply. People never really knew how they would react in such a situation until they found themselves there. Often, people who took part in self-defence classes were more likely to fight for their lives. It saddened her to think that those seldom in contact with violence were more likely to freeze up with fear.

'I'll do anything to help.' Tessa glanced up as a woman entered the room with a tray. 'This is my sister, Ellen,' she said by means of introduction. 'She's staying with me for a few days.'

Ellen seemed the image of Tessa, apart from a few extra wrinkles, which revealed her age. She smiled in acknowledgement, her long blonde hair falling over her face as she laid the tray down. 'Please, help yourself,' she said, in a northern accent, before sitting across from them both. The smell of fresh coffee rose up from the mugs, and Tessa plopped three sugar cubes into her cup before meeting Amy's gaze. 'This is the only thing keeping me going right now.' 'World's Best Mum' was printed on the side of the mug, along with a photo of Tessa squeezing Hermione in a warm embrace. Similar pictures were framed and displayed on the Victorian fireplace and there were canvas prints on the walls.

'Thank you.' Amy smiled, pouring a little cream into her cup before giving her coffee a stir. 'Can I ask you . . . how does your daughter cope during times of stress? Is she good in emergencies?'

'Hermione takes after her father: she deals well with pressure.' Tessa wrapped her fingers around the mug. 'When she was six, Harry Potter swept the nation, and she was teased mercilessly in school. She didn't mind. She liked the idea of having magical powers, being different to everyone else.'

'Would you say she's resourceful? Good at reading people's moods?'

'Very.' Tessa nodded. 'Which is why I know she'll be OK. She's a clever girl, and she's strong like her dad. Whatever's happening to her' – Tessa's chin wobbled – 'she'll get through this. Whatever happens, we can start again.'

Ellen leaned forward and gave her sister's shoulder a squeeze.

'You've not had any ransom demand of any kind?' Locking her gaze onto Tessa's, Amy searched for the truth. 'Are you absolutely sure?'

'I swear on Hemmy's life. I've had nothing. I'd tell you if I had.'

'Have you had any stalkers? Any strange phone calls, letters or requests?'

Tessa shook her head vehemently. 'Nothing. I keep my family life private. I'm not on Facebook and the only time I share a family photo is at Christmas. The BBC like to do this online piece about their presenters over the festive season. But that was months ago.' Her mouth dropped open as she paused, reading the expression on Amy's face. 'You don't think that's how they found her, do you? If they've been planning it that long she'll have no chance of getting away.'

'Let's not jump the gun,' Amy said, keeping her tone even. 'You said yourself she's resourceful. Best to stay positive until we know more.'

'She's a good judge of character, too,' Ellen interrupted. 'Which is why we can't understand why she left the house.'

'You're absolutely sure there was no sign of forced entry?' Amy looked to Tessa for the answer.

'Positive. It's so unlike her. Our front door was wide open, and her shoes were in the hall where she kicked them off. What made her go outside? And why leave to go two doors down? It's completely against her nature.'

Amy frowned. If Hermione was as responsible as they both made out, then they were right, it didn't make sense. She had seen the chain on the door, the spy hole embedded in the wood. What would make a sensible fifteen-year-old go running to her neighbour and cast caution to the wind? 'And there were no phone calls? Have you checked your answer machine?'

'The police have taken her mobile and I checked the answer machine. Hemmy had—' She corrected herself. '*Has* this habit of deleting messages after she listens. If she did pick up a message, she wouldn't have left it there.'

'So she was routinely alone for an hour before you came home from work? No friends came back with her? No boyfriend or neighbours called in during that time?'

Tessa shook her head. 'She hasn't got a boyfriend . . . At least, not yet. Most of our neighbours are at work during the day, and she walks home with her friend Paige, but she doesn't come in.'

Amy frowned. The fact that Tessa had spoken of her daughter in the past tense made a prickle of unease run through her. 'Do you have pets?' she asked, picking up a fine white hair from the arm of the sofa.

'Oh, that's Purdy's,' Tessa said flatly. 'We got her six months ago.'

'Purdy?' Amy's frown deepened. This was news to her.

'Hemmy's cat. I thought I told the officers, but maybe I didn't. She's the least of my worries right now.' Bowing her head, Tessa pressed the tips of her fingers against her forehead. 'My head is all over the place.'

'It's OK, take your time,' Amy replied, with as much reassurance as she could convey.

'She was a gift for Hemmy's fifteenth birthday. They're smitten with each other.'

Amy glanced around the room. 'Where is she now?' Her colleagues would laugh at her. Ask if she were going to question a cat. But her intuition told her to press on. Sometimes the most insignificant detail could lead to a clue.

'Gone,' Tessa said. 'She must have got out through the front door after Hemmy left. I've been waiting for her to come back, but there's no sign. I hope she's not been run over, Hemmy will be devastated.'

The comment sparked an idea in Amy's mind. 'Do you have a cat flap or is Purdy confined during the day?'

'There's a small cat flap in the back door. She only leaves for a few minutes to do her business then comes straight back. She's never gone out the front before. To be honest, I've been so worried about Hemmy, I've barely given Purdy a second thought.'

Amy nodded. 'You said that Hemmy never answers the door when she's in the house on her own. What if Purdy wasn't here when she got home? Would she have gone outside to look for her?'

'I hadn't thought of that,' Tessa said. 'But she'd open the back door, not the front. And she wouldn't have gone out without shoes.'

'She might in an emergency,' Amy said. A flutter of excitement rose as she explored the theory. 'Think about it. You said yourself, she's a bright girl. What would bring her running outside in her bare feet? Is it possible someone could have taken her cat?'

'Maybe. Actually . . .' She paused for a few seconds. 'You could be right. Our address is on Purdy's collar. Someone could have stolen her, then knocked on the door and pretended they'd found her.'

'It looks like there was some sense of panic as Hermione left. Our witness reports hearing screaming just before four o clock. It's possible that the suspect used Purdy to get her to leave the house.'

'The more I think about it, the more I think you're right. She wouldn't have answered for anything less,' Tessa said.

Killers could be inventive. Amy did not inform Tessa that the infamous serial killer Ted Bundy coaxed young women into his vehicle by feigning injury and asking for help. She mulled it over, finishing her coffee, which had now gone cold. 'It's just a theory,' she said. 'I own a pug, Dotty. There's nothing I wouldn't do for her.'

'Hemmy is animal mad. She wants to be a vet.' Tessa's bottom lip trembled, fresh tears forming in her eyes. 'She'll be all right, won't she? I couldn't bear it if . . . if . . .'

'Try not to think the worst,' Amy said. 'Most missing teenagers return home safely.' But Hermione was not just any teenager. She was a sensible girl with a decent family life and no reason to run away from home. The theory she had been snatched was growing stronger by the minute. It had to be her screams her neighbour heard that day. But why take the risk of abducting her in broad daylight? And what was their next move? After updating Tessa on the rest of their enquiries, Amy stood, projecting her best poker face. The truth was, she was scared for this girl.

'Let us know if Purdy turns up. We'd appreciate a picture if you've got one. We'll make some checks of the animal shelters as well.'

'I've got some pictures on my phone,' Tessa said. 'Floyd will be back soon, I'll pass them on.'

Amy nodded. She would have a word with Floyd later on. The absence of the family pet could be a vital clue. His failure to ask could cost them dearly. The next step would be to seize some of Hermione's belongings, take her fingerprints and see if they could match them with the ones taken two doors down.

Tessa led Amy to the front door, resting her hand on the latch as she prepared to show her out. Amy watched her face contorting as she desperately tried to keep her emotions in check. Hovering behind her, her sister watched them both. The two women were lost. Powerless. Whoever had taken Hemmy had robbed them of everything. Involuntary spectators, all they could do was stand by and watch events pan out.

'Please,' Tessa said, her words choked by a sob. 'Bring her home.'

'Shh. C'mon, sis, let's get you away from that door,' Ellen said.

Grim-faced, Amy ignored the journalists and paparazzi as she walked down the steps to her car. The feeling of grief and helplessness was one she remembered. Sally-Ann's resemblance to Hermione had not been lost on her: both girls fifteen, both caring and kind.

Her heels echoing on the pavement, Amy felt that this was a path she was walking very much alone. She had let one fifteen-year-old girl down. It could not happen a second time. She had to bring Hermione home.

CHAPTER TWENTY-SEVEN

1986

'You're shaking,' Marjorie said. 'Is everything all right?' Each time the woman from the social leaned forward, a gentle flowery fragrance was released. It was preferable to the sickly air freshener that Poppy had sprayed, and a lot less frightening than what it masked.

Poppy tried to think of an excuse for her trembling, given her mother was listening on the other side of the door. She glanced at the paint-streaked wood, imagining Lillian's face pressed against it on the other side. 'C . . . c . . . cold,' she stuttered, her teeth chattering from fear.

Marjorie and Thomas exchanged a glance. 'It's sunny outside,' Marjorie said, her bangles jangling as she gesticulated. 'Do you fancy coming out to the car? It's a shame to be cooped up in the house on such a lovely day.'

Poppy's eyes widened. Was the social taking her away? She had not said anything. She had been a good girl.

As if reading her mind, Thomas gently spoke. 'We won't go any-where, I promise. Your mummy will be able to see the car from the house, but when we talk, nobody else will be able to hear.'

As her eyes darted to the door and back, Poppy was not so sure. She folded her arms high on her chest, but still the trembling continued. Sitting with her legs and arms tightly crossed, she felt like one big knot.

Marjorie shuffled towards her on the sofa, her generous bosom moving from left to right. She was a big lady, and taller than Mummy, but Poppy liked that. It made her seem strong. She smiled, her teeth pearly white. 'Our car has lots of comfy seats, and it smells really nice.' She wrinkled her nose as she inhaled another breath.

Poppy knew the lady was too polite to say that her house stank. Each day the stench from the floorboards became more rotten and putrid than the day before. She swallowed, hoping they would not ask her what it was. She knew it had something to do with the soiled sheets and the things that Daddy did in the basement before the ladies disappeared.

Sensing her hesitation, Thomas leaned forward and whispered, 'How about I give you the keys to the car? You can look after them while we're there. I might even have some stickers you can play with – do you like unicorns?'

Poppy nodded, a gap-toothed smile breaking out on her face. She'd never had anything all to herself before. She had been wrong about Thomas. She could see now that he had a gentle face, very unlike her father's. He opened the palm of his hand to reveal a set of car keys. Tentatively, Poppy took them, enjoying the feel of the leather key ring in her hand.

Standing up, she took Thomas by the hand. His skin was soft, so unlike the roughly calloused flesh of her father's palms. Marjorie's face broke into a smile, and Poppy knew she had been a good girl.

'We'll only be a few minutes,' she explained to Lillian as Poppy jangled the keys of the car.

Lillian was standing in the hall, confirming Poppy's suspicions that she had been listening in all along. Her stomach flipped as she wondered whom to trust. Her mother was staring daggers, her lips a tight white line slashed across her mouth. 'I don't see why you can't talk to her here,' she said, failing to hide her displeasure.

But Marjorie was not to be put off. She was chunkier than her mother, and Poppy felt a warm glow of protection as Marjorie spoke in a firm voice. 'As you know, we have a right to speak to your child alone. We can do that now, or we can wait for a court order to take her into our care. Which would you prefer?'

Lillian glared at Marjorie, her knuckles whitening as she rested her hands on her hips. Poppy's grip on Thomas's hand tightened as the women stared each other out.

'I'm sure you don't want it to come to that.' Marjorie's voice softened. 'We're just going to have a little chat and Poppy will be back here in a matter of minutes.'

'Fine,' Lillian said, unblinking as she watched them leave. Poppy was grateful that her father had stayed in the kitchen, though her mother's eyes bore into her back like lasers. The heat of her gaze lingered long after she got into the car.

'No need for your seat belt,' Thomas said. 'We're not going anywhere.' He averted his gaze. 'Do you like our windows? They're tinted. It means you can see out, but nobody can see in. Isn't that clever?' Poppy's shaking subsided as she looked at the glass in wonderment. Marjorie had been truthful about the weather. The car was comfortably warm.

'How about I put on some music?' Marjorie said, turning it down low enough so they could speak. A tune about the wheels on the bus going round and round set Poppy slightly at ease. She liked this car. It felt safe and smelt of cookies. She looked out the window, her heart faltering as she saw the curtains twitch. She reminded herself that nobody could see her. She was safely cocooned – for now, at least.

'Look what I found,' Thomas said.

Poppy stared longingly at the sheet of bright pink and white stickers. But she did not immediately accept his gift. People who gave you things for free usually wanted something in return. At least, that's the way it was with the visitors who came to their home. But Mandy said the social were nothing like the visitors, didn't she?

'It's OK,' Marjorie said. 'You can have them. They're yours.'

Tentatively Poppy reached out and accepted the gift. She comforted herself that the car keys were safely nestled in her dress pocket and she had sat beside the door, should she need to escape. The music changed to a cheerful tune about mother goose, and Poppy relaxed into her seat. She peeled back a unicorn sticker, pressing it against her dress. After a few minutes of playing, she smiled shyly at Thomas and Marjorie. 'T-th-thank you,' she said, her eyes dropping to the rows of shiny stickers that were hers. Once back inside, Mandy would take them and ignore her cries to have them returned. But for now, they belonged to her. She thought about Sally-Ann and how pleased she would have been that Poppy received a gift.

'You like those, don't you?' Thomas said. 'Does Sally-Ann like stickers too?'

Poppy nodded, her expression growing sad as she wondered why he was talking about her in the present. Her sister was gone, and nothing would bring her back. She loved her more than Mummy and missed her so much that it hurt.

'When's the last time you saw her?' Marjorie said, her head tilted to one side. But Poppy didn't like that question because the last time she saw her sister . . . She pushed the thought away, her chin wobbling slightly as she strained to keep her tears at bay. Crying was bad. Sally-Ann had told her so.

'It smells a bit nicer in here, doesn't it?' Thomas said. 'Do you have any pets? I have a dog at home, and he gets very stinky. His name's Charlie. Would you like to see a picture?'

Nodding, Poppy tore her eyes away from the stickers to look at the photo Thomas produced from his jacket pocket. A shaggy white dog was snapped in mid-pant, its pink tongue lolling from its mouth.

'Do you have any pets?' Thomas asked.

'A h-ham-hamster,' Poppy said. 'Hammy.' She was pleased she managed to get that final word out in one piece.

'Ooh. I like hamsters. Where does he live?'

Poppy shook her head. 'He's gone. Daddy squished him.' She thought about the last time she looked for him. When she crept down into the basement and hid from her father. It was her fault that Sally-Ann was dead. Her mummy had told her that the social took bad people away and they put them in this place called jail. She did not want to go to jail.

'Has your daddy hurt other things too?' Thomas said.

Poppy nodded, wondering if you could get into trouble just from nodding and shaking her head. If she didn't say the words out loud, then she hadn't told anything, had she? Her face brightened, having come up with this all by herself.

'Has he hurt Sally-Ann?' Thomas said, speaking even softer this time.

Poppy nodded vigorously, her head bobbing up and down. Unblinkingly she stared at him, wondering if he was worthy of her trust.

'Open questions,' Marjorie whispered to Thomas, but Poppy did not know what that meant.

'What can you tell me about that?' Thomas said, his face flushed pink.

But Poppy shook her head, returning to her stickers. If she spoke, then she would go to jail. Bad people lived there. Maybe worse than the ones who visited her house. Poppy bit her bottom lip, swallowing back the words that threatened to spill out.

'You're not in any trouble, Poppy,' Thomas continued. 'Has someone told you not to talk to us?'

Poppy nodded, clambering off her seat to pick up a sticker she had dropped.

Marjorie whispered into Thomas's ear. 'You can't lead her. It's got to be open questions.'

'She's petrified,' Thomas whispered back. 'It's the only way to find out what's going on.'

As Poppy rose, Marjorie greeted her with a smile. 'We're not here to hurt you, sweetheart, we just want to keep you safe.'

Safe. The word hung tantalisingly in the air. To be safe was what Poppy wanted most in the world. 'Daddy,' she said, 'hurt S-S . . . Sally-Ann.' She peeled off another sticker. This one had glitter. She held it up on one finger. She liked the way it caught the light. Intently, she stared at it, allowing the words to tumble off her tongue. 'He . . .' She swallowed, replacing the sticker exactly where she had removed it. 'He made her dead.'

CHAPTER TWENTY-EIGHT

Standing in the background, Amy absorbed the office banter that was part of everyday life. They were a small team and it helped them to deal with the darkness inflicted upon them. She liked the new addition: DC Gary Wilkes was just twenty-five but had progressed well since joining the police. His colourful shirts made him easy to spot, and his cheerful demeanour was welcome. Having previously worked with Molly, he was integrating well. Amy watched as she laughed in response to his jibes.

'Well, that's the last date we go on,' Molly said. 'Blooming breadcrumber.'

'A breadcrumber? What the hell is that?' Gary paused at the printer to collect copies of the latest statements to read.

'A tease,' Molly said, clicking her mouse. 'They put out little crumbs to lure you in, won't take no for an answer. But the minute you take the bait they run for the hills.'

'Well if you ever get tired of playing with boys there are some real men in this office.' The proposal came from DC Steve Moss from the far side of the room.

Amy stiffened. She was trying to reserve judgement about Steve, but sometimes he was a little too nice to her face. While he seemed keen to please, she often caught his reflection as she turned. His narrow-eyed glare had taken her off guard. The jury was out when it came to him, and she could see by Molly's withering gaze that she shared her thoughts. Out of everyone in her team, she sensed that Steve would be the first to turn on her if things took a turn for the worse. *Manage your team well. It only takes one bad apple.* Her father's words rose in her memory. From what she had heard, Steve had no problem rubbing people up the wrong way.

'There's nothing wrong with being single,' Amy said, making her presence known. 'You don't have to please anyone but yourself.'

'True,' Molly replied. 'But I'm not ready for a hot-water bottle to warm the bed just yet.'

Amy smiled. Dotty was *her* hot-water bottle, but she would keep that nugget of information to herself. 'Have you any updates for me?' She wisely steered the conversation away from sex. The last thing she needed was Steve putting a word in, although his smile had faded as soon as she stepped in. He was old enough to be Molly's father, not that that would put him off.

Molly was good at her job but had no filter when it came to office banter. Amy was reluctant to rein her in. Since joining them she had lightened their days and provided some much-needed relief. Their job did not afford them lunch breaks, bonuses or perks. If they were lucky enough to eat, then they did it on the go. Computer keyboards were littered with crumbs, mugs of coffee left to go cold. Too many families had to learn to live with their partner's commitment or walk away from it all. 'Join the force and get a divorce' was a phrase Amy heard more than once. You married your profession or let it kill you. But regardless of it all, there was nowhere she would rather be.

She walked around to Molly's side of the desk, watching as she brought up a series of sites on her screen. Social media was Molly's forte, and she had been allocated with fake accounts to infiltrate it when the need arose.

'There's been a lot of activity online, but there's one group that stands out.' She clicked onto Facebook and Twitter, using the hashtag #FindHermione. 'See here?' she said, pointing at a series of tweets.

> #FindHermione We all eat lies when our hearts are hungry.

> #FindHermione The truth may hurt for a little while, but a lie lasts forever.

> #FindHermione Denying the truth doesn't change the facts.

> #FindHermione Better to be slapped with the truth than kissed with a lie.

> #FindHermione It's hard to accept the truth when lies are what you want to hear.

'There's hundreds of tweets, all referencing quotes about truth.'

'I recognise some of those,' Amy said, peering at the screen.

'Most of the quotes can be found online. It's the group tweeting it that worries me – The Keepers of Truth.'

She brought up Facebook, and a plethora of similar comments. 'They're here, too. They're heavily into conspiracy theories, but every now and again they'll get their teeth into a cause and not let go.'

'Over ten thousand followers,' Amy said. 'I take it they're known to us?'

'Yes, ma'am,' Molly said, using the formality as she sometimes did. 'We've got tonnes of intel on them for violence offences. Last year they set fire to an abortion clinic after a very nasty protest. Two people died.'

'I remember that,' Amy said, recalling the news report. 'Didn't they beat up an MP for taking backhanders, too?'

'Amongst other things,' Molly nodded. 'I'm trying to infiltrate the group, but they're very choosy about who they let in.'

'They can't be that choosy if they've got ten thousand followers.' Amy straightened her posture, rubbing the base of her spine to ease the twinge of pain. She made a mental note to arrange another gym session with Pike when she had the chance.

'They're just followers though,' Molly said. 'They've got a private Facebook group with a dozen people who carry out the proactive stuff.' She clicked on the group name, which came up as 'private' on Facebook. 'They're slippery bastards,' she muttered under her breath. 'They work together, providing alibis and backing each other up.'

Amy nodded, although the inner workings of social media went over her head. 'How do you know all this?'

'Just reading between the lines. I've been trying to wangle an invite into their group.'

Amy knew Molly was thinking the same as her. Why would a hard-core conspiracy group like The Keepers of Truth be interested in a fifteen-year-old girl? The persistent ring of her mobile ended their conversation, and she strode to her office, picking it up on the third ring.

DI Donovan's name flashed up on the screen. She liked him, probably more than she should, but after her experience with Adam, she had sworn off men. 'DI Winter,' she answered, because she did not want him to know she had saved his number on her phone.

'We've found her.' His voice was warm, ruffled by the breeze filtering down the line.

Amy paused as she took in the news, but Donovan must have taken her silence as confusion.

'Sorry,' he said. 'It's Donovan here, I'm at the burial site. We—'

'But it's only been a few hours,' Amy interrupted, unable to believe they had found Vivian – body number two.

'I had people on standby to dig the grave.'

'I'm impressed,' Amy said.

'We would have dug them all if we had to. I'm just glad she's come good.'

'Are you sure it's her?'

'We've found the clasp of a handbag she carried and a few other bits. It's enough to go on for now.'

'I'll have to inform the family.' Amy's heart plummeted at the thought. She was still feeling guilty about seeing the Price family, but a visit to Viv Holden's next of kin would have to be organised. She had made it clear to Donovan: she had to be the one to break the news.

'I don't think your budget will stretch that far,' Donovan said. 'They emigrated to Australia last year.'

'Oh.' Amy raised her right hand, kneading her forehead as she tried to work out her next move. 'Have we got their number?'

'We do,' Donovan said, 'but they're already aware. Some of their friends came to the graveyard. They've been keeping a close eye since Barbara was found.'

'Don't tell me. Facebook?' Amy groaned.

'Yep, I'm afraid so. The press were here, too. Bloody vultures. We've had a job keeping them away.'

'The main thing is that you've found her. I can't thank you enough for your help.'

'My pleasure. It's not every day I get to make progress in a case as big as this.'

It was more than a case to Amy, but she was not about to tell him that.

'Hopefully, we'll get news of Wendy soon. I'll up the pressure this end. Keep you in the loop.' Amy felt her insides churn. What would Lillian want in exchange for the last piece of information? Surely she was saving the best for last.

CHAPTER TWENTY-NINE

Hemmy murmured in her sleep, feeling the soft stroke of hands against her hair. At weekends, Mum would wake her gently: touching the crown of her head before placing a cup of tea next to her bed. Yet as she awoke, the stench of fish and rotting timbers reminded her that she was not at home.

Her head pounding, she surfaced from the fog. This wasn't a normal awakening. Her tongue felt too big for her mouth, her body ill at ease with itself. Gloved hands caressed her cheek, before moving onto her shoulders and finally, pulling a blanket over the dip of her waist. Hemmy shrieked as she realised what was going on. Pulling her knees up, she scooted back on the bed. 'Get off me!' she cried, grabbing the grubby woollen blanket and drawing it up to her chest.

Her captor was not peering through the hatch, but sitting on the edge of her bed. A dry rattle pierced the air as they drew in a breath through the black latex mask.

'Shh . . . Hemmy needs to be quiet.' Again that muffled, distorted voice and the rattle of their breath. Hemmy's heart hammered against her ribcage, her eyes darting around the room. If she could get away . . . could she make it out the door?

'Purdy is here. If Hemmy is good, Purdy lives.' Leaning towards the end of the bed, her captor lifted the pet cage containing her beloved cat.

Purdy was a pathetic sight, her white fur smeared with patches of yellow. As she caught sight of Hemmy, she meowed loudly, clawing her cage door. Inching towards the cage, Hemmy grimaced, sucking air between her teeth as her head pounded in pain.

'Does Hemmy's head hurt?' her captor said, opening his combat jacket, which looked too big for his frame.

At least, she thought he was a man. Every inch of his body was covered, making it almost impossible to tell. For the briefest of seconds, Hemmy felt hope. He did not appear all that strong. So how had he managed to get her here? Had there been more than one person behind her when it happened? The whole episode seemed fuzzy and distant, but her senses quickly sharpened as the handle of a scalpel caught her eye. The slim blade protruding from her captor's jacket pocket was more terrifying than any hunting knife. She dropped her gaze as all hope of escape fizzled and died.

The pop of foil was followed by two paracetamols being placed onto the bed. Leaning over, her kidnapper picked up a plastic bag from the floor and laid it at her feet. More food. But what about her cat? Opening the wrapper, she tore off a piece of tuna and cucumber sandwich and stretched to the cage at the side of the bed. Still clinging to the blanket, she looked at her captor for permission.

He nodded, eyes glinting behind the mask. Fascinated, he watched as she pushed half of her sandwich between the rusted cage bars. A small tin container was secured to the inside. Moving slowly and carefully, Hemmy placed her stockinged feet on the floor. After a cautious sideways glance, she unscrewed the water bottle and poured a generous amount into the tin bowl. Purdy swallowed down the last of the bread before diving for the water, parched.

Hemmy swallowed back her tears as she retreated to the corner of the bed. Quickly she assessed the cage. It was spring bolted. Purdy would not be able to escape without help.

'Who are you?' Hemmy asked, too scared to ask what he wanted from her, for fear of what he might say.

'No talking,' he replied. Outside, a sudden whoop of wind caused the boat to creak and sway. Hemmy had forgotten about the outside world. It was just her, Purdy, her captor, and the incessant pounding in her head. 'Who are you?' she asked again, desperate to understand. She froze as her captor leaned towards her, sliding the blade from his pocket. She wanted to run, to hammer on the door and escape. But something deep inside told her to remain very, very still. Her breath shallow, she stiffened as he brought the scalpel to her face. 'I'm sorry,' she uttered, gripping onto the blankets. 'Please don't hurt me.' Squeezing her eyes shut, she winced as effortlessly, he sliced off a length of her hair.

Taking slow, noisy breaths, he pocketed the long blonde strands. 'Next time Hemmy breaks the rules, Purdy gets cut.'

A sharp nod of understanding conveyed Hemmy's willingness to behave.

As they rose, she took a breath to ask if she could keep Purdy with her, but then remembered his instruction to be quiet. He was gone in seconds, taking the cat along with him, her meows filling the vessel's hollow spaces before drifting away. She waited until she heard his steps above her before getting up. Crawling to the end of the bed, she caught sight of the bucket and pack of wet wipes. How had she not awoken when he came in and left them here? She thought back to when she was kidnapped, how a mask had been pressed over her face. Was he gassing her? She could not remember falling asleep last night, just crying as she curled up on the metal bed.

She cast an eye over the sandwich wrapper lying crumpled on her bed. The expiry date hadn't passed. Had her kidnapper left her alone long enough to buy fresh food? Her jaw tightened in determination. The time for crying was over. She was not staying here to become another statistic. And whoever her captor was, he sure as hell wasn't killing her cat.

CHAPTER THIRTY

As always during her phone calls with Lillian, Amy had closed her office door. She sat at her desk with her head bowed low, her desk lamp casting a shadow in the room.

'What do you want?' she snapped, in no mood for games.

But Lillian seemed oblivious to her curt tone. 'Why have you let your chief inspector take all the credit? Is it because you don't feel worthy of the praise?' Lillian paused for a sly breath. 'Or is the truth finally sinking in?'

'It's not your concern how we handle our investigation. When are you giving me Wendy Thompson's location?'

'My dear Poppy,' Lillian said, using the opportunity to call her by her old name. 'Always so impatient. I'm still waiting for my thank you for giving you the last two.'

'Thanks? You're the one who put them there.' Amy shook her head incredulously. Lillian possessed little or no conscience, and the only way to persuade her to help was to make her think there was something in it for her. 'Mrs Thompson hasn't got long. Think of how good you'll look in the press if you tell us where Wendy is before she dies.'

'Don't forget probation,' Lillian replied. 'It'll impress them, too; especially if they know I have a supportive daughter on the outside.'

'Mandy?' Amy snorted. 'She just about tolerates you.'

'We both know I wasn't talking about Mandy,' Lillian said. 'Now, are you going to sulk forever? I'm helping your career, yet still you show no respect. What do you want from me? Blood?'

'You could start by telling me why you called,' Amy said, ignoring the platitudes. Given the late hour, Lillian must have had her reasons. How was she even getting access to a phone? 'Have you got the address?'

'Oh, come on now, you know it's not that easy. I can't just give away secrets I've been holding onto for years. Not without something in return.'

'What?' Amy said, wanting their conversation over as quickly as possible.

'Another family reunion,' Lillian replied. 'You must have been expecting it. It's time you and Damien were reacquainted. You have a lot to catch up on.'

'I presume he's aware?' Amy said, sliding a pen from across her desk and opening her jotter to scribble the address.

'Of course. You'll meet him tomorrow. And don't give me all that guff about not being able to take time off. Your DCI Pike is all hot in her pants over this. She'll give you whatever you need.'

'The address?' Amy said. She wasn't going to disagree. She had never seen Pike so pleased. And the sooner she could get this meeting over with the better. Lately it felt like Lillian was invading every aspect of her life. She couldn't eat, she could barely sleep, and she felt sick to her stomach every minute of the day. All she wanted was for things to get back to how they were. But she should have known that Lillian was not going to make things easy.

'I want him to come to your house,' Lillian said. 'I do live for what goes on in the outside world. I want to hear all about you and your mummy dearest.'

'No deal.' Amy's voice was firm.

'I think you'll find there is. That's if you want that Thompson bitch to find what's left of her daughter.'

'You disgust me,' Amy spat, unable to hold back her anger. She had seen the press images of Wendy Thompson, a beautiful twelve-year-old girl. Her emotions dictated her words. 'You're a piece of shit, you know that?'

'I love you too, Daughter dear,' Lillian replied tersely. 'I'm going to count to three. And don't for a second think I'm bluffing, because I'm not. There's far more at stake here than you know.'

Silence fell between them as Amy gathered up her thoughts. Lillian took a breath to speak. 'It's his birthday tomorrow, so I want you to make him tea and scones with clotted cream. We don't get nice things on the inside, but I'd love to hear about your afternoon tea.'

'You want me to play happy families and have him report back to you? I'm not doing it,' Amy said. 'You're not part of my life.'

'But it's not me, is it?' Lillian was quick to reply. 'It's your brother – your flesh and blood. He's done nothing to you. None of this is his fault . . . unless you're saying he's guilty by association. In which case that would also apply to you.' A tinkle of laughter sprinkled her words. 'You can't run away forever. And by turning your back on him, you're the biggest hypocrite of all.'

Lillian's words rang with a hint of truth that cut Amy to the bone. 'I'll buy him a pastry in Starbucks. Take it or leave it.'

'In that case I'll leave it, and your Mrs Thompson will die without knowing if her daughter was ever found. Can you imagine it? Looking into the bottomless pit of nothingness, deprived of the comfort of knowing your little girl can rest in peace.'

A beat passed between them before Lillian spoke again. 'Shame it has to end like this. I suppose two out of three ain't bad, as the song goes. Tell you what, I'm feeling generous. I'll give you three seconds to decide.'

Amy rubbed her face, dragging her skin. How she wished she could step into someone else's shoes and be anywhere but here. Was this why Robert had tried to protect her all these years? This woman was a monster. But what choice did she have?

'One.' Lillian began the countdown.

Amy swallowed. Could she really invite Damien into her mother's home? She had sublet her old flat. There was nowhere else she could go.

'Two.' Lillian cut through her thoughts.

What about Flora? She would have to get her out of the house for an hour. But then again, what about Wendy Thompson's mother? Didn't she deserve peace? She belonged to the family that had inflicted such horrors. She owed her.

'Three,' Lillian said.

'All right, all right. I'll do it!' Amy shouted into the phone. She took a breath, cursing her outburst. She knew Lillian enjoyed getting under her skin. 'Just me and Damien. I'm not having Mum tangled up in all of this.' Amy gained a small satisfaction from calling Flora mum.

'Deal,' Lillian replied.

'Wait,' Amy said before she hung up the phone. 'How's he going to know where to meet me?'

'He'll call your office in the morning. You can give him your address then. You never know, you might end up thanking me. And I'll sleep easier knowing I've brought my family that bit closer together.'

Amy shook her head. Her biological mother had more faces than Medusa. 'Can't you tell me where Wendy is now? We don't have much time.'

'Well, Mrs Thompson's managed to keep going for all her newspaper and television appearances,' Lillian said, as if somehow *she* was the victim in all of this. 'A proper little celebrity. I'll be glad when she's dead. You should be, too, the way she casts aspersions on our family name.'

'Show her some mercy. You can put an end to this now.'

'Mercy?' Lillian snorted. 'It's because of her that I get so much hatred from the press, her and that son of hers. Poor Wendy's mother who's been dying for what feels like forever. If you ask me, it's all put on.' The heat of Lillian's anger rose as she ranted down the phone. 'The cheek of it, when *I* was the victim in all of this. *I* was the one trying to keep my family safe.'

Amy licked her lips, tasting bitterness on her tongue as bile rose in her throat. Speaking to Lillian was making her physically ill. 'I've got to go. So, unless there's anything else you can tell me . . .'

'I can't wait to hear how you and Damien get on. You wouldn't believe the lengths I would go to, to keep my family together. One day soon you'll understand.'

As the phone clicked with the buzz of a dead line Amy wondered just how delusional Lillian Grimes was. What was her fascination with introducing Amy to her birth siblings? Was it really to impress probation in the hope of leniency? Recent events had hit the press hard, the newspapers capitalising on the story of the innocent lives lost. Yet some had produced a mildly sympathetic report on Lillian's life, presenting a different point of view. Late-night television programmes debated whether she deserved sympathy due to her remorse. Amy had wanted to scream at the television, to tell them to remember the victims. To remember Sally-Ann. It was strange that when mentioning the innocent victims, her sister's name was rarely brought up. She was tainted. They all were. A sudden helplessness washed over her. She hated dealing with cold cases. It left her with such a feeling of emptiness because there was nobody left to save. All Amy could do was speak up for the voiceless dead and help the families of those involved as best she could. She switched off her desk light and sat in the shadows, alone with her thoughts. Rehashing the past brought its own particular kind of pain.

CHAPTER THIRTY-ONE

'Hard day at the office?' Elaine asked, kneading Paddy's shoulders as she tried to loosen a knot.

'I wouldn't know where to start,' Paddy moaned softly as Elaine worked her magic. He was glad to be home and sitting at their small kitchen table. His dinner was reheating in the oven, the gravy to accompany his roast beef bubbling on the hob. He was three hours late but, as always, Elaine understood. Sighing in contentment, he sipped his can of beer. Being with her made everything else bearable. He winced as her fingers slid around his neck.

'Sorry,' she said, her pink cardigan brushing against his cheek as she kissed the top of his head. 'That burn is taking time to heal. And here was me thinking you worked in a nice safe office.'

Paddy smiled, forcing out yet another lie. 'You know me love, can't resist a tussle.'

'You can say that again, the number of bruises you come home with. What does your DI make of all this?' She turned to stir the gravy. Given the size of their kitchen, she was never very far away.

'She's troubled. Distracted.' He sighed heavily, wrapping his fingers around his can. 'I don't know what's going on with her lately. I mean, she's always been a closed book, so it must be getting to her, whatever it is.'

'Pressures of work?' Elaine said, turning off the gas and slipping on her oven gloves.

'I've seen her handle worse cases than this. You know today, she stuttered mid-sentence during briefing. It was odd.'

'She was probably just tripping over her words,' Elaine said, her back to Paddy as she held the oven tray mid-air. 'She must be under a lot of pressure with that Lillian Grimes case, and she's only just lost her dad, too.'

Paddy watched her plate up dinner, grateful for the wisdom of her words. 'Maybe.'

'No news on Hermione Parker?' she said. 'I don't suppose that's making things any easier.'

'How did you know we're handling her case?' Paddy said, his fingers tensing around his knife and fork. He tried not to get drawn into pillow talk. The rules were clear, particularly with high-profile cases. He was forbidden to discuss work with anyone other than his colleagues.

Elaine placed the plate before him. On the table was a fresh bouquet of flowers, a small gesture of thanks for everything she did. Pulling out a chair, she joined him. She had once said there was something satisfying about looking after your other half. She was being kind. The truth was, he was a terrible cook, so he tried to spoil her in other ways. Which is why he found it hard not to answer her questions while she was plying him with food.

'You work in the high-profile team. It's kind of obvious it's your case . . . isn't it?' She leaned her chin on her palm as she watched him pile roast beef onto his fork. 'I take it you've no clues where she is then?'

'Lovely grub,' Paddy said, chewing the somewhat tough beef. The clock on the wall ticked loudly as seconds passed between them.

Elaine took a breath, her blue eyes twinkling in amusement. 'If you'd rather change the subject then you only have to say. My patients don't exactly provide scintillating conversation, but if you'd rather talk about bed baths and farting, then I'm game.' Her part-time job in the private hospital helped pay the bills and was another example of her caring nature.

'Sorry.' Paddy grinned. 'I don't deserve you. And you didn't have to cook. I could have grabbed us some fish and chips on the way home.'

'It's no trouble. I finished at three. Cooking gives me something to do. Is it too late for some apple crumble?' she asked, casting an eye over to the clock on the wall.

'It's never too late for that,' Paddy replied, despite the late hour. 'And no, nothing on Hermione so far.' It felt only fair to provide her with an answer, given all the trouble she had gone to for him. 'We've gone through witness statements, CCTV, re-enactments and appeals. Do you know how many positive leads we've turned up?'

Elaine raised an eyebrow. 'Enlighten me.'

'None. At least, nothing concrete. We recovered a fingerprint on a light switch two doors down. It ties in with a necklace that was left at the scene. One of the neighbours heard screaming and saw a van driving away, but after that . . . nothing. It's like she's disappeared into thin air.'

'Leave that, love, it looks as tough as old boots,' Elaine said, watching him prod the meat on his plate. Within seconds of the microwave pinging, a bowl of hot crumble and homemade custard was placed under his nose. Plucking a second dessert spoon from the drawer, Elaine shared the generous portion. 'That poor girl, her mum must be in bits. It's all over the papers, you know. If they're not reporting on her, they're fixated on Lillian Grimes. I don't know how you do it. Gives me the shudders thinking about it.'

'This is good, thanks,' Paddy said, pointing at the dessert with his spoon.

'Let's hope it doesn't keep you awake,' Elaine replied, taking the hint that the topic of work had come to an end.

Paddy smiled softly before tucking in. There were far worse things than apple crumble keeping him awake at night. Tomorrow, he was due to go back to Geraldine. His throat felt tight as he swallowed. He had fallen into this double life and knew that it was wrong. He had succumbed to the whirlwind romance all too quickly. It was hard to believe he had only known Elaine for a year. Paddy took another bite, savouring the dessert that was made with love. He had been selfish, but most of all he was a coward. It was his fault his marriage to Geraldine disintegrated. His fault that their beloved daughter had died. Would Elaine still want him if she knew what sort of man he was? Without her, life would not be worth living. Perhaps Geraldine sensed he was gearing up to leave. Up until now, guilt and shame had kept him there. She had agoraphobia. How could he leave her alone? Yet there was a bigger, uglier truth. For the last few years, his wife had been beating him, and the violence was getting worse. In reality, he was scared. And he didn't know where to turn.

CHAPTER THIRTY-TWO

Amy picked up the teaspoon, rubbed it on the leg of her suit trousers, and laid it back on the table. It was gleaming, as was the rest of the cutlery, yet something was amiss. Seeing Damien again felt wrong. It was more than their shared history that was making her uneasy. Flora's comment about her siblings being too 'damaged' to adopt had been playing on a loop in Amy's brain. It intermingled with Lillian's words about going to any lengths to keep her family together. *Why* was it so important to bring them together? Just what was Lillian's end game? Her comments about wanting to impress probation rang true, but a growing sense of foreboding warned her there was something more at stake.

Last night sleep had evaded her again, and she had struggled to concentrate at work this morning. As Lillian had predicted, DCI Pike had been only too happy to grant permission for the meeting, as long as it was related to the case. She was beaming in the aftermath of the positive publicity, but the pressure was on to find the last burial site. When it came to Hemmy, it was a different story. More detectives had been drafted in to help with the case, and Amy had a meeting with specialist officers later today. Thirty minutes had been scheduled in for this lunchtime with Damien. She hoped it would be worth the inevitable discomfort they were both bound to feel.

The past is over. It can't hurt you anymore, she reminded herself. *But what if Damien doesn't feel the same?* A small spike of irritation grew as she checked her watch. He was seven minutes late. The echo of a memory emerged: Lillian musing he would be late for his own funeral one day. The letters from his teachers, complaining that Damien was the last person to arrive to class and always the first to leave.

At four, Amy had been desperate to follow her siblings to school. Instead, she was forced to stay in her room. More than once she had played at the window with her Raggedy Ann doll to the backdrop of her father slicing a shovel through soil.

Lost in the memory, Amy tried to fix the kink in her hair, smoothing the mahogany strands by sliding them between her fingers as if her hands were straightening irons. It immediately sprang back up. A sudden rap on the door made her jump, and she cast an eye over the spread she had prepared before leaving the room.

Taking a deep breath, she opened the door, her face neutral, her posture straight. She felt a pang of recognition as Damien stood before her, shoulders slouched. He gazed at her as if she was a stranger and shuffled awkwardly on the step before she told him to come inside. His curly brown hair was cut short, a few days of beard growth on his face. He was of slim build and lacked his father's definition, but his features carried a chilling similarity to Jack's. He was taller than Amy, but gangly with it, and dressed in a sweatshirt and jeans.

'Come in.' Amy smiled. There was no need for introductions. 'Happy birthday, by the way. I've made us some tea.'

Following her into the kitchen, Damien rolled his dark eyes from left to right as he took in every inch of the house. The air was filled with the aroma of percolating coffee, alongside scones bought from a nearby bakery. Notting Hill was filled with up-market bakeries, delis and coffee shops, so they hadn't been hard to find. A jug of fresh orange juice sat on the table next to saucers, clotted cream and jam.

Pulling out the chair, he waited for her to sit before taking a seat.

'Do you drink coffee?' Amy said, unaccustomed to feeling so nervous. 'I can make tea if you prefer.'

'Have you anything stronger?' Damien replied, his expression taut.

'Sorry,' Amy lied. She had hidden away the spirits before he came. Perhaps a bit of Dutch courage was what he was after, but she wanted their conversation short, sober and to the point.

'Coffee is fine,' he said flatly.

As she poured the beverage, Amy's eyes flicked up, catching his mistrustful gaze. She had a habit of finding people out when their guard was down. Averting his eyes, Damien placed a scone on his plate, scooping jam then cream onto the cake before taking a bite. Amy waited until he was finished, picking at her own. There was no point in small talk in such bizarre circumstances and Damien was obviously not a talker. She figured she might as well get straight to the point. 'Why did you ask to meet me here?' The question had burned on her lips ever since the request.

Damien shrugged, swallowing down the scone he had eaten in three bites. 'Why not? It's your home, isn't it?'

'It's where I currently live. My flat's being sub-let. Mum doesn't know about any of this. I'd rather keep it that way.' She had persuaded Flora to go to the hairdressers for an hour or two. Dotty, her pug, was sleeping in her room. Amy did not want any part of her old life to collide with her new one, and she was sure Dotty would disapprove of her new guest.

Damien slurped his coffee before giving Amy a quizzical look. 'It was her idea, wasn't it?' Her brother was only a few years older than her, but his weathered skin held the expression of someone fated to a hard life.

'No, I mean my adoptive mum,' Amy replied. 'My dad died recently. She's been through the wringer. I don't want to upset her any more.'

Tilting his head slightly, Damien regarded her. 'You're ashamed of us.'

Now Amy knew she had not imagined the earlier disdain in his voice. He was annoyed when he had come here. The heat of his aggression rose as he took a sandwich from the pile of food and slammed it onto his plate.

Quickly, she orchestrated a reply. The last thing she wanted was to argue. 'Everything's happened so fast. I've not had a chance to explain things to her yet.' She topped up her coffee and stirred it with a silver spoon. 'Help yourself to more food. I know I've made too much.' The smile slid from her face as her glance met his.

'Very fancy,' he said, taking a bite of the sandwich and swallowing after a couple of chews.

Amy sighed, having lost an appetite that was barely there to begin with. The clock on the mantelpiece loudly ticked away the seconds and she shifted uncomfortably in her chair. 'I don't know what to say. You're obviously pissed off at me, but I don't know what I've done.'

Damien wiped his mouth with the back of his hand, his face flushed. 'I heard all about your private schooling and high-paying job. You've forgotten your roots. No wonder you don't want to hear from the likes of us.'

'Sounds like someone's been stirring the pot,' Amy said, wondering how Lillian found out about her education. 'I'm not going to apologise for who I am. We've all had to learn to put the pieces back together again.'

'Only some of us have had it easier than others.'

'But you don't know me, do you? Therefore, you're in no position to judge.'

A bitter laugh left Damien's lips. 'You're only seeing me because you were forced to.'

'Nobody forces me into anything. I'm trying to undo some of the damage our family has caused.' Amy could feel her temper rising as the stress of the last few weeks took its toll. 'If you're angry about your life then focus on the person whose job it was to keep us safe.' She waited for a response, but none came. 'I watched Jack murder our sister before my eyes.' Amy took a breath, gaining her composure. 'But I don't wear my scars as a badge of honour. I'm grateful to the people who raised me and proud to be in a job that makes a difference to people's lives.'

Damien regarded her silently. Taking the coffee pot, he filled his cup, the tinkle of spoon against china reverberating throughout the room. 'That's some speech.' He paused to take a sip. 'But you had two sisters and a brother. You could have tried to get in touch. The problem is, you only care about yourself.'

'I was four when the police took me away. Blocking everything out was the only way I could carry on. Besides, it wasn't just a matter of picking up the phone or finding your address.'

'You knew where Mum was,' Damien said, his lip arched into a sneer. 'Oh, and I mean our real mum. The one you put behind bars.'

Amy shook her head in disbelief. Damien was blinkered. It was like talking to a brick wall. He had gathered up all his hate and resentment and was directing it towards her. The trouble was, he was blaming a four-year-old child. It was evident that Lillian had been pouring poison into his ear. As the atmosphere thickened, Amy fought the urge to leave the room.

'I get it. You're angry because I was placed with Flora and Robert.' She sighed. 'I wish they could have taken all three of us. Perhaps things would have been different then.'

Damien's features creased in a frown. 'I'm angry because you turned your back on our mum. Do you know how long she worked on that letter before she sent it? She's been taking English lessons so you wouldn't be ashamed. All she ever does is talk about you. She said she was scared that you'd knock her back. I told her to try because the Poppy I knew cared about her family. Goes to show I was wrong.'

Amy's mouth dropped open. 'You're serious, aren't you? You've really forgiven her for what she's done?'

'Of course I have, she's my mum. If you listened to her, you'd know none of this was her fault.'

'She's a murderer,' Amy said, heat rising to her face. 'All those sex parties, the people she invited into our home. Are you saying I imagined it all?'

Damien put his cup to one side, his features earnest as he spoke. 'It was Dad, all of it. She was scared of him just like us. She shouldn't be in prison. We need to get her out.'

'What do you mean, get her out?' Amy said incredulously. 'She's guilty. You can't argue with the evidence.'

Damien wagged his finger, his fingernail chewed to the quick. 'You can when she was set up. She was leaving him. She'd sorted it with the women's refuge. But then you went and blabbed to the social. If you'd have waited just one more week . . .'

'Ahh, now I get it. This is why she wanted us to meet. To talk about an appeal. It's all becoming clear now.' Amy smiled, but there was a fire in her grey eyes. 'Well, it's not happening. Not on my watch.' The thoughts of Lillian being released from prison made her blood run cold.

'The truth needs to be told,' Damien said, rising from his chair.

Amy stood, her words firm. 'You can tell her from me. She's guilty, and I hope she rots in hell.'

'Tell her yourself,' Damien replied. 'She wants another visit. You won't want to miss this one.'

'No more visits,' Amy replied, walking to the front door to show him out. 'This was a bad idea. I've carried out my side of the deal. She's not getting any more out of me.'

Damien's smile was razor sharp, his eyes cold. As Amy raised her hand to the door latch, he grabbed her wrist and squeezed hard. 'If you value your job, you'll see her.'

It took all of Amy's self-restraint not to knee him in the groin. 'Get your hands off me.' She pulled back her wrist before opening the door. 'I want you to leave. Now.'

'It's hard to accept the truth, isn't it? When lies are all you want to hear.' Damien glared at Amy before throwing open the door. Outside, the clouds had gathered, their bellies pregnant with unshed rain.

Amy stood as if entranced. She had heard his words before.

Her hands shaking, she slipped her mobile phone from her pocket and searched Twitter. The quote she was looking for flashed up the screen.

#FindHermione It's hard to accept the truth when lies are what you want to hear.

Amy paled. Was Damien connected to Hermione's disappearance? She stared down the road, but he was gone. She patted her suit jacket for her car keys. It was time to get back to work.

CHAPTER THIRTY-THREE

Returning to her office, Amy's head was filled with conflicting thoughts. What did Damien mean about the next prison visit? Her outburst could have cost her Wendy's location, but listening to Damien defend Lillian felt as torturous as needles being pushed under her skin. Just when she thought this was all coming to an end. Her footsteps echoed in the office corridor, her mood as gloomy as the windowless space. In the side rooms, teams of officers worked, their minds on their next case. But it was not so easy for Amy as her personal and work lives merged. What would DCI Pike say if she knew? More to the point, what should she do next? Damien's comments about truth had left her uneasy. He didn't seem the type to reel off quotes. Not unless he had looked them up first. Was he connected to Hemmy's disappearance? But why? What would possess him to do such a thing? A background check was needed, but by conducting one, it would link him to the case. Could she live with what she would find? She took a breath, her thoughts crowding in. She had been blamed for putting her mother in prison. Could she do the same to her brother, too?

Nodding to her colleagues, she joined her team. Her eyes narrowed at the sight of DC Molly Baxter bending down to pick up a sheet of paper. DC Steve Moss was behind her, grinning as he spoke. His words were out of Amy's range, but when Molly stood, her face was flushed.

'Molly, can I have a word?' Amy said, gaining a smidgen of satisfaction as the smile dropped from Steve's face. She had vowed to give him the benefit of the doubt, but found she liked him less and less every day.

Following Amy inside, Molly instinctively closed the door behind her. She held tightly onto the piece of paper as she sat in the swivel chair.

'Is everything all right?' Amy said, taking up position on the other side of the desk. 'You looked a bit uncomfortable out there. Has Steve been hassling you?'

Molly's round cheeks were now bright pink, her discomfort evident. 'It's nothing,' she said. 'Just a bit of office banter. You know how it is.'

'I know how it used to be,' Amy said firmly. 'But it doesn't need to be like that anymore.' Amy's father had been instrumental in cutting down on workplace sexism. His initiatives in reporting incidents had helped both male and female officers, and new training programmes had made it clear that such behaviour was no longer tolerated in the police. But certain old-school officers, like Steve, were slow to learn.

'It's nothing I can't handle, honestly. If I have any problems, I'll come to you, but he's just a bit over-friendly.'

Amy frowned as she tried to read between the lines. 'Has he touched you inappropriately?'

'No,' Molly said, her eyes dropping to her lap. 'At least, not on purpose.' She swallowed. 'He might have brushed up against me a couple of times.'

Amy's nostrils flared as she inhaled a sudden breath. The last thing she wanted was a predator on her team. 'Are you willing to make a complaint?'

A flicker of fear crossed Molly's face. 'Please, ma'am, I don't want to make a big thing of this. He probably hasn't a clue that he's done anything wrong.'

'Oh, he knows all right,' Amy replied, her lips thinning. 'And I'll be marking his card.'

'Please don't,' Molly said, her features crumpling. 'I mean, I'm a right flirt at the best of times. Mum's always telling me off for giving people the wrong idea. If it comes out that I've complained about sexual harassment, nobody will want to work with me again.'

'That's ridiculous,' Amy replied. 'If we don't stand up against it, how are we going to make it stop? The old fool. He's old enough to be your dad.'

But Molly was vehement. 'I appreciate you looking out for me but, honestly, there's nothing to report. He's just keen to fit in. It can't be easy coming to a new team after being demoted. One minute you're an inspector and the next you're a DC.'

'That was of his own doing. He's privileged to be in this team, and he needs to make an effort to integrate in the right way. I'll speak to him when the time is right, but I won't mention you by name.'

Molly exhaled in relief. 'Thank you, ma'am.'

'Less of the ma'am. It makes me feel old.' Amy smiled. 'Just remember, my door is always open if you need to talk.' It was hard having time to chat when they worked in such a demanding role, but her father had always managed it, and it was essential to Amy that she did, too.

'I'll remember that,' Molly said. Her phone pinged in her pocket, bringing a blush to her cheeks as she read her texts. Her mouth moved silently, a glint of mischief in her eyes. 'It's a dating app. Guess I won't be needing the hot-water bottle tonight.'

Amy smiled as she left. Not all officers would be quite so candid about their personal lives. But like Amy, Molly's father was a police officer, and she was relaxed around the higher ranks. She could tell by Molly's behaviour that Steve had crossed boundaries, and a few sexual innuendos did not make her a flirt. She also knew that Steve was going to feel ridiculous when he found out Molly was gay.

'Office politics.' She spoke her thoughts aloud before heaving a sigh. Standing by her window she glared at Steve, knowing he could feel the intensity of her stare. *Yeah, roll your eyes*, she thought as she caught the movement. *You might find a brain back there.* She would speak to Paddy about it later and keep an eye on them both. As her desk phone rang, she tore her gaze away. Right now, all she wanted was a strong coffee and time to sort out the planner on her desk. Her heart faltered as DCI Pike's name flashed up on the screen.

'Ma'am,' Amy said respectfully. 'What can I do for you?'

'Plenty,' Pike replied. 'I've just had a fascinating conversation with Lillian Grimes.'

Amy froze as she gripped the phone. This afternoon's meeting with Damien had not gone well. Had Lillian been angered because she didn't welcome him with open arms? Had she called Pike to inform her of Amy's true identity? She formed her words carefully, making every effort to disguise her concerns. 'You spoke to Lillian? Why?'

'I asked myself the same thing when I accepted the call. She wants us to organise another drive. She's giving you Wendy Thompson's burial site. Well done. Your meeting with her son must have been a productive one.'

The enthusiasm in Pike's voice told Amy all was well. She presumed they had met in a cafe. Amy did not tell her otherwise.

'It was odd,' Amy said truthfully. 'He wanted to talk about organising an appeal for Lillian. I told him there was little chance of that. I'm glad she's agreed to give us Wendy's whereabouts.'

'That can't have been easy,' Pike replied. 'That whole family must be deranged.'

Amy stiffened. 'I still don't understand why she called you.'

'She said she knew Wendy's mother was on her "last legs" as she put it, and every second counted. We're making arrangements with the prison so you can take her out today.'

'So soon?' Amy's stomach churned at the thought of seeing Lillian again. Could she face two family members in the same day? 'I've got a meeting with a specialist officer, DI Victoria Summer. She's handled high-profile missing person cases and had some good results.'

'Reschedule. Hermione's case is in good hands.' Pike's words were firm as she switched into leadership mode. 'I've had to pull in a lot of favours to get Lillian released today, and she insisted you be the one to accompany her.'

I bet she did, Amy thought bitterly. She could never resist twisting the knife. 'Yes ma'am,' Amy replied. She could have mentioned her concerns regarding Damien's comments about truth and lies, but she did not know if they carried any substance yet. She smoothed a hand over her diary, crossed out her scheduled meeting with Victoria, and wrote Lillian's name beneath.

'What time am I leaving for the prison?' Amy asked, her pen poised. 'Have we got a driver? Backup?'

'It's all arranged,' Pike replied. 'You leave in an hour. But there's someone very important I need you to see first.'

CHAPTER THIRTY-FOUR

'Thank you for coming,' Gladys Thompson said, looking frail and washed out as she pressed the button to lift her recliner bed. She was not in a hospital as Amy had presumed, but at home receiving specialist care. By her side, her son John catered to her every need. He was younger than Amy, with a full beard and short brown hair. Amy could not imagine what it must have felt like, to grow up in the shadow of such grief.

'I know you're a busy woman, but I wanted to see you . . .' Gladys's words drifted as she paused for breath. She blinked, the strain of the action clear to see. 'To thank you for everything you've done. Your father was such a kind man. He promised to bring my Wendy home. Of all the people to find her . . . I'm glad it's you.' She reached out her hand, and tentatively, Amy took it.

Usually, she kept contact to a minimum, but today was different. She could not think of her real parentage now. She would not taint the visit with such evil. She smiled gently at the woman. It was important to say what was needed. She could not deprive Gladys of the precious time she had left. The sitting room was on the ground floor and had been converted to a bedroom for easy access. With soft carpeting and a large bay window, the scent of fresh blooms lingered in the air. Alongside the vase of flowers was a framed photograph of a twelve-year-old Wendy. With her cheeky smile and soft blonde curls, her innocence was enough to make Amy weep.

'I'm just glad we're making progress at last,' Amy said, clearing her throat. 'I have no doubt that we'll bring her home.'

'I haven't got long, dear,' Gladys said, her eyes full of knowing. 'I've tried to hang on as long as I can.'

'I'm sorry,' Amy said quietly. For once, she was at a loss for what to say.

'It would bring me peace to know that Wendy's body can be put to rest. Perhaps when I die, I'll see her again.'

'How are your family coping?' Amy said as John excused himself from the room, not before Amy caught the tears forming in his eyes.

'Good.' Gladys smiled. 'I've been blessed to see my grandchildren today. I told my daughter I want my headstone to offer free Wi-Fi, so they'll come and visit me more often.'

Amy's soft chuckle brought some light into the room.

'You've got a lovely smile,' Gladys said. 'A young woman like you, going out and dealing with all these terrible people. I don't know how you do it.'

The truth was that Amy had been drawn to it, but now her fascination with serial killers frightened her. *Takes one to know one.* Her smile faded. She patted Gladys's hand, the network of veins revealed beneath the thin, almost transparent skin. 'As soon as I hear anything, I'll let you know. We're travelling to Essex. There's a woodland graveyard in Ingrave, a beautiful place, with flowers and a meadow. There's every chance that's where Wendy has been laid.' Her research uncovered that Jack had worked in Ingrave for a few months, but she prayed she wasn't setting Gladys up for a fall.

'I hope so,' Gladys said, her voice growing weary. 'She loved the countryside. That's where she was going the day she ran away. She was always flouncing off, but she'd be back again the same day. It was like a game she used to play.'

'I know,' Amy said, watching Gladys's strength fade as her eyelids drooped shut. 'Why don't you get some rest, so you'll be at full strength when I call. I promise I'll do everything I can to bring her home.'

'If anything happens . . . I want my little girl to be buried with me, so she'll never be alone again.'

Amy nodded, a lump rising in her throat. She swallowed it back down, giving Gladys's hand a final squeeze before letting go.

Her breath shallow, Gladys seemed to fade before her very eyes. Amy leaned into her ear to whisper a promise her father had made years ago. 'I'll bring her back to you.' But the words felt hollow. For the first time in her career she made a promise she might be unable to keep.

CHAPTER THIRTY-FIVE

1986

Mummy had been right about the social. They *were* bad people, and now they were tearing her home apart. The drum of heavy boots hitting their basement steps made Poppy feel scared. Mummy had tried to lock the door when they first rapped for her to answer, but they had forced their way in. Damien and Mandy had already gone with the social to their car, but Poppy had wriggled free and run back inside.

As police officers searched the basement, all hell seemed to break loose. Police radios buzzed into life as officers spoke about remains being found. Daddy, pale-faced and silent, raised his wrists as police clamped handcuffs on. They weren't the handcuffs Mummy and Daddy had used in the basement either. These were proper ones. What did that mean, Daddy was under a rest? And why was he leaving without saying a word?

Her heart fluttering like a caged bird, Poppy ran up the stairs into the bedroom she had once shared with Sally-Ann. Pulling back the candlewick bedspread, she grabbed the Raggedy Ann doll beneath. She traced her finger over the embroidered heart stitched into the body of the toy. The last link to her sister, it was something to cling on to as her mother's screams rose from below. Pressing her nose against the fabric, Poppy closed her eyes before inhaling deeply. She could still smell traces of her sister if she tried really hard. But not today. Today all she could smell was fear and the sick, rotting stench of what lay beneath their home. She wanted to cry, but Sally-Ann's last words rang true. *Not a sound. Don't cry. Or you'll be a goner for sure.* They were jumbled now. She could not remember the exact order of her warning but the meaning was clear just the same. Crying was bad. But still, tears edged forward. She could feel them, beneath the brim of her eyelids, and her chin wobbled as she tried to push them down. Squeezing her eyes shut, she swallowed them back. Mummy wasn't crying today. Mummy was angry. Really angry. Perhaps she should be like Mummy instead. Holding her doll, she tiptoed down the stairs. As a gentle hand was placed on her shoulder, Poppy looked into the eyes of the woman who was to blame. The social.

'Sweetheart, you shouldn't run off like that.' Marjorie held out her hand. 'There's no need to be afraid, I'm going to bring you somewhere safe.'

Poppy narrowed her grey eyes. She had changed her mind. She was somewhere safe. She was home. Heat grew in her belly as sorrow was replaced by flaring anger. A sudden hatred rose for the woman before her. 'Fuck off,' she shouted, the words sounding alien as they left her lips. 'Sod off, bitch. I ain't going nowhere with you!'

A sharp, shrill cackle ensued, which made Poppy jump. It was her mother in the doorway, still wrestling with police officers as they tried to drag her out. 'You tell 'em, Poppy! You tell them fuckers what for!'

Poppy's eyes widened. Despite growing up hearing what Sally-Ann had called 'bad language', Poppy had rarely used it because Sally-Ann did not approve. She felt tall, like she had gained a set of armour, the wide-eyed expression of the woman from 'the social' relaying that her words had hit home. But Mummy approved. And Mummy had been right about them so far. Swearing blindly, Poppy recounted every bad word she had ever heard. Arms flailing and legs kicking, she screamed at the top of her lungs as Marjorie tried to hold onto her.

'Hey, hey, little girl, you're going to knock your dolly's head off if you keep that up.' The words were soft and gentle and Poppy stared into the warm hazel eyes of the man before her. She drew in her Raggedy Ann, checking she was still intact. Pausing for breath, Poppy stilled, taking in the policeman's form. He was different to the others, his skin dark, and his hair much bigger than any she had ever seen.

'My name's Dougie,' he said softly, kneeling down to her level. 'What's yours?'

'P . . . P . . . Poppy,' she said, shaking his hand as it was offered. She looked over his shoulder to see that Mummy and Daddy were now gone. There was nobody left from her family but her, and Sally-Ann who was buried somewhere nearby.

'Nice to meet you, Poppy,' Dougie said. 'Have you had breakfast yet? Because Marjorie here makes some lovely hot buttered toast. If you're really good, she'll get you a glass of fresh orange juice, too.'

Right on cue, Poppy's stomach grumbled. But there was one thing holding her back. Her sister. She could not leave her alone. 'Sa . . . Sa . . . Sally-Ann,' Poppy stuttered, her speech impediment dictated by her stress levels, which were now through the roof.

Dougie rested his hand on Poppy's shoulders. 'We'll look after her. I promise. I won't leave here until she does, and I'll be there every step of the way.' He sighed, shaking his head. 'She can't stay here, sweetheart. She deserves better. And so do you.'

Poppy nodded, absorbing his kindness. He understood. She turned to face Marjorie, slipping her hand through hers. A pang of guilt enveloped her as she saw the scratches she had made on the woman's hands. She had not stuttered once during her outburst. Just the same, she had been bad. Mummy and Daddy had been bad, too. That's why the police were taking them away. Giving one last sad glance towards Dougie, she allowed Marjorie to lead her back to the car. But what would happen to her? Mandy and Damien had already been driven away. Silently, she hugged her doll close to her chest. She would rename her Sally-Ann. Mummy had warned her not to speak to the social, told her she would never see her family again. But the nice policeman with the big hair had said what she needed to hear. She watched through the car window as more police cars parked up outside her home. The neighbours were standing on the pavement now, being told to move back by police as they taped off the road. Sally-Ann would be found, and Mummy and Daddy would not be able to hurt anyone else. But what would happen to her?

CHAPTER THIRTY-SIX

Amy tried to keep a lid on her emotions, but her anger was eating her up inside. As before, she stared straight ahead, trying not to inhale Lillian's sickeningly sweet deodorant as they sat in the back of the unmarked police car. Today was a day filled with contrasts. Seeing Lillian on the same day as Gladys had only served to fuel her disgust and guilt. It had been hard enough coming to terms with Damien's visit. Their reunion served to unlock another memory from the past – being taken away by social care as the police raided her home. Damien's unwavering belief in his mother had made Amy wonder if Lillian's story held a seed of truth. It had warranted further investigation. A quick phone call to prison liaison told her what she had suspected all along. Lillian had lied to Damien about taking classes in prison, just as she had lied about being in touch with a women's refuge before social services became involved. The original investigating officers had been thorough when investigating Lillian's claims. Staff at the refuge she had mentioned confirmed no such call had been made – but Damien would not have known that. What other lies had she spun him? And for what cause?

Lillian and Jack had made for a dangerous pairing, two psychopaths wired differently to the outside world. They had taken what they wanted without a thought for their victims. Despite her protests of innocence, Amy knew without doubt that Lillian felt no empathy for the families involved. She tilted her head to the window, still watching Lillian from the corner of her eye. Roadside trees merged into a blur of green and brown as they sped through Essex. They only had a few hours of daylight left, but more than the night was closing in: death was beating a path to Gladys Thompson's door. Amy had memorised the route to the Ingrave cemetery. It was why her heart plummeted when Lillian gave directions that took them the other way.

'I thought we were going to Ingrave?' Amy said, remembering her promise to Gladys earlier that day.

'Where did you get that idea?' Lillian replied, her voice alight with amusement. 'Did your detective skills lead you down the wrong path?'

Amy's lips thinned as she tried to conceal her disappointment. 'Why did you do it?' she said, unable to keep her questions at bay. 'Wendy was twelve, just a child. Why did you take her? I need to know.'

'That was Jack's doing,' Lillian said, her expression blank. 'He was a monster. I told you before. You can't pin that on me.' She leaned forward, giving further directions to the officer before sitting back in her seat. An Essex Police detective constable, he had been offered up by DI Donovan as they were unable to spare Molly to conduct the drive.

'Besides,' Lillian added for good measure. 'If I killed Wendy Thompson I wouldn't be telling you where she is, now would I?'

Her statement made little sense to Amy. 'But you didn't tell us where she is. All these years you've kept it to yourself.'

'Until I met you. I could have asked for a nicer cell, money, a more comfortable bed. But I haven't. I've done all this for you. To bring the family together.'

Pressing her fingers to her lips, Amy mimed a shush as she glared from Lillian to the back of the driver's head. The last thing she wanted was details of their relationship getting out.

'You asked.' Sullenly, Lillian shrugged.

She *had* asked. And there was a lot more she needed to know. She leaned into Lillian, speaking in a harsh whisper. 'What did Damien mean when he said, "It's hard to accept the truth when lies are all you want to hear?"'

'What do you think he meant?' Lillian said cryptically, seeming unsurprised by the words.

Amy frowned. She should have known better than to expect an explanation. 'Is he connected to Hermione Parker's case? She's a missing person . . .'

'I know who she is,' Lillian interrupted. 'But wouldn't you be better off asking Damien about that?'

'So you're saying he's involved? What do you know?' Amy's thoughts raced as she tried to connect the dots.

'I'm saying I can only focus on one thing at a time.' She smiled at Amy before directing the driver down a dirt track. Behind them, a police escort followed. Uniformed backup was on the way, with DI Donovan in tow.

Straightening her posture, Amy tried to get her bearings as she stared through the dirt-speckled window. 'What is this place?' she said, as the car bumped along the uneven path.

'A farm where Jack used to work. He had all sorts of odd jobs. The graveyard shifts didn't last very long.'

'We're going to someone's home? You should have warned us beforehand. We'll need to speak to the landowner.'

'It's been vacant for years.' Lillian bumped in her seat as the back tyre hit a pothole. 'The owners are living in Spain. I know where they are.'

'How?' Amy said, peering at the farmhouse in the distance.

'We used to be friends. We had similar . . . interests.'

Amy's eyebrows rose, and she was unable to resist the quip that followed. 'Were they child killers too?'

'Of course not,' Lillian said, taking it in her stride. 'They were swingers. We had a lot of fun together. But when they moved, Jack still had access to the farm. I remember him telling me where he'd buried Wendy's body. I felt terrible. But there was nothing I could do.'

Amy's disgust grew as she listened to Lillian speak. 'Felt terrible' was an expression you might use if you mixed someone's whites with colours in the wash. 'Did he rape her?' Amy said, the words feeling like dirt on her tongue.

Lillian sniffed. 'Your father liked to push the boundaries in every way he could.'

As they bumped along the farm road, Amy's thoughts grew dark. Why was this woman still alive after all the awful things she'd done? She resisted the urge to open the car door and push Lillian out. She did not believe her protests of innocence. Lillian was just as much a part of this as Jack was.

The long dirt driveway led them to a property that consisted of a rundown stone building and a series of outhouses dotted around the overgrown land. Fencing the property were rows of mature trees. High gusts of wind tested autumn leaves as their branches shook in protest. Passing through the farmyard gate, Amy caught sight of the weathered 'Trespassers Will Be Shot' sign bent to one side. Exiting the car, she updated control, requesting her officers conduct intelligence checks on the owners of the farm. If Wendy had been brought here, there was every chance they were involved.

'We meet again,' DI Donovan said, approaching Amy's car. She had told Lillian to remain inside while officers scoped the property. This was to be Lillian's last departure from prison, and given Damien's recent behaviour, the last thing she wanted was any surprises ahead.

'Thanks again for moving quickly with Barbara and Viv,' Amy replied, taking a soothing breath of country air. She checked her watch, consoled by the fact they were ahead of schedule.

'Hopefully, today's visit will bear fruit,' Donovan said. 'We make a good team.' He drove his hands into his trouser pockets as he smiled. His suit looked new, and Amy appreciated the spiced aroma of his aftershave, which carried on the breeze. She cleared her throat, her cheeks flushing.

'Yes, well, we only have a few hours of daylight left. Let's get her out and see what she has to say.'

Opening the car door, she clasped the handcuffs that would tether them together. How different this journey had been to their first when they had barely spoken. It was a blessed relief it was coming to an end.

'This way,' Lillian said, with the knowledge of somebody who had been there before. Walking with confidence, she led them to a galvanised roofed outbuilding that had seen better days. It whistled and groaned loudly against the force of the wind. It was an eerie sound, enhanced by the desolate landscape, the sound of a soul ill at rest. Amy drew back her windswept hair. Had little Wendy walked this land? Or was she already dead when she was brought here?

It seemed that Jack Grimes was not the only one who liked to push boundaries. There were several outhouses here, yet as Lillian picked her way along the muddied path, she seemed to know precisely where the burial site was. A uniformed officer walked ahead to keep watch as Lillian directed them around the back. Sombrely, they walked, startled rabbits bounding ahead of them as Amy's heels dug into the soil. Her thoughts were with Wendy's mother; she prayed they would come to a hill with lush grass and autumn flowers. But as she turned the corner, she was horrified at what she found.

The dump site consisted of a deep, gaping pit gouged into the mud. Rusted farm machinery littered the grounds, giving it a post-apocalyptic feel. This was not the gentle countryside filled with birdsong that Amy had described. It was a rubbish tip. A wave of nausea overcame her as she contemplated what lay ahead.

'She's down there,' Lillian said, yanking Amy's left hand in the air as she pulled on the handcuffs. 'In an old freezer.' She peered through the dead trees and moss-covered rocks taking up space in the pit. 'There. You can see it sticking out. It's still there, after all these years.'

'Christ,' DI Donovan whispered under his breath.

Amy felt her legs weaken from the horror, bile rising in her throat. Why hadn't the original investigators uncovered this lair? Another wave of nausea rolled over her, stronger this time. She had dealt with many murder cases and the most heinous crimes, but none had been committed by her own flesh and blood. As she stood tethered to Lillian, the onset of emotions flooding her system was too much to bear.

A firm hand took her elbow as she felt her legs give way.

'The ground's a bit torn up here, isn't it?' Donovan said, helping her regain her balance. 'Did you bring any wellington boots?'

Amy gave him a grateful smile as he helped her save face. They both knew it was more than her unsuitable footwear making her falter. Had he known of her relationship to the woman beside her, he may have just let her go.

'They called it the sinkhole,' Lillian said, her voice void of emotion. 'They used to throw everything in here: rocks, furniture, anything they couldn't burn.'

'And Wendy?' Amy replied. 'Please tell me you're not serious. Wendy's not down there.'

'You asked me to take you to where she was. I didn't promise it would be pretty.' A hint of a smile touched her lips. 'At least now you can go back and tell old Gladys where she is.'

Amy's jaw clenched. So that was why she was happy to help. Lillian wanted Gladys to die knowing her twelve-year-old daughter had been abused and thrown into a rubbish tip. Something snapped inside her. 'You evil bitch,' she growled, pushing Lillian on the chest. 'You vile waste of skin.' She shrugged off Donovan's hand as he placed it on her shoulder. He spoke her name, but his voice seemed very far away.

'Steady on,' Lillian said, looking nervous as she took a step back. But she had not seen the tree root jutting out from the dirt.

Yanked forward by the handcuff, Amy landed on top of her as she fell, both of them hitting the ground with a thud. Scrambling to straddle her, Amy grabbed her wrists and pinned her to the ground. With Lillian's head edging near the precipice, the soil began to crumble beneath their weight. 'You want her to know, don't you? To stick the knife in, even now. You're a monster. An evil . . .'

Lillian's eyes flashed wide. 'Now, Poppy, You're in no position to . . .'

But her words were cut short as Amy drew back her fist.

CHAPTER THIRTY-SEVEN

Amy wrung her hands as she waited to enter Gladys's room. The house was warm, too warm for her liking. Her mind had been torturing her with questions since her visit to the farm. Had the landowners been involved in a paedophile ring? It seemed possible, given the way they had abandoned their home.

Shame reigned as she recalled her behaviour. To say the red mist had come down was an understatement. It was too much, and Lillian's gloating face had been the final straw. It was lucky that DI Donovan had pulled her off before she landed a punch. Crime scene investigators had promptly attended. Under strong lamps and a precariously assembled tent, they had found their answers. Sealed in an airless tomb, Wendy's body had been preserved better than many found underground.

Amy had returned Lillian to the prison in silence, without uttering a word, despite her attempts to engage her in conversation. Instead, her thoughts wandered to the memories that continued to flood her consciousness. Had she really first encountered Dougie all those years ago? The sweet, kind man who had calmed her down and told her he would stay with Sally-Ann throughout? She thought of her promised weekly visits and wondered what day it was. Had she broken her vow?

Bit by bit, her routine was falling down around her. Lillian was invading every aspect of her life. But it would all be over soon. Wouldn't it? A creeping sense of foreboding drove a chill down her spine, despite the warmth of the room.

Amy's footsteps stalled as she approached Gladys's door. How could she send her to her death with the knowledge that her daughter had been left in such a way? Once again, she felt like a fraud. She had no right to be there, let alone to be the one to break the news. She pressed her hand against the door, taken aback by what greeted her. The family had told her to call with the news, no matter what time of the day or night. But as she entered to find them gathered around the bed, she prayed she had not been too late.

Drawing apart, they made a path for her to reach Gladys's side. Amy was shocked to see just how much she had deteriorated since that morning. Even breathing seemed a monumental effort now. Tears fell on the faces of her sons and daughters as they waited for news. Gladys's eyes flickered open, her skin like parchment, her lips dry. She parted them to speak, but her voice was so frail that Amy had to lean down to take her words in.

'Have you found her?' she whispered, reaching out for Amy's hand.

'Yes.' Amy squeezed her fingers. On the surface, it appeared Lillian had done everything she could to assist the police, but Amy knew that such things came with very dark intent. Amy thought of the small folded-up remains they had found in the freezer buried under so much junk. Scooped up from the street, Wendy would never have got into the car if Jack had been on his own. Amy could not imagine what they had done to her before they ended her life. Had she been there too? The thought made her stomach churn. To imagine Wendy's body like that, entombed in a disused freezer, was too much for anyone to bear.

'Tell . . . me . . . everything,' Gladys said. And for the first time in her career, Amy prepared to lie.

As she left the room, she took a soothing breath, not realising that she had been followed by Gladys's son, John. Hooking his thumbs into the loops of his chinos, he called for Amy to wait.

'You didn't find Wendy in the forest, did you?' he said sadly, regarding her with red-rimmed eyes.

Amy cleared her throat, her words feeling as heavy as stones. 'I'm sorry,' she said. 'Details of the burial site will come out later, but I didn't see the benefit in upsetting her at this time.'

'Well . . . I just wanted to say thanks. At least now she can have some peace.' He sighed, pinching the bridge of his nose. 'I know you've got procedures, but she wants Wendy's remains buried with her when the time comes.'

'I understand.' Amy nodded. Judging by Gladys's condition, that time was not far away.

'I don't know how you did it, getting that monster to talk. For years we've tried. You should see some of the horrible responses to our letters over the years. Prison's too good for the likes of her. She deserves a taste of her own medicine.' A thunderous shadow crossed his face as he spoke.

'Hopefully, you'll be able to turn a corner now,' Amy said, inwardly cursing her platitudes. There were no words strong enough to heal the pain inflicted upon them.

'I'd best get back inside,' John said. 'She hasn't got long left.'

◆ ◆ ◆

Walking to her car, Amy paused to stare up at the blood-red sky. Was it an omen? Would both Wendy's and Gladys's souls be at peace tonight? She checked her phone, flicking through the missed calls. Calling up DI Donovan's number, she smiled as she spoke. She could not help but warm to him and took comfort in his strength.

'I've passed on the news,' she said as he answered. 'Are you free to talk?'

'I'm always free for you,' he replied, his words ending in a yawn. 'Sorry, I'm still at the scene. I've just been updating DCI Pike.'

'Did you mention what happened earlier? With Lillian, I mean.' She paced the concrete path, wishing she did not sound as stupid as she felt. 'I was out of order. I don't know what came over me.'

'You're human. You only did what the rest of us wanted to do. I saw the smile on her face. She was goading you from the off.'

'I only hope Pike feels the same way.'

'I didn't think it was relevant,' Donovan replied. 'As far as we're concerned, Lillian tripped over a tree root and pulled you down with her. You've done nothing wrong.'

'I don't know what to say.' Amy's voice wobbled as she struggled to keep her emotions at bay.

'We should meet up for debriefing . . .' Donovan chuckled. 'I didn't mean it in that way.'

'Are you sure about that?' Amy smiled, glad of the opportunity to escape her problems just for a moment or two.

'A drink would be nice.'

'I could certainly do with it, after the day I've had. But it's going to be past closing by the time I catch up with my work tonight.'

'Another time,' Donovan said. 'Before you go, there's something I've been meaning to ask you . . .'

'Two propositions in one night.' Amy smiled. 'Fire away.'

'I was wondering. Why did Lillian call you Poppy?'

CHAPTER THIRTY-EIGHT

Every bone in Hemmy's body ached. Sleeping on a damp bed made her explode in coughing fits, so she slept sitting up, her back slouched against the metal frame. Her hair, now greasy and stringy, fell into her face. In the darkness, her thoughts had been wild and wandering, her eyes puffy from crying when all hope seemed lost. It was in the night, with the water softly lapping, that her father had spoken. It was a dream, it had to be, but his words rang clear in her mind.

'You've got a lion inside you, Hemmy. Now c'mon, let me hear you roar.'

He had first spoken the words when she was twelve and strapped to a zip line. At five hundred feet high and a mile long, it had been described as the nearest thing to flying. Her dad always encouraged her to push past her fears, and the memory of that experience gave her strength.

She had to keep going because the police weren't going to find her anytime soon. The sirens she had heard earlier continued with strange regularity. She must be moored within earshot of busy city streets. Under the light of the moon, she had searched every inch of her confinement for a makeshift weapon of some kind. Her palm ached from where she had pulled out the splinter, and her skin was red and angry from the hole it had left behind. She had used precious drops of water to rinse it, but the skin was already crusting over with a yellow pus beneath. Not that she could think about it now. Time was precious, and she could hear her father's voice telling her to carry on.

Hunched beside the bedpost, the tips of her fingers throbbed as she spent hours working on loosening the long, rusted metal screw. It may not be much on its own, but if she could break the porthole glass . . . a gasp of relief escaped her lips as it loosened between her fingers.

She stiffened at the creak of footsteps hitting the floorboards above. Her captor's actions followed a pattern. Leaving her alone at night, he returned morning and evening to provide her with food. But Hemmy could not take anything for granted. Today might be the day he came to finish her off. 'Come on,' she grunted, twisting the screw free. The creaking footsteps grew closer, and fear hastened her movements as her captor approached the door.

She clenched the screw tightly in her palm just as the bolt shot across the door. Fizzing with pins and needles, her legs buckled beneath her as she struggled to get to her feet. Choppy waters made the boat bob, tipping her towards the bucket planted in the middle of the floor. Hemmy howled in frustration as urine spilt from the overflowing vessel. Seeping into the floorboards, the stench of ammonia rose up around her, making her gag.

Tensing as he drew nearer, she scooted back onto the mattress. Her heart faltered as his footsteps creaked down the steps. She was panting now, trying to regulate her panicked breath.

From above, Purdy meowed, and Hemmy bit back her tears. She had to do something. Her cat would not survive much longer without proper care. Adrenaline racing, she plumped up her pillow, covering it with the blankets on her bed. If her kidnapper thought she was sleeping, it might buy her some time. He was going to kill her – that's if he didn't rape her first. Down here, amongst the damp and rotting wood, she'd had time to think. The blackouts, followed by the headaches: he'd been drugging her. That's what the gas mask was for. He was building up to something. How else would he have known she had a headache, and produced painkillers before she even asked? She looked at the bucket, still half full of urine. A plan formed. She was not going to wait for a second longer. Even if she was at sea, her captor might have a phone. Holding her breath, she gripped the lip of the bucket and tiptoed behind the door. It would provide a useful distraction as he entered, giving her time to get away. She thought of the scalpel nestling in his pocket, but the only other option was to give in. She set her jaw and prepared for the fight of her life. Slowly, the door creaked open. In her hand, the rusted screw peeped through the first and second fingers of her clenched fist.

CHAPTER THIRTY-NINE

Reversing his wheelchair, Dougie opened his front door and welcomed Amy inside. 'You look like you've seen a ghost. Are you all right?'

A sliver of night air crept into the hallway. Amy's silence spoke volumes as she closed the door behind her and slid the security chain across.

'Something's happened, hasn't it?' Dougie said. 'Say something, girl.'

'I'm OK.' Amy sighed. 'Are you sure it's not too late for a chat?'

She had been pleased when Dougie replied to her text telling her to pop in after work. Given his insomnia, he rarely went to bed before three.

'I'm glad of the company,' Dougie replied, wheeling his chair into the living room. As always, it was warm and inviting, the open fire crackling and the lights dimmed low. A book lay open on the coffee table, a half-eaten digestive biscuit next to a cup of tea.

'Take off your coat,' he said. 'Come, sit beside the fire and I'll pour us both a drink.' Amy offered him a watery smile as she held up a paper bag containing a bottle of rum. 'It's my treat this time. I can't keep draining yours.'

Within a couple of minutes, her legs were warmed by the fire as she cradled a crystal tumbler of rum in her hands. She liked the way the ice clinked in the glass, it reminded her of her father enjoying an occasional tipple at home.

'Tough day at work?' Dougie said, concern etched on his face.

Amy was horrified to find her voice trembling as the enormity of recent events took hold. 'I di . . . didn't know who else to talk to,' she said, feeling the edge of a stutter in her words. It was becoming more frequent lately, a physical manifestation of the stress she was trying to push down. She paused to sip her rum, the warmth of the spirit lubricating her words. 'I hate bringing this to your door, but I feel like I'm going to explode if I don't get it off my chest.'

'I take it you're talking about the delightful Lillian Grimes. It's been on all the news channels, and the papers are having a field day.'

Amy nodded, recalling the journalists gathered outside the police station. Apparently, renewed efforts had been made to speak to Lillian on the inside. The thought drove another pang of worry into Amy's chest as she brought Dougie up to speed.

He shook his head in dismay. 'Why didn't you tell me? You shouldn't have to shoulder all this on your own.'

Amy shrugged. 'It's been awful. Just today I've met Damien Grimes over cream tea, taken Lillian out of prison, found the body of Wendy Thompson and visited her dying mother to break the news. All of that, and I'm supervising a kidnap case involving a fifteen-year-old girl.' She'd also had to wriggle out of some awkward questions from DI Donovan as to why Lillian had called her Poppy earlier on.

'It's too much for anyone under normal circumstances, but given your background . . .' Dougie's words trailed away.

Amy nodded in understanding. 'The families, they were so grateful, but—' Her words came to a sudden halt, and she took a breath to accommodate the cold and harsh truth. 'I can't bear the thought of that blood running through my veins. My parents are serial killers.' She stared into the flames, recalling earlier events. 'I lost my temper today, almost punched Lillian in the face. What if I carry the same gene?'

'Don't be daft—' Dougie began to say.

'I'm starting to remember, but every time I do, I lose a piece of who I am.' Amy interrupted. 'Worst of all . . .' She paused to sip her rum. 'I don't know if I'm a good enough person to do the job that I do.' Exhaling slowly, she was scared to look at Dougie for fear of what she might see. But she need not have worried, for his face carried nothing but kindness and sympathy for her plight.

'What would your father say if he was here now?' Dougie said. 'And I mean your real father, the man who taught you right from wrong.'

'I don't know. We never spoke about it.' Amy shook her head. 'Sure, he adopted me in good faith, but what if he realised that I would revert to my old ways?'

'And what old ways would they be?' Dougie chided her. 'You were four when you left that place, nothing but a baby.'

'I remember . . .' Amy said, a brief smile touching her lips. 'And I remember you, too. How kind you were, how you told me you'd stay with Sally-Ann.'

'You remember that?' Dougie's eyebrows raised, and he emitted a low chuckle at the thought. 'I don't suppose there were many coppers with afros in your house that day.'

'Not long ago you said it was a wonder I turned out well, given my upbringing.'

'That was a silly off-the-cuff remark.' Dougie rolled his eyes at his own insensitivity. 'You've been a credit to Robert and Flora. You exceeded their expectations and they're so proud of you. They had a bumpy few months when they took you in. But you're not that child anymore.'

'I suppose,' Amy said, unconvinced.

'Do you think I'm the same person as when I was running around my mother's skirts at the age of four? I've been shaped by my life experiences and the people around me. You're a strong leader, Amy, and perhaps you *have* been affected by the past. But it's not because of any fascination with serial killers, it's the sense of injustice in it all.'

Amy nodded at Dougie's words. 'I've always known I was different. Maybe some good can come from this if I use my insight to make things right.'

'Exactly,' Dougie replied. 'You could have torn up Lillian's letter and walked away, but you didn't. You sacrificed your own well-being to help the families involved.'

'Thank you,' Amy said. 'I needed to hear that. The toughest thing about all of this is not having anyone to talk to.'

'Have you spoken to Flora?' Dougie said.

'I don't want to upset her,' Amy replied. 'She's been through enough.'

'But so have you. It's best not to keep it bottled up. There's only so much you can keep down until that lid comes popping off.' Dougie raised the bottle to top Amy up, but she placed her hand over her glass.

'Not for me, thanks. It's time I headed off.' Draining her glass, she placed it on the coffee table before catching sight of today's newspaper headlines. 'See that?' she said, shaking her head in disgust. 'The papers are reporting that the "Beast of Brentwood" has had a change of heart. The truth is, she doesn't feel remorse. She pretends she wants to keep her family together, but it's all lies.'

'It's a miracle you've managed to keep it out of the papers. Your DCI still doesn't know?'

'You think I'd be working the case if she did?' Amy said, with a half-smile. 'It's when I break contact with Lillian that I'm most at risk.' Amy knew from experience that victims of domestic abuse were at their most vulnerable when they tried to leave. 'She's not going to let me walk away.'

'You've got to shut the door on it. For the sake of your sanity if nothing else.' Leaning forward, Dougie threw a log onto the fire and it crackled and spat in response.

'It frightens me to know that . . .' Amy stared into the flames, her face pale, 'that I'll never be able to go back to who I was.'

'Then you move forward. You're stronger than you think. Take control.'

'You're right,' Amy said, rising to leave. 'I've got a prison visit tomorrow. I'm telling Lillian I won't be seeing her again.'

'Every time I speak to you, I know we've done the right thing,' Dougie mumbled under his breath.

'What was that?' Amy said.

Dougie raised an eyebrow, seeming surprised she had caught his words.

'Nothing, just thinking out loud,' he replied. 'Oh, and don't forget to put my new home number on your phone. I don't always have my mobile switched on.'

'New number?' Amy replied.

'Yes, I got a private one to stop the cold calls. If it wasn't PPI claims, it was asking if I'd been in an accident. Bit late for all that,' he said.

'Do you want to write it down for me?' Amy replied. 'My mobile's dead.'

'No need,' Dougie said. 'Your mum has it.'

Amy turned to pick up her coat, which was resting on the back of the sofa. She didn't know that Flora kept in touch with Dougie. She turned to face him, her brow creased. 'If there were anything wrong, you'd tell me, wouldn't you?'

'Of course I would.' Dougie smiled. 'I'm fine.'

But as Amy said goodbye she was not so convinced. For the first time that night, Dougie was unable to meet her eyes.

CHAPTER FORTY

In the darkness, Lillian paced her cell, nibbling on her thumbnail as she thought things through. Everyone was assembled like pieces on a chessboard, ready for her next move. True, she had not expected Amy to lash out like that, but detective inspector or not, even she had her limits it seemed. Not that Lillian would have done things any differently. It had been a joy to spend time in the outside world. But it wasn't the wildlife she was interested in, or the kiss of the autumn breeze on her skin. Revisiting the girls' final resting places had helped her relive those moments all over again. She smiled, inhaling deeply as her eyelids fluttered shut. Oh, the sweetness and innocence of those young girls. Taking their lives had been a pleasure like no other. How she missed those heady days of self-gratification, exploring the darkness and giving it full control. And Jack, her insatiable husband, who, in the early days, had thought that threesomes were as far as he could go. How she had opened his eyes over the years and introduced him to the pleasures of the flesh.

Even killing his own daughter was something she had encouraged, whispering in his ear that she was all set to report them to the police. Sally-Ann had been developing, catching the eyes of their regular guests.

Where Mandy was dull and plain, Sally-Ann was voluptuous and sickly sweet. She could not allow another woman in the household to shine brighter than her. But she had underestimated little Poppy, the Judas of the family.

Lillian was not afforded a conventional upbringing. Introduced to sex long before her body was equipped for it, she had learned to cope the only way she could – by exercising control and bending others to her will. True, there were plenty of fools to manipulate in prison, and a well-timed beating could evoke sympathy when visitors cast their eyes over the bruises on her face. It was worth the discomfort. Nothing was as tantalising as the prospect of freedom and being able to relive her youth. According to Damien, the internet had opened up vast possibilities she could have only dreamed of before. Apps that located 'fuck-buddies' who wanted to meet up for sex. Online groups of likeminded people who would have hung on her every word. After years of protesting her so-called innocence, she had almost given up on her dream of being freed, but when she read of Robert Winter's demise, a plan hatched in her brain.

She lay on her bed, staring but not seeing, thoughts of her children at the forefront of her mind. Dim-witted Damien and Maggoty Mandy. She chuckled at the nicknames she appointed for them both. They were easily manipulated, but sadly had inherited their father's brains. It wasn't until Amy came on the scene that hope flared. She had worked on them, each one in turn. Damien infiltrated The Keepers of Truth, garnering support for his poor innocent mother. It was wise to use the group as a scapegoat. As much as she liked to toy with him, Damien was no good to her in jail. As for Mandy, she was happy to carry out her bidding as long as it led to a few quid at the end. And now Amy, who had granted her momentary satisfaction by driving the last nail into Gladys Thompson's coffin. Surely news that she had dumped her daughter's body in a freezer would kill the bitch off?

She had revelled in details of Hermione Parker's kidnapping and would make Amy jump through a few more hoops yet. Then, when Amy was wrung out and Hermione turned up dead, she would finish her off for good. Her daughter had chosen sides when she had shopped them to social services, and she would have to live with the consequences of her acts. Her friends, family and finally her career – Lillian would not rest until she tore it all down. But she had to be free to see it. Lillian's eyelids grew heavy as sleep drew close and she breathed a contented sigh. She could almost smell freedom. It would happen, as long as everything came together. She had one more ace up her sleeve.

CHAPTER FORTY-ONE

Every inch of Hemmy's body trembled. She held the bucket tightly as she prepared to take action, her feet planted firmly on the floor. The stench of urine did not bother her anymore. She was too busy concentrating on the person behind the door. Could she buy enough time to get away? As the door creaked open, she drew back the bucket and launched it at her captor's head. Having gained the element of surprise, she pushed him to the floor before stumbling through the door and towards the stairs. The metal bedstead rattled as his head bounced against the frame on the way down.

Forcing one foot before the other, Hemmy heaved for breath as she clambered up the steps. But her escape was hampered by the closed trapdoor at the top. 'No,' she gasped. Weak from lack of food and water, she strained to push back the wooden hatch.

'You . . . bitch!' The muffled voice roared from below, timbers creaking as he clambered to his feet.

Hemmy thought of the blade and how it had cut through her hair like butter. She had to get out. She would rather take her chances in the water than face punishment for trying to run away. The screw was coarse against her fingers, but she could not let it go. Pushing hard, she felt the trapdoor give. Just one more push . . .

'Come back here!' the voice rasped behind her, a gloved hand biting into her ankles. Hemmy kicked it away. 'Help me!' she screamed, praying to be heard. 'Someone, please help!' She glared down at her masked captor. Blood smeared inside the lens, blinding his left eye. Snarling like a wounded animal, he swiped at her ankles to pull her back down.

Her muscles shaking from the exertion, Hemmy shoved back the trap door and poked her head through. The rush of fresh air hit her, making her hair fly over her face. *Almost there*, she thought, gripping the ledge as she struggled to climb the steps. A whimper escaped her lips as she saw Purdy in her cage near the mouth of the trap door, but a gloved hand tugged on her ankle and began pulling her down. Screaming for help, she gripped the hatch for balance as she swivelled her head from left to right. But all she could see were the walls of the boat. Where was she? She needed to haul herself up. 'Help!' she shouted, heaving air into her lungs. Without shoes, her kicks were not enough to keep her kidnapper at bay for long. A piercing meow responded to her distress. Hermione's heart ached for her cat, weak and emaciated in her cage. She grappled for the lock. If *she* couldn't escape, she would see to it that her Purdy did. The sound of traffic in the distance told her they must be moored near dry land. Hope flared inside her. Fiddling with the cage, she struggled to pull the latch across, her feet still on the steps below. But her captor was upon her.

'Help me! Please, someone, help!' Hemmy screamed, fear sharpening her words. As she lost her fight to clamber onto the deck, the door of Purdy's cage flew open. 'Shoo!' Hemmy screamed at her pet. 'Go! Get out!' Then with a sudden yank, she was pulled back down, cracking her chin against the lip of the trap door.

Blood streamed from her tongue as she caught it between her teeth, but Hemmy was not going down without a fight.

His breath rattling loudly, her kidnapper dragged her back to her bed.

Spitting blood, Hemmy wriggled under his grip, screaming at the top of her breath. Her fingers tightened over the screw, still pressed into the palm of her hand. If she could gouge his neck, make a run for it . . . If she didn't, she knew what would come next.

A cold blade pressed against her cheek brought her movements to a halt.

'Shut your mouth, or I'll cut you from ear to ear.' Panting, he tried to catch his breath.

Hemmy lowered her hands, slipping the rusted screw into her skirt pocket. 'Please, don't hurt me,' she whispered, swallowing back the blood trickling into her mouth.

CHAPTER FORTY-TWO

Evening briefing had drained Paddy of energy, and he barely felt equipped to deal with what lay ahead. Thoughts of Geraldine had haunted his working day. He had tried to get his act together to make up for his recent lateness and now it was time to sort things out at home.

Anxiety had always clouded Geraldine's life, but they had managed, right up until that horrific day. His suggestion they try for another child was met with outright hostility. He remembered it clearly, and still had the scar on his thigh from where she'd swiped at him with a knife. She hadn't meant it, of course; it was just bad timing. She had been peeling the potatoes, and lashed out in response. In her eyes, his suggestion was akin to asking if they could sleep together again. In the heat of their argument she told him how repulsive she found him and banished him to the spare room.

Paddy turned off for the road where they lived. Geraldine's rejection that day had hurt more than the knife wound, which he had managed to patch up on his own. Yet every time he packed his bags, she insisted that he stay. She needed him: to pay the bills, clean the house, do the gardening and buy food. Being with Elaine had taught him that a loving relationship was born of mutual love and respect. It was time for Geraldine to stand on her own two feet.

His trip home wasn't planned, but he could not wait to sort things out. It was why he had brought a handful of support leaflets he'd been squirrelling away in his office drawer. Tonight would be about getting Geraldine help. Only then could he face leaving for good. She must have felt *something* for him. Why else would she be so paranoid and jealous all the time?

Heaving a deep sigh, he shoved the leaflets into his coat pocket before ambling up their overgrown drive. The sight of it was another depressing reminder of how he had let things go. Sometimes it was easier to live a fantasy than face up to how bad things had got. Fumbling for his lighter, he gave in to his craving and quickly lit a cigarette to calm his nerves. The circular orange glow of his cigarette tip reminded him of an injury Geraldine had dealt to the back of his hand. The pock-marked burn was faded now; a result of her catching him smoking after they'd had a row.

They could sell the house, split the proceeds and set Geraldine up in a nice little flat. Maybe get her a pet. As long as it wasn't a cat: she hated them. It was hard to believe she was once a London property developer. It was some small relief that they owned their own home. A sergeant's wage would only stretch so far, but if she downsized to a smaller property it should help until she found her feet. If only he hadn't spent his inheritance on buying a new Jag. It was a temporary plaster over the pain of his father's death – typical of his impulsive nature, another thing that drove Geraldine mad. Stubbing out his cigarette, he checked the time: it was almost eleven. She never went to bed before twelve. So why was the house cloaked in darkness as he entered through the door?

'Geraldine?' he called out, his face tilted towards the stairs. 'It's me, I'm home.' But no response came. His shoulders inched higher at the bite of the cold and he clicked on the heating timer. Behind the door lay today's post. Next to that was a pair of Geraldine's boots, the soles edged with fresh mud. When had she been outside? Silence laid claim to the house, broken by the trickle of heating pipes filling inside the walls. 'Geraldine?' he called a second time, his pulse quickening as his fears grew. What if she had hurt herself? He had spoken to her this morning, and all had seemed well. Slowly, he trudged towards the kitchen, feeling as if his shoes were made of lead. The guilt of his daughter's death had all but consumed him; he could not bear to lose Geraldine too.

Switching on the light, he found the kitchen empty. A day's worth of dirty plates were piled in the sink and the smell of decaying food emanated from an overflowing bin. Resting his palm against the electric kettle, Paddy found it was cold. He rattled the key in the back door. Locked.

After checking the bathroom and living room, he forced himself up the stairs. Was she lying on the bed with an empty pill bottle in her hand? Perhaps she had left a note, told the world it was all his fault. It was no more than he deserved.

Inhaling deeply, he stood on the landing, grateful to smell nothing more than the scent of damp clothes. Geraldine was too frightened to go outside and use the washing line, but why wouldn't she turn on the heat? Paddy was continually puzzled by her seeming desire to live in such dark and miserable conditions. As always, the bedroom curtains were closed. Still filled with dread, he searched each room, unable to bring himself to enter hers until last. Slowly, he twisted the doorknob. The flicker of a desktop computer glowed from a desk in the corner of the room. Paddy's eyebrows shot up in surprise. 'Hello?' he called out. With some relief, he found her bed unmade but bare.

'Geraldine, love, it's me, Paddy.' It seemed ridiculous introducing himself, but what if she thought he was a burglar? With that thought in mind, he switched on the light. He hated to admit it, but he was scared of his wife.

Groaning, he rubbed his back as he straightened from checking beneath the bed. She was gone. Falling into police mode, he scouted the room for further clues.

His eyes crept over the make-up on the dresser table that he had not seen before. As for the desktop computer, she had always claimed that technology was beyond her. Had she been lying to him all these years? Shaking the mouse, he brought the screen to life. 'What have you been up to?' he murmured under his breath.

Within seconds, he had her browsing history up. What he saw made him gasp. After all these years, he thought he knew her. Paddy shook his head. He was wrong.

CHAPTER FORTY-THREE

After her chat with Dougie, Amy experienced the best night's sleep she'd had all week. She felt like a physical weight had lifted off her shoulders. She was strong. She could deal with this. None of it was her fault. Regardless of her internal pep talk, she still found herself hovering outside her office door. Having opened it an inch, she was too scared to go in.

It was with relief and surprise that she found Paddy at his desk. She knew he was trying to make up for his recent tardiness, but it was six am.

'Who kicked you out of bed?' Her smile faded as she took in his crumpled features. There were dark shadows beneath his eyes, and he was wearing yesterday's clothes.

He plucked his tie – a black design with an image of a penguin on the front – from his jacket pocket and began to slide it on. 'I'm just in. I was about to put the kettle on. Fancy a cuppa?'

'In a minute. I need you to do me a favour first.' She grimaced, mortified at what she was about to say.

'Everything all right?' Paddy said, a smile rising to his lips. He knew her well enough to guess what the request entailed.

'A spider.' Amy's words were followed by a sharp exhalation. 'There's a spider in my office. Freakishly huge. Monstrous, in fact. Can you get rid of it?'

'You only had to ask.' Paddy smirked, grabbing a glass and a piece of card from his desk drawer. Within a couple of minutes, the intruder had been humanely sent on his travels through her office window.

Amy slammed the window shut in case he decided to pay her a second visit. She had managed to keep her fear of spiders a secret from everyone but Paddy, who was more than happy to kick them out when the need arose. 'If you tell anyone . . .' her words trailed behind her as she followed him back to his computer.

'You'll kill me. Yeah, I know. I didn't blab when you were a probationer, I'm hardly going to now you're my DI.'

Amy threw him a wry smile. 'I've been meaning to talk to you alone. Now seems as good a time as any.'

He nodded towards his screen as he tightened the knot on his tie. 'I'm bringing up the outstanding tasks now,' he said seriously. 'I'll be able to update you when I've had a chance to read through them.'

'It's not about work.' Pulling up a swivel chair, Amy took a seat beside him. 'Who's been sitting on this?' She fumbled for the fittings as her feet dangled from the chair. A soft hiss escaped the mechanism as she pulled the lever to lower the seat. Satisfied, she placed her feet flat on the floor.

'Is this about Steve?' Paddy said. 'I've had a word. He said the whole thing with Molly was a misunderstanding. Promises to keep his distance from now on.'

'Huh. You've got more confidence in him than me.' Amy had spoken to his previous colleagues and did not like what she had heard. 'Do you know what they called him in his last department? Mr Tickle. If he crosses the line . . . in fact, if he *approaches* the line, he'll be transferred to prisoner processing so fast his feet won't hit the ground.'

It was not a hollow threat. The prisoner processing department dealt with petty crimes. Usually a stomping ground for probationers, it would be the last thing Steve would want. 'Anyway,' Amy said, 'that wasn't what I wanted to talk you about, at least, not yet.'

'I'm all ears.' Minimising his computer program, Paddy turned to face her.

'I'm not one to stick my nose in, but I get the feeling you've got problems at home.'

'You're not far wrong there.' Paddy rubbed his stubbled chin. 'But I'm sorting it. You've got enough to get through, without taking on my worries.'

'You're my right-hand man. Whatever it is, you can talk to me.' She arched an eyebrow in an *it's now or never* manner. Seconds passed before Paddy delivered a defeated exhalation.

'You know Geraldine has agoraphobia.' He paused as Amy nodded in understanding. 'Well, last night I went home, and she was gone.'

'I see,' Amy replied, remembering that Paddy had mentioned her condition in the past. Things had been tough for them, but until lately, she thought they were muddling through. 'Is she OK?'

'She's fine. But she said she's not been outside in years. She's been lying to me.' He glanced around the empty office before continuing. On the floor above them, a hoover whirred as the cleaning ladies got on with their work. 'Promise me this won't go any further, not until I know more.'

'Go on,' Amy said.

'We sleep in separate rooms. I didn't know she had a computer until I searched her bedroom last night.' He exhaled a deep sigh. 'I checked her browser history. I couldn't bloody well believe what I found.'

'What people do in the privacy of their own homes . . .' Amy offered him a shrug. 'Women look at porn, too.'

'But it wasn't porn,' Paddy replied, mumbling something about a zero sex drive. 'It was all Facebook groups and conspiracy sites. She's a troll.'

Of all the things Amy had expected Paddy to say, this was last on her list. The point of this conversation was to bring up the topic of domestic abuse. She knew his excuses about car problems were fabricated, much like the explanations he manufactured for the bruises and injuries to his skin. This had not factored at all. 'I don't understand,' she found herself saying, as she waited for him to explain.

'She's nasty. Vile. Part of all these online groups. They target certain causes and post tweets and Facebook comments. Then there are the conspiracy theorists, all UFOs and Elvis lives. She's lost the plot.'

'Wait,' Amy interrupted. 'Is she part of The Keepers of Truth? Has she tweeted with the "Find Hermione" hashtag?'

'Amongst others. She's got this notebook in her drawer listing hundreds of sites. No wonder she never gets anything done. She's on there day and night.'

'Have you said anything?'

Paddy shook his head. 'Not yet.'

'Where was she?' Amy replied. 'You said she was missing when you came home.'

Paddy shrugged. 'I don't know. I parked my car around the corner and waited until she came back. I followed her in after a few minutes, and she said nothing about being out.'

'Keep me updated,' Amy said, wondering how scared Paddy must have been to take such measures. It was on her lips to ask him about his injuries when her office phone rang.

'I'd better get that,' she said. 'Why don't you make us both a coffee and we can carry on with our chat?'

'I'll put the kettle on.' Paddy smiled as they both rose. 'But I've pretty much covered it all.'

As she answered the phone, Amy scribbled a note to speak to Paddy later. She took comfort in her note taking, even though she wasn't likely to forget.

The call was from the front counter. Amy waited for the unwelcome sound of Lillian's voice.

'Ah, good morning. I didn't know if you'd be in.'

The caller did not come from prison as Amy had predicted.

'My name's Michelle Baldwin, and I'm calling from Paws Animal Shelter.'

'Good morning, what can I do for you?' Amy replied before holding her breath. Dare she hope for news?

'I've got a white Persian cat here that matches the description of the one you called about. Well, when I say white . . . She's been through the wars, bless her. Dehydrated and undernourished, but she'll pull through.'

'Where did you find her?' Amy said, on high alert. *Could this be Hemmy's cat?*

'She was handed in by a member of the public who said they found her wandering around Canary Wharf. I found an address on her collar, but then I remembered your enquiry and thought I'd call you direct.'

'I'm so glad you did.' Amy smiled. 'The address . . . it's the one I gave you?'

'Yes, it is. Do you tell the owner, or will I?'

'I will, thanks. Are you OK to provide a statement if I send an officer round? And . . . can you not wash her yet? I know it sounds odd, but I'd like to get my scenes of crime officer to pay you a visit, too.'

'Of course, anything to help,' Michelle replied.

'Oh, and if you could keep it to yourself, I'd really appreciate it.' Amy's smile widened. 'I'm so glad Purdy's OK.'

Michelle assured her she was happy to oblige. As she hung up the phone, Amy silently punched the air. Purdy was alive, and what's more, she had escaped her confinement. It may only be a small lead, but Amy had a good feeling about it. Sometimes, the smallest of seeds bore the biggest fruit. Taking out her phone, she looked up the mobile number of a colleague for whom she held an immense amount of respect. If anyone could find a fresh lead from a tired cat, it was CSI Malcolm Webber.

CHAPTER FORTY-FOUR

As the Senior Investigating Officer, Pike dictated Amy's movements and insisted she visit Lillian in prison one more time. 'You never know, she might have another confession,' she had said, her eyes bright as buttons as they trained in the gym that morning.

Pre-empting Amy's reluctance, Lillian had phoned DCI Pike, hinting she had more to tell. Usually, Pike left Amy to her own devices, but this week she was feeling like a puppet on the end of a string. 'Keep the visit informal,' Pike told her as they pounded their treadmills. 'She wants it just like before.'

Amy's face soured, thinking back to Pike's words. Since when did Lillian Grimes call the shots?

Her earlier optimism had faded after more tweets appeared with the Find Hermione hashtag from the Keepers of Truth. As well as their usual spiel, it came with a new set of hashtags, #ThreeDays #TickTock. #TickTock was especially worrying, something they had used in the past. It suggested that if their demands were not met within a certain time, there would be hell to pay. But all attempts to communicate with them had proved fruitless. Just what the hell did they want? Molly and the team were doing everything they could but the media had gone crazy with reports. It felt like the eyes of the world were upon them. But Amy could not feel pressured – this was exactly what her team were there for.

Now, her glance swept across the children in the prison visitation room. Did Lillian look upon them with sick fascination as she had with Wendy Thompson? Did she think about them in bed at night? Repulsion forced the thought away. As she approached her, she was taken aback to see the man sitting in the next seat. It was Damien, wearing jeans and a scuffed leather biker jacket that had seen better days. Unlike Lillian, her sibling was free, and his unpredictability made her stomach bubble up with nerves. She had yet to question him about Hermione, but was waiting for the results of his background checks. She knew she could trust Molly to be discreet and had tasked her with speaking to the divisional intelligence unit earlier in the day. Taking a deep breath, she sank into the foamy blue chair, her back rigid as she smoothed the crease in her suit skirt. As always, she was perfectly poised. Her hair had grown long enough to tie back, kept in place with an antique clip, anything to differentiate herself from the woman before her. Seeing Lillian and Damien together made the hairs rise on the back of her neck.

'Nice of you to join us at last,' Lillian said. She seemed pleased with herself, which was cause for concern. A light application of rouge coloured her cheekbones, a coating of lip gloss disguising the paleness of her mouth.

Amy checked her watch. The search had delayed her by four minutes on the way in. It felt like a bad omen for what was to come. 'What are you doing here?' she said to Damien, as he regarded her, stony-faced.

'It's not a crime to visit your mum, is it? Unlike you, I only have the one.'

'Well, in that case, I'll leave you to it,' Amy replied tersely, the memory of their last meeting still fresh in her mind. 'I only came to say goodbye. We've identified the body at the farm as Wendy Thompson.

Thank you for your cooperation.' Robotically, Amy tried to keep every ounce of emotion out of her voice.

'Now the investigation is complete, I won't need to see you again.' Yet Damien's previous comment about finding the truth hung like a loose thread.

'Are you sure about that?' Lillian said, her eyes like two black pearls.

'I am unless you have something else to tell me,' Amy said, refusing to back down. From her peripheral vision, she could see Damien observing her. An undercurrent of aggression emanated from him, an expression of disgust evident on his face.

'Tell me,' Lillian replied, folding her arms. 'How do you feel about people being framed for murder? Have you ever done that? Set someone up?'

Amy's lips thinned. She was about to cross her arms but not wanting to mirror Lillian, she folded her hands in her lap. 'You had your trial. You were found guilty.'

'Only because your so-called father set me up.'

'Prove it.'

'Oh, I think you'll find that's down to you.' Lillian looked from Damien to Amy, a smug smile playing on her lips.

Pulling back her shirtsleeve, Amy checked the time. Turning to Lillian, she made a conscious effort to instil professionalism into her words. 'If you have a problem then hire a solicitor, take your concerns to them.'

As Amy rose to leave, her brother grabbed her by the wrist. Snatching back her hand, she cut him in two with a glare. 'Touch me again and you'll be sorry.'

Damien raised his hands in mock surrender. 'All right, firecracker. Just listen to what she has to say.'

Amy grimaced, her patience lost. 'She's winding you up, can't you see? I've checked about her English classes and so called enquiries with the refuge. It's all lies.'

Dismissing her words with a snort, Damien and Lillian shared a conspiratorial glance.

Amy straightened, feeling a sense of satisfaction that she could turn and walk away. 'You've run out of things to trade. You've no control over me anymore.'

'That's where you're wrong . . . tick tock,' Lillian said, tapping the side of her nose with childish glee. 'I know something you don't know.' Singing the words, she attracted curious glances from the children in the room.

Briefly, Amy closed her eyes, taking a breath as she sat back down. Lillian's constant toying was a rope around her neck that was beginning to fray. Had she seen the posts on social media?

'Remember that nice little blonde bit that went missing?' Damien said. 'I bet you'd love to know where she is.'

'You're lying.' Amy's voice hardened. Despite her best efforts, her name had been publicly linked to the case.

A smile formed on Lillian's lips. 'Willing to take that risk, are you? Because time is running out, and unlike Wendy Thompson, this little temptress is very much alive.' Her features darkened as she kept her voice low. 'You've got three days to find answers. If you don't, Hermione Parker will die.'

'Bullshit,' Amy spat, wishing she could swallow back the swearword that rolled off her tongue. To hear her refer to a child as a 'temptress' made her stomach churn.

'Listen,' Damien said. 'She's telling the truth.'

Amy stared in disbelief. 'Are you involved in this? Because if you are . . .'

'You can't pin this on me,' he replied. But the expression on his face told her otherwise.

'If you've anything to do with her abduction I'll be arresting you both,' Amy said, cursing the fact she had left her voice recorder at work.

'I've got an alibi,' Damien raised his chin in defiance. 'And who the fuck do you think you are, threatening to arrest me?'

Lillian cackled as she set the two of them against each other. 'Aw, look at you, my Poppy back to her old self. Even at the age of four, you were happy to have your family locked away. Here you are now, ready to do it all over again.' She tilted her head to one side, her eyes narrowing. 'What's wrong? Not content with killing your dad and locking up your mum, you want your brother banged up too?'

Amy's jaw tightened. 'You've just admitted to arranging Hermione Parker's kidnapping. I'm a police officer. What do you expect me to do?'

Tutting, Lillian wagged a finger in a tick-tock fashion. 'There she goes again, skewing the truth. How could I kidnap some snotty schoolgirl when I'm in prison?' She exhaled theatrically. 'I've been nothing but helpful, despite everything you've done. But if you don't want to know where she is . . .' Pushing back her chair, Lillian pressed her palms against the table as she rose to leave.

'Sit down,' Amy commanded. 'I'm listening.'

'Good. Then we have an understanding,' Lillian said smugly. 'You've got three days to prove that I've been framed for murder. They're hungry for justice, as the tweets say. Arrest Damien and that's sure to piss them off.'

'You threatened to kill her,' Amy replied. 'You're the one who should be under arrest.'

Damien silently watched as Lillian replied with a shrug. 'I've got quite the following in the real world. A lot of people aren't happy with how I've been treated. I can't help it if there's a revolt.'

'The Keepers of Truth,' Amy said, the words rolling off her tongue. 'They're using Hermione as a bargaining chip to set you free. And what about you?' She turned to Damien. 'Are you part of this group?'

'It's not against the law to go on Facebook,' Damien replied noncommittally. 'If they're trying to help Mum, then it sounds like a good idea to me.'

'Then where is she?' Amy leaned across the table. 'Tell me, and I'll look into your case.'

'Call me a bad mother, but I've got some trust issues with you,' Lillian replied. 'As I said, you've got three days.'

'And if I don't find what you want?'

'Then her blood is on your hands.'

CHAPTER FORTY-FIVE

Sipping her takeaway coffee, Amy's footsteps were heavy as she walked across the police car park. She'd had more than her fair share of revelations and was still reeling from her prison visit. But at least she had her answer. Now she knew the real reason why Lillian had got back in touch. Providing the burial sites was just a warm-up for what was to come. She had drawn entertainment from watching Amy squirm, but at the heart of it all, the woman wanted her freedom – at any cost. Amy sighed. In what parallel universe would the 'Beast of Brentwood' be released from prison? And where did that leave Hermione?

Damien had been quick to bring up his alibi, furiously backtracking on any involvement as visiting time came to a close. It had felt strange leaving the building together, out of Lillian's sight. Looking back on their conversation, he had simply told her to listen to what Lillian had to say. At a stretch, they could arrest her, but would the ends justify the means? Given she was in prison, there would be no premises search, no seizure of telephone records, no CSI to attend the scene or computers to infiltrate. Was it worth inflaming the situation? The Keepers of Truth did not mess around. Lillian had played ball so far. She had no reason to doubt she would again.

From the corner of her eye, she caught sight of two uniformed officers stepping out, a pack of cigarettes in their hands. Thanks to new regulations they weren't allowed to smoke in the car park anymore. As she approached the building, she smiled in response to their respectful nod. Was she deserving of her rank?

She knew what she had to do – come clean with DCI Pike. God, she would have her guts for garters for this. Withholding information was serious. It could even get her kicked off the team. Her stomach churned as she imagined the consequences. Why hadn't she been honest all along? She knew the answer to that. Her friendship with Pike was by proxy, built on her history with Robert, but now her father was gone. As soon as Pike found out Amy wasn't blood related, she could cast her in a different light. This was what Lillian wanted: for Amy to feel the fear of rejection and uncertainty, just as she had done.

She had little time to dwell; her mobile rang the second she entered her office. It was Malcolm, her lead CSI. Her team had nicknamed him the Nigel Havers of the forensic world. 'Amy, darling, how are you?'

Amy warmed at the sound of his voice. Classical music rose in the background, and it sounded like he was in his car. Born and bred in Westminster, he had several degrees to his name. Why he left his job as a high court judge to get down and dirty in crime scenes was a mystery to Amy.

'I've had better days,' she replied dryly, 'but I'm hoping you're calling with good news?'

'Depends on how you'd like to look at it. I've had a fascinating chat with Purdy this morning. Very interesting indeed.'

'Did she talk back?' Amy replied, visions of his meeting with the cat making her grin.

'She certainly did. She told me she'd been caged all this time. The poor lamb's fur was matted with urine and excrement. She's a very clean lady, you know. She would never have lain on it if she weren't confined.'

'So it's unlikely she's been wandering the streets all this time?'

'*Highly* unlikely. According to the vet, she would only have survived a few more days at the most. It's doubtful her abductor was present when she fled. She was too weak to run at any great speed.'

'Any idea of location?'

'The urine and faeces matting her fur were relatively fresh, so I'm estimating she'd escaped no more than a couple of hours before she was found.'

'Which narrows down her location . . .' Amy thought aloud.

'At the speed she was travelling, it was not very far away. That is, unless she was dumped.' He paused. 'There's something else you may find of interest.'

'Do tell,' Amy replied, feeling a small frisson of hope. If they got to Hemmy now, there was a chance they would find her alive.

'I went slightly beyond the call of duty when I met Purdy, but thankfully we're both refined creatures and hit it off. I persuaded her to climb up on my lap, and I buried my nose in her fur.'

Amy arched an eyebrow. 'And the purpose of that was?'

'To give it a jolly good sniff of course, why else? As expected, I came back with the pungent aroma of excrement and urine, but there was another rather heady bouquet . . .'

'Cigarettes?' Amy hazarded a guess.

'On the contrary, and before I disclose it, I must tell you that I have very refined olfactory senses. They've not let me down yet.'

'I'm all ears,' Amy replied. A showman, Malcolm liked to draw things out.

'Fish. I smelt fish. There was no mistaking it. If I were you, I'd instruct the team to start searching the docklands. I'd also consider fish shops, markets, fishing vessels. Not so much restaurants as they tend to get in fresh stock. This was very pungent. It's worth a shot.'

'You little beauty,' Amy replied. 'Anything else?'

'I've seized some cat hairs. If the search team find a location, tell them to watch out for them. I don't want them carrying evidence away on their clothes. I was reading about a veterinary genetics laboratory in California. They've helped Scotland Yard with homicide cases in the past. Mind you, at two thousand dollars a pop, it's not cheap. One of their first cases involved the hairs of a white cat.'

Amy nodded, one eye on the clock. Malcolm could talk all day, but she needed to put the information to good use. 'Sounds fascinating,' she said. 'Will you forward me on your report?'

'It's winging its way as we speak.' His tone grew serious. 'If Purdy's anything to go by, I doubt Hermione's in a good way.'

CHAPTER FORTY-SIX

1986

The man standing over her seemed like an angel, the summer sun forming a halo behind his head. Behind them, a tall grey building loomed. It smelt of stale air and was filled with serious-looking people who talked over Poppy's head. Bored, she had begged to come outside after the paperwork was complete. The lady from the social seemed happy today, as she told Poppy she was going to a new home. She had almost sung the news, and Poppy had wondered how that could be a good thing. And now she found herself with her hand over her forehead as she assessed her new guardian's form. Tall and wiry with silver blonde hair, he was so unlike Daddy, who was twice his width. Speaking all posh and proper, he said he was bringing her home. His voice was soft and comforting, and with a sense of resignation Poppy accepted her fate.

He told her his name was Robert and she made an effort to commit it to memory. So many people had come into her life since she spoke to the social. Like Dougie, he knelt down on one knee to speak to her, but where Dougie's eyes were like hazelnuts, Robert's were grey, like hers. Poppy stood tongue-tied, until the woman next to him began touching her short brown hair. Overcome by her heady perfume, Poppy coughed as it hit the back of her throat.

'My name's Flora,' she said, patting Poppy's head like a dog. 'We're both named after flowers.' But then Robert mumbled something about changing her name and Poppy's chest tightened all over again.

Flora did not notice, her words tripping over each other as she explained excitedly all the things they were going to do. Visits to the hairdressers, shopping, pony club, ballet lessons. It was enough to make Poppy's head spin. She frowned, nestling closer to Robert. It felt like the safest place. She watched as he reached for Flora's arm, telling her to slow down.

'We're going to have so much fun,' she said, grinning with pink lipstick stained teeth. 'You're going to be our little girl.'

Recoiling, Poppy took a step back, nestling into the crook of Robert's arm. She had been told by the social about her new foster family, that they might even adopt her one day too. Until now, she had not believed it was true. She thought about what Mummy would do. Her lips pinched as she sucked them inwards, her fists bunched beneath the sleeves of her dress. She leaned forward to speak.

Flora threw Robert a smug smile before bending down at the waist. 'What is it, sweetie? What do you want to say?'

'Suck my cock, bitch,' Poppy said. She did not know what the words meant, but she had heard such things said at home. Flora froze, her mouth dropping open.

Poppy frowned. Hadn't she heard her? She decided to put the actions in place to drive her anger home. Holding her hand to her mouth, she pushed her tongue against the inside of her cheek in a gesture of eating a banana. At least that's what she thought it meant. But she knew it was a bad thing. A rude thing. Something to drive this woman away for good. Her palms damp with sweat, Poppy's heart beat like a moth trapped in her chest. After failing to get enough of a reaction, she called her the worst word of all. The 'c' word. The word that

Sally-Ann had told her she must *never* say. It was so short and snappy; Poppy couldn't understand why it was so bad, or even what it meant. But Flora did. The blood draining from her face, she gasped in horror as she backed away.

'She . . . how can she say these things?' she said to Robert, jerking him by the arm. In the absence of an answer, she turned to Poppy, waggling her finger in her face. 'That's a bad word. Rude. Little girls don't talk like that.'

'Eff off,' Poppy shrilled, thrilled by the effect of her words. 'Slag! Cow! Bitch!' As the expletives rolled off her tongue, she found herself unable to stop. From the corner of her eye, she could see the woman from the social approach. She was in trouble now. Big trouble – but it was too late to stop. Raising his hand, Robert asked her to wait as he kneeled to face Poppy once more.

But instead of being angry, his features softened into a smile – Poppy's expletives seemingly having no effect at all. 'I know you're scared, I would be too,' he said softly. 'But I promise we will keep you safe. I also know people have let you down . . .'

Poppy stopped swearing as she took in his words.

'But I'm going to make a vow . . . do you know what a vow is?'

Poppy shook her head, toeing the gravel beneath her feet.

'It's the biggest, most serious promise anyone can make. It means that once they say it, they *have* to do it. Forever. Do you understand now?'

Poppy nodded.

'OK. Well, firstly I have to raise my hand like this.' His face sombre, he held up his palm. 'I vow to keep you safe. Always. And nobody is going to make you do anything you don't want to.' He lowered his voice to a whisper. 'If saying bad words makes you feel a little better inside, then that's fine, too. Hopefully, soon you won't need them anymore.' He lowered his palm. 'You miss your family, don't you?'

Poppy sighed.

'We're not trying to take their place. But we would like to look after you. I know how scary it is because when I was your age, I got a new mummy and daddy, too.'

Poppy's lips parted, but the words would not come. Did the same thing happen to him?

His smile widened, showing a row of white teeth, and it felt like warm sunshine beaming down on her face. 'Flora's just excited. We've got a lovely room all set up for you, and she can't wait to show it off. You can sit there in peace and quiet if you like, or just watch TV.' He held out his hand. 'So how about it? Would you like to come and see your new home?'

Nodding softly, Poppy wiped her palms on her dress before taking his hand.

CHAPTER FORTY-SEVEN

'I see you haven't found her yet,' Lillian said, during yet another phone call. 'Your DCI looked very cool during the press appeal. She was friendly over the phone, mind, but I reckon she's a hard-faced cow beneath it all.'

'You're not to ring me at work again. Not me, not my DCI,' Amy replied in exasperation. Another memory had returned, leaving Amy more grateful than ever she had been adopted by such a kind and caring couple. Inwardly cringing, she recalled the swearwords she used as a child. Yet Robert had handled it with good grace. And now the source of all Amy's misery was badgering her over the phone. She'd had enough of her for one day. 'How are you even making all these calls?' Amy said, returning her attention to Lillian. 'Have you smuggled a phone into your cell?'

'Makes me wonder,' Lillian chuckled, ignoring her outburst. 'Wouldn't it be hilarious if po-faced Pike found out who you were? And what would the papers make of it all?'

'What do you want from me?' Amy said. The barely veiled threat was a warning to pay heed, and she had no choice but to comply. Outside her office, the team were busy following leads on Hermione

Parker's case. With press attention hotting up, extra officers had been drafted in to carry out premises searches in locations recommended by CSI.

'Can't you spare your mother ten minutes, or do I have to get your attention by other means?'

'If there's one thing you have, it's my attention,' Amy admitted, sagging back into her office chair. She was tired of telling Lillian that she did not regard her as her mother. She threw the remainder of her salad sandwich in the bin. Her appetite had disappeared as soon as she took the call.

'Good!' Lillian said, her delight evident in her tone. 'Have you spoken to your brother since?'

'If you mean Damien, then no.' Amy's brother was Craig, the boy she grew up with under Robert and Flora's roof. Damien's dark eyes and aggressive manner reminded her too much of Jack Grimes. Being in his presence both saddened and unsettled her. Ever the manipulator, Lillian picked up her hesitancy.

'Have you done one of those police checks on him yet? You might be surprised at what you'd find.'

Amy frowned. What game was she playing now? 'Why would you want that? You worked so hard to get us all all together. What are you up to?'

Lillian sniffed. 'I've been feeling off all week. I think I've come down with a cold. Some families send their loved ones things through the post. Even a get-well card can mean a lot when you're on the inside. It's nice to know somebody cares.'

Amy's frown deepened as she tried to decipher the conversation. 'I'm not with you.'

'That much I know,' Lillian sneered. 'In fact, you've not been on the ball for some time. Are you really suited to policing? How will your workmates react when they find out who you are?'

'I don't plan on telling anyone.'

A sudden titter speared the phone line, making Amy question Lillian's mental health. 'You were always creative with the truth, but then that's how psychopaths work.'

'Are you calling me a psychopath?' Amy said, itching to hang up.

'Like mother, like daughter.' Lillian paused for effect. 'Do you think it's unfair? I certainly did when I was labelled the "Beast of Brentwood".'

'Have you taken your medication today? Because you don't seem very lucid?'

'Tell me,' Lillian said, ignoring her barbed comment. 'When you find out what Damien is, are you going to hang him out to dry, too?'

'What do you mean, *what* he is?' Amy rubbed the back of her neck. Lillian's presence was so strong she could almost feel her breath tickling her skin.

'He's a chip off the old block, just like his dad. I told him, it's in his blood. He can't escape it so he's better off making peace with it. Accept what he is and move on.'

'OK, I'm going now,' Amy said. 'So unless you've something of value to say . . .'

'You're not cut out to be a copper . . . They can sense it, can't they? That you're different. They put up with you because they think you're a Winter. But as soon as they find out who you are, it'll all be blown to hell.'

'I *am* a Winter,' Amy replied. 'It's my legal name and I'm proud to use it. Don't call me here again.'

'I want that appeal.' Lillian's voice rose a notch. 'If you don't prove my innocence, I'm taking you with me, and Hermione Parker will die.' A dead ring tone followed and Amy swore under her breath. Her DCI had told her . . . no, *ordered* her to keep Lillian Grimes talking when she rang. She was correct when she guessed the woman had more to give. She seemed convinced that Robert had framed her. But her father would *never* plant evidence to secure a conviction. She glanced at the silver-framed picture on her desk and saw an honest and kind man.

But sometimes people with pure intentions were driven to do terrible things . . .

A knock on her office door pulled her from her thoughts. It was Paddy, and the printout in his hand told her his visit was timely. 'Come in,' Amy said. 'What have you got?'

'That intel on Damien Grimes you asked for. He's got previous. Lots of it. A bit of a deviant by all accounts.'

Amy gestured at Paddy to take a seat, pushing an open packet of Werther's Originals towards him. She may have tasked Molly with obtaining the intelligence, but as her sergeant, Paddy needed to be kept in the loop.

He slipped a toffee from its wrapping before popping it in his mouth. 'We first came across him during a bust at a sex party where drugs were in use,' he said, parking the toffee in his cheek. 'He didn't get done for anything, but his details were uploaded to Intel. He was only sixteen when it happened and not the youngest one there.'

'He would have still been in care, wouldn't he?'

Paddy nodded. 'He was taken back to his foster home, but kept running away. There's intel on him making a nuisance of himself with schoolgirls in particular, and he's had previous for drugs and petty crime.'

Amy thumbed through the report. 'He was found in possession of Rohypnol?'

'Yup.' Paddy nodded. 'Hardly surprising, given his background.'

Amy had to stop herself physically wincing from his remark. It was a fair comment, and Paddy would never have said it if he had known the truth.

'Really?' she asked, unable to hold back the question on her lips. 'Do you think if you're born to serial killer parents you're destined to turn out the same way?'

'Maybe not destined, but those kids were bound to be messed up in the head. The stuff that went on in that house . . . it wasn't just the murders, was it? There were sex parties, too. A lot of people came and went. Maybe Damien's finding it hard to shake it off. It's no excuse for what he's done, but it's there just the same.'

It is there, Amy thought, like a stain on his soul. And it made him a dangerous man. She thought of the times he defended Lillian, justifying her actions and acting like Amy was in the wrong. She turned the page, her heart sinking as she read the markers for his mental health.

'I've been talking to Lillian Grimes. She's hinted that Damien is in The Keepers of Truth.'

Paddy blew out his cheeks. 'Bloody hell, dobbing in her own son? That's a new low.'

Amy flushed. 'She's trying to make herself look good to probation. She doesn't care who she hurts.' The irony was not lost on her. She sipped her coffee, which had now turned cold. Any excuse to avert her gaze. In prison, Lillian had defended Damien, but as soon as his back was turned, she was ringing Amy, suggesting he was guilty as hell. More proof that she was toying with them. Amy almost felt sorry for him.

'Makes sense, I suppose.' Paddy rolled the sweet on his tongue. 'I didn't believe that rubbish in the papers about her seeing the light. People like that never do. But it seems a bit far-fetched to point the finger at her son.'

'But does it?' Amy asked, her eyes scanning the lines of text. 'Look at his previous. Possession of a date-rape drug, a history of sexual offences and mental health issues to boot.' Amy filled him in on details of her conversation with Lillian Grimes.

'Best we go and lift him then,' Paddy replied. It was not that simple, and they both knew it. A full arrest package would need to be put in place.

'Don't do a thing until I speak to the DCI. This needs to be handled with care.'

'But you said yourself, we've got suspicion . . .'

Amy frowned. It was unlike her to be so indecisive, but the Grimes's involvement in Hemmy's case had tied her up in knots. 'If we have him on a loose lead, we can keep track of his movements. He might bring us straight to her. Then we've got all the evidence we need.'

'Good luck with getting a surveillance team together. Our budget is stretched as it is.'

Amy knew that more than anyone. 'Which is why I need to speak to Pike.'

'Maybe you can tap his phone line while you're at it,' Paddy replied. 'But I'm not holding my breath.'

Amy's jaw tightened. Thoughts of officers listening to his calls made her blood run cold. Lillian was not averse to ringing her. What if Damien did too? Time was running out. But it wasn't just herself she was worried about. It was the allegations against her father too.

'Lillian could be just getting off on the attention. As for Damien: you can't help the family you're born into. We can't automatically suspect him just because of that.'

'Whatever you say, guv'nor,' Paddy said, tipping an imaginary hat.

'Best we keep this locked down until we come up with a strategy. The last thing we need is to set people galloping off in the wrong direction.' Amy glanced up at the corners of her ceiling, instinctively checking for spiders. Would she ever be free of the past?

CHAPTER FORTY-EIGHT

Hemmy felt her captor's eyes burning through her back long before she turned around. She groaned, blinking her one good eye. Her left was almost sealed shut. Her kidnapper's fist had felt like an iron bar as it made contact with her face. Through searing pain, a hundred sparks exploded in her vision as he pinned her back on the bed. 'Stupid! Stupid! Stupid!' he had rasped. Panting, he bound her wrists, before pressing a clear plastic mask over her face. Fear immobilised her limbs and scattered her thoughts. What would become of her now? Through muffled sobs she had inhaled, grateful for the darkness that overtook her, as the boat creaked and swayed beneath her weight.

Consciousness brought a renewed sense of danger. Had Purdy got away? It was a minor victory but a welcome one. She remembered the tiny bell on her collar tinkling as she ambled through the cage door. Hemmy had insisted on it, to warn the birds inhabiting their back garden. Also on her collar was a tiny silver tube containing her home address. A tiny spark of hope ignited within her. If nothing else, at least her pet was free to start again. She shuffled on the bed, the scent of her own sweat competing with the stench of urine still lingering in the air.

Sitting on the upturned bucket, her silent companion watched, the scalpel protruding from his gloved hands. Today he was dressed differently, baggy clothes further disguising his form. The black latex gas mask served the double purpose of keeping his identity secret and frightening Hemmy to the core.

She blinked, praying for an ounce of sympathy, anything that would keep her alive.

'Sorry,' she croaked, before clearing her throat. 'I just want to go home. Can you untie me? Please?'

Shaking his head, her kidnapper almost unbalanced himself as a sudden wave made the boat bob.

Hemmy narrowed her good eye. There was something clumsy about his movements. Something that told her he had not done this before. During her escape, he had been taken aback and, just before punching her, she noticed that he had stalled his fist mid-air. These were not the actions of a seasoned criminal. He was nervous. Yet she sensed impending danger just the same.

'I need the toilet,' she said, her voice growing stronger. 'Untie me. Please.'

Another raking breath as he looked from her to the blade. 'Hemmy disobeyed the rules. Purdy has gone. Now Hemmy's got to go.'

'What do you mean, I've got to go?' Hemmy said, her heartbeat picking up.

'Hemmy wouldn't listen,' he replied simply, in a dark tone.

'Please, let me go. I won't tell anyone.' Tears pricked Hermione's eyelids, stinging her bruised socket. 'I won't say a word.'

Rising from the bucket, her captor gripped the scalpel.

'Please don't hurt me,' Hemmy cried, hope evaporating as she yanked at her bindings. 'I won't say anything. Please.'

With a hint of longing, the kidnapper sighed through his mask, giving her one last glance before walking out the door. The sound of the bolt being pulled across brought a terrifying sense of finality. Boat timbers groaned, as if in warning. They were going to leave her here to rot. Overhead, footsteps creaked. With her good eye, she peered at the end of the bed. There was no sandwich, no drink. The bucket was left upside down. Even the wipes had not been replenished. Her time here had come to an end.

CHAPTER FORTY-NINE

'Cheers.' Amy raised her gin and tonic and chinked it against Paddy's pint. She hoped that a drink at The Ladbroke Arms would encourage him to open up. Just a stone's throw from the police station, on a quiet residential road, the cosy local was furnished with pretty swinging baskets and a traditional wooden bar. She used to meet her father here and, even now, she half expected him to walk in through the door. With some effort, she returned her focus to Paddy. She knew she was being hypocritical, expecting him to confide in her when her own personal life was off limits, but it felt good to spend time out of the station and it was a respite from what was going on at home.

'It's good to get out,' Amy said, voicing her thoughts. 'After the week I've had, I'm running on fumes.'

Paddy stared into his pint. His features creased, his inner struggle evident on his face.

Seconds passed as she waited for a response. 'Are things that tough at home?'

The depth of Paddy's sigh provided her with the answer. 'This needs to be a conversation as friends, not colleagues,' he said.

'Why, have you murdered someone?' Amy joked, toying with a beer mat.

'No, but . . . it's personal.'

'Is this you telling me where your bruises have come from? That burn on the back of your neck?'

Paddy nodded before knocking back a mouthful of beer.

Amy squeezed his arm, an uncharacteristic show of physical contact. 'Whatever's going on, we can sort this.'

His shoulders heavy, Paddy sipped his pint. 'I've dealt with victims of domestic abuse before. All these years, I've never put myself in the same category.'

'Lots of men are victims,' Amy said sadly. 'Far too many, in fact.'

Glasses clinked in the background as a group of revellers at the bar raised a toast. The atmosphere felt strangely cheery, at odds with their conversation. 'Up until now, I've always believed it was my fault,' Paddy said. 'You know I lost a daughter, don't you?'

Amy nodded.

'Geraldine . . . she blames me. The thing is, she has good reason to.' Paddy raised a hand as Amy opened her mouth to speak. 'If I hadn't bought her that bike . . .' He hung his head. 'Christ.' He exhaled. 'Of all the people, I never thought I'd tell you.'

'That's because you know I'll give it to you straight. I'll tell you what to do and insist that you do it.'

'I think that's what I need right now.' A faraway look crossed his face as he smoothed his penguin tie. 'You know, I wear these in her memory. She loved them, the sillier the better. She was such a sweet girl . . .' His eyes moistened, and he took a steadying sip of his drink. 'It's daft, but I still can't talk about her without welling up.'

'It's not daft when you've lost the centre of your world,' Amy said. 'As coppers, we're expected to get over things, push trauma aside. But we're not robots. Grief is a pain like no other, especially when you lose someone at such an early age.' Amy spoke with an authority that made

Paddy narrow his eyes. She caught his glance and responded with a cramped smile. That would have to be a conversation for later.

'It happened on a summer evening,' Paddy said, staring into his pint. 'It was nine o'clock but still bright. I'd taken the stabilisers off Suzy's bike and she begged me to bring her down the road before bed. She'd been waiting all day. The missus . . . she hated the outdoors, even then. She said it was too late and we should wait until tomorrow . . . If only I'd listened.' Pausing, he cleared his throat. 'I promised Geraldine I'd make Suzy ride on the path and wear her protective gear.'

Behind them, a burst of laughter erupted from the group at the bar. Paddy didn't notice. His thoughts were in the past.

'I remember her giggling as she cycled ahead of me, the roads slippery from the rain. She kept pedalling faster and I shouted at her to slow down. But then she came to a bend and I couldn't see her anymore.' His eyes filled with tears, he inhaled a shuddering breath. 'I called her . . . God I wish I hadn't called her . . .'

'Keep going,' Amy said firmly. As painful as it was, she knew he needed to finish it. To allow the pain an outlet.

'She looked around, came off the pavement in front of an oncoming car. The driver had been drinking, a family dinner apparently . . . didn't realise how much they'd had.' Paddy closed his eyes as the memory came into view. 'It flipped her up in the air like a rag doll. And when she hit the ground she was dead.'

'You're nearly there. Keep going,' Amy said softly, her glass growing warm as she cupped it in her hand.

Paddy nodded, his chin trembling from the effort of swallowing back his tears. 'Geraldine blamed me for everything. She was right, of course, it *was* all my fault. The driver served time. She had kids of her own. So many lives ruined because of my stupidity. It ended our marriage.'

'But you stayed together?'

A crooked smile was offered. 'I couldn't leave. Geraldine's agora-phobia worsened, leaving her permanently trapped inside. All we did was argue. When I stopped listening she turned to violence to get my attention.' Paddy lifted the pint glass to his lips and drained the last of his drink. 'She said she'd kill herself if I tried to leave. So, we came to an agreement. I'd flat share with a colleague near work and go home a couple of days a week. But each time I went back, things got worse.'

Amy raised her eyebrows as she waited for an explanation. Paddy was putting her in a difficult situation. By providing her with details of physical assaults, she was duty bound to look into it.

'I won't go into detail,' Paddy said, as if reading her thoughts. 'Criminalising her won't help.'

'How many bruises do we justify because we love the person dol-ing them out?' Amy said, her voice low. It was something she'd heard a victim once say. Someone who had learned to be strong.

'I became very good at hiding it.' Paddy took a deep breath. 'The thing is . . . I've met someone else. She's kind, caring . . .'

'Not another copper?' Amy frowned, trying to work out who it could be.

'No . . . not at all. Her name's Elaine. She's a nurse in a private hospital not far from here.'

'Been offering you a bit of TLC, has she?' It was good to lighten the mood, if only for a second or two.

'Get your mind out of the gutter, Winter.' Paddy's smile lingered on his lips before fading away. 'It's time to divorce Geraldine. But what right do I have to start again?'

'Come on now, Paddy, this isn't your fault.' Amy paused to sip her gin. 'Is this what Suzy would want? For you to be battered, beaten and burnt?'

Paddy shook his head.

'You know how this is going to end if you stay. Escalating violence has only one way to go.' Pushing her empty glass aside, Amy picked up her bag from the floor. Flipping it open, she pulled out a notepad and pen.

'Please tell me you're not making a to-do list,' Paddy replied.

'Don't knock it till you've tried it,' Amy said, knowing Paddy's impulsive nature shied from order. She flipped the notebook to a new page. 'Right, number one. We need to fill out a report of domestic abuse. Don't worry,' she added in response to Paddy's dismayed expression. 'We'll keep it sensitive so it won't show up on the system. That way, if Geraldine makes a counter allegation, then you've got there first. I want you to speak to an IDVA. Take advantage of any counselling offered. It won't come back to us, but at least a record has been made.' The Independent Domestic Violence Advocators worked separately from the police and supported high-risk victims of such abuse.

'I've told you before. No arrests.'

'There won't be, not unless you list specific assaults with the police. But then you already know that.' She raised her eyes from the notepad. 'Agree?'

Grimacing, Paddy nodded. His pint glass stood empty, but Amy did not want to break momentum by ordering another round. 'Good.' She ticked the box she had created beside number one. 'One down, two to go. I want you to pack a bag or have someone pack it for you and leave without fanfare. Tell her you're going to a conference if you want, but don't allow things to escalate.'

Paddy released an exasperated sigh. 'I'll tell her face-to-face. There's no way I can end my marriage by text or over the phone.'

'Sounds to me like your marriage ended a long time ago,' Amy murmured. She hated domestic violence. There was no justification for hurting the person you claimed to love. Her short stint on the unit a few years previously left her permanently frustrated in her role. She poised her pen over the page, waiting to tick the next box. 'I'll assign a uniformed officer to come with you and prevent a breach of the peace. We'll use a male officer. We don't want her getting any ideas that there's something going on. If you've been seeing someone else, it may well have crossed her mind.'

'I know,' Paddy said. 'But I don't want this going all around the station.'

'It won't,' Amy replied, her words firm. 'Especially not if it comes from me. It'll be a brave officer who goes against my wishes.'

Paddy grinned. 'That much we agree on.'

'Good. Then that's another box ticked.' Amy smiled in satisfaction. 'Right,' she said, circling number three. 'Aftercare. We'll sort you out with an IDVA . . .'

'Do I have to?' Paddy replied.

'Non-negotiable.' Amy gave him a hard stare. 'We've ticked the box, there's no backing out now.' She returned her attention to the pad and scribbled. 'Number three is for Geraldine. We can't leave her in such a state. You'll have to arrange for support.'

'Believe me I've tried. She refused victim support after Suzy died. She's thrown away all the leaflets I brought home. She won't see her doctor either.'

'Then you'll have to get her family involved.'

'They're estranged. I think it's half the reason she suffers from anxiety. They wouldn't even come to Suzy's funeral. I can't see them getting involved now.'

Amy tapped her pen against her bottom lip. 'I take it she's not working? Doesn't have any friends or work colleagues.'

'She doesn't leave the house . . . at least, she didn't,' Paddy said. 'And she's got no friends apart from her online ones.'

'Then family it is,' Amy said, writing the words on her list. 'There must be one family member she can talk to. A sibling? Cousin? Parent?'

'I have her sister's number but they've not spoken in years.'

'Then you'll have to bite the bullet. Don't look at me like that, you've been sniffing around someone else, remember? You can't just wash your hands of her. Agreed? I've got to hear you say it, a nod doesn't count.'

'Agreed,' Paddy replied.

Amy ticked the box she had created beside the third point. 'See? Don't you feel a sense of accomplishment now we've written it all down?'

'I suppose so,' Paddy said begrudgingly, staring at the notebook. He *did* feel lighter.

'Good.' Amy scribbled the word 'deadline' next to a date on the page. 'I'm giving you one week to sort this out. And if you don't, I'll be visiting her myself. Officially this time.'

'You're not serious.'

'Does a duck have a watertight bum?'

'There's more to you than meets the eye, isn't there?' Paddy chuckled, a bemused smile on his face. 'Just when I think I've got you all figured out, I see another side.'

'You don't know the half of it,' Amy said in total honesty.

She'd meant to put a smile on Paddy's face, but his response had made her pause. If she could help Paddy, then she could sort her own life out. It was why she found herself making another list after he left. Her number one task was to negate Lillian's claims that Robert had set her up. Unable to find anything in the case files, she knew where she had to go. Into the dusty recesses of her parents' loft.

CHAPTER FIFTY

Perching on the edge of the open loft hatch, Amy wished for the hundredth time that her father was still alive. She masked a yawn with the back of her hand. It was almost two in the morning, and she should be tucked up in bed.

She peered down the length of the gloomy space. The cobwebs hanging from the low beams had kept her away until now. Tonight, a couple of gin and tonics had provided some Dutch courage. Things would be so much easier if Robert were here. She closed her eyes briefly, recalling his face. But his expression was uneasy, pained. Was her subconscious trying to prepare her for what was to come?

Shoulders hunched, she edged into the loft space, squeaking as the top of her hair brushed against the beams. Pausing, she swept away imaginary spiders, telling herself to calm down. Her heart was hammering now, her armpits sticky as the stifling heat beaded her forehead with sweat. She was looking for old diaries or paperwork, anything that could harbour a clue. Like her, Robert was not allowed to bring home case files from work, but he had kept a journal. Could he have made notes?

Her iPhone torch held mid-air, she sorted through boxes of old blankets, unwanted curtains . . . stumbling upon a stack of old newspapers that made her heart stall. Brushing off the dust, she unfolded the first yellowed paper. Peering at the faded print, she found the date she had been looking for: 29th October 1987. The Beasts of Brentwood headlines screamed from the front cover of the newspaper and she shuddered at what felt like icy fingertips caressing the nape of her neck; it was a breeze filtering through the roof, it had to be. Just the same, she needed to get out. Bowing her head, she dragged the box to the loft hatch, searching the ceiling for spiders as she went. After another quick look around the loft, she found a second box with 'Poppy' written in black marker on the outside flap. Balancing the first one against her chest she carefully slid down the set of steps before going back up and retrieving the second.

As she descended, a figure stood watching in the doorway, making her start.

'Mum, you frightened the life out of me.' Amy exhaled. Flora's long white nightdress and dressing gown had done little to ease Amy's frayed nerves.

'Dotty woke me,' she said, her eyes on the box in Amy's arms. 'What are you doing up there?'

'Snitch,' Amy said, as her beloved pet sauntered over to her, tongue lolling to one side. 'I'm just going through some stuff.'

'Bring it into the living room, dear,' Flora said. 'I've made you a hot chocolate.'

Amy had wanted to do this on her own, but she did not have the heart to send her mother away. Gratefully, she took the mug, declining the offer of shortbread, which was placed on the coffee table next to the box on the floor. Silently, she opened the box labelled 'Poppy', picking through the clothing it contained. She held a white-collared red dress to the light. Musty air emanated from the fabric that had been placed there decades ago.

'You loved that dress,' Flora said quietly. 'The social worker said you refused to leave without it, even though it was too big for you. But you never wore it. We couldn't understand why you kept it so close but wouldn't put it on.'

'It was Sally-Ann's,' Amy said, a deep-rooted sadness touching her words. 'I thought if I kept it safe, she might come back for it one day. Silly really.'

'I'm sorry,' Flora said, her face ashen. Flora had been protected from the ugly side of life. Encountering the Grimes family and their misdemeanours had been a shock to her system, to say the least.

'You've nothing to be sorry for. I know how hard it must have been when I came to live here.' Amy lowered the dress to her lap. 'I'm starting to remember. I didn't make it easy for you.'

Flora smiled. 'Don't let the past change who you are today.'

Amy turned back to the box, lifting each item out and placing it on the coffee table. A Cabbage Patch doll stared at her with blank, soulless eyes. Tentatively, she plucked it from the box, touching the yellow woollen hair.

'You slept with that doll for six months before you decided you didn't need it anymore,' Flora said, observing her movements. 'One day I found it hidden in the bottom of the dirty linen basket. We knew that was a turning point because you didn't want to be reminded of it. I put it away, and you never asked for it again.'

Amy nodded, another memory sloping across her consciousness. 'I felt like she was judging me, all nicely tucked up in bed while Sally-Ann lay buried in the ground.' She swallowed, unable to believe she had uttered the words aloud. Despite all the councellors she had spoken to as a child, she had never disclosed her guilt. 'But it wasn't this doll, it was a Raggedy-Ann.'

'Raggedy-Ann?' Flora echoed her words. 'I'm afraid not, love. This is the only doll you had. It was so sad, you used to call her . . .'

'. . . Sally-Ann,' Amy whispered. How could this be? The memory that was once lucid, felt like it was breaking away. 'It can't be.' Pulling up the doll's dress, Amy searched for the embroidered love heart that was only found on a Raggedy-Ann. But instead, drawn in pen was a hastily scribbled heart. She frowned, closing her eyes as she tried to recall the memory: Sally-Ann drawing the heart and getting red ink on her fingers. Smiling as she turned to show Poppy, because now she was a 'living doll'.

'Are you all right, love?' Flora's words dragged her from the recesses of her memory.

'Fine. I'm . . . fine. I remembered differently. I suppose it's to be . . . expected.' Her words faltered as she straddled past and present. If she was wrong about the doll, what else had she misremembered? False memory was commonplace when dealing with victims of crime. Three witnesses could see the same person and describe them in completely different ways. But not her, she had been staunch in her convictions. But what if she was wrong?

She turned back to the box, making an effort to hide her shock. All that was left was notebooks, schoolbooks, reading manuals and diaries. Amy refilled the container, gently placing her doll on top. Reaching for the second box, she paused as she absorbed Flora's expression.

She looked as if she had seen a ghost. 'Darling . . . haven't you had enough for one night? It's almost three in the morning.' Flora touched her hand. 'Why don't you leave this for now, eh? We can go through it tomorrow when you get back from work.'

Amy frowned. 'What is it, mum? What are you hiding?' Only now was she confident enough to challenge her. She had not imagined the phone call she had overheard. The same fear had been in Flora's voice then, when she had spoken about being scared that 'she' would find out. But it was Flora's turn to be quiet now, and she dropped her gaze to the floor.

Silently, Amy transferred the newspapers and clippings from the second box to the coffee table. These would not help with what she needed to know. She drew her attention to a thick red file, inhaling the scent of musty paperwork as she pulled back the lid. Lying on top were photocopies of crime reports – the same paperwork that Essex Police had furnished her with. She flicked through copies of autopsy reports, maps of the house she had once lived in, burial sites and more. Why had he kept it? He had been taking a risk, bringing it back here. From the corner of her eye, she watched Flora pick up her cup, a slight tremble in her hands.

'What's this?' Amy said, lifting out the last item. The label on the side of the box suggested it housed a pair of size eleven boots, but judging by her mother's reaction, there was something far more interesting inside. Flora shifted in her chair, still silent.

It's time to bite the bullet. Amy pulled back the lid, her mouth dropping open at what she found inside.

CHAPTER FIFTY-ONE

'I was wondering, would you mind if I got a cat?' Elaine breathed a sigh of contentment, snuggling in the crook of Paddy's arm. 'It would be nice to have some company when you're not here.'

As they lay in bed, Paddy enjoyed the sensation of Elaine's head resting on his bare chest. His conversation with Amy had drained him emotionally, and sex with Elaine had put the world to rights again. For now, everything was back as it should be.

'What's put that into your head?' he said, not averse to the idea. After confiding in Amy, he was so grateful just to have Elaine in his life. She had worked hard to make their home perfect. He gazed at the ceiling as he counted his blessings, the room glowing from the fairy lights hung over their bed.

Elaine's fingers crept to his chest, tracing circles on his skin. 'I heard they found Hermione's cat. It must be of some comfort to her mother, now she's back.'

'What?' He nudged back his head to look her in the eye. 'How do you know that? It's meant to be confidential.'

'Don't be cross.' Elaine smiled, knowing he was anything but. 'One of the girls in the hospital told me. Her mum runs the shelter where the cat was handed in. She said they had this really odd chap from the police turn up. He was wearing a dicky bow . . .'

'Malcolm.' Paddy sighed.

'Yes, well he caused quite a stir. Asked to be left alone with the cat in one of the kennels. First, he started crawling around beside her, then he started sniffing her fur. They could see him on CCTV.'

The thought of Malcolm on all fours incited a chuckle from Paddy's lips. 'He's a crime scene officer, and believe me, that's not the most unusual thing he's done.'

'The mind boggles,' Elaine replied. 'Have you had any news on the case?'

Paddy gave her the look which conveyed she should know better than to ask. But Hermione Parker haunted his thoughts, too. Such a beautiful young girl, with long, blonde hair just like Suzy's had been. She would have been the same age as Hermione, had she been alive today. He blinked, focusing on their conversation. It would not do to have details of the case leaked. 'Do me a favour, love, ask your friend to keep things quiet. Out of respect for the family if nothing else. You know what social media's like.'

'I'll try, but she does love a gossip. Anyway, about that cat. I was thinking, we could try the shelter ourselves. She said they've got plenty looking for new homes.'

'Sounds like a plan,' Paddy said, kissing the top of her head. 'As long as I don't have to clean up its poop.'

'You don't need to worry,' she said with a wry grin. 'Its farts will probably smell of roses, like yours.'

'Good.' Paddy smiled. 'Our new pet will fit right in. Besides . . .' He took a breath, composing his words. 'You'll be seeing a lot more of me soon.'

'Really? Are you knocking all those courses on the head?'

'Pretty much,' Paddy lied. Another pang of guilt. There was a fourth tick box that needed to be added to Amy's list. Tell Elaine. The thought brought a frisson of worry. He had lied to her for so long. 'I love you,' he blurted, needing to hear her reciprocate.

'Mmm? Sorry, love, I was almost asleep there.' She yawned, cupping her hand as she moved away to plump her pillow. 'Look at the time, it's gone midnight.'

'Do you?' Paddy asked, hating the insecurity in his voice.

'Do I what?' Elaine replied, her gaze dreamy as she lay on her pillow.

'Love me, too.'

'Of course I do, you daft thing. What's brought this on?'

'Nothing. I just needed to hear you say it. Elaine . . .'

'Yes?'

'We'll always be together, won't we? No matter what.'

'Of course we will. I told you, I love you. And when you love someone you never let them go.'

CHAPTER FIFTY-TWO

'I don't believe it.' On the coffee table, faded graph paper featured hand-drawn outlines of where Lillian and Jack Grimes's victims' bodies had been found. But it was not the wild meanderings and scribbled notes that stole Amy's breath, it was the items housed in the shoebox. The contents of this box had nothing to do with her – but they had everything to do with Lillian Grimes.

'What is it?' Flora asked, peering over her shoulder. Despite her shock, Amy had the presence of mind to use a pen and not her fingers to poke the contents around. She recognised the hairbrush instantly. It had provoked much amusement between Jack and Lillian; at the time she had not been able to work out why. Seeing its phallic handle now, she understood. A bright-red toothbrush was housed in a clear plastic bag, a handful of woollen fibres in another. They were also red, the same colour as the cardigan Lillian had been wearing when the bodies were found. Her passion for the colour was reflected in her lipstick, nail varnish, shoes and clothes. Even the walls of her bedroom had been candy-apple red. Amy frowned as she recalled details of the investigation that she had read about. Fibres from Lillian's clothes had been found on the bodies later recovered. Back in 1987, DNA testing was a new tool in police forces across the UK. It had been these fibres, along with hairs and an earring, which had proven instrumental in charging Lillian with the crimes. 'It's from the crime scene,' Amy said, her voice breaking. She cleared her throat as she turned to Flora. 'Did you know about this?'

'Of course not,' she said, her glance furtive.

Amy was not convinced. 'It's plans to plant evidence. Enough to put Lillian Grimes away for good.' Saying it aloud made her sick to the core. Had Lillian been telling the truth all along?

Amy sealed the box shut, resting her arms on top of it as emotional and physical exhaustion rushed in. 'Tell me straight, Mum. Is this Dad's?'

Flora paled. 'Those boxes have been up there for years. I don't remember how that one got there.'

'Why keep this stuff? Why not destroy it after she was jailed?' She turned to Flora, eyes narrowed. 'Are you sure you weren't in on this?' She knew how ludicrous it sounded but had to ask just the same.

'How can I be in on something when I don't even know what it is!' Flora's voice raised an octave, her fists clenched.

Dotty snuffled, her head resting on Amy's feet as she was awoken from her sleep. Absentmindedly, Amy reached down to comfort her, stroking her head. Dotty had been a present from her father, someone to keep her company at night. His kindness came in many forms, and he had touched the heart of almost everyone he met. She could not equate such a compassionate man with someone so readily capable of breaking the law. But how could she not when the evidence was staring her in the face?

She turned to face Flora. 'The jury convicted Lillian because of forensic evidence and information leaked to the press. Without forensics, the evidence would have been circumstantial, she could have been set free.'

'I . . . I don't know how it got there,' Flora said, twiddling with the belt on her dressing gown.

Amy set the box on the table, her expression grim. 'I wish Dad were here to explain this mess.'

'It's that Lillian,' Flora said. 'She's twisting everything, just like I said she would.'

'I don't like her any more than you do, but if she's been set up for those murders . . .' Amy could barely contemplate what she was about to say.

'See?' Flora snapped. 'She does that – reels you in. Before you know it, you're believing everything she says. That woman is a monster, and if she's set free, she'll kill again.'

Amy shook her head. 'She's a great-grandmother who's spent half her life in prison. I can't be a party to this.'

'Surely you're not serious?' Flora said, grabbing her by the hand and squeezing hard. 'Your father was a good man. If you go to the police, you'll ruin his reputation.'

'I *am* the police,' Amy said, pulling back her hand. But Flora dug her nails in further, her eyes wide with conviction as she spoke.

'And how do you think that came to be? Would you have got anywhere if they knew who you really were?'

'I can't believe you said that,' Amy replied, a chilling smile on her lips. It was an expression she wore in the tensest of circumstances and often misconstrued by those she did not know.

Flora released her grip. 'Sorry. I didn't mean it. Please, Amy, I didn't mean what I said.'

'You meant it all right,' Amy said, gathering the shoebox under her arm. 'But don't worry, I'm not going to stab you in your sleep.'

'Where are you going?' Flora said, panic lacing her words.

Amy paused at the door. 'To my room. I need to work out how to break this to my DCI.'

CHAPTER FIFTY-THREE

Amy pulled the loose thread hanging from her cuff. She had picked up the shirt from the dry cleaners, along with four identical ones the day before. She alternated the crisp white shirts with occasional bursts of colour to break the monotony. She was holding the shoebox under her arm: she would need it for what lay ahead. Today The Keepers of Truth Twitter feed simply said: #FindHermione #TwoDays #TickTock. The presence of a clock ticking downwards added a heightened sense of urgency to her tasks.

After raking through previous intel on them, she found they rarely carried out their threats. Yet their vagueness made her uneasy. Were they trying to avoid arrest or were they leading her up the garden path? She raised her knuckle to her DCI's office door, delivering a gentle knock.

'Thanks for seeing me at such short notice,' she said, having rung ahead. Rising at six, she had showered and crept out long before her mother had awoken. Flora's words about her being promoted had bitten deep, but it was not as distressing as the possibility of her father being involved in setting Lillian up. She was in way over her head. It was time to come clean. Taking a seat, she rested the box on her lap as she faced DCI Pike.

'You're more than welcome,' Pike replied, her eyes flicking to the shoebox on her lap. 'Fancy the gym tomorrow? I've been a bit slack this week.'

'Sure,' Amy said, feeling breathless as she prepared to confess. What she was about to say would change everything. How would her colleagues react? If she were to preach about honesty, she would have to start with herself. She took a deep breath. Her intestines felt twisted in knots. 'I'm afraid I haven't been totally honest with you.'

A flicker of concern crossed Pike's face. 'Go on.'

'I should have come to you straight away.' Reaching into her jacket pocket, Amy pulled out the letter that had started it all. She pushed it across the desk by means of explanation.

Pike's eyes moved from left to right as she read Lillian's writing. She paused, her lips parting as she inhaled suddenly. Amy knew exactly which bit she was reading because she knew the words off by heart. *I am your birth mother. The person who gave you life.*

After what felt like a lifetime, Pike returned her gaze to Amy. Her features had tightened, and she looked far from amused. 'Is this some kind of joke?'

'No ma'am, it's not,' Amy replied, shrinking in her seat. 'I was adopted. Jack and Lillian Grimes are my biological parents.'

Returning the letter, Pike held her with a gaze. Amy refused to look away. 'Is this why she told you about the bodies? The real reason she wanted to see you in private?'

Amy nodded.

'Then why didn't you come to me the second you found out?'

Amy folded the letter before sliding it back into her pocket. 'I was shocked, ashamed . . . in denial,' she said truthfully. 'Everyone was so pleased about finding the burial sites. I didn't want to ruin it. Then the longer I left it, the harder it became. I couldn't bear for my colleagues to associate me with those people. I'm nothing like them.'

'I can't believe Robert didn't tell me,' Pike said, leaning on her elbows as she clasped her hands together.

Amy's features creased in a frown. If she didn't know better, she would think that Pike was hurt. What business was it of hers? Her gaze fell on the shoebox sitting on Pike's desk waiting to be opened. But Pike's eyes were still firmly fixed on Amy, gluing her to her chair. Things were about to get a whole lot worse.

'I'm afraid that's not all.' Slipping a pair of latex gloves from her pocket, Amy pulled one on before opening the lid of the box. 'You might want to wear this,' she said, resting the other glove on the desk as she nodded towards the box. 'I found this in the loft at home. It's evidence crucial to Lillian Grimes's case.'

'Evidence?' Pike said, making little movement. 'What sort of evidence?'

It felt as if all the air had been sucked out of the office. Amy inhaled a breath to deliver the next revelation. 'Lillian claims she's been set up. In exchange for helping prove her innocence, she's promised to give me something in return.'

'Hang on,' Pike replied, her mouth downturned. 'You're saying you've found evidence in your parents' loft?'

'Lillian believes DNA evidence was planted to send her down.' The words sent a chill down Amy's spine. How different everything would have been had Lillian been freed. As awful as it sounded, her life now was far better than the alternative.

'And this is the evidence?' Pike pointed towards the box. In its bright-red covering, it felt like a bomb about to explode. She had yet to look inside, which seemed bizarre.

'Mum swears she has no knowledge of it, which means Dad must have been involved.' Amy's forehead creased. 'There are copies of case files, notes . . . I don't want to believe it, but how else did it get in our loft?'

'You're suggesting that Robert Winter planted this evidence to incarcerate Lillian Grimes?'

Amy nodded, feeling as if she was on trial. Suddenly everything felt formal, their friendship evaporating into thin air.

'Do you know what would happen if this came out?'

Amy looked from the box back to her senior officer, confusion crossing her face. Surely it was a matter of when not if? 'I don't understand. This is evidence . . .'

'Evidence that would ruin your father's reputation.' Pike leaned across the table and fixed Amy with a glare. 'Robert was a good man. I, for one, don't believe he was capable of such a thing. It's a terrible shame that you don't afford him the same loyalty.'

'But we can't just say nothing. Lillian knows she's been framed . . .'

'When did we start dealing with terrorists? Because that's what this woman is: a person capable of inflicting terror on innocent women and children. I know she's your mother, but have you any idea what she's done?'

'She's not my mother.' Amy's voice raised an octave. 'She disgusts me.' In the corridor, her superintendent's voice carried loudly as he chatted on the phone. Amy took a calming breath as she reminded herself where she was. Pike's floor housed only senior officers – many of whom knew her father.

'Have you told anyone else?' Pike said, waiting until he had passed.

'Only my mother.'

'You mean Flora? I take it she's not keen to drag Robert's good name through the mud?'

'No,' Amy said, feeling as if she had been punched in the gut.

'Then you need to decide where your loyalties lie. If you've any sense, you'll put this back where you found it and forget we ever had this conversation.' A pause. 'Don't look at me like that. I'm not suggesting you conceal evidence, I'm telling you you're wrong.'

'How can you be so sure?' Amy said, nodding towards the shoebox. 'You've not even looked.'

'I don't need to,' Pike replied, her eyes alight with conviction. 'I knew Robert. He was a good man who made many sacrifices to keep you in a happy and secure home. More than you can imagine. He . . . he . . .' She dropped her gaze, her eyes filling with tears. As her DCI's emotions were laid bare, Amy was hit by the truth.

'Oh my god,' she said, her hand raised to her mouth. 'You loved him, didn't you?' Amy remembered a period in her father's life when Pike was constantly demanding his attention. Then there was the time he had told her off for calling him at home. Working out of the same station, they were bound to be in close contact, but their friendship went way beyond that. Why hadn't she picked up on it before?

'Now you listen to me.' Pike jabbed the air with her forefinger. 'Go home, put that box where you found it, and we won't say another word.'

'She's promised me Hermione Parker's location if I clear her name.'

'Clear Lillian Grimes?' Pike barked a harsh laugh. 'Don't be so stupid. You've got more chance of making her Pope.'

Amy shook her head in disbelief. 'All those questions you asked me about my family life. You were pumping me for information all along.' Amy rose, snatching the box from her desk. 'Don't worry, I won't say anything about you and Dad. I've had enough revelations to last me a lifetime.'

Pike stood, her knuckles white as she rested them on her desk. Her response told Amy she was crossing the line. 'Go home. Put the box back. We'll discuss Hermione when you've calmed down.'

Like hell, Amy thought. Scooping the box under her arm she turned and strode out the door.

CHAPTER FIFTY-FOUR

'All right, all right, keep your hair on!' Dougie's voice rose from behind the front door. He was slightly out of breath as he opened it, no doubt from the exertion of manoeuvring his wheelchair at such a pace.

'Sorry,' Amy said, looking forlorn. 'I need to talk, and I don't know where else to go.' She clung to the red shoebox as if it contained untold wealth instead of the secrets and lies held within.

Dougie's eyes fell on the box and back to Amy. Without wasting another moment, he invited her inside. Regardless of the early hour he was freshly shaved and wearing clean pressed clothes. Amy had never seen him any other way.

'Sit down. Can I get you a drink?' Dougie said, positioning his wheelchair next to the sofa where Amy usually sat. Picking up the remote, he muted the breakfast TV that was on.

'No thanks,' Amy replied. 'It's a flying visit. I've got to get back to work.'

'You're shaking.' Dougie's eyebrows knotted in concern. 'What's wrong?'

'I don't know where to start.' Holding the box on her lap, she tried to regain her composure. She knew she could not go home and hide the evidence away. Her DCI was wrong. She took a deep breath as she tried to explain. 'I should have known I couldn't just walk away from Lillian. She has something else up her sleeve.'

'That woman always does.' Dougie's words were carried on a sigh. 'I take it she's upset you?'

'Indirectly. She claims she's innocent . . . I believe her.'

'You mustn't,' Dougie said. 'She's no stranger to twisting the truth.'

'Neither is my dad, so it seems,' Amy replied listlessly. She rested the box on the coffee table before them. Like Pike, Dougie seemed reluctant to touch it.

'I found this in the loft.' She tipped her head towards the box. Seconds passed, but Dougie did not speak. Slowly, Amy lifted the lid and moved it forward in his direction.

Dougie peered inside before sitting back in his chair. 'What is it?'

'Evidence Lillian Grimes was set up for murder. She was telling the truth.'

'And you think your father was involved? Robert would never do that.' Dougie's words were firm.

'That's what DCI Pike said,' Amy replied. 'I'd be inclined to believe her if I hadn't found it in our loft.'

'You went to Pike with this?'

Amy nodded. 'She wouldn't look in the box, never mind acknowledge what I said. Did you know she had an affair with my dad?'

Dougie sighed heavily. 'Oh, Amy, it's not what you think.'

'Does everyone at the station know?' She felt sick at the thought.

'Not at all. It happened just once, and he regretted it straight away. It was Pike that kept pushing for more. She was obsessed. Wouldn't leave him alone.'

'And here was me thinking I earned my promotion.' Amy laughed without humour as her world tumbled down. 'She told me to get rid of the evidence, can you believe that? I loved my father, he was good to me. But I need to get to the bottom of this.' Amy stared at her feet as she turned things over in her mind. 'I don't get why he held on to it though, Dad would never have . . .' She trailed off as a piece of the puzzle fell into place. 'Unless it was someone else.' The overheard phone call. Her mother stressing over a secret. *What if she finds it?* She glanced at Dougie's feet. They were several sizes bigger than her father's size seven. Her gaze flickered to the side of the shoebox with its size eleven label before meeting Dougie's eyes.

'It wasn't your dad that planted the evidence . . .' He looked at her longingly, as if sensing her judgement. She knew exactly how he felt.

'Oh, Dougie,' Amy said, because she had worked it out for herself. 'What have you done?'

'This house is so much smaller than my last one.' He glanced up at the ceiling, as if invoking old memories. 'After I moved in, your dad offered to store some of my stuff in his loft. Just bric-a-brac mainly, sentimental stuff I couldn't bear to throw away.'

Amy could imagine it. Another example of her father's kindness towards an old friend. 'Weren't you afraid he'd find the shoebox?'

'I was counting on it,' Dougie said. 'I didn't have the courage to tell him straight out. But my guilt was mounting. I left it in the lap of the gods.'

'Why hold onto it all these years?'

'Because I knew deep down I was wrong,' Dougie said wearily. 'I waited, and nothing happened. Then one day Flora called. I thought she was ready to blow the whistle, but she came to thank me instead.'

'She kept your secret,' Amy replied.

'Yes, and I'd do it again if I had to. I'd bet anything Lillian encouraged Jack to rape those girls.' His face soured at the thought. 'She's monstrous, grotesque. She deserves the electric chair.'

'How did you do it?' Amy said, steering him from his anger.

'I didn't expect to get away with it at first.' Dougie shifted in his chair. 'It wasn't even that hard. I snagged a few threads from her cardigan when I was at the house for the search. Things were different then, we weren't as conscientious about forensics and cross-contamination for a start. Then I found a hairbrush in her bedroom and took some of her jewellery. I planted bits of evidence in the burial sites. When I got home, I made notes.'

'And you leaked the story to the press?'

'People needed to know what kind of monsters they were.'

'Couldn't you have trusted the justice system?'

Dougie tutted under his breath. 'Where was justice when those poor girls were being raped and tortured? Do you really want me to tell you what they did?'

Amy shook her head. She had skimmed the finer details in the case files, unwilling to take it in. On the television, a muted presenter was discussing autumn wear. How simple some people's lives were, Amy thought, when all they had to worry about was whether to wear green or brown. 'Lillian promised to tell me where Hermione Parker is if I help her with an appeal. I'll go back to Pike, insist that she listen. There must be a way around this, without any more people getting hurt.'

Dougie smiled, placing his hand on Amy's. His skin was warm and comforting to the touch. 'I knew the truth would come out in the end. I'm glad it's come from you.' Reaching forward, he took the box from the coffee table. 'I'll hand myself in today. You don't need to be involved.'

'What if you end up in prison?' Amy sighed. 'I can't let you do that.'

'It's for the best.' He looked her in the eye, his expression resolute. 'I'll call them after lunch, tell them I've had the box all along.'

'After lunch?' Amy said, wondering why the delay.

'I've got a nice steak in the fridge waiting to be cooked. I'm going to have a bath and change into my best suit. When I leave this place, I'll do it with grace. All I ask is that you promise to keep out of it. Don't risk your career for me.'

'I can come with you if you like, ease the wheels,' Amy said, feeling a pang of sadness for her father's old friend. 'That's if you're sure . . .'

'Promise me,' Dougie said, his words firm.

Amy nodded. *Was he doing the right thing?* She looked at Dougie, helpless in his wheelchair. But Lillian had kept her word so far. Coming forward with the evidence could save Hermione's life.

'This will be all sorted by this evening. You can call Lillian Grimes and she can get her appeal underway,' Dougie said.

Amy opened her mouth to protest, to say none of this was for Lillian Grimes. But he raised his finger to silence her. He already knew.

CHAPTER FIFTY-FIVE

'I wish you'd told me you were coming,' Geraldine said, meeting Paddy in the hall. 'I would have made you breakfast. Have you got time off work? I've got eggs. I could make pancakes . . .'

'Stop. Just . . . stop.' Paddy raised his palms in the air. 'We need to talk.' He sniffed the air, inhaling the harsh smell of bleach. It appeared she had been cleaning. She had been lying about her inability to leave the house. Had she sensed he was planning something? Was that what all the cleaning was about?

'We can talk over breakfast,' Geraldine insisted, tightening her dressing gown as she searched his face. 'Why are you standing there? What's wrong?'

But Paddy shook his head. The kitchen was filled with implements that could easily be used against him – potentially end his life. 'I'm sorry love. I can't do this anymore.' He sighed wearily.

'Do what? Come home to a clean house and have your wife make you breakfast? I'm sorry, am I going to too much trouble for you?'

And there it was: the acidic tone. She could only be nice for so long before the timer kicked in. He could almost hear it, beneath the surface. *Tick, tick, tick* . . . an unexploded bomb waiting to detonate.

It made what he had to say a whole lot easier. Taking a deep breath, he prepared to voice the words he had rehearsed for so long. 'I'm leaving you. I want a divorce.'

Raising her hands to her ears, Geraldine simultaneously shook her head. 'No. I don't want to hear it.' A pause. Abruptly she nodded as if responding to her thoughts. 'Pancakes, that's what I'll make. With maple syrup and blueberries. I have some nice filter coffee and . . .'

'I could have just texted you,' Paddy interrupted, turning towards the stairs. 'God knows it would have been safer. I'm in more danger with you than the people I deal with in work.'

'All couples argue . . .' Geraldine's slippered feet slapped against the wooden stairs as she followed him up to his bedroom. 'This is your fault, not mine!'

'My fault?' Paddy said incredulously. Pulling his suit from the wardrobe, he laid it on the bed. It was the one he wore to Suzy's funeral – too precious to be chopped into pieces by his angry wife. Reaching onto the top shelf, he slid out the box containing his old ties. They were his last link to his daughter, apart from the memories he had stored away. Beneath the ties was a packet of printed photographs. Geraldine had burned every one she could find after Suzy died. It had been done to provoke him, to inflict as much pain as possible. It had worked. He had wanted to hurt her that night. To repay her for every harsh word, every cut and every bruise. His self-control was only kept intact because of the pack of photos kept in a cupboard she had forgotten to search. Such bitter memories rolled over in his brain as he grabbed the last of his belongings. Standing in the doorway, Geraldine watched his every move.

He had vowed to leave without argument, but his words came, low and rumbling just the same. 'At first I thought I deserved it. That it was *my* fault Suzy died. But I loved her . . .' He swallowed, determined to finish. 'Loved her more than anything in the world.' He looked pointedly at his wife. 'I thought it might work with us seeing less of each other, but it's actually got worse. It's like you store it all up for when I come home.' Grabbing his belongings, he turned towards the door. 'You're going to end up killing me if we carry on like this.'

'Boo hoo, poor you,' Geraldine said, blocking his exit. 'Dread coming home, do you? You pathetic, feeble excuse for a man.' Her words were punctuated with spittle that caught Paddy on the face. 'You can shrug off the blame all you like. It's your fault Suzy's dead.'

Paddy tried not to take the bait. He had already spoken to an IDVA, who was on her way over right now.

Gesticulating wildly, Geraldine rolled her eyes. 'If you were a real man . . .'

'I'd what? Hit you back?' Paddy stepped towards her. 'Because that's what you want, isn't it? To be punished. But I don't work that way. It's over. You won't see me again.'

'You're not leaving, I won't let you!' Turning on her heel, she ran ahead of him down the stairs. Briefly, she disappeared into the kitchen. It set Paddy on guard. But he would not rush out the door. He still had a little pride left.

'There's a police officer outside. If I'm not out in five minutes, they'll be knocking on the door.' Paddy checked his watch as he descended the steps into the hall. He cast an eye on the crooked pictures that Geraldine had once thrown to the floor, the dent in the door from where she had kicked it after he left. But it was the atmosphere in their home that disturbed him most of all. Everything was cold and grey. It was as if the house had withered and died the day Suzy was killed.

Shuffling into the hall, Geraldine returned, her hands behind her back. Her hair was wild and unkempt, her eyes filled with a hatred that made Paddy stall.

'Given them some sob story, have you? Poor Paddy with his nasty wife, ironing his shirts and cooking him breakfast while he gallivants to his fancy piece during the week.' She glanced over his shoulder and pointed at the door. 'I should go out there and make one of those . . . what do you call it? Counter allegations?'

'Except you're not able to go outside, are you?' Paddy said. 'Or at least that's what you've been telling me all these years.'

For once, Geraldine stood, devoid of words.

'I know you've left the house. Bought yourself a computer, too. Why did you lie about having agoraphobia? If you hate me so much, why keep me here?'

'I didn't lie!' She blurted the words as Paddy made a move towards the door. 'My sister . . . she's been helping me to get out. I was going to surprise you. I was going to . . .' Tears streamed down her face as she fought for composure. 'Please, Paddy. I'll get counselling, I . . . I'll do whatever you want. Every couple has rows. We can sort this out.'

Her sister? Paddy frowned. Was she having him on? Did he even care anymore? Her pleading had won him around in the past, but Paddy felt stronger now. It always followed the same cycle: sorrow, regret, blame, and violence. But this morning her moods were changing rapidly to suit the progression of events. He checked his watch. 'This is as much for your good as it is mine.'

She revealed the weapon behind her back. The knife was small but sharp, used to peel potatoes, but deadly if she stabbed him in the right place. 'You're off to shack up with that Winter tart, aren't you? That's what this is about.'

Over the years Paddy had been accused of having an affair with anyone from the postwoman to their next-door neighbour. But Amy Winter . . . She was wide off the mark. 'You're wrong,' Paddy said, although unable to deny having an affair. 'She's not interested in an old codger like me.'

As he approached the door, Geraldine blocked his exit, her hand shaking as she held her weapon aloft. 'Don't try and deny it. You think I'm going to let you walk away after everything you've done?' A vein throbbed on the side of her forehead, her knuckles tightening around the knife.

'Put the knife down,' Paddy said, as they came to a standoff in the hall. It was pride that had made him ask the accompanying officer to wait in the car. That and the fact he didn't want Geraldine arrested. Even now, he still cared. But moving her aside involved physical contact, and only God knew where that would end.

She stood, a twisted smile playing on her face. She was goading him. But he was wise to her and could recognise the signs. A sharp knock on the door made her jump, and she pocketed the knife.

As he pulled the door open, Paddy wore a hesitant smile.

'Everything OK, Sarge?' the uniformed officer said, casting a concerned eye over them both. At a well-built six foot three, his presence was useful, to say the least.

'What about money? How am I going to manage on my own?' Geraldine wailed, ignoring the officer standing on the step.

Grateful for the blast of fresh air, Paddy inhaled a lungful before turning to his wife. 'I'll send it as normal until we sort things out.'

He turned to the officer. 'It's time we were off.' Grasping his belongings under his arm, he followed him down the drive.

Lunging forward, Geraldine took two steps outside and hissed in Paddy's ear. 'I'll say you assaulted me. I'll have you locked up.'

'Which is why I'm recording our conversation. Oh, and every bruise, every cut, every injury has been logged. Say one lie about me, and I'll report the lot.'

Geraldine withered before his eyes like a deflated balloon. Defeated, she sloped back inside and closed the door. Paddy was lying. He would never have reported her. But at least now things were over. He inhaled another lungful of fresh morning air. It was time to begin again.

CHAPTER FIFTY-SIX

DCI Hazel Pike would have made a terrible poker player. Her failure to conceal her emotions was the same reason she performed badly in suspect interviews when she was a DC. Having said that, her inability to mask her thoughts did have its advantages. It left people in no doubt when she was mad at them. As she entered Amy's office, her annoyance was clear. Without saying a word, she clicked the door firmly shut.

Amy rose from her chair. It was a mark of respect that most probationers seemed to forget these days. She knew that Pike was awaiting an update, but she needed time to catch her breath.

'I take it our little matter this morning has been dealt with?' Pike said, her harsh eyeliner and coffee-coloured lipstick making her skin look drawn and pale.

Amy wished she would sit down. It felt like a showdown at the OK Corral as they stood across from each other, feet planted wide. Any minute now she would draw her gun and *bam, you're dead.*

'Winter? Are you all right?' Pike's features softened, one eyebrow raised.

Amy took a breath as she reined in her thoughts. Lack of sleep had taken its toll, and her office was uncomfortably warm, the window tightly shut.

'Sorry, ma'am,' she said huskily before clearing her throat. 'Can you spare five minutes so I can explain?'

Checking her watch, Pike sighed. 'I'll give you four. I've got a conference call in ten. Where's your sergeant by the way? Late again?'

As Pike took a seat, Amy mirrored her movements. It felt strange to be on the other side of the desk. 'No, he had a domestic matter to clear up. Something that couldn't wait. He's got TOIL, so I authorised him to come in an hour late.'

Time owed in lieu was easily accumulated when you were working on their team. Pike nodded, seeming satisfied with the explanation, and waited for Amy to speak.

'I've spoken to Dougie Griffiths, Dad's old shift partner.'

'I know who Dougie is,' Pike replied with authority. 'What's he got to do with this?'

'The shoebox was his. He planted the evidence – not Dad.' Amy paused. Given Pike's feelings for her father, it was unwise to mention Flora's knowledge of events. Pike was bound to feel animosity towards her, and her mum had been through enough. 'Dougie's going to hand himself in. We might even get Lillian's cooperation. Hermione's what matters after all.'

'That's who I came to speak to you about.' Pike crossed her legs, picking at an invisible thread, her way of buying time to think. 'Do you think Lillian is connected to The Keepers of Truth?'

'It's possible. She's promised to give me her location if she gets enough evidence for an appeal.' Amy wondered how much to tell. Too much information and Pike would insist on arrests. Too little and she would steer the investigation the wrong way. Amy wished she had more faith in Pike's decision making, but the truth was, she didn't.

'How are you documenting this?' Pike said.

'Dougie's asked that I keep out of it. It was his shoebox, and as far as he's concerned, he's had it all these years.' The statement felt bitter on Amy's tongue. She had wrestled with the prospect of omitting the truth, but it was the only way of keeping her mum safe. Flora would crumble in a police interview and perverting the course of justice was a serious crime. It was not going to happen. Not on her watch.

'In that case, contact Lillian Grimes. Tell her you've found evidence which should form the basis for an appeal. As far as you're concerned, Mr Griffiths has informed you he's going to hand himself in. Granted, it would have been better if you'd arrested him there and then . . .' She paused as Amy's eyebrows rose in response. 'But you understood there were mobility issues so you've left to follow it up with Essex Police.'

Amy nodded. 'I've already rung the prison. Lillian's with the doctor – routine check-up. I'm waiting for a call back.'

'Good. I'll inform the command team in the meantime. Update Lillian, then call Griffiths. Make sure he hands himself in.'

Amy rose as Pike stood. 'You're a good detective, Winter. As long as we agree on things, then I don't have a problem with your parentage. If anything, it makes me admire Robert even more.'

Amy baulked at the backhanded compliment. *As long as we agree? My parentage?* She clenched her jaw, delivering a strained smile.

It was another half an hour before Lillian called and the heat of Amy's anger still blazed. 'I've got what you wanted,' she said begrudgingly. 'It's time for you to deliver your side of the bargain.'

'I need more than your word for it,' Lillian said. 'Where's my proof?' Her words sounded tinny, and crackles interfered on the line.

Crossing her ankles beneath her chair, Amy leaned forward on her desk. 'I'll speak to your solicitor, get the ball rolling. But only if you tell me where Hermione Parker is.'

'Tell me what you've got first,' Lillian replied. She sounded less sure of herself. Amy pressed the phone close to her ear as the arrogance drained from her voice.

'Notes. Plans, drawings,' Amy recounted. 'Written evidence as well as items that were taken from your home. By the end of today, a written confession from a witness involved in the case. You've got it all. Now tell me where she is.'

'Must be a shock for you, to discover I've been telling the truth all along. Makes you wonder what other lies Robert told. Seems he's not Mr Perfect after all.' The words were familiar but again, lacked her usual mocking tone. Amy did not have time to correct her. Hermione's life was on the line.

'You told me to deliver within three days and you would call your fanatics off.'

'No need to panic, she's still there, safe and sound.'

'Tell me where she is, or I'll bury it,' Amy lied. Even talking about bending the law made her break out in a cold sweat. But Hermione's time was running out.

'You wouldn't.'

Amy's eyes narrowed, her chair creaking as she leaned forward in her seat. Unlike before, Lillian was not asking for a trip out of prison, or even hinting that she knew the address. 'Do you even know where she is? Because wasting police time is a criminal offence.'

A pause.

'Lillian, are you there? Diverting the investigation will add time to your sentence, not take it away.'

'I have to go,' Lillian said. 'Someone's waiting to use the phone.'

'Where is she?'

'Um . . . talk to my solicitor, then we'll see where we go from there.'

'But that makes no sense. Time is running out.' The call went dead. As she put down the phone, clarity struck. Pike was not the only person who could ill conceal their emotions. The hesitancy in Lillian's voice came through loud and clear.

'She doesn't know,' Amy whispered aloud. 'She doesn't have a clue where Hermione is.'

A sharp knock at the door made her jump.

A chequered tie hung from Paddy's neck as he poked his head through. 'Sorry, ma'am, but we've got something.'

'Yes?' Amy placed the phone back on the receiver.

'The search team. They're at India Docks. They've got a result.'

CHAPTER FIFTY-SEVEN

Of all the crime scenes Amy had attended over the years, this was her first visit to a fishing vessel of this kind. No stranger to seedy back alley locations, she had attended public toilets, seen bodies hanging in the woods and once suffered the indignity of her trousers ripping as she climbed into a tiny tree house.

West India Docks was both historic and modern, with Canary Wharf and its glittering skyscrapers, restaurants and shops. With the trundle of the light railway and the atmospheric docks, it was a blend of centuries old and new. But today the beauty of the area was surpassed by Amy's sense of urgency as she rushed to the scene.

As she slipped on the white over suit, Lillian's words still rang in her ears, compounding her hunch. The Keepers of Truth may have been involved on her behalf, but it wasn't Lillian guiding them. As for Damien – surely if he had kidnapped Hemmy then his mother would have been more in the know? 'She's still there, safe and sound,' Lillian had said. But from what crime scene officers had gathered, Hermione was long gone.

Rusted and rotting, the fishing vessel was moored to the dock by long thick ropes. Malcolm's eccentricities had brought them here. As he gave her an update, Amy stood on solid ground, waiting to go in.

'The good news is, we've found blood at the scene, but not enough to make us believe our victim has been stabbed or seriously injured.'

'And the bad news?' Amy said. When it came to crime scenes such as this, there was always bad news.

'We've found enough gas to knock out a horse.'

'Gas?' That, she had not been expecting. Her forensic suit rustled as she folded her arms.

'Yes, darling,' Malcolm replied, his brown wavy hair ruffled by the wind. There was no need for titles with Malcolm, when 'darling' and 'lovie' would do. 'It's some kind of sedative,' he continued. 'We're sending it off to the lab for testing, as well as the blood samples of course. Looks like they left in a hurry.'

'They must have known we were on to them.'

'Or they were worried about the cat being traced back.'

Amy nodded. 'Any evidence of Purdy actually being here?'

'The cage is still on the boat.'

'Wow. Sloppy,' Amy replied. She had been right: this was the work of an amateur. The fact there was so much evidence at the scene gave her a fragment of hope. DNA would be in abundance. But were they too late? Stepping forward on the dock, she stared into the murky waters and felt her spirits dampen. Was Hermione lying beneath the surface? Had her kidnapper finished her off and run?

'Let's try to remain hopeful,' Malcolm said, reading her expression. 'If they've murdered her then it's unlikely they would have left so much evidence at the scene.'

'You're presuming they used rational thought,' Amy said wryly. 'It's quite rare in this line of work. OK to go aboard?' She did not need to ask permission, but their working relationship was based on mutual respect. She wished the same could be said for her DCI, whose words still stung. *As long as you agree with me* indeed, Amy thought, snapping on her gloves. *We'll see about that.*

It took several seconds for Amy to acclimatise herself to the gentle rocking of the boat. From the moment she stepped on board, she put herself in the kidnapper's shoes. Why had they brought her here of all places? And why bring the cat? She stared at the animal cage, its bars matted with white fur. In the corner, a rotting fish head sat next to an empty water bowl. Another wave bobbed the boat from one side to the other.

The smell of fish grew stronger as she stepped into the bowels of the boat. What must Hermione have felt, waking dizzy and disorientated in this gloom? Had she screamed? Cried out? Why had nobody heard her? Or had they walked swiftly past, their head down as they distanced themselves from the sound? It annoyed her that Purdy was taken in and fussed over, yet nobody had seen fit to report what was happening in the boat. But then so much goes on in plain sight, with people turning a blind eye. Being born into the Grimes household had taught her that. People who closed their eyes to injustice were almost as bad as those taking part. How many had shut their eyes to Jack and Lillian Grimes's wrongdoings over the years?

Tentatively, she balanced herself as she took in the dingy space. In the corner, a bucket lay tipped to one side. Urine pooled in a pocket of timbers, and next to it was an empty pack of wet wipes. Empty sandwich cartons littered the floor, along with a discarded plastic bottle. And the smell . . . Amy raised a hand to her nose. She was never eating fish again.

After speaking to his colleagues, Malcolm followed her down. He appeared almost ghostly in his white forensic suit, illuminated by the shaft of light from the grubby porthole. Amy turned her attention to the rusted single bed.

'Look at this,' Malcolm said, pulling back a blanket. He shifted the damp, spored mattress to reveal something scraped into the wood panelling. Leaning forward, Amy peered at what looked to be letters H and E scraped in the wood. 'Hermione?'

'Or help,' Malcolm said. 'Either way, it looks recent.'

'She didn't do this with her nails, did she?'

Malcolm shook his head. 'There's a screw missing from the bed frame.'

'Clever girl.' But it was too early in proceedings to carry too much hope. 'Any sign of it?'

Malcolm shook his head. 'We've gone over every inch, and it's not here. Could be that he's taken it off her . . .'

'Or she's keeping it hidden in case she needs it.' She sighed as her thoughts grew dark. 'Any blood on the sheets? Signs of sexual activity?'

'No,' Malcolm replied. 'We're seizing the bedding, but the blood stains were found here . . .' He pointed to the door. 'And on the top of the steps. Looks like someone gripped them with blood on their hand. Thankfully it's not enough to have come from any great injury. We'll know more when the test results come in.'

'Fast-tracked?' Amy said. It would take a chunk of their budget, but it was imperative they find their suspect. If they had been arrested in the past, then their DNA would be on the system, and this could bring the case to a quick conclusion. That's if the blood wasn't Hermione's, of course. She thought of Damien and his previous convictions. Soon she may know once and for all.

◆　◆　◆

Perching on her office chair, Amy listened to the unanswered ring of Dougie's home phone. She had imagined him calmly dressing in his smartest suit and tie before calling Essex Police and asking to speak to DI Donovan before handing himself in. She still struggled to believe he had framed Lillian for her crimes.

Amy needed to update Lillian's solicitor, in the slim chance Lillian knew where Hemmy was. Why hadn't Donovan rung her with an update? Was he peeved with her for her short response the last time they spoke? His inquisitiveness about Lillian had cut their fledgling friendship short. There was no update on the system. From what she could tell, DCI Pike wanted to give Dougie's past misdemeanours a wide berth. The sense of guilt was overwhelming. Was she sentencing her father's best friend to spending the rest of his years in prison?

'Amy, nice to hear from you,' DI Donovan replied after the second ring. Amy's frown deepened at his familiarity. She should have used the work phone instead of her mobile, but she did not want the call logged.

'I was wondering if you'd processed Douglas Griffiths yet,' she said, seeing no point in small talk. 'He was due to get in touch. It's about the Lillian Grimes case.'

'Oh . . .' Donovan replied, a hint of disappointment in his voice. 'I've not heard anything . . . Just a second, let me check my emails . . .' Time passed as his mouse clicked in the background. 'Nope, nothing there either. I've been around most of the day. Was it important?'

'Very. He's coming with a shoebox full of evidence – evidence he used to frame Lillian Grimes.' She stood from her chair, her frown deepening. 'Dammit, I should have called you to give you the heads up.'

'I'm looking through the STORM reports, we've had nothing from anyone of that name.' What the Met called CAD, Essex Police called STORM. It was an acronym for logged incidents and calls. The ringing of her desk phone drew her attention away, and Amy blew a loud exhalation into the mobile phone. 'It's my DCI. I've got to go. If you hear anything call me straight away.'

'Sure,' he said, taking a breath to say more, but Amy hurriedly hung up the phone. She did not mean to be so short with him, but perhaps it was better that way.

DCI Pike's voice had an urgent tone as Amy answered her desk phone. 'I'd like a word with you, please. Now.'

Amy stared at the phone as Pike hung up. 'Bye then.' She sniffed, miffed at Pike's abruptness before remembering she had done the same to Donovan just seconds before. Why couldn't Pike come down here and speak to her? Did she feel she had more authority in her own setting? The friendship they had enjoyed was clearly coming to an end. She would fix this, she had to. For now, her main priority was finding Hermione and getting her home safe.

Her brow was furrowed as she took a seat behind her DCI's desk.

'I've got some bad news, I'm afraid,' Pike said, her fingers intertwined. Behind her, the clock seemed to tick unnaturally loudly. *Tick, tick, tick,* the seconds passed mercilessly as time ran away.

Amy sat bolt upright, her muscles clenched. 'Have they found Hermione?' she said, preparing herself for the worst. 'Is she dead?'

'No.' Pike sighed, taking a measured breath. 'I wanted to tell you before you picked it up on the system.'

'An incident has come in?'

Pike nodded. 'Officers have attended and confirmed it. I'm afraid Dougie Griffiths is dead.'

CHAPTER FIFTY-EIGHT

Amy stared into the distance as she gripped the steering wheel of her car. Dougie was gone. She did not want to believe it, but she *could* understand it. Prison was far worse if you were a police officer, particularly if you were wheelchair-bound. You could easily encounter people you had convicted over the years. Why hadn't she just left things alone?

'At some point, you're going to have to tell me what's going on.' Paddy's voice was gentle as he sat next to her, waiting for her to gather her thoughts. He had found her in the station car park, unable to get out of the car. Pike had authorised her attendance at Dougie's home. The duty inspector had already declared his death as non-suspicious, but she could not rest until she saw the scene for herself. She barely remembered driving back to the station. All she could see was Dougie lying face down on his bed. *I'm going to have a bath and change into my best suit. When I leave this place, I'll do it with grace.* Amy recalled his words. Had he been gearing up to this all along? The empty pill bottle by his side explained as much as the suicide note he left behind. Amy felt the world close in, until it got to the point where she was unable to step out of her car. She needed to release the floodgates and have a good cry. But she couldn't because if she started, she might not be able to stop.

'He was a close friend of my father's,' Amy said, giving Paddy the sanitised version of the truth; the version that did not include her connection to Lillian, or the evidence stored in their loft.

'So, you really think one of Lillian's supporters kidnapped Hermione to draw attention to her case?'

Amy gave him a weak smile. Steering the conversation to work was the best way of helping her right now. 'It's possible,' she said, grateful for his presence. 'But I'm loath to direct too much attention to it. Do we focus on this and ignore the other veins of enquiry?'

'This investigation has more holes than a block of Swiss cheese.' Paddy smiled back.

An understanding passed between them. He knew she hated hugs. His presence was enough for now. 'I take it Molly's had no luck with infiltrating the group on Facebook?'

Paddy shook his head. 'Apart from the "two days" countdown on Twitter, there's nothing about any kidnap attempt. I suppose I'd best be getting inside . . . Will you be OK?' He gave her a look filled with empathy, a look from someone who understood tough times.

'I'm fine,' she said, not wanting to burden him. 'I meant to ask, how did things go with Geraldine?'

'As well as expected. I asked Jenny, the IDVA, to call in on her. She said Geraldine's been in touch with her sister, she's getting support from her.'

'And you believe her?' Amy replied, referring to Geraldine.

'I've no reason not to. That's where she was the other night – with her sister. Where else would she be at that hour?' He drew in a heavy sigh. 'What happened to your friend Dougie . . . it got me thinking. I don't want Geraldine to end up the same way.'

Amy could sympathise. The weight of responsibility was a heavy one. 'I've tasked an officer to speak to her about trolling. They'll say they picked it up from her IP address.'

Paddy nodded, reaching for the door latch. 'Fine by me. Are you coming in?'

'Stick the kettle on,' Amy replied. 'I'll be in by the time it's boiled.' Gently she slipped an envelope from her pocket. 'Dougie left me a note. I want to read it before I go in.'

'Oh. Of course . . .' Paddy said, a flush rising to his cheeks as he tried to find the right words. 'Well, um . . . if you need anything, just give me a shout.'

'Thanks,' Amy said, grateful for his kindness. She meant it. With Paddy, there was no ulterior motive. Their friendship was genuine, built upon their mutual love for the job. As she watched him leave, she felt grateful to have him in her life. As for Dougie, the kindness he had displayed towards her when she was a child was marred by his behaviour during Lillian's case. How could he plant evidence, knowing she may not have committed those crimes? Had he so little faith in the justice system that he served? Inhaling a deep breath, she opened the envelope as she prepared to read Dougie's words.

> Dear Amy,
> I'm sorry it has to end this way. As you know, I have taken the death of your father quite hard, and after losing my own parents recently I find no reason to carry on anymore. It was very kind of you to visit me, and I'm ashamed that I had a part to play in Lillian Grimes's case all those years ago. You advised me to go to the authorities, giving me enough time to gather my dignity and prepare myself for what lay ahead.
> I kept the shoebox of evidence because I was too ashamed to throw it away. Perhaps one day I knew I

would be held accountable for my actions, but hand on heart, I would do it all over again. Lillian Grimes is guilty of the murders of those women. She should spend the rest of her days in prison. But I admit that I gave the investigation the help it needed when it came to charging her. In the box, you will find some threads from the red cardigan she was wearing. I planted some of those on the bodies to ensure that she was found guilty in court. This is the only time I have ever planted evidence during my career as a DC. I also planted hairs from her hairbrush as well as an earring in the burial sites in the house. I could not risk her being set free.

I do not regret my actions. I am a hundred per cent sure of her guilt. However, I know where such an admission would lead me, and I am not prepared to spend the rest of my days in a prison cell. I hope this will help give you some closure. Everybody else on the team worked incredibly hard and with total honesty, including your father. I am sorry to have let him down. I am going to sleep now. It will be one from which I will not awake. You are young and strong and will pick up the pieces of your life. Robert would want you to begin again. I hope you can forgive me. Please send my love to my relatives, for whom I have also left notes. My funeral plan is in my bedside locker, and everything is paid for. My will is beneath it. As you can see, I have been prepared for this day for some time. This was my decision and mine alone.

Amy, don't be a coward like me. Make your life count.

Dougie

CHAPTER FIFTY-NINE

'I already know,' Flora said, as Amy tried to break the news over the phone. 'I spoke to the police officer guarding his front door.'

'Why didn't you call me?' Amy was taken aback by Flora's sudden show of strength. She wasn't aware of her mother's visit to Dougie, and it made her wonder what else had been going on.

'I knew you'd find out soon enough.' Flora's voice was cold. Distant. The Flora she thought she knew would have fallen apart. Was she annoyed with her for telling Dougie to hand himself in?

'Had a falling out with your DCI, have you?' Flora's words bridged the silence. She was trying to act casual, but as she skirted around the idea, Amy could hear that something weighed heavy on her mind.

'Why do you ask?'

'Because you don't spend any time with her anymore. But then I expected her to lose interest after Robert died.' Again, Flora's voice was slow and mocking. It didn't sound like her at all.

'Her job is very pressured.' Amy chose her words carefully. 'We've got a lot on.' Perhaps Flora was in shock? It was hardly surprising, given all the bad feelings that had been stirred up.

'That's not what I meant. I know what went on between them. I've known for a very long time.'

Amy's heart lunged in her chest. To play dumb would only add insult to injury. 'I only just found out,' she said softly. 'I wasn't sure whether to believe it or not.' She paused for breath, hearing the clink of a bottle against glass on the other end of the line. Was that why Flora sounded so strange? Had she been drinking to ease her grief? 'Why didn't you tell me?' she asked, feeling guilty for not being there.

'You adored your father. We all did things to please him. He liked my dependency, it made him feel like the big man. But I'm stronger than any of you know.'

'Have you been drinking?' Amy said, bewildered by her mother's change in tone.

'I'm well entitled to, don't you think?' She paused to swallow whatever spirit had filled her glass. 'He didn't love Pike, not really. He tried to shake her off, but she used *you* to get to *him*. Even after he died, she kept sniffing around to find out what was going on at home.'

'I never told her anything,' Amy said. 'And I wish I'd known because I wouldn't have spent time with her.'

'But it's not that easy, is it?' Flora paused to take another sip. 'Not when your career is at stake.'

'I could have got a transfer. I still can.'

'No. I don't want you being posted far away. You deserve your promotion, but you need to prove yourself, too. That's why you need to find that Hermione girl.'

But Amy barely heard her mother's words; she was too busy picking over the bones of her past. 'You shouldn't have put up with it. You should have told Dad how you felt.'

'Like you told him how you felt about watching all those James Bond movies?' Flora emitted an intoxicated giggle. 'You only pretended to like them so you could spend time together. See? We all put him on a pedestal. But he was human, he made his mistakes, just like us.'

It was true. Their Sundays together watching 007 films were precious only because of the time they shared. They could have just as easily watched hours of wrestling for all she cared.

'The adoption agency approved us the week your parents were arrested. It seemed like fate,' Flora said wistfully. 'When we adopted you, I thought it would bring the family closer together, but it made me feel like an outsider even more. I was so jealous of what you both had.'

'Oh, Mum,' Amy said, dismayed to hear such a painful confession.

'It's not your fault there was distance between us, Amy; it was mine. There were plenty of times I could have reached out to gain your trust . . .' She heaved a sigh. 'But it's not too late to make things right.'

Amy checked her watch, night was closing in and she had been away from the office for far too long. But she couldn't leave her mum in such a state. 'Are you going to be OK? Would you like me to call Craig, ask him to come over?' Unlike her, Craig had finished his shift hours ago.

'I'm not going to do anything daft, if that's what you're worried about. I'm just a bit drunk. No law against it, is there, ossifer?' A giggle bubbled up her throat as she slurred the word.

But Amy did not take Flora's word for it. After telling her mother she loved her, she quickly called Craig and arranged for him to pop around. He was more than amused to hear that their normally teetotal parent was drunk.

As her phone buzzed in her hand, Amy's grip on the car door handle loosened. Paddy's name flashed up on the screen, and she wasted no time in answering it.

'Sorry to trouble you, ma'am. Are you still in the car park?'

'I'm coming in now,' she said, her fringe flying into her eyes as a sudden gust of wind hit her full on. 'What's wrong?'

'Gladys Thompson's died.'

'I see,' Amy replied. Given the woman had a terminal illness, the news was not entirely unexpected.

'Her son is here,' Paddy said. 'He said he won't leave until he speaks to you.'

CHAPTER SIXTY

Amy wondered if the full moon had anything to do with the recent spate of events. She had come across such anomalies before, how a change in lunar energy could result in a wave of vicious attacks. She believed in the power of the unknown. The fact she was not always grounded helped her sense things when others could not. She had been expecting news of Gladys Thompson's passing since she had awoken that morning.

Shoulders slumped, John Thompson waited patiently at the front counter, his hands deep in the pockets of his creased black suit. Directing him into a side room, Amy passed on her sympathies for the loss of his mother.

With a nod of the head, he thanked her, pulling out the hard plastic chair to take a seat. The shadows beneath his eyes suggested sleep had been a stranger, and the new sprinkle of silver hairs in his sandy beard revealed the depth of his stress. The family liaison officer had since provided John with the ugly truth of his sister's death and disposal. Losing his mother so soon after the news must have inflicted unbearable pain.

'Thanks for dropping everything to talk to me,' he said. 'I got myself in such a state. I hope you don't mind.'

'Of course I don't mind,' Amy replied. 'I'm just sorry it has to be under such sad circumstances. Can I get you a cup of tea? It's vending machine brew, I'm afraid . . .' They were sitting in one of the rooms off reception, often used for quick enquiries. She could have brought him further into the building, but that would risk exposing him to information she did not want to share. Uniformed officers had been known to openly discuss cases in their offices, and pictures of offenders were pinned up on walls. Their room may smell strongly of its last occupant, but it was the most sensible place to talk for now.

'I've had a million cups already, thank you,' John said. 'Mum . . . she's still at the house. People have been coming all day to pay their respects.'

'Then your time must be precious,' Amy said, grateful for the excuse to speed things along. 'What can I help you with?'

'I've seen something online.' John delivered a heartfelt sigh. 'And I can't rest until I know if it's true.'

'What would that be?'

'Is Lillian Grimes launching an appeal?' John's face grew taut at the mention of her name.

'Where did you hear that?' Amy replied, neither confirming nor denying it.

'On social media. There's this group called The Keepers of Truth something or other. They said they're working on setting her free.'

'Right . . . How do they intend doing that?' Amy said, giving nothing away.

'They said . . .' John swallowed, his throat clicking as he tried to clear it. 'Well, they said they're responsible for kidnapping Hemmy Parker, you know, the daughter of the TV presenter? They're holding her hostage until Lillian can appeal. I can't believe these people. After everything she's done . . .'

'It's news to me.' Amy's grey eyes remained cool, despite her accelerating heartbeat. 'Did you take a note of the conversation? Screenshot it maybe? Can you show me on your phone?'

'Sorry,' John said, leaning back in his chair. 'I saw it just before Mum took a turn for the worse. I would have told you straight away, but . . .' His words faded.

'Please, don't apologise,' Amy said. 'It was good of you to tell us at all.'

'To be honest, I needed the excuse to leave the house for a few minutes. It's all getting a bit much. People say they're sorry, but they've no idea what that woman put Mum through.'

'Can you remember exactly where you saw this information?' Amy said, gently steering him back.

'In a Facebook group,' John replied, giving her an empty smile. 'It's a bit embarrassing, I can't imagine what you think of me, looking at Facebook when my mum was so ill.'

'No judgement here,' Amy replied. 'I think I'm the only person in the world who doesn't use it. Can you show me the group if I log on to my computer?'

'Sorry.' He shook his head. 'I tried searching for it on my phone, but it's gone. Some conspiracy theory site I think.'

'How did you find it?' Amy wished he would stop apologising. After everything that had happened to his family, the police were the ones who had let him down.

'I typed in the search term "Lillian Grimes", and all sorts of things showed up.' He cast his eyes downward. 'You haven't been very forthcoming, I just wanted to know what was going on.'

'We have to wait until information is substantiated before we share. You're not going to get an accurate account from social media. We've all heard of fake news, right?'

John nodded but did not seem convinced. 'Can you tell me, is Lillian's case being reopened, or not?' He surveyed her with interest, and

Amy felt the temperature between them cool. He was bound to hold bitterness towards the police, given what had happened over the years. The stress of not being able to bury Wendy had eaten his mother up inside. She deflected his question with one of her own. 'This Facebook conversation, can you tell me anything more? Who was talking, for example?'

'She's not going to be freed, is she? After all the pain she's caused . . . murdering my sister and then dumping her in that fridge. What sort of a woman does that?' Silence lengthened between them until sharply, he inhaled, as if he had been drowning and suddenly found air. 'She put my family through hell. I can't bear the thought.' His eyes wet with tears, he looked at her pleadingly, a man broken by a lifetime of grief.

Amy realised it was too soon to question him. 'I can't see it happening.' It was the best she could give him for now.

John blinked, dragging himself from his painful past up to present day. 'I mean, this is just a stunt to get attention. They don't really have Hemmy, and if they do, they'll let her go.' He glanced up at Amy, his expression a question. 'Won't they?'

She delivered a tight smile. 'Thanks for coming in. We'll need to take a statement covering what you've said just the same. Can I book an appointment for a more convenient time?' She rose from the chair, fighting to keep her expression neutral.

'Anything to help,' John said, following her to the front counter.

Something had changed during their short conversation. She could sense it deep down, but was yet to figure out what. All she knew was that for Hemmy, Amy felt suddenly afraid.

CHAPTER SIXTY-ONE

'There's something I need to tell you.' Paddy spoke into his car mirror, trying out the words for size. The lines around his eyes were more pronounced, and he felt as if he had aged ten years.

'It's just that . . . well, you know I love you, don't you?' He swallowed, tugging at his tie before popping open his shirt collar button. 'It's just . . .' The words died in his throat. Swearing, he cursed his ineptitude. If he could not say it aloud then how would he persuade Elaine to give him a chance? Most people would get a divorce before meeting someone new. He had been selfish. He dropped his gaze from the mirror, unable to meet his own eyes. The solitary life had been thrust upon Geraldine without a moment's notice. He could have handled things better. *You're weak, a spineless coward. Why didn't you die instead of her?* Geraldine's voice echoed in the corridors of his mind. It would take a long time for her to quieten. One thing at a time, he reminded himself. His heart thumped in his chest as he tried to rehearse his speech to Elaine. How do you jazz up the fact that you're married to someone else? Describing Geraldine as violent made her sound like a monster. But blaming himself would surely make him a loser in Elaine's eyes. He thought of Amy Winter, and how she had faced things head on.

Geraldine was wrong; his feelings for Amy were paternal, although he would never admit such a thing. Had his daughter been alive, Amy was just how he hoped Suzy would have been: strong, self-sufficient and on the ball.

'Honey, I'm home!' he shouted from the hall, knowing he sounded like a character in a cheesy old movie. Hanging up his coat, he closed his eyes and inhaled. Gravy . . . maybe beef pie? His stomach churned. The last thing he wanted was food. He waited until she had dished up before trying to voice his confession. As she slid their heated plates from the oven, she took the opportunity to ask him about his day. 'Any news on Hermione Parker?' she said, dishing up what turned out to be beef stew.

'We're closing in. Our DI reckons it's only a matter of time.'

'Really?' Elaine said, turning away to pour some water into a jug. 'How's she coping with it all?'

'She's not had it easy,' Paddy said, wondering how they'd ended up on this subject. 'The DCI seems to have turned on her for some reason. I reckon she could do with a friend right about now.'

Elaine took a seat, her smile fading. 'Oh dear. Still, as you say. It won't be long until you find that missing girl.'

Paddy nodded, trying but failing to enjoy his meal. What should have melted on his tongue tasted bitter and fermented; but it was not the quality of the food troubling him, it was what he was due to say. And was it just his imagination, or had the atmosphere between them changed? He regarded Elaine with a sideways glance. She was also picking at her meal.

'Elaine, love,' he said, dropping his knife and fork and gently placing them either side of his plate. 'There's something I need to tell you.' It surprised him to see her eyes were dewy when she looked up to meet his gaze.

'I need to talk to you, too,' she said, her words followed by a soft sigh.

For what felt like a lifetime, they stared at each other, waiting for the other to speak. Paddy felt like a cartoon character, about to push the handle on a box of TNT. *Kaboom, your life is over.* Dismissing his thoughts, he took a sharp breath. 'I've been lying to you, but it's only because I love you. I was trying to protect what we had.'

'I know,' she said, the colour fading from her cheeks as she pushed away her plate.

'You know?'

Elaine nodded.

'I was married when I met you. But it's over. I've left her for good.' Tilting his head, Paddy checked for understanding. But Elaine did not flinch. Behind her eyes was blank nothingness. Paddy grasped for the words needed to make this better, but her eyes . . . A chill drove its way down his back as she regarded him with the look of a stranger.

'I said I know,' Elaine replied, her words firmer this time. 'I've always known. I thought we could make a go of this, and for a while, it was nice to live in a happy home.' She sighed, swiping away a tear as if it were an errant fly. 'But it's lies, all of it. Which is why I have to go.'

'You're leaving me?' Paddy's chair screeched against the floor tiles as he stood. 'No. Please. We can work this out. Please don't go.' His stomach lurched as he heard himself echo Geraldine's earlier pleas.

'I was never meant to fall for you. For a while, it was nice . . . But you don't know me. Not really. If you knew the truth . . .' Her words were hollow, disjointed. As if a piece of her had already left.

'Then tell me,' Paddy said. 'Please. We can fix this. Whatever you've done, I don't care. We can wipe the slate clean and start again.' Paddy gripped the back of the chair. He could not bear the prospect of Elaine walking away.

'I'm a bad person,' she said, the vacant expression returning to her eyes. 'And you're better off without me. I'm sorry. I didn't mean for things to go this far.'

'I won't let you go.' Paddy stepped forward as she moved towards the door.

'You have no choice,' Elaine sighed, gently moving him aside. 'I've paid the rent until the end of the month. You can take over the lease if you like, all the details are in the drawer.'

Instead of going upstairs to pack, Elaine pulled a heavy-looking suitcase from the cupboard beneath the stairs. 'I was going to go when you were out, but I couldn't leave without saying goodbye.'

'Is there someone else? Is that what this is?' Paddy stood at the door, painfully aware of the irony of it all.

'You could say that . . . but it's not what you think,' Elaine replied. 'You're better off without me. The best thing you can do is to let me go.'

Outside, a car beeped. 'That'll be my taxi,' she said, blinking back her tears as she checked her watch for the time. 'Goodbye, Paddy . . . and . . .' Her voice broke as she squeezed his arm for the very last time. 'I'm sorry . . . for everything.'

Paddy stood aghast. Her taxi? She had planned this all along. Yet he could not find the words to make her change her mind. He'd always had a feeling that his relationship with Elaine was too good to be true and far more than he deserved. She had finally seen through him. Seen him for the failure Geraldine knew he was. Standing motionlessly at the door, an awful hollowness overcame him as his whole world walked away.

CHAPTER SIXTY-TWO

1985

New Year was a time of celebration and the house was never as full as it was tonight. Usually, Poppy had to be in bed by seven, but Mummy was out, and Daddy was in a good mood. Sally-Ann said that 'anything goes' when it came to Christmas, although Poppy did not understand what it meant. Tired from cleaning all day, Sally-Ann had gone to bed with a set of earplugs firmly embedded in her ears to blot out the music downstairs. Sally-Ann did not appreciate 'Agadoo' followed by 'Rock-the-boat' – songs Poppy had come to love. Tonight, as things got really loud, her sister wore white furry ear muffs, too. They belonged to one of the girls that visited their house, but she stopped coming around ages ago. Poppy had noticed her mummy wearing the silver chain the girl had once worn, too. It was not unusual for trinkets to be left behind.

Mandy and Damien were on sleepovers and Poppy's spirits were high. She loved the Christmas decorations hanging from the ceiling, and the colourful tinsel that spiralled around their staircase. When she had asked Sally-Ann what everyone was so happy about, she said it was because of the New Year. Poppy hoped that it meant Mummy and

Daddy would come to a truce. Poppy knew all about truces, given the amount of fighting under their roof. This time Mummy didn't like Daddy's new friend, Viv, because she was clingy, whatever that meant. Poppy had met Viv lots of times, and although she sometimes gave her Smarties, she didn't cling to anything, as far as Poppy could see. Viv did like her daddy though. She liked to kiss him on the lips. Before, Mummy asked to join in, but Viv said she didn't like kissing girls. Poppy supposed Mummy was upset because Viv wanted to be Daddy's friend and not hers. Sometimes they would go up to Daddy's bedroom and play wrestle on the bed with no clothes on. Poppy couldn't see much fun in that, not when it was so cold.

Slipping into the living room, Poppy weaved through the bodies of sweaty party-goers, and crouched down in her secret place. The thick, floor-length red curtain was the perfect place to hide. Poppy had been clever. Having stuffed her pillow under her bedclothes, she made it look like she was asleep. Her face smeared with chocolate, she felt warmth in her tummy as she washed it down with the honey-coloured liquid someone had left behind. With music still blaring, she fell asleep, hunched up and drowsy from the drink that burnt her throat on the way down.

By the time she awoke, all remnants of the earlier celebrations had ceased. *What time is it?* Poppy thought, wiping the chocolate-stained drool from her mouth. Her heart fluttered as she peeped out from behind the curtain and caught sight of her mother's angry face. That was, until she realised the focus of her mum's attention wasn't her. Her eyes blazing, Mummy's attention was wholly on Viv, who was sprawled across the sofa in her knickers and bra. Softly, the young woman snored, a dreamy smile on her face. Poppy peered around the room. Crisps had been ground into the carpet and empty beer cans and streamers littered the floor.

Grabbing a handful of Viv's bleached-blonde hair, Mummy woke her in an instant, a loud yelp emitting from between Viv's lips.

'You bitch. I told you not to come back!' Lillian yelled, dragging the young woman off the sofa.

Still yelping loudly, Viv tried to find her feet as Lillian released her hold. 'Where's Jack?' she said breathlessly, buttoning up her blouse.

'Don't worry about him,' Lillian shouted. 'What are you doing in my home?'

'I would have thought that was obvious,' Viv sneered, rubbing her head as Lillian released her grip. 'He invited me. Said you weren't due back until tomorrow.'

'It *is* tomorrow, you silly bitch. And this is my house. Now get the fuck out and don't come back.'

'Jack!' Viv shouted in a high-pitched squeal. 'Come and sort out your missus!'

Biting her lip, Poppy ignored the fact that she was desperate for a wee. She curled herself even tighter into a ball, her fists clenched. She knew that her father's good moods did not last, and things were going to get bad. She wished she could leave, but no one knew she was here. She had no choice but to stay and watch.

'What's all the fuss?' Jack said, rubbing his head as he walked in. His expression changed as he caught sight of Viv, who was pulling on her mini skirt. 'What are you doing here? I thought I told you to go home?'

'I fell back asleep,' she said, but her words sounded weak, and the pinkness of her cheeks told Poppy she was lying.

'Why is she here in the first place?' Lillian jabbed a finger in Jack's direction. 'You know the rules, no fun without me.'

'I didn't invite her,' Jack said. But his words were met with dismay.

'Yes, you did!' Viv shouted, tugging the zip on her skirt. 'Come on, Jack, tell her the truth.' She turned to Lillian. 'We love each other. He don't want you no more.'

Poppy was wide awake now. This was bad. Really bad. Like a temperature gauge, the redness rose from her mother's chest up to her throat. She looked as if she were going to explode.

But instead of shouting and screaming, her mother simply turned to Jack. 'You go back to bed. Me and Viv here are gonna have a little chat.'

Jack shuffled in the doorway, his shirttail hanging out of his trousers as he looked from one woman to the other. 'Lils, there's no need for—'

'What?' Lillian cocked an eyebrow. 'You want to stay here and argue it out? Cos I'm up for that an' all!'

Jack raised his hands to his temples as if fending off a swarm of bees instead of his wife's high-pitched commands. 'All right, all right! Just keep the noise down.' Without looking back, he turned and went upstairs to bed.

'Jack. Where are you going? Jack!' Viv called, her mouth dropping open in dismay.

Baring her teeth in a chilling smile, Lillian turned and locked the door.

Poppy bunched up her fists into the sleeves of her nightdress. Her insides felt all twisted in knots, too. She did not want to be here anymore. She could try to sneak out, but the door was locked, and her mum would see her leave. Mum might be short, but she was strong, and when she was mad, you kept out of her way.

The muscles in Lillian's face tensed as she spoke. 'You should have left when I gave you the chance.'

'He don't love you.' As she groped for her belongings, Viv's confidence seemed to fade. 'You . . . You don't scare me.'

'Well, I should.' Lillian advanced towards her, the veins in her neck protruding like cables ready to snap.

Viv retreated until the back of her knees hit the sofa with a muffled thud. 'Lay one finger on me and I'm calling the social. I'll tell them exactly what goes on.'

'You wouldn't,' Lillian said, temporarily stalled.

A smile broadened on Viv's face as her bravado was restored. 'Yeah, well, I meant every word. And you can say goodbye to your husband. He'll be following me soon enough.'

'I wish you hadn't said that,' Lillian replied, making no move to get out of her way.

'The truth hurts,' Viv said, slipping her feet into her kitten heel shoes.

'No . . .' Lillian smirked. 'I mean I can't be bothered to clean up the mess.'

'What mess . . .'

A loud cracking sound was followed by a violent spurt of blood as Lillian head-butted her on the nose. With both hands outstretched, she pushed Viv hard until she hit the carpeted floor with a thud. 'My naagh!' Viv gurgled, cupping her nose with both hands. Gasping, she fought for breath as blood travelled back up her nose.

Her eyes alight with terror, Poppy watched as her mother kicked Viv in the stomach, each blow coinciding with a swearword on her lips. Panting, she blew her fringe from her forehead, before dropping to straddle Viv's chest. Splattered across their red carpet, Viv's blood merged with the fibres and broken crisps. Rigid with fear, Poppy prayed for the violence to end.

Viv was weak now, her movements limp as a dull moan drizzled from her lips, but Lillian did not stop there. Sweat glistened on her forehead as she pinched Viv's bloodied nose and clamped her left hand over her mouth. 'You think you can come in here and threaten me,' Lillian muttered as Viv bucked beneath her weight.

Viv's eyes bulged with disbelief as Lillian pressed down hard, cutting off her air supply. It seemed to take forever until, devoid of strength, her limbs flopped like dying fish.

Wincing, Poppy pushed her face into her knees, which were drawn tightly up to her chest. Her own breath was coming faster now. If

Mummy heard, she would silence her for good. As the movements subsided, Lillian rose, complaining about the carpet stains as she unlocked the door. Tentatively, Poppy peeped at the aftermath, her heart still clacking like a wind-up toy. Arms outstretched, Viv stared unblinkingly in her direction. In strange wonderment, Poppy watched the Christmas tree fairy lights blink on and off as they reflected in her eyes. She knew that no breath passed Viv's lips because her mummy had taken it away.

CHAPTER SIXTY-THREE

'Hello, Daughter dear, I thought you would have been in to see me today.'

Usually the sound of Lillian's voice made Amy's skin crawl, but today she had awoken with a new understanding. Overnight, another horrifying piece of her memory had slotted into place.

'Why would I visit you?' Amy said. 'I've spoken to your solicitor. According to him, you don't have a clue where Hermione Parker is.'

'Is that any way to speak to your mother?' Lillian tutted down the phone. 'I had no choice but to use her as a bargaining chip. If I didn't, you'd have left me here to rot.'

'Ever the victim,' Amy said. 'But you're wasting your time with me. I know what you did.' As the line fell silent, Amy could almost hear the cogs in Lillian's brain whirr.

'What's this? Something Robert told you when you were a child?' Sly and mocking, Lillian's voice greased the line. 'The bent copper twists the knife from the grave. Put yourself in my shoes. That man took my kids, my dignity and my freedom. It's only natural I'd fight back.'

'I could *never* put myself in your shoes,' Amy said, unable to conceal her disgust.

'You already are. You're part of me.' She paused for breath. 'Those people who took you in . . . they're not your parents. You're mine, mine and your father's. You have my skin, his smile. Our blood runs through your veins.'

Her voice was dark, almost hypnotic as it lured her in. Amy stiffened in her chair. She had given this woman far too much of herself already. 'Let me tell you something. I am my thoughts, my words and, most of all, my actions – which means I have *nothing* to do with you.' A wave of disgust rolled over her as she recalled her memory from the night before. 'That's why I could never put myself in your shoes – because I know what you did to Viv Holden. I was there.'

'Rubbish,' Lillian spat. 'You were barely four years old. Whatever you *think* you remember is wrong.'

'I remember seeing Jack and Viv on the sofa, cuddling up when you weren't there. You didn't like that, did you? The fact he saw her alone.'

'It's a fake memory,' Lillian said, temper rattling her words. 'Where do you think I was that day? Trying to find us a new home away from him.' She exhaled an exasperated breath. 'I'm not asking for much, just the truth to be told.'

'Then why don't you let me tell it?' It was Amy's turn to mock. She was sure this time. Regardless of her mix-up with the doll, the memory of Viv's murder was too lucid to be anything but real. Gripping the bannisters as she crept downstairs on New Year's Eve. The warmth invading her stomach as she tipped a mouthful of spirits down her throat, mistaking it for apple juice.

'God, when I think of it now, the way we were brought up,' Amy thought aloud. 'People look after their dogs better than you cared for us.'

'How would you know?' Lillian said indignantly. 'You're not a mother. You don't know how tough it is.'

But Amy deflected the comment. 'I know how to treat another human being, especially one as small and vulnerable as a child. I remember falling asleep that night, wrapped up in those awful red, floor-length curtains I used to hide behind. It was dark when you came home, and none of us heard you slip in. Were you trying to catch them out?'

'Lies, it's all lies.'

'Well, somebody killed her, and it sure wasn't Jack. That's why you hated her. It wasn't the fact she wouldn't let you join in, but because he wanted her around without *you*. That look on Viv's face when Jack turned and left you both to it. She was terrified when you locked the door.'

'Terrified my arse, she was hard as nails that one,' Lillian said, forgetting her earlier claim that their meeting never took place.

'She wanted to leave but you wouldn't let her,' Amy replied. 'Even as a child, I knew you'd kill her because you had killed before. You orchestrated everything. You were the driving force behind it all.' Amy knew that there were more memories that had not yet been revealed. Ones which would appear in time, when she was strong enough to cope with them. She bowed her head, her elbows on her desk as she held the phone to her ear. For now, this dreadful knowing was enough.

'Maybe I *did* want to catch them out because I knew something was going on,' Lillian replied. 'We had a row, I slapped her around, but I didn't kill her, I swear.'

'It was real,' Amy said. 'I know how I felt.'

'I've no doubt you were there, sticking your nose in where it wasn't wanted, yet again. But it wasn't me that throttled Viv. I went to bed after our argument. I don't know what happened to her after that. All I know is that I never saw her again. That night, Jack was digging in the garden . . .'

Amy raised her hand to her temple. The sound of a shovel slicing through soil echoed in her mind. 'I never said she was throttled,' she said flatly.

'What?' Lillian replied.

'I never said you choked her. And it didn't show up on the autopsy because all they found were bones.'

Lillian fell silent.

Amy felt the familiar sense of satisfaction she had gained during suspect interviews in the past. She had led her suspect to the scene but omitted the crucial damning detail, winding Lillian up enough to get her to blurt it out herself. There was an audible click as she switched off the device recording their conversation. It was her last tool in the battle to keep the woman imprisoned. She could not allow Dougie's death to be for nothing, and she knew that somewhere far away, her father would be proud.

'Thank you for the confession,' Amy said, tiredness seeping into her bones. 'Don't call me again unless it's with Hermione's address.'

CHAPTER SIXTY-FOUR

With a sharp inhalation of breath, Hemmy awoke, her forehead slick with sweat. Sleep was becoming her enemy, making her vulnerable and unable to fight. Silently it had crept through the cracks in the timber carrying on the air like a ghost. The gas mask wasn't just for concealing her kidnapper's identity. Just the same, there was something familiar about him. Something she had seen before.

She had seen the indecision in his eyes after Purdy escaped. Knew it would be easier for them to get rid of her rather than move her again. Her face was bound to be all over the newspapers and on TV. The risk of getting caught was very real. Yet something was holding him back, strong enough to transfer her from that awful boat to the dank, oppressive space she now found herself in. Running the length of the walls, piping was stripped bare and hot to the touch. In the distance, a constant trickle of water provided a backdrop to her sobs. She had no memory of being transported to this windowless space, but the bruises on her knees and arms told her she had not been handled with care.

Apart from the whiff that still hung on her clothes, the stench of fish had all but evaporated. But there was no bed to lie on this time, no bucket for a toilet. No food to eat. She tugged at her ankle, the rattle of her chains echoing down the long hollow space. The pipe the padlock was attached to hissed with steam and water dripped endlessly down the slimy walls.

Vaguely, she recalled a mask being pressed upon her face and holding her breath until her lungs burned. *Maybe I'm in hell,* she thought listlessly. *Maybe I'm already dead.*

Something told her that life after death did not come with shackles, and the pain she felt seemed very real. She rubbed her ankle, torn and tender from where the chain bit into her skin. 'Help!' she cried listlessly, the word taunting her as it echoed around the room. 'Please, someone help me—' Her voice broke as she choked back a cough. The splinter wound on her hand was now a full-blown infection, and it felt like molten lava was flooding through the veins in her palm. Sweat trickled down her back as the world swam in and out of focus, blurred through red-rimmed eyes.

As she lay on her side, she felt the dig of the rusted screw poke into her hip. She had hidden it in her knickers. It provided small reassurance that her captor had not sexually assaulted her while she had been unconscious. There was no way her captor would allow her to conceal a weapon of any kind. Had the police found the letters she had gouged into the wood of the boat? At least she had tried. But now she had lost all sense of time and felt so very alone.

Tears pricked her eyelids and she winced as she shifted on the floor. Still bruised and puffy, her skin was painful to the touch, but at least she could see through both eyes now. She gazed at the roof, so high above her head, and the network of cables and pipes above. A rumbling sound vibrated through the building. At first, it sounded like the bass and drum of a stereo system playing too loud as it delivered a *thump, thump, thump.* It occurred with such regularity that it could be the same song on loop. She had settled on the idea of it being an industrial dryer before realising nothing that big could make the floor vibrate beneath her feet. Grateful for something to take her mind off her fears, she counted the seconds between each rumble. *Of course.* A frisson of hope sparked in her weary brain. Only a tube train could come with such regularity as it negotiated the underground network. She was still in London, maybe not even that far from home. The thought warmed her as her eyelids grew heavy and the darkness closed in.

CHAPTER SIXTY-FIVE

'I waited outside the gym.' Amy tried to sound nonchalant. She already guessed their training sessions had come to an end. Given Pike's motives, it was no significant loss, but she was not letting her DCI off the hook that easily. She wanted to hear her say the words aloud.

'I'm cutting the gym out for now,' Pike said, diverting her gaze as she answered the phone in her office.

Amy knew it was a lie. Pike's new gym partner would soon be selected, someone she could manipulate for her own needs. With Robert dead and Amy tarnished, there was little chance Pike would want to meet socially again. 'The smiling assassin', Paddy had once called her, and Amy was beginning to see why.

Amy used to believe that, no matter what life threw at her, she was in control. It was only now that she accepted that she was fallible like everyone else. All the timekeeping and scheduling in the world couldn't stop her messing up every now and again. But strength lay in facing her challenges head on.

'Was there anything else?' Pike said, ending her call.

'I've been speaking to Malcolm about the evidence seized from the boat. The results have come back on the contents of those gas canisters. It's some kind of sedative . . .'

'I'm well aware,' Pike replied. 'And we've got details of the person leasing the fishing boat.'

'Really?' A smile formed on Amy's face. 'That's excellent. Anyone we know?'

'It's your brother. Which is why you're no longer running this case.'

The announcement rooted Amy to the floor. 'There's got to be some mistake. Craig hasn't leased any boat.' She had guessed Pike was referring to Damien, but mentioned Craig to make her point. She hated how Pike continually referred to the Grimeses as her family.

'I was talking about Damien.' Pike arched an eyebrow, as if to say she knew what Amy was up to. 'And I'd appreciate it if you don't put officers in an awkward position by asking them about the investigation. I'll tell them you've got a lot on due to your recent bereavement and I'm just helping you out.'

Amy shook her head. It wasn't the fact her DCI was jumping in to take the credit that irked her: Pike's behaviour bordered on bullying. 'His alibi is solid. He was working the day Hermione was kidnapped.' The information had been confirmed in a follow-up to the intelligence package she had tasked DC Molly Baxter with.

'There were gaps.' Pike paused to take an apple from her drawer and placed it on her desk. 'Enough time for him to have left and come back.'

'All the way from his workplace to Hermione's house and then over to India Docks?' She folded her arms. She could tell by Pike's expression that she was barely tolerating her presence as it was. 'And why Hermione? Her mother's very protective of her home life. How would Damien know about her, much less where she lives?'

'We've got a possible connection to that Facebook group for starters . . .' She raised her hand as Amy attempted to interrupt. Amy knew the hashtag had changed. It now read #FindHermione #OneDayLeft #TickTock.

'But if that's not enough for you, we have a further statement from Tessa, too. She's admitted to using a dating app on her phone last year. Well, when I say dating . . .' Pike snorted, her eyebrows raised. 'It's basically for hook-ups. No-strings sex.'

Amy's mouth fell open at the revelation. She had not expected this. 'She brought strangers back to the house? While Hermione was there?'

Pike shook her head. 'Only when she was on sleepovers with friends. She did it two, three times. Had sex and then kicked them out. She was so drunk at the time she doesn't remember their descriptions, much less their names.'

'That's so dangerous . . .' Amy replied. No wonder she had been slow in coming forward. Their Family Liaison Officer must have pried the words from her mouth. 'Still, you said it was a year ago . . .'

'Enough time for one of them to plan and execute a kidnap attempt.'

'Malcolm was telling me about this case.' Amy changed tack, unwilling to give up on her theory just yet. 'The ghost rapes of Bolivia. Women used to wake up with blood and semen stains on their sheets, with no memory of the night before. Then police discovered that some of the townsmen had leaked gas into their rooms to make them sleep.'

'From what I've heard, Tessa Parker was a more than willing participant.' Pike's expression hardened as she bit into her fruit. 'Now, if you'll excuse me . . .'

'I'm sure she was, but I'm talking about Hermione and the gas we found on the boat. The person who manufactured the sedative in Bolivia was a vet. Damien's unlikely to know about things like that.' Amy voiced her thoughts as they came to mind. 'Damien's evaded arrest plenty of times. Would he really put his name on the lease of the boat? I've been investigating links with medical professionals . . .'

'Damien Grimes is a deviant, just like the rest of his family, and they can be very inventive when they need to be.' Pike took another bite of her apple.

Amy regarded her coolly, refusing to rise to the bait, but deep within her was an angry little girl who wanted to ram the damn apple down her throat. 'There's no need to take me off the case. Apart from my DNA, I have no connection to Damien Grimes.'

'Really?' Pike arched an eyebrow as she chewed. 'I seem to recollect you meeting up with him for tea not very long ago. And it's not as if you've made any great breakthroughs. A new set of eyes is what this investigation needs.'

'No breakthroughs? Are you kidding me? I gave you Lillian's last three victims.'

'And now I understand why she was so keen to comply. This has all worked out rather nicely for her, wouldn't you say? She has you to thank for the appeal.'

Amy rose from her chair, her jaw rigid. 'Are you punishing me? Or are you just grieving for my father? Because I'm grieving, too.'

'I have work to do,' Pike replied, a knot forming between her brows. 'And it's best you leave before you cross the line.'

'But, ma'am, I have a theory . . .' Amy said, using her title a little too late.

'Put it in an email.' Rising, Pike rested her apple core on the desk and opened the office door to see Amy out. Her expression tightened as she caught the look of defiance in Amy's eyes. It was only there because Amy wanted her to see it. The women stood head to head, Pike with her hand on the door.

'Remember what I said, Winter? You're either with me or you're in my way. I expect you to support this arrest.'

'I *would* agree with you . . .' Amy said tersely. 'But then we'd *both* be wrong. Now if you excuse me, I've got some enquiries to make.'

Turning on her heel, Amy marched down the corridor, her mind racing ahead. She had knocked on Pike's door for advice and been dismissed like a petulant child. #Onedayleft. The hashtag was branded on her brain with a digital clock counting backwards at frightening speed. She had less than twenty-four hours to find Hemmy and bring her home alive. The more she thought about her hunch, the more her instinct screamed to follow it up. But after what had happened with Dougie, could she ever trust herself again? She had believed him when he said he was going to hand himself in. Now he was dead. Today she had a new suspect in her sights. But what if she was wrong?

CHAPTER SIXTY-SIX

In truth, if Amy had enough belief in her hunch, then she would not have left Pike's office so soon. But there seemed something ludicrous about her suspicions. It was *so* ridiculous that she had to check it out for herself before telling anyone else. Where was their motivation? There was a time when she would have listed the validity of her suspicions and ticked off each bullet point. She may even have crossed the suspect's name off her list. But the last couple of weeks had taught her that not everything was so easily figured out. Particularly people, who could surprise you when you expected it the least. Which was why she had followed her suspect to work today.

The fact they were dressed in black raised another flag of suspicion. As she watched them furtively sneak into the plant entrance, that flag turned red. The hospital was a large building, housing many patients. Privately owned, its occupants were afforded the very best of care. But something told Amy her suspect was not there to comfort patients. As they swung the rucksack upon their back, it was obvious they were up to no good. Just the same, she held off calling for backup, dialling Paddy's number instead. Had she been wrong about her suspect and called the police, there would be hell to pay.

'Yes?' Paddy replied, his tone strident.

'Hello, my little ray of pitch black. Everything all right?' Amy tried to hide her concerns. If this lead turned out to be nothing, she could not afford to look like a fool.

Paddy sighed. 'I feel like my head's going to come off. Damien Grimes has gone AWOL, and now I'm being told that Pike is the SIO. What happened?'

'I'll tell you later,' Amy replied, figuring that now may not be the best time to ask for his help after all. 'Are you sure that's all that's wrong?' It was unlike Paddy to get in a flap over his caseload: his relaxed attitude to work usually drove her mad. There was a pause before he continued, and she could hear the sound of a closing door.

'It's Elaine, my girlfriend,' Paddy said. 'She's left me.'

'Oh, Paddy, I'm sorry,' Amy said. She was about to say more when he interrupted her.

'I told her about Geraldine last night over dinner, but the thing is . . . she already knew.'

Now it was Amy's turn to sigh. At least he was at work, which was the safest place to be. Her suspect had darted into the rear of the building, and she was losing precious seconds. 'I can't talk right now. Can I speak to you later?'

In the background, a voice demanded Paddy's attention. 'No worries,' he said. 'I'll see you when you get back. We're working on an interview plan.'

After putting her phone on silent, Amy shoved it into her pocket and got out of the car. She would have to do this alone. She crept past the chain-link fence, her shoes squelching on the muddy path. The fact that the gate had been left open suggested that her suspect was planning to be speedy. Gazing left and right, she scanned for CCTV cameras, but this part of the building was yet to benefit from the security measures in place for its more modern counterpart. The slate-grey building housed generators, heating and plumbing, and her suspect had no reason to be there. Silently, she hurried down the weed-infested path and through the back door, which had been left slightly ajar. Stepping into the murky corridor, she wrinkled her nose at the smell of engine oil and machinery fumes. She would have to quicken her steps if she hoped to catch up. Blinking, she accustomed her eyes to the dimness, the glow of the late afternoon sun barely visible through dirt-stained windows high on the wall. Amy strained for sounds, her heartbeat thundering as blood and adrenaline pulsed through her veins. It was hard to believe they were in central London, although the sound of the underground station served as a reminder as a tube train rumbled from below. Stilling her movements, she strained to hear footsteps and followed them to the end of the corridor.

She paused at a half-open door. Slowly, she unclipped a pouch on her shoulder harness and released her baton from its belt. She flicked it open, and the Asp extended fully in her hand. She took comfort from its weight as she flexed her fingers around the handle. Peering into the darkness, Amy felt four years old all over again.

With each step inside, Amy's eyes crept around her, just as they had in her basement all those years ago: to the cobwebs hanging from the ceiling; to the boxes stored against the walls. 'Hemmy?' she whispered. But instead of scratching, she could hear the gentle clanking of chains. Muggy heat vibrated from plant machinery, making her tense as it emitted a hiss of steam. In the distance, another low rumble from below made the ceiling vibrate, speckling dust in her hair. It did not seem to disturb the many spiders hanging from their nests. Amy felt herself visibly shrink. Get a grip, she thought. Her steps measured, she held her Asp above her shoulder. A noise from the end of the building made her squint into the distance. Turning on the lights would only notify her suspect that she was here.

It was all too perfect. The gate left open, the door left unlocked. She had followed her suspect into the bowels of this building with nothing but her equipment to keep her safe. Amy was walking into a trap. She was about to take a step back when she heard moaning from the far corner of the room.

'Hermione,' she whispered, peering into the darkness. 'Are you there?' A memory rose of a sudden scratching noise from a chest in the corner. Her hamster . . . Amy's heart faltered. Hammy. What were the odds of that? She was reliving that day all over again. Except Sally-Ann would not come tapping down the steps to save her. This time, she was on her own. This time she could put things right.

Gripping her baton, she followed the clink of chains drawing her in. With her free hand, she slid her phone from her pocket, the back-light stinging her eyes. No signal. She needed to get to high ground, call for backup, but Hermione could be dying down here. She could not leave her alone.

Another moan, growing louder as Amy approached. And then she saw her: a bruised and battered figure huddled in the corner, connected by chains to a pipe. Amy's footsteps echoed as she raced towards her. But all too late, she saw Hermione's eyes flash a warning. The glint of a blade edged Amy's vision, blinding pain filling her senses as it sliced into her skin.

CHAPTER SIXTY-SEVEN

He watched Amy creep down the stairs, her eyes wide as she took in the scene. From his vantage point, he worked out it would take three minutes for her to reach Hemmy. Three minutes to confront him for what he had done.

He hated the way Hemmy cringed when he touched her. As if he would ever abuse her in that way. He was no rapist or paedophile. His actions were necessary and just. He remembered the first time he saw her, how the light reflected on her blonde hair. Such a pretty girl, with a caring nature; but beauty and charm did not protect you from a brutal world. He had been careful to hide his identity and imagined her gratitude when he 'rescued' her after the three days were up. But now his plan had come apart at the seams – thanks to that Winter bitch. He had caught the spark of suspicion in her eyes when they last met. The detective had figured it out, and too late, she had come looking for him.

For a while it had worked, securing an appeal for Lillian Grimes. Prison was no place for her, and he could not wait to see her when she was released. But liberating Lillian was only half the plan. Three days, that's all it was meant to be. Three days in Hemmy's company, keeping her safe and watching her sleep. But somewhere along the line it all went dangerously wrong. He was not a violent man, but what choice did he have? He was not going to prison. Things could still go to plan, but not while Amy Winter was alive.

He watched as she negotiated the corridor, slightly crouched, her police baton drawn. She was toned but short in stature. He had the advantage over her. Having grown used to the dark, it was second nature to him now. Slowly and without sound he pulled on the gas mask, gently picking up the rucksack he had brought. The small white canister peeped out from the top. This one was marked in red letters. DANGER. It would drag her into a sleep from which she would never wake. Amy was the loose thread in his plan. Once she was removed, everything else would fall into place. Tugging on the mask, he found comfort in the rubbery smell. Silently, he crept towards her, holding his breath as he drew near. He slid the scalpel from his inside pocket and gripped it in his right hand. Every plan needed a backup. He would slit her throat if it came to it. It would be worth it if it meant setting Lillian free. Nothing would come between him and his goal.

CHAPTER SIXTY-EIGHT

As the scalpel pierced through her skin, Amy cried out in pain. She had glimpsed her attacker barely seconds before he struck. Swiftly, he disarmed her, slicing her flesh. Her pulse pounding, she stemmed her bleeding forearm. A small stream of blood trickled through her fingers and dripped steadily to the floor.

'I wouldn't,' her suspect said as she moved to release her incapacitant spray from her harness.

Dropping his left shoulder, he shrugged off his rucksack and slid it to the floor. 'Don't be fooled by its size,' he said, sliding out the canister peeping out from the top of the bag. 'This contains enough poison to kill you both. Now throw me your harness.' Still holding the scalpel, he kicked her baton away. Skittering into the darkness, it flew into the far corner, rebounding against a metal pipe with a clang.

Amy considered her options as she diverted her gaze to Hermione. Lying on the floor tethered by a length of chain, her face was streaked with sweat. Even without her bindings, it was clear she was in no fit state to get to her feet. Barely conscious, her eyes blinked open as she softly mewed in pain. If Amy was right about her suspect, it would be beyond him to kill such a defenceless young girl. Especially one only three years older than his own sister was when she died. She could talk her way out of this. She had to. Slowly, Amy raised her palms. Blood dripped down towards her elbow, streaking her shirt in jagged red paths. She gritted her teeth. It may be a surface wound, but it stung like hell.

'Relax,' she said, doing her best to sound calm. 'I'm here to help. She needs a doctor. Why don't you let me . . .' Walking backwards, she approached the young girl.

'Stay where you are.' The man's words rattled through the mask. He was bigger than Amy, but she had encountered far worse than John Thompson in her career.

'She's innocent, just like your sister. Please, John, take your mask off and call for an ambulance. She needs our help.'

Hemmy's eyes fluttered open a second time, her lips parting as she heard her captor's name.

'I'm not John,' he replied angrily, sucking in a harsh breath. 'I'm Damien Grimes. He . . . I set this all up.'

'You're a good few inches taller than Damien,' Amy said, looking over her shoulder. 'And he's in custody as far as I know.' Placing her palm on Hermione's forehead, she winced at the fiery heat of her skin. The eerie rattle of the gas mask grew louder as John advanced. In order to get them both out of here, Amy had to shatter his plans. She also had to pretend she didn't view him as a threat. Both were a lie. Now she could see that John had been trying to set Damien up all along.

'You're no murderer,' Amy said. 'You're a vet. Hardly the type to kill someone in cold blood.' But he *was* the sort of person to write hundreds of letters to Lillian in prison. It wasn't Gladys who had been harassing Lillian Grimes for years; John was behind it all. *I could paper my cell walls with the letters*, Lillian had said. It was only when Amy read them for herself that her concerns grew. Vicious and nasty, they wished a slow torturous death on the woman who had killed his sister. On the few times that Gladys did write, it was to say she forgave Lillian for her sins.

Both he and his mother had been victims in all of this. That's what put Amy off all along. Why would he want Lillian set free?

John raised his voice to be heard through the mask. 'You don't know me.'

Despite the weird acoustics, Amy could easily make his words out. 'It got me wondering when you used her nickname. Only close friends and family call her Hemmy. It made me see you in a different light.' She glanced back at the young girl, who was struggling to keep conscious. 'Why help Lillian though?' Amy returned her attention to her advancing attacker. She needed to keep him talking. Lure him into a false sense of security as she worked out her next move. 'After everything your poor mother went through. And what she did to your sister . . . dumping her in that freezer without any remorse. Why would you want Lillian freed?'

'I don't want to *help* her.' John's words were torn now, etched with pain. 'I want to *kill* her. Prison is too good for the likes of Lillian Grimes. She deserves a slow, painful death, with her remains scattered in a rubbish pit.'

Amy noted the present tense. He had not abandoned his plans. He would take her here, into the basement of the animal hospital and make her pay for what she had done. 'And you befriended Damien through Facebook?'

John did not deny her theory. 'For hours he used to bang on about his mum, and how the police set her up. I wanted that bitch freed, so I could sort her out myself.'

Amy stiffened as a sudden expulsion of steam caused the pipe behind her to hiss. Now it made sense. After kidnapping Hermione, John joined The Keepers group and used it as leverage to reopen Lillian's case. It served a double purpose: setting Damien up for the kidnapping and giving Lillian a taste of her own medicine when she was free.

'It almost worked.' John tightened his grip on the gas cylinder. 'It still can.'

A trickle of sweat ran down Amy's back as she tried to buy some time. 'You must have known we'd find out you were Hermione's vet.' It was only when Amy researched the veterinary practice online that she recognised John's face.

'But you said Damien's in custody, so no one else knows about me yet.' Twitching, John fixed his mask. Perspiration stained the armpits of his sweatshirt.

Amy had already worked out that Mrs Cotterill had given him a key. With his recent home visits to the old woman's poorly Yorkshire terrier, it was easy for John to work out Hermione's routine. Her eyes rested on the scalpel in his hand.

'I was meant to keep Hemmy for three days and then we'd . . .' his words trailed away, tired from the effort of speaking through the mask.

The heat was stifling now, and Amy swiped the perspiration from her forehead, leaving a bloodied trail. 'It's not too late to turn this around. Hemmy's a good kid. She doesn't deserve this.'

'Neither did my sister.' John's breath quickened as Amy stood her ground. 'Now move it. Throw me your harness or I'll gas you both.'

Given John's mask, Amy knew that there was no point in holding onto her CS spray. Hermione was fading and there seemed little chance of talking him around. She had to disarm him, and she had to do it fast.

Bunching her harness in her hands, an idea formed as she felt the weight of the handcuffs from within their pouch. With as much strength she could gather, she launched the shoulder harness at John's head. Holding the scalpel in his right hand and the canister in the left, something had to give. A loud clang erupted as the gas can fell and rolled away. Amy had to make a decision. Should she run for help or stay and fight? There was no way she was abandoning Hermione now. She had seen the mad glint in John's eyes. After years of living beneath the shadow of his dead sister, he was hungry for revenge. He may have liked Hermione, but he had left her in a shocking state. Blinded by his own motivations, he was thinking of himself right now. There was only one thing she could do: fight her way out.

Hermione's chain rattled as she struggled to rise. Amy's heart broke for the young girl all over again. To see her there, defenceless and chained – she was representative of every girl that Jack and Lillian harmed.

Raising her fists, Amy glared at John, planting her feet steadily on the ground. *Go ahead*, she thought, as she heard his mocking sneer. *Underestimate me.*

A foot taller, John needed to be brought down to size. Drawing back her foot Amy didn't hold back as she kicked him hard between the legs.

'Ooof!' he gasped. Struggling for breath beneath his mask, he dropped to his knees onto the cement floor.

Drawing back her right fist, Amy pumped all her frustration into a right hook, catching him squarely on the jaw. Pounding her fist against the latex, she ducked and dived against his flailing gloved hands as he tried to gain control of her wrists. Quickly she stepped back, her left hand slippery with blood as she grasped for the rucksack lying on its side on the floor. She had heard the jangle of keys as he dropped it. She had to get Hermione free. But as John lunged towards her, the next punch was misguided. Blinding pain seared through her knuckles as she shattered the glass eyepiece of the mask with her fist. They cried out simultaneously, Amy shaking her fist furiously to recover some feeling in her fingers, John falling back onto his knees clutching his face.

'Hemmy,' Amy said, rummaging through the rucksack. 'I'm the police, but I'm on my own. Can you get to your feet?' But her words were met with a listless moan. Gasping with relief Amy wrapped her fingers around a hard metal key ring. If she could loosen Hermione's chains, then she might have some chance of breaking free. But hope was short lived as John got to his feet, throwing his mask across the floor.

'You bitch,' he screamed, clutching his left eye. A viscous substance oozed from the gouged socket, his face slick with blood. Roaring in anger he advanced upon her, a fire of fury on his face.

Slipping in her own blood, Amy staggered to her feet. The effort of getting to her feet and her painful injuries evoked a cluster of white stars that flashed before her eyes. 'Drop the blade!' she demanded, with more confidence than she felt. From her peripheral vision, she saw Hermione's fingers curl around the keys on the floor. Hope flared. If she could undo the lock and get to her feet they might still stand a chance. But could Amy fend off their attacker for that long? Clenching her fists, she prepared to fight.

As John lunged towards her, Amy drew upwards with her left fist, wincing as her knuckles made contact with his chin. But her punch was not sent with its earlier force, her injury weakening the blow.

There was no time to recover as John barrelled on top of her. Falling backwards, another flash of stars danced in her vision as her skull rebounded against the ground.

With his full weight upon her, she was barely able to breathe, and walls of pain pushed in from every side. Heaving for breath, Amy bucked beneath his weight. 'I'm going to cut your throat,' John snarled, flecks of blood and spit raining down on Amy's face. His left eye socket was a gaping wound, but he seemed oblivious to the pain. Helpless, she kicked out, praying Hermione was still conscious. Another rattle of chains told her she was moving, but would she get out in time? 'Get off me!' Amy screamed. 'Kill me and you're going to jail!'

But reasoning was beyond him. Grasping for the blade, John positioned it above Amy's face. 'The thing about being a vet,' he sneered, spitting blood onto the floor, 'is that I know exactly where to cut.'

But the thing about being a police officer was that Amy was trained in the art of self-defence. Clasping his wrists, she drew them together, until he bore down with all his might. As the scalpel trembled in his grip, it hung above her like a guillotine waiting to seal her fate. One wrong move could bring it slicing through her throat. Dropping her right arm, she wrapped her legs around his body and rolled them both to the side. Unbalanced by the sudden momentum, John found himself thrown to the ground.

Clambering on top, Amy fought for control, punching him hard in the face. Having lost his scalpel in the tussle, John wrapped his hands around her neck and squeezed.

Panic set in as Amy felt the sudden shock of her breath locking in her throat. She clawed for her life, digging her nails into his wrists. But her lungs burned in her chest, void of the oxygen she desperately needed to carry on. A flash of recollection took her: Lillian, choking the life out of Viv as they lay on the living room floor. Would John be pleased when he found out who Amy was? The irony taunted her. Her eyes bulged, her sight tinted red as the driving pressure made her blood vessels burst. Tighter, John squeezed, gritting his teeth against the pain.

Amy did not see Hermione creep up behind her until John's eye rolled upwards from where he lay on the ground. Without mercy, Hermione slammed the rusted screw into his good eye. John's grip fell away from Amy's throat, his savage outcry filling the air.

Clambering to one side, Amy heaved in a lungful of warm breath.

On her knees, Hermione blinked from behind sweat-laced hair, splatters of blood dappling her school shirt. 'On my back,' Amy rasped. 'Let's go.'

'My eyes!' John screamed. 'I'm blind, I'm blind!' Clawing at his face, he rolled around on the floor.

Gently, Amy lifted Hermione, shocked at how little she weighed. Piggyback was a game Sally-Ann used to play with her as a child. Wearily, she made her way down the corridor and followed the beam of light coming from the door.

CHAPTER SIXTY-NINE

Pushing her hair from her face, Amy stared at the words engraved on the lime-eaten tombstone. Judging by the weeds creeping up around its base, she was its only visitor.

Three days had passed since she found Hermione. Enough time for the girl to begin to heal. Her physical injuries would fade in time, but the mental scarring would prove harder to escape. As for John . . . doctors feared he would lose the sight in one eye. Sympathy did not come as easily for the man who had almost ended her life and Amy hated the fact that, in that moment, one of her last thoughts had been of Lillian and the awful things she had done.

She knelt to lay down the bunch of white roses she had purchased on the way. It was an acknowledgement of her sister, buried beneath the ground. 'The winter is past, flowers appear on the earth, the rain is over and gone.' The tribute on the tombstone lingered on her lips as she read the inscription aloud. A memory played in her mind, a horrendous vivid re-enactment she could not escape.

Sally-Ann, her legs crumbling beneath her as she was struck on the back of the head. Lillian's face when she discovered what Jack had done. How could they be so heartless? They cared more about the strangers coming to their house than their own flesh and blood, the same blood that ran through her veins.

Amy had always felt different, but she could barely comprehend being a part of something as horrific as this. Now her thoughts were filled with blame and regret. If she hadn't entered the basement that night, Sally-Ann would still be alive. Kissing her fingers, she pressed them against the cold concrete headstone.

'I'm sorry,' she whispered. Lillian had almost broken her, and now she barely knew who she was. But her sister would want her to carry on. Her chest tightened as Sally-Ann's last moments replayed once more. It would have been better if they had killed her instead. At least then she would not have to undergo the pain of . . .

'Amy?' A soft voice spoke from behind, breaking into her thoughts. Amy straightened, annoyance wrinkling her brow. Couldn't she have five minutes alone? Gathering her composure, she squinted against the sunlight breaking through the clouds as she turned around.

'Elaine?' She recognised the woman from a blurry photograph that Paddy had shown her on his phone. He had been out of his mind with worry since her disappearance and lodged a missing person's report. But there was something about this woman's features, something that made Amy's heart clamber up her throat. It was her mind playing tricks on her, her thoughts so full of Sally-Ann that she believed she saw something of her sister in her. Her kindly face, her blue-grey eyes . . . but instead of long chestnut hair, Elaine's was blonde and cut into a bob. The woman touched her forearm as if checking she was real. Amy flinched from the contact.

'I'm not Elaine,' she said, delivering a kindly smile.

'You're not P . . . Paddy's Elaine?' Amy flushed. Just what was wrong with her? Horrified, she swallowed back the stammer she thought she had conquered.

'I'm more than that,' the woman said. 'Look again.'

Amy blinked. Those warm eyes, the gentle smile and the patient voice – it couldn't be. It was only when Elaine smiled and her dimples became apparent that she knew for sure.

'It's me. I'm your sister. I'm Sally-Ann.'

'Are you a ghost?' Amy gaped, long repressed tears finally making a path down her face.

'Sweetheart, I didn't die,' Elaine chuckled, placing a warm arm around her. 'I ran away. But I'm never leaving you again.'

CHAPTER SEVENTY

Two Weeks Later

'Don't look so nervous.' DI Amy Winter glanced at Paddy over the roof of the car. 'Anyone would think you were going before the firing squad.' She peered at his navy tie which was dotted with small gold legal scales.

Smoothing it over, Paddy threw her an appealing gaze. 'Shouldn't you fill me in? I don't like going in unprepared.' Playing things by ear had never bothered DS Patrick Byrne in the past. An ex firearms officer, he was used to responding at a moment's notice, strengthened by the adrenaline pumping through his veins. But this afternoon was different. It was their day off for one thing, and Paddy seemed more frightened by what lay ahead than anything he had faced in his career.

'I'll leave the explaining to Elaine,' she said with a smile. They were standing outside Amy's usual haunt, The Ladbroke Arms.

Being involved in their domestics was the last thing Amy wanted, but given that Paddy had chosen her sister over his wife, she had little choice. Ever since Elaine had come forward, her head had been full of conflicted thoughts. The fact she was adopted and Elaine was her sister was as much as she had been able to share with Paddy until now.

'She's leaving me, isn't she?' His face was solemn as they both approached the pub. 'Properly, I mean.'

Amy glared up at him, wondering how she could politely tell him to grow some balls. 'Saved by the bell,' she said, reaching into her coat pocket to answer the insistent ring of her phone. 'Yes, we're outside.' She nodded. 'See you in a minute.'

She tilted her head back upwards to look him squarely in the eyes. 'Just keep an open mind – whatever she says.'

'It's a big enough shock to hear you're related.' Paddy's hands were deep in his pockets, his right leg jigging. The disparity of his behaviour was strange to see. With a gun in his hand, he was cool, focused and under control.

Amy rolled her eyes. 'Listen. You can fix this. She wants you to stay together. She's here to put things right.'

'Really?' Paddy said, hope lighting up his face. He had lost weight since Elaine had left him, but it had not done him any harm. The belly that once hung over his work trousers had shrunk, the double chin all but disappeared. His face was weather worn and a few grey hairs had crept in, but all in all, he was not a bad-looking man. 'A face full of character', was how DC Molly Baxter had once described him. God knows he had had enough turmoil in his life to shape it.

Amy forced a smile as she realised Paddy was waiting for reassurance. 'But . . . and this is a big but . . . you've got to listen to what she has to say and don't make any big decisions until it's sunk in.'

Taking a quick puff of his electronic cigarette, Paddy blew a ribbon of tobacco-scented vapour into the air.

'After you,' she said, opening the door.

As they entered the pub, Amy raised an eyebrow to see a bottle of Prosecco in an ice bucket. Elaine was sitting near the window behind a long, wooden table, with padded seats against the inner wall. Amy still felt a pang of disbelief at being in the presence of her biological sister.

Awkwardly, Paddy stood, the love clearly evident in his face. He hesitated for only seconds before stepping forward and taking Elaine in his arms. Holding her close, he kissed the crown of her head. As he pulled back, his eyes were moist with tears, his voice gravelly with emotion. 'I've missed you.'

Amy swallowed, feeling a swell of affection for them both. Having her sister in her life made the world feel like a warmer place. Perhaps it was why Elaine had been drawn to Paddy. She was adept at saving souls.

'I'm sorry I left. I thought you were better off without me,' Elaine said, her face haunted with remorse. Her generous figure made her all the more motherly, and Amy thought it was a shame that she had never had children of her own.

Amy's eyes flicked from Elaine to Paddy as she waited for the bombshell to drop. How was he going to take the news? She hoped her sister's purchase of Prosecco had not been a premature one.

Paddy shifted in his seat. 'You have something to tell me?'

Elaine took a deep breath, her face flushed. 'Well, Amy's told you that we're sisters?'

'Yes,' he said, 'but I've a feeling there's something more.'

'There is,' Elaine said, steeling herself. 'Our birth parents were Jack and Lillian Grimes.' She looked at him for understanding, then carried on when there was none. 'As in the serial killers.'

Paddy stared, unblinking as he absorbed the double blow. 'This is a wind-up, right?'

Elaine shook her head. 'My birth name is Sally-Ann Grimes.'

'But you're . . .' He paused, looking from Elaine to Amy. 'She's dead. Sally-Ann was murdered.'

Tentatively, Elaine reached across the table. Her words were soft as she cupped Paddy's hand. 'I didn't die, I ran away.'

'It's true,' Amy said, feeling a frisson of worry as another facet of her past was laid bare. She crossed her legs, her fingers tightening as she laced them together over her knee of her jeans. She missed the reassurance of her starched work suit and leather boots, hated the focus being on her personal life instead of her latest job. But if she was going to have a brother-in-law one day, she could not ask for a better one than Paddy Byrne. Amy glanced at her sister, who was struggling to find the right words. Who would want to admit to such a parentage? That the 'Beasts of Brentwood' had produced them both. Up until now, the world had thought that Sally-Ann was another of their victims. Their own daughter – killed when she was barely a teen. Amy took a breath to speak. 'That night, I thought Jack killed Sally-Ann. But instead, she woke up dumped under some tarpaulin in our freezing cold shed. She'd been saving to run away for ages and had hidden her suitcase behind some boxes at the back. We had relatives in London who kept her safe – and kept her secret too.'

'But they must have noticed you were gone.' Paddy turned to Elaine for answers.

Elaine nodded, finally finding her voice. 'Killing had become a routine for them. Lillian must have thought that Jack buried me, and he thought the same of her. They both stayed quiet about it because they knew it was wrong to kill one of their own.'

'Who was buried behind the fireplace if it wasn't you?' Paddy's questions were identical to those Amy had asked her sister when she first discovered the truth.

'A young runaway,' Elaine replied. 'Our home was like a halfway house at times, so many of them came and went. Jack burnt her body. We were the same height, the same age. She had stolen my necklace. She was wearing it when she died.'

'But we earmarked her body as yours. Why didn't Jack say it was her?'

'He was building up to it. It's all in the transcripts of the interview,' Amy replied, ready to fill in the gaps. 'He mentioned Sally-Ann more than once, saying that we'd have to ask Lillian where she was buried.

Then later, he said he wanted to come clean, saying the police had got things wrong.'

'But he died before he could explain,' Paddy said, raising his glass and knocking back a mouthful of fizz. News like this warranted a stronger drink. 'I can't believe it.' He rested his half empty glass on the table. His face clouded over as another thought entered his mind. 'When we met . . . you spilling your drink on me in this very pub. That was more than a coincidence, wasn't it?'

'Try to understand,' Elaine said, lowering her voice as a woman passed by, rattling her car keys from her bag before leaving through the front door. 'After Amy was adopted, I told myself she was better off without me, but she never left my thoughts. I found Damien on Facebook. He was very open about his identity. He didn't care who knew he was a Grimes.'

'You friended him?' Amy asked. This was news to her.

Elaine nodded. 'I said I was his cousin and gave details of the family I'd stayed with. He told me you were adopted by the police officer who handled Lillian's case. It wasn't difficult to track you down after that.'

'How did he find me?'

'Lillian hired a private detective to track Robert Winter down. She wanted to send him hate mail but she got a lot more than she bargained for when the detective showed her pictures of you.'

Amy's stomach lurched. If her biological brother was so free with the truth then it was only a matter of time before it became public knowledge and her job was further compromised. She turned her attention back to Elaine, who was unaware of her inner turmoil.

'And me?' Paddy said, squeezing Elaine's hand.

'At first . . .' Elaine confessed, 'at first I got to know you because you worked with Amy. I never meant to fall in love.'

Paddy exhaled a long, tired sigh. 'So what now?'

'I'm ready to come back, if you'll let me.'

Paddy nodded, deep in thought. 'We've got lots to talk about.'

Amy smiled. It was just like Paddy, displaying steady acceptance in the face of the chaos around him. She rose from the table. 'In that case, my work here is done. Hey, Paddy, you do realise this makes you almost my brother-in-law.'

He smiled, looking happy at the prospect. 'Suits me just fine.'

EPILOGUE

As she sat at the table, Lillian gripped the pen in her hand. It was time for another roll of the dice. Her solicitor had informed her that police were reopening her case. Her youngest daughter held no value to her anymore, but . . . she could not end things like this, with her thinking she had the upper hand. It was time to bring that girl back to her roots. She smiled, just as she had when she started the ball rolling after Robert Winter's death.

> Dear Adam,
> I imagine my correspondence will come as a surprise. I have been following your newspaper reports with interest. I feel that we're going to get along.
> Did you know we were almost related, you and I? It's a shame your engagement to Amy failed. It would have been nice to have a journalist in the family. Then again, perhaps when you know who she really is, you'll count your parting as a blessing.

I have arranged for you to visit me tomorrow. I'm sure you'll find it useful, and I'm prepared to tell all. There's just something I need you to do for me first.

Yours always,

Lillian Grimes

ACKNOWLEDGMENTS

Thanks to the fantastic team of professionals at Thomas & Mercer, particularly editors Jack Butler, Sophie Missing and Laura Deacon, who have done an amazing job in making this book the very best it could be. A special thanks to the cover designer Tom Sanderson, who has done a magnificent job on my cover, the only person capable of rendering me speechless as it was revealed.

To Madeleine Milburn, Hayley Steed and the rest of the literary agency team. I feel hugely fortunate to have them guiding my writing career.

To the fantastic band of authors whom I am very fortunate to know, in particular Mel Sherratt, Teresa Driscoll and Angela Marsons. It's true what they say: crime authors are the nicest people you could meet.

To my ex-colleagues in the police, you are still very much in my thoughts. Also, to the book reviewers, bloggers, readers and book clubs who have championed my books from the beginning. I am hugely grateful, as always, for your support.

Last but not least, to my family and friends. Thank you for believing in me.

ABOUT THE AUTHOR

A former police detective, Caroline Mitchell now writes full-time.

She has worked in CID and specialised in roles dealing with vulnerable victims – high-risk victims of domestic abuse and serious sexual offences. The mental strength shown by the victims of these crimes is a constant source of inspiration to her, and Mitchell combines their tenacity with her knowledge of police procedure to create tense psychological thrillers.

Originally from Ireland, she now lives in a pretty village on the coast of Essex with her husband and three children.

You can find out more about her at www.caroline-writes.com, or follow her on Twitter (@caroline_writes) or Facebook (www.facebook.com/CMitchellAuthor).